REEL
Sexy

Jenna Baker

Cover Design: Jessie Smillie
Cover Design Concept: Lauren Borgersen Ras
Copy Editor: Keidi Keating

DEDICATION

To my diamond boy, Austin and my golden girl, Avery.
I love you to the moon and back.

1.

Earning a day off in my industry was about as likely as winning an Emmy award. It was possible and we all aspired to it, but it was a rare occurrence. In my case, the honor was bestowed upon me out of sympathy, after I was poisoned and left for dead.

I was working as a reality television producer on a show where I documented detectives with the Los Angeles Police Department as they solved crimes. This meant that being shot or stabbed or maimed was a distinct possibility for me. The fact that I was poisoned during our latest episode represented a real legal risk to my employer. My boss Lenny initially offered me and my crew two days off to recover, but the show's legal counsel stepped in and extended it to a week.

Over the past five days I had cleaned my apartment, restocked my fridge, visited my family, and even went out to dinner a few times. In reality television, the life of a producer was one of feast or famine. You were either working like a dog around the clock, or you were without work and hustling to try to get your next gig. In either case, it was unusual to be this carefree, with no obligations. It was a luxury and I was grateful, but I didn't know what to do with myself anymore.

Most of the people I knew worked during the day, so I found myself sitting around my apartment, without much purpose. I decided to take a drive around the neighborhood as a cure for my boredom.

Los Angeles was very hot. In particular, the San Fernando Valley where I was currently living. There were days when I questioned my sanity for driving around in a car with no air conditioning. The '92 Miata was a convertible, so I always reasoned that it didn't need air conditioning, but when the thermostat was pushing one hundred degrees, that argument held little weight. I must have been really bored to be driving around in this heat.

During the course of today's travels, I found myself driving through a residential area complete with picket fences and tree-lined streets. As I wiped the sweat off my brow for the millionth time, I started to feel frustrated. How could anyone live in this heat? I could barely see with the constant stream of sweat pouring into my eyes.

Ahead, I spotted a house with the sprinklers turned on. It was one of those sprinklers that hooked to a garden hose and moved backwards and forwards casting a wide spray. The water looked so cool, so inviting. Without giving it a second thought, I pulled my car over and parked right in front of that glorious stream. The sprinkler turned towards me and I could feel the cold drops dampening my skin.

I sat there for a few minutes, enjoying the coolness, not worrying about what damage this was causing to my car. It was so hot that the water was probably evaporating as soon as it fell, but it felt great.

"What the hell are you doing lady?" I heard a voice call out.

I jumped and turned to see the owner of the sprinkler sitting on his front porch. Had he been there the whole time?

"Are you crazy?" he shouted.

"Shoot," I whispered as I quickly put the car in gear and pulled away.

Being called "crazy" wasn't a new thing for me, but later that night as I sat across the table from one of the hottest men I had ever known, I wondered if perhaps I was. This guy had strong arms and a strong chest with pectoral muscles that I could see through his black T-shirt. His hair was dark, just like his eyes, framed by long lashes and thick eyebrows. He was a cop with movie-star good looks and a track record of honesty and integrity to boot. The guy sitting across from me was liquid sex, so why wasn't I ripping off his clothes right now? Why, instead of jumping across the table and taking him right there, was I collecting eights in a card game? Yup. I was crazy all right.

Detective Bradley Reid and I had met a few weeks ago on the show I was producing called *Murder Live!* He had been an unwilling participant while I was the pushy producer. We started off as bitter enemies, but soon realized the tension between us wasn't because we didn't like each other. It was because we did.

For years I had lacked the confidence to feel like I was doing a good job as a television producer. My mother was an entertainment newscaster and had made a career of hosting *LA Incorporated.* I had gotten my first job through my famous mother's connections and had always felt like my last name was the only thing opening the doors for me. I had always considered myself to be mediocre at best when it came to my craft, but somehow this particular show seemed to be appealing to all my strengths. I was aggressive, pushy, and had almost gotten myself killed to solve a case. That may have sounded like a recipe for disaster but it wasn't. I was delivering good episodes and people were watching them.

My first *Murder Live!* episode starred Reid and his partner Dustin "Foxy" Flanagan, cracking a case involving human trafficking across the Mexican border. I admit that Reid's looks contributed to the success of the episode, but my killer instincts did too. My second blockbuster was with two different cops and involved me and my crew getting poisoned by a crazed killer. We survived, obviously, and the episode got national attention. The network was so pleased that they pulled the show from their cable partner over to the big leagues. This was my first primetime network show ever and it was hard not to get excited about it.

The idea of *Murder Live!* was that most murders were solved within the first 48-hours. Once a murder occurred, we would follow the detectives around as they pulled together the clues to solve the crime. Our timelines were short and our instructions were clear – if the case seemed solvable, cover it. If it didn't, ditch it and move on. It seemed simple enough, but I was never one to follow instructions. I pushed hard to solve the cases that no one thought could be solved. And it paid off – twice.

While we were frigid towards each other at the outset, me and Detective Bradley Reid, who went by "Reid," warmed towards each other in the end. In fact, we came to discover that we had a lot in common, including some very close connections. Reid's father was a talent agent who represented my mother. She was retired from entertainment reporting now, but was finding her new groove as the face of Burt's Hemorrhoid cream.

My relationship with Reid was complicated. The sexual attraction was there and it was intense, but every time things started to heat up between us, something or someone seemed to get in the way. We were paired together for the first episode but not the second when I was hospitalized.

After that, Reid wanted me to give up the job, but of course I wasn't willing. My near-death experience had given me a new lease on life, but it didn't make me shy away from the job. Instead, it made me shy away from Reid. I discovered that I cared for him on a deep level and worried his attraction to me was more sexual and short-term. We had gotten very close a number of times to consummating our relationship, but I finally pumped the brakes. I wanted to know if we could make it as a couple before we complicated things with sex. That may have been a backwards approach, but I really liked him and I didn't want to lose him. Was I withholding sex from him to keep him in my life longer? Maybe.

Sitting across from this gorgeous man, I knew I was an idiot. The fact that he was sitting here, playing cards on a work night should have told me he was committed. Still, I felt confused about where this relationship would end up.

Between picking up and putting down my cards, collecting my eights, I stole glances at Reid. Growing up in Malibu with the rich and famous, it was a wonder he became a cop. His looks were another thing. How did his talent-agent father not force him to become an actor? I glanced at his lips which were full and plump. He ran his tongue over them, thinking about his next move. When he kissed me with those lips my body tingled all the way down to my toes. He was so sexy, I still couldn't believe he was interested in me.

On the looks scale, I would probably give myself a B+. I wasn't the type of girl that would turn every head in the room, but that didn't mean men didn't notice me. My blonde, wavy hair was a little past my shoulders. My eyes were blue and I was about five and a half feet tall. I was thin enough that I could look good in most things, but not thin enough that I would feel comfortable in a bikini. I was too modest to wear something like that anyway, especially now that I was thirty. In general, I dressed pretty casually, but I blamed that on my job. My work days were long and so comfort took priority over fashion. Besides, I lived in LA. Everyone dressed down.

Reid, on the other hand, was smoking hot. A guy like this could bed a new girl every night, but he didn't. In fact, he hadn't had sex in quite some time. The poor guy was waiting on me, banking that I would finally come around. The fact that he was waiting patiently made it all the more difficult to resist him.

"What?" Reid asked, breaking my concentration.

"Huh?" I asked, startled.

"You're staring at my lips."

"No, I'm not."

Reid stood up, revealing a tight torso well-defined beneath a T-shirt that seemed like it was made for him. Every part of him was firm and toned. I felt myself staring again. I couldn't seem to look away.

Reid walked over to me and took my hand, pulling me up to my feet. As I stood up, his hands found my waist. He was taller than me and as he pulled me to him, I enjoyed the way we fit. I looked up at him, focusing on his lips again, watching as they curved into a slight smile. "Am I making you nervous?"

"No," I lied, letting my arms reach around him, resting on his waist. I was only a few inches from some of his better parts, but I kept my hands planted where they were. The truth was, even sitting across the table from Reid, the electricity between us was palpable. Now with him standing this close to me, I started to feel my hormones winding up like a clock. One false move and they would unwind and explode, ripping his clothes off in the process.

His head dipped down to me and his lips met mine. It wasn't long before I was opening my mouth to him, taking in his tongue. His full lips covered mine and took my mouth in completely, submerging me in the kiss. I moved my arms around his waist, preparing to move them down towards his perfect backside, when he pulled back and stared down at me.

"It's getting late," he said.

I looked at him, startled. I wasn't wearing a watch, but instinctively looked down at my wrist anyway. "Oh yeah, I guess it is."

It took me a moment to gain my composure, but when I did, I felt a little silly. I stepped away from him, grabbed my purse and headed to the front door. As I opened it, he met me there, pressing my back against it.

"Thanks for having me," I told him.

Reid looked at me, studying me before placing his hands on the sides of my face and pulling me in for another kiss. I was grateful to be leaning against the door as it was providing a much-needed support system. I finally understood what people meant when they said a man made them weak in the knees. Mine seemed to be jelly at the moment.

Reid moved his lips to my neck and whispered to me, "I'm not a big fan of your rules. They're actually pretty difficult to follow."

I smiled, knowing what he meant. My "rules" allowed us to get this close, but not much further. We both knew that if we got too carried away it would be impossible to stop ourselves. His lips connected with mine again and the kiss intensified. Before we knew it, our hands were all over each other. I kept trying to draw him deeper into my mouth and closer to my body, but I felt like I couldn't get close enough to him.

Reid pulled back again and licked his lips. "When you change your mind, I'll be waiting."

"Right," I said. "I'll see you tomorrow." I felt like such an idiot. I was definitely crazy. This guy was delicious and delectable and I was depriving myself. I was scared, I knew that. That was part of the problem. I was going to have to get over my fears. I knew that too.

I headed out to my car, hot and bothered. The heatwave seemed to be present during both day and night, which meant the night air wouldn't help much. I planned to take a very cold shower when I got back to my apartment.

*****

During the short ride between Reid's place and mine, my sister Ginny called my cell phone.

"Hello?"

"Wanna meet me at the Beverly Center?" Ginny asked.

"I can't, it's late," I told her.

"What are you, an old lady now? It's seven-thirty."

"It is?" I looked at the clock and was surprised to realize she was right. In fact, it was still light outside. Reid saying it was "late" had thrown me off. Apparently playing crazy eights wasn't his favorite pastime.

The Beverly Center was located in Beverly Hills, about half way between where Ginny lived and where I lived, so I agreed I would meet her. I didn't have anything better to do. It was the last day of my vacation and knowing I had to go back to work tomorrow was kind of disappointing.

After my near-death experience, Reid insisted that if I was going to remain on the show I had to be paired with him and Foxy. He said it was the only way he could keep me safe. Reid being there tomorrow was something to look forward to, but that was about it. Going back meant getting back into the grind – working eighteen-hour days, living off junk food, and hanging out with a bunch of criminals and degenerates. It was cool that my name appeared on the show's credits, especially on a network show, but that was where the glamour and the glory ended. The rest was exhausting, thankless grunt work.

I pulled into the garage at the Beverly Center and parked my car. I walked into the mall and found Ginny browsing in a lingerie shop.

Ginny was my younger sister by a few years and had been living with my parents until recently, when she married an entertainment attorney. My parents were wealthy thanks both to my mother's career and the success of my father as a set-designer. They used their money to spoil Ginny, their baby, rotten. I worked hard for my paychecks while Ginny simply batted her eyes. She landed herself a workaholic named Bob, who brought home a handsome salary. She was petite and pretty and the perfect trophy wife to have at his company parties. As for Bob, he was kind of a jerk and below average in the looks department, but wealthy and generous with his money. I wasn't a huge fan of my sister to begin with and I liked Bob even less. I resented the fact that I was out in the field working like a dog, while she stressed over whether her shoes coordinated with her dress and which philanthropic initiative required the least amount of effort.

Ginny held up a pale blue padded bra and examined it. "Do you think this is sexy?"

"Trying to keep the romance alive?" I asked, trying to sound interested. In truth, picturing her and Bob sleeping together totally turned my stomach. Once she slipped and told me that he cried after having sex. She found it endearing, assuming he was weeping because he loved her so much. I just thought it was strange. Perhaps he was crying over the shambles his life was in after marrying such a lunatic.

"I'm not as experienced as you are, Vicky. That's why I'm looking for some advice."

I punched her in the arm. "Don't say that! You make me sound like a tramp!"

Some of the customers in the store turned and looked at me. I lowered my voice. "I'm older than you, so yes, I've slept with more people than you have – that's basic math. But that doesn't mean I have all this experience. Do I have to remind you that I have remained celibate with Reid?"

Ginny placed the bra down and looked at me. "And why is that Vicky?"

"Don't ask that, you know why."

"Yeah, because you're in love with him," Ginny answered.

My eyes bulged and my mouth opened. "What?" I gasped. "That isn't true!"

"Of course it is. You're afraid of losing him so you're using sex as your weapon."

"I'm not in love with him and I'm not using sex as my weapon!" I scolded. A few more shoppers looked over at me and giggled under their breath. "Move on please," I instructed them. I took Ginny's arm and walked her to another area of the store. There was some silk underwear lying on a display table and I thumbed through it, looking for my size.

"Look, I don't want to fight," Ginny said. "I need some new underwear and I thought you might too."

I looked at the price tag. "And you feel I need to spend forty dollars on it?"

Ginny smiled. "Consider it a gift from me."

"More like a gift from Bob. I don't think I like him buying me underwear." I thought for a moment. "But I do like spending his money."

"Perfect. Me too."

"So how is married life going?" I asked. "Is it true that your sex life dries up?"

"Victoria, I've been married for three weeks," Ginny reminded me. "The sex area is okay, I just think we need to spice it up or something. It gets boring doing the same old thing, you know?"

"Not really. I can barely remember the last time I had sex actually."

I grabbed a few pairs of underwear then turned to a wall display for the matching bras. They were silk with lace across the tops of the cups. I smiled to myself. Reid would like these. I searched for my size and grabbed a few. The bras were twice the price of the panties, but Bob was paying anyway.

"Maybe I'm scared. You've seen Reid – he's probably really good in bed."

Ginny smiled dreamily. "Yeah, he probably is."

I smiled and slapped her playfully. "You're married, Gin."

"That's exactly why you need to close the deal and give me all the juicy details."

"Soon," I promised. Across the store I noticed a couple shopping for a bustier, giggling and kissing each other. "Mac?"

Mac seemed startled to hear his name. Ginny and I walked over to see my cameraman Mac, red-faced, and holding a leather push-up bra. I recognized the woman he was with, too. Terry had been one of the detectives on our last case and she and Mac had been dating ever since. It was an occupational hazard of our business; too much time together, combined with intense exhaustion and constant proximity could make you feel something. That was another reason I wasn't convinced my relationship with Reid was real. Almost nothing in reality television was.

"Sharpe, hi," Mac said, calling me by my last name. It was the name I went by and had for a long time. Only my immediate family called me Victoria or Vicky at this point. Even Reid called me Sharpe almost exclusively. Of course, I called him Reid and that was his last name too. "We were just shopping," Mac explained.

"I see that. Nice to see you, Terry," I said. Terry was drop-dead gorgeous with auburn hair and piercing green eyes. She was dressed in a green wrap dress, which emphasized her tiny waist and ample cleavage. I would have hated her for her looks if she wasn't so self-conscious about them. She was stunning but also painfully shy; a combination I found endearing.

Terry smiled. "Have you been enjoying your time off? We have."

Terry, Mac, my sound operator Manny and me all unknowing ingested cyanide and miraculously survived. The woman who poisoned us deserved most of the blame, but I was partly responsible too. I had this idea that it would make great TV if we confronted the killer. I didn't consider that she might try to kill us too.

"Yeah, I've been relaxing mostly. Just laying low," I explained. "How about you?"

"Mac and I went up to Napa for a few days."

"Nice," Ginny said, chiming in. "Bob's parents have a house up there. It's beautiful this time of year."

Mac had found something special with Terry. In all the years I had known him I had never seen him so openly affectionate with someone. I was genuinely happy for him.

Mac had earned his nickname because he was a real-life MacGyver. He was like a boy scout – always prepared. He focused on his work, his body, and his intellect. He was also pretty deep and frequently participated in meditation, spiritual healing circles, and hot yoga. It wasn't like him to lose himself in a woman the way he had with Terry. I was convinced the near-death experience had changed him too. Maybe it had changed us all.

I smiled. "I'll let you two get back to your shopping. Mac, I'll see you at the station tomorrow."

"Back to work," Mac lamented.

I nodded. "Back to work."

2.

I arrived at the station bright and early. By now I was a known-entity so the cops at the front desk let me walk around, unescorted. Reid worked in Receda, which was deep in the heart of the San Fernando Valley. The station was beat-up and run-down and looked like it hadn't been cleaned since the seventies. I gave Mac and Manny a call-time of 9 a.m. and picked up some coffee and donuts on my way. Experience told me not to bother with the sludge they called coffee at the station. I bought enough for my crew, the cops, and anyone else who might want a cup. Bribery with food was highly encouraged at the precinct.

The first time I had arrived at this particular station, my reception was icy. In fact, most of the cops chose to ridicule me. When I complained about my unfair treatment, the female captain told me to put on my big girl panties and suck it up. Reid had acted like my mere existence disgusted him and Foxy didn't pay me much mind. Well times had changed, hadn't they? I was practically family at this point. It didn't hurt that I had portrayed two of their detectives as absolute heroes in the premiere episode of *Murder Live!* That good PR for a station used to dealing with prostitution and immigration crimes, went a long way.

"Good morning!" I cooed as I entered the precinct, opening up the donut box to let the front desk cops grab a few. I passed through a series of doors into the workroom where Reid and Foxy sat. Foxy was a good cop and a good man and could always be counted on to make a joke at the absolute worst time. Reid and I had become the prime target for him lately as he joked and jabbed about our relationship. In the beginning it was especially exciting for Foxy to try and embarrass us as we tried to sort out how we felt about each other. Now he tended to favor more sexually charged jokes, still with the intention of humiliating us. Foxy was like a kid in a candy store and he teased us mercilessly.

"Well look who it is!" Foxy smiled. "The welcome wagon and she brings treats."

"I was worried you were getting thin," I teased Foxy who could probably stand to lose fifty pounds. I dropped the donuts on a desk along with the coffee and invited everyone to dig in.

Foxy had been partnered with Reid for about two years now and they were a great team. Foxy married his high school sweetheart Sherry, and had two kids at home. His real name was Dustin Flannigan, but like the rest of us, he went by another name. He had strawberry blonde hair and pale freckled skin, and he was Irish all the way.

"Donut, Mac?" I offered, not surprised to see that my camera man had arrived before call time and was already working.

"My body is a temple, Sharpe," he teased, walking by me carrying a roll of gaffers tape.

I didn't see Reid or Manny so I followed Mac to see what he had already gotten accomplished. This wasn't Mac's first time rigging this place for sight and sound and he had already made some quick work of the interrogation room. He mounted a camera from the ceiling and wired it into the "observation room," which sat between the two interrogation rooms. The cops called them interview rooms, but we all knew what they really were. The rooms had two-way glass and when they interviewed suspects we could sit in the middle room and watch, unnoticed. When Manny arrived with his sound equipment he would wire the room for sound as well.

Mac was in the process of hanging some lights from the ceiling, creating more moody lighting. The existing florescent bulbs were a cinematographer's nightmare, so Mac turned them off, preferring a softer glow.

"Hey guys!" I heard from behind me.

I turned to see Manny walking towards us. He was dressed in his usual attire – a pair of long jean-shorts and a T-shirt depicting a Latin band. Manny was Mexican and spoke with a thick accent. He was pretty short for a guy, about the same height as me, but he had strong legs and arms for carrying equipment. His black hair hung in a long braid down his back and his legs were covered in tattoos.

"Hey man," Mac said and slapped hands with him, pulling him in for a chest bump.

I went for the more traditional hug. "How are you, Manny?" I asked. "How was your time off?"

"Chica, it was amazing," Manny said. "I went to this Native American tribal camp out in the dessert. They put us in a teepee with these hot lava rocks and we just had to sweat in there until we started hallucinating. Then we got high and talked about our fears. It was deep."

"I've done that," Mac said. "Of course, without the drugs. It's pretty transformational."

It was no surprise to me that Mac had sweated in a teepee. He was the type of guy who could always one-up you when you were telling a story. You were attacked by a bear? Mac would say he was attacked by a lion. You jumped out of an airplane? Mac would say he did too, but his parachute failed and he had to find a way to survive. The stories were true, too. When he wasn't working with me he was usually doing much cooler things like back-packing through Africa for the Documentary Channel. But that didn't mean this work was beneath him. Without this show, Mac wouldn't be able to say he was poisoned by a deranged killer. That story had become a recent favorite of his.

"Yeah man, I got all those toxins out of my body," Manny continued. "All of that poison from that perra mujer who tried to kill us. How about you, Sharpe?"

"Oh, I just hung around and took it easy," I said, feeling like a loser. "I probably should have sweated out my toxins, but instead I caught up on my sleep."

Manny winked. "Probably spent lots of time in bed with the detective, right? I get you, Chica."

"Mac was just setting up the rooms for video," I said, changing the subject. "Do you want to get going on sound? I have to talk to the cops and see if there are any cases brewing."

"You got it babe," Manny told me.

*****

13

I wandered back into the bullpen to see if Reid had arrived yet. I found him sitting at his desk, his face buried in a file. It was hot today and he had taken his dress shirt off and hung it on the back of his chair like he usually did. He was wearing a white T-shirt and I couldn't help but notice how nicely it clung to his biceps. He was leaning on his elbows, supporting his head with his hand. His big lips were pursed as he read the case file he was looking at.

"Take a picture, it'll last longer." Foxy teased me from his desk. I hadn't realized I was standing there staring at Reid, but obviously I was.

Reid looked up to me and smiled slowly. "Hey."

"Hey," I said back. "How was the rest of your night?"

Reid shrugged. "Lonely."

I tilted my head, giving him a half-smile. "You kicked me out."

Reid turned his head to look at Foxy, who was sitting at his desk with his head perched between his hands. He had a goofy smile on his face. "Oh, don't worry about me. Keep talking, it's turning me on."

Reid sat up in his chair. "So, what's the plan for today?"

"Right," I said, snapping into producer mode. "We'll follow your lead. Is there anything hot at the moment?"

"Just the tension between you two," Foxy joked.

Reid ignored his partner and pointed at the file he was reviewing. "I've got another dead hooker case."

I shook my head. "No more hookers. Missy just aired your hooker episode last week. We can't do the same story again."

"But that's our specialty!" Foxy whined.

Missy was another one of the producers assigned to the show that I had the misfortune of working with. She and I were competitive and aggressive when it came to snatching up the greatest number of episodes. Now that the show had made it onto network TV, the budget had gotten much bigger. My boss Lenny was able to hire a few more producers allowing us more time to pull our stories together and more time to get them edited. Missy and I had a rivalry to see who could out-produce the other. It intensified during the last episode, when she was paired with Foxy and Reid. I won that battle, even Missy would agree, but the mention of her name still sent a shot of anger through my system.

"Hookers are all I've got right now," Reid said.

"Okay," I said. "We can continue to set up and maybe do some talking heads later."

"She talks to it, man?" Foxy said to Reid, eyes widening.

"I'm talking about interviews, Foxy," I scolded, grabbing a donut and shoving it in my mouth. If I wasn't going to have sex, I was at least going to have donuts.

*****

Thirty minutes later, I found myself getting restless. Mac and Manny had finished getting everything rigged and set in the interrogation rooms and had also lit an area for my on-camera interviews with the cops. Talking heads were typically framed as a medium shot, including the subject's head, neck and shoulders. During these sessions, I would sit very close to the lens of the camera and fire off questions. The idea was to make it look like the subjects were talking to the camera, instead of talking to me. If this were a normal shoot, with brand new cops, I would have been interviewing them now. But with these two, I had the footage already and I knew their backstories, so there was really no point. All I could do was sit there and wait for someone to die.

I sat at a desk near Reid and Foxy, fooling around on my smart phone and stealing glances at Reid. I opened up an email that I received from the *Daily Buzz*, the news authority in Hollywood, scanning it for anything interesting. There was an article on Hollywood producer Mark Stosky's newest project. It was a film he had picked up recently that involved my neighbor Kelly and Hollywood Johnson, the cop I had worked with on the last episode. They were going into production in a few months in Canada.

The article managed to distract me for a few minutes before I started staring at the clock. It was nine-thirty. This felt like it was going to be a long day. We had elected to start our week on a Tuesday to give the cops some time on Monday to snag us a juicy case. But all they had come up with were dead prostitutes. "Were any of the prostitutes male?" I asked the guys hopefully.

"No Sharpe," Foxy answered, in a way that suggested my question was stupid.

I sighed and returned back to sneaking glances at Reid. I wasn't sure how to act around him. Everyone knew we were seeing each other, but we had never had the experience of working together while we were involved. The dating part of our relationship, if that was what you wanted to call it, didn't start until the first show ended. I didn't know if we should act like we were strangers or openly display our affection. I needed to have a conversation with Reid about it to see if he was feeling as awkward as I was.

I walked over to Reid's desk and he looked up at me, his dark lashes revealing chocolate brown eyes. "We're all set in the interview rooms. Do you want to check it out?" I asked.

Reid looked at me and then over at Foxy. "Sure."

"Should I come too Sharpe, or are you guys planning on making out in there?" Foxy asked.

Sometimes he was really annoying. I smiled. "We'll be fine alone."

I turned and silently led Reid into one of the interrogation rooms. When we were both inside, I closed the door behind him and looked up into his dark eyes. I moved close to him and ran my fingers over his chest. "I felt weird kissing you hello this morning," I told him. "So I didn't."

Reid placed his hands on my hips and exhaled. "Yeah, me too." His breath smelled like sex and I found it drawing me into him.

"We'll probably have to sneak around a little. Find secret spots or something. I don't really know how to act around you when other people are around," I admitted.

"I don't either. I mean, I'm working right now. Having you here is… a distraction for sure," Reid said, leaning in.

Having him this close to me was intoxicating. I raised my lips to his and lightly brushed them with mine. That one brush of our lips became two and three, until I gripped my fingers around his shirt and pulled him in. The kiss started tender and soft but it soon turned more heated and hungry. It was a familiar pattern for us.

I could feel Reid's lips curl into a smile. "What are you doing to me honey? You're gonna kill me."

I smiled and went in for another kiss. I could do this all day. I was so wrapped up in Reid that I completely forgot where I was or that anyone else might be around. I also forgot about the two-way glass in the interrogation room, and the video camera.

Suddenly, there was a sharp rap at the door. "We can see you," the voice on the other side said.

I froze momentarily and then Reid and I pulled apart. I would have expected the voice to be Foxy's, but it sounded more like a woman's voice.

Reid and I gazed at our reflections in the two-way glass. I released my grip from his shirt while Reid smoothed it out. Reid turned towards the door and opened it to find Captain Harris standing on the other side.

My eyes went wide. This was not good. Reid could get in trouble for this.

"Captain Harris, we were just..." I began.

"Save it," she shot back. "Last I understood your show was about solving cases, not making love connections." Captain Harris was beefy and tough with dark brown hair pulled into a tight bun and a plain, make-up free face.

"Captain, I'm really sorry," Reid said. He was embarrassed and it was my fault.

Captain Harris seemed to take some pleasure in the fact that she had just humiliated us. Her lips twisted into a devilish grin as she held out a brown case file. "Boy do I have a case for you."

Reid looked down at the folder and opened it.

"They just called it in," Harris explained. "Victim was found dead in his underwear. A gold and black thong to be exact."

"Is he an escort?" Reid asked.

Harris grinned grandly. "He's a porn star, detective. The murder happened while he was on set."

Reid stared at her for a moment, not sure if she was being serious or not.

Captain Harris looked at me. "As for you, hot stuff, remember that your job is to observe the officers doing their work. No more vigilante stuff like last time."

"Of course," I confirmed, kind of enjoying being called "hot stuff."

"There's going to be a lot of temptation in that studio," Harris continued, staring directly at Reid. "When you're on duty, keep your relationship professional."

Reid's face flushed. I had never seen him look so small. "Captain, I, uh…"

"That's all," she said, then she turned and walked away, chuckling under her breath.

A lot had gone on during that brief exchange, enough to throw me off my game and nearly miss the point. I stood there paralyzed for a moment, feeling both mortified and extremely guilty. After a brief moment I returned to my senses and turned to Reid with a burst of energy. "Let's roll!"

Without waiting for his reply, I charged past him to collect the crew. "Guys, we have a murder!" I announced as I ran back into the bullpen. Mac and Foxy were sitting near each other and both popped their heads up upon hearing the news. I scanned the room for Manny but I didn't see him.

"Who's the victim?" Mac asked me.

"Dead porn star," I announced, trying to sound somber, barely able to disguise my grin.

Reid walked up behind me, but he wasn't grinning like I was. Foxy looked over at him, taking this seriously. "What do we know?"

"Not much," Reid and I said in unison.

I flinched as the words came out of my mouth. The captain told me not to get involved and here I was up to my old tricks. I looked away, afraid to meet Reid's judgmental gaze.

Reid cleared his throat and then walked past me to speak to his partner. "Let's get rolling. Murder was in Burbank, but they asked us to take it."

Foxy smiled. "Well, they called on the right people. I certainly know a thing or two about pornography."

"I wouldn't brag about that, man," Mac chided.

Foxy shrugged. "Why not?"

Reid pulled his dress shirt on over his T-shirt. He grabbed his badge and his gun and headed out the door. Foxy followed suit, collecting his items and following behind his partner.

I turned to Mac. "Where the hell is Manny?"

Mac shrugged. "Where do you think?"

I knew that meant he was either smoking up behind the police station or smoking up in our van. "Come on, let's go."

Mac picked up his camera while I grabbed my clipboard and we headed out of the station. I knew Reid was upset with me. He took his job seriously and I was already mucking it up. The memories of working with Reid and Foxy during our first shoot came flooding back. They had regarded us as a general nuisance. We slowed them down, we asked them to do retakes, and we interfered with their police work. I was worried that by the time we got to the parking lot, Reid and Foxy would be gone and we'd have to scramble to figure out where they went. Luckily and somewhat miraculously, they were waiting for us outside.

Manny was outside too, sleeping in the back of our SUV. He hadn't smoked up; instead, he had popped a medical marijuana pill and passed out. At least there was less odor.

Reid sat in the driver's seat of their unmarked, yet still very obvious, Ford Taurus. Foxy was in the passenger's seat and they were idling in the parking lot. I looked left at our production vehicle and right at the cop car and hesitated, not sure which vehicle to get into. Normally I would ride with the cops and fire off questions to them as we drove, but I was nervous because I felt like Reid was mad at me. I had embarrassed him in front of his superior and I felt like an idiot. I had acted like some sex-crazed teenager back there.

Reid's stony demeanor and not-so-subtle glare was not exactly new. When we first started working together he was rude, abrasive, and a complete asshole to me and everyone around. Was I going to have to deal with the same treatment all over again? I may have put up with it last time but I wasn't about to put up with it again.

"Sharpe, are you coming?" Reid called out to me.

"Oh," I smiled, feeling a wave of relief. "Yes, coming."

"Five fifteen, Magnolia Boulevard in Burbank," Reid called out to Mac.

"Got it." Mac nodded from behind the wheel of the SUV. The fact that we had worked with these cops before made things much easier. They knew the drill and so did we.

Mac had already mounted a small camera on the rearview mirror that captured an angle of Reid and Foxy as they drove. There was also a microphone to capture their audio. I sat behind Reid in the camera's blind spot so I would not be filmed. My role was to ask thought-provoking questions that would get the guys talking. It would appear to the viewers at home that they were talking to each other, even though I was the one driving the conversation. It wasn't as if these guys didn't talk to each other when they drove, but I needed them to be clear and articulate and to properly describe what was going on.

Once we started driving I threw out my questions. "Can you tell me what you know so far?"

"Sharpe, we know as much as you do," Foxy answered.

"Seriously, Foxy?" I said, gesturing towards the camera on his rearview mirror. "You worked with Missy like two weeks ago and already you've forgotten how this all works?"

"Missy didn't ride with us," Foxy informed me. "My partner here didn't allow it."

I raised my eyebrow. "Oh really? I suppose I should consider myself quite lucky then."

"She just wasn't as pushy as you are," Foxy explained.

"Look, if we're gonna do an interview let's just get it over with, okay?" Reid grumbled.

"Sure," I said. "Reid, can you talk to Foxy about what you know so far?"

Reid looked at his partner and smiled. "So Foxy, let me tell you about this case." He was being kind of obnoxious, which irked me a bit. "We got a call from the Burbank PD about a male victim found dead. We don't have a lot of details, but apparently he was on a porn set. We aren't sure if he was an actor or what. We're heading there now."

"Oh, is that where we're going?" Foxy joked. "I was wondering why we were driving around! But I do know how much you like your afternoon drives partner."

"Okay, let's try this another way," I said, not amused by these two wise guys. "Foxy, this question is for you. How do you approach a case like this?"

Foxy smiled and turned to his partner. "You know Reid, I have a feeling this is going to be a *hard* case. We need to seek out the *naked* truth to *expose* the killer." Foxy turned and looked at me, smiling. "Better?"

"Very nice," I told him sarcastically. "Can we expect these kinds of jokes the whole time?"

"When we get there, I'll *cock* my weapon in order to avoid any *premature* gunfire," Foxy answered, still smiling.

"Make sure there are no barriers to our *entry*," Reid said to his partner. "We'll have to *penetrate* deep to get the facts."

Foxy considered Reid's comments. "You're getting there. Not bad."

"Detective work can be a *pain* in the *butt*," Reid said and Foxy let out a shriek of laughter.

"Okay, so the answer is yes, I can expect these jokes the whole time," I muttered.

"We'll be on our *breast* behavior, Sharpe," Foxy told me.

I looked out the back window and saw Mac and Manny following behind us. Manny apparently had woken up at some point and made his way from the back seat up to the passenger's seat. Reid and Foxy continued to one-up each other with the porn-speak while I looked out the window.

I gazed out as we drove past a series of rundown shops and mini strip malls. Burbank had great shopping, good food outlets, and it was family oriented. But not all sections of Burbank were created equal. As we crossed through North Hollywood on Magnolia Boulevard and into Burbank I observed a series of low-end studios. From the street, they looked like office buildings with junky signs hanging on them. The streets were almost empty with no cars parked out front and there were no restaurants or coffee shops. The whole area screamed "Something underground is going on here" and we were about to find out exactly what that was.

I pulled out my phone and sent a text to my boss, Lenny. While I preferred to keep contact with my sleazebag boss to a minimum, I wanted to keep him informed. Considering his lust for all things female, except me luckily, I figured something like this would be right up his alley. I wasn't sure how well it would play on TV and what we could and couldn't show, but generally America responded positively to filth and smut. I typed into my phone: *Heading to a porn set for a murder case. Dead guy was wearing a thong.*

How was that for a text? If that didn't pique his interest, nothing would. Despite my general disdain for the man, I enjoyed when he recognized me for my good work. I got a little thrill out of feeling like I was doing things well.

"This is it, on the right," Foxy told Reid, pointing out the window.

Reid put on his turn signal and pulled over in front of a black stucco one-story building. It had bars across the windows and a small sign on the door that read, "Happy Day Studios." The bleak building adorned with the rusty sign was the perfect contrast to the sunny name of the studio.

Mac and Manny pulled up behind Reid and parked. Manny jumped out and opened the trunk to retrieve his recording equipment.

Reid turned around and looked at me. "You ready for this?"

I smiled, "Yeah sure."

Foxy shook his head. "This might be some crazy shit. Sharpe, you're not gonna freak out, right?"

"Shut up, Foxy," I said and got out of the car.

"Whoa, whoa, whoa. Let me get you guys micked up before you go in there," Manny told the cops. "I just need a minute."

Foxy smiled, turned his back to Manny, and lifted his arms. Manny rolled his eyes as he clipped the mic pack to the back of Foxy's pants and threaded the lavaliere up his shirt.

"You missed this ass, didn't you?' Foxy joked.

"You know most people clip their own mics," Manny whined.

"I know. You tell me that every single time, Manny. But I really enjoy getting the star treatment."

"Come on man, you're all sweaty," Manny complained. "All you were doing is sitting on your ass in an air-conditioned car!"

Reid was next and clipped his own microphone to his pants and threaded it up his own shirt. If he had needed someone to assist, I would have been happy to help. Manny slung his recording equipment over his shoulder and did some audio tests.

"Sharpe, it could be gross inside," Foxy told me. "You're not going to throw up again, right?"

"Shut up already, Foxy!" I said punching him in the arm. "This isn't my first rodeo, I'm good now."

Manny continued to test his equipment. Once everything was working well, he grabbed his boom mic and looked at me expectantly. "Ready."

I noted that the group dynamics were as they should be. Mac and Manny were looking to me for guidance, while Foxy was looking to Reid. It needed to stay that way, which meant I had to fight my usual urges to take over. I reminded myself that I had to be careful about crossing that line.

We headed toward the door, camera and sound rolling. I hung back, allowing my crew to capture the action. Mac's camera used the time of day as timecode so I made a note on my clipboard that it was 10.30 a.m. as we approached the building. My notes would help my editor later as he tried to pull hours and hours of footage together.

Reid and Foxy approached the front door and rang the bell. A moment later, the door swung open and we suddenly came face-to-face with Rose Ortez, the very same woman we had put behind bars a few weeks earlier.

3.

Rose was a striking Latina, both because of her gorgeous flowing black hair and because of the voluptuous figure she enjoyed flaunting. She wore red leather boots laced up to her thighs attached to six-inch heels. Her eyes were large, lined with dark eyeliner, and her lips were red and glossy. On her body she wore a red leather corset and matching mini skirt to coordinate with her boots. Her enormous breasts were busting out of the top of her corset, her nipples desperately close to making an appearance. Even though I had just noted on my clipboard that the time was ten-thirty, I felt the urge to check again. Was this her day-look now? While Rose's wardrobe wasn't one that I would ever wear, it seemed especially strange for the morning.

Rose's lips curled into a smile when she saw us. "Well, look what the gato dragged in." She was from Mexico originally and spoke with a thick accent.

I heard a thud behind me and turned to see that Manny had dropped his boom microphone on the floor. He didn't seem to notice, his eyes were transfixed on Rose. "I didn't think I'd see you again," he managed to mumble, practically drooling at the sight of her.

Rose looked him up and down and squinted, trying to remember. "We had sex, right?"

Foxy let out a laugh. It had been maybe three weeks since she and Manny had done it, twice, and she barely remembered. Foxy placed a hand on Manny's shoulder. "I guess you didn't rock her world, dude."

Manny looked shocked and slightly embarrassed but I wasn't

24

surprised. Rose had probably been with fifty guys since then and that was no exaggeration. The woman had an addiction to sex and a line of conquests a mile long. No wonder she ended up on a porn set.

"I remember you," Rose said, scrutinizing my body up and down. She shook her head. "We *didn't* have sex."

Foxy laughed again. "She would have remembered you, Sharpe."

I straightened up, feeling annoyed and naked under her glare. Did she seriously think I would be interested in her? "You're not my type," I told her.

Rose nodded. "That's right." She moved towards Reid and ran a hand across his chest. "You liked this one. Me too."

I felt my blood start to boil. It irked me to the core that she thought she could control Reid like he was some moronic puppet that couldn't resist her charms. Reid slapped her hand away just as I was about to erupt. "How the hell did you get out?" Reid wanted to know.

On my first episode of *Murder Live!* Reid and Foxy investigated a case involving an underground drag racer who had been killed during a hit and run. Rose was the dead guy's girlfriend and had gotten him involved in smuggling Mexicans across the U.S. border for a price. When a job went wrong, her boyfriend Chaser was killed. Chaser's best friend Kitt, who Rose was also sleeping with, was also involved and was also later killed. Although Rose may not have intended for the men to be killed, she was involved in informing their killers about their locations and also formulating a lie that resulted in one of their deaths. The last time I saw her she was being hauled off to jail as an accomplice to murder.

"I got off," Rose said, answering Reid's question.

"How the hell did you do that?" Reid asked.

Rose smiled. "I got the judge off."

I must have looked like I had just swallowed a bug or something as an expression of distaste crossed my mouth. How screwed up could the criminal justice system possibly be?

"You're shitting me," Reid said, not believing her either.

Rose raised her hands. "Seeing me in handcuffs turned you on, didn't it? Sorry to disappoint."

I felt my blood heating up again, but I needed to remember we were filming this. I was supposed to be an observer and if I walked over and decked her, it would ruin everything. I had never decked anyone in my life, but with Rose it was tempting.

Foxy shook his head like he was disappointed in a young child. "So you're fresh out of jail and already you're mixed up in another murder?"

Rose leaned in to Foxy, her lips curving into a sneaky smile. "Coincidence."

"So, pornography is your new gig, Rose? That's a step-up from human smuggling I think," Foxy told her.

"It's adult film," Rose corrected.

I felt myself physically gag. This environment was uncomfortable to begin with, now I had this sexpot standing in front of us doing everything possible to make it more awkward.

"Did you find the victim?' Reid asked.

Rose looked at Mac's camera. Manny had managed to pick up the sound equipment he had dropped on the floor and he was now holding the boom microphone over Rose's head. "Are you recording this?"

"Don't play stupid, Rose," I interrupted, forgetting my place as a silent listener. "You know we are."

"I didn't give my consent," Rose smirked.

Reid glared at her. "We have you on camera confessing to obstructing justice with a federal judge. You'll give your consent."

Rose puffed her chest. "Fine, I have nothing to hide."

"Then answer the question," Reid said. "Did you find the victim?"

"Yes."

"Were you sleeping with the victim?"

"No."

"Yeah right," Foxy said. "Another poor schmuck who got mixed up with the wrong girl. This case should be open and shut."

Rose didn't look phased. "I didn't kill him."

"Sure, you did," Foxy argued. "It's a classic case. You got away with murder once, so now you think you're invincible. Don't tell me it's a coincidence that everyone you hang around with ends up dead."

I stepped behind Mac and watched as he zoomed in on Rose's face, recording her reaction. She was stone cold. She knew how to play this – she wasn't going to give up anything. She had almost fooled us the last time. She knew how to manipulate things to get her way.

Behind me, I heard the sound of kids laughing. I turned to see two young girls, maybe thirteen years old, pointing at Rose and giggling. "Nice outfit," one of them said to her.

Rose narrowed her eyes at the girls. "That's what your Daddy told me last night."

I saw their faces drop. They looked at each other, horrified, then ran off crying. "Is that why your parents are getting divorced?" one girl asked the other as they ran.

"I don't know!" the other cried.

"That was low Rose, even for you," Foxy told her.

Rose shrugged her shoulders. She didn't care, it wasn't her style.

"Looks like the film crew is here," a voice from behind us said. We turned to see the Medical Examiner Lou, approaching us.

"Hey buddy," Foxy said by way of greeting.

Lou looked at me. "You again, huh?"

The last time we were together I had vomited after seeing a bloody and bruised victim lying on the ground. It was my first dead body. I had managed to retch right next to the crime scene, so Lou had to smell the contents of my stomach for the rest of the night. Understandably he was not a big fan.

I pulled out a release, snapped it to my clipboard, and handed it to him. "Would you mind?"

"Does this mean I get another three seconds of fame? I counted last time you know. I was on air for three seconds exactly."

"Maybe I'll keep you on for four this time," I offered.

Lou shook his head before grabbing my pen and signing.

"Why don't you take us inside and show us around?" Foxy said, turning back to Rose.

"This isn't my shop. You can talk to Vinnie," Rose said. "Vinnie! The cops are here."

With that, Rose turned around, exposing her barely-covered rear end and walked back into the studio, slamming the door shut behind her.

"Well that was rude," Foxy announced to our group.

Manny looked crest fallen. "*Did we have sex?* What kind of a question is that? She doesn't even remember?"

"She's a sex addict," Mac reminded him. "Sex has no meaning to her, man. She's probably been with hundreds of guys."

"And so have you," Foxy said to Manny placing a hand on his shoulder. "They say when you sleep with someone you're sleeping with everyone before you too. You've been with like a thousand guys, dude."

Manny grunted, slapping Foxy's hand off his shoulder. "She's still hot," he lamented.

The front door opened again and a greasy, short Italian man stepped out. He looked to be in his late thirties and he wore a plaid button-down shirt with a pair of old jeans. In LA, people didn't dress for the weather, they dressed for status and style. The worse you looked, the wealthier people believed you to be. Was it strange that this guy was wearing a flannel shirt on a scorching hot day? Not really.

"How you guys doin? I'm Vinnie Sputello, the director here."

"Detective Flanagan," Foxy said, extending a hand. "This is my partner Detective Reid, and this is Lou Meyers, our medical examiner. Can we come inside?"

"What's with the film crew?" Vinnie wanted to know.

I put a hand on Mac's arm, signaling to him that he should stop filming while I jumped in. "Hi Vinnie, my name is Victoria Sharpe. Can I talk to you a minute?"

"Oh, come on," Lou whined, wanting to get this thing over with.

"Just give us a minute," I told him.

I pulled Vinnie aside and walked a few steps down the street before starting my speech. "We're doing a show called *Murder Live!* Have you heard of it?"

"Oh yeah, you guys did that story about the actress that got killed in the hills, right? It was on the news I think."

"That's right," I said proudly, "and guess what? You are our next story. Cool, right?"

Vinnie hesitated. "I don't know. I mean, what if one of my guys did this or something?"

I was a little surprised by the comment. "Wait, do you know who killed the victim?"

"No, no," Vinnie said quickly holding up his hands. I was just thinking I wouldn't want to get anyone in trouble."

"Well if they killed someone I think they're going to be in pretty big trouble with or without the show. Don't you?"

"It's sweeps you know. Maybe this could be good for us."

I stopped walking and turned to him. "Sweeps?"

"Yeah, you know sweeps season. Where they decide what shows are going to be picked up for the year. We're shooting a television pilot called *Babes in Space* right now for the Lush network."

I shook my head. "They have a sweeps season for pornography?"

Vinnie's eyes narrowed. "Let's get something straight here, I'm not a pornographer. We do soft core television shows for major cable networks. There's a difference."

"Oh." I thought to myself for a moment. "What's the difference?"

"No penetration and no genitals. We only show boobs and butts."

He answered me with a straight face but it was hard not to laugh. Actually, I felt relieved when he said it was only 'boobs and butts.' When I saw Rose in that ridiculous outfit I figured it was some sort of S&M thing. Boobs and butts was better, I could handle that. "Well then that's good news. That will play better on the network too. So, you'll sign my release?"

Vinnie nodded. "Why not?"

"I'll need to get the rest of your cast and crew released too," I said.

Vinnie nodded again, indicating that he would help. We returned to the group that was waiting for us by the door.

"Can we go inside now?" Lou complained. "I don't have all day."

"Yup, we're all set," I said, giving my crew a nod. Mac and Manny re-fired their equipment and we all followed Vinnie as he led us in towards whatever evil lurked inside.

4.

Television sets were not new to me. I had grown up the daughter of one of the most recognizable faces in entertainment news. In my mother's heyday, kids were not something you showed off or even mentioned you had. A woman working in Hollywood kept her kids out of sight, not wanting anything to jeopardize her career. But as my sister and I got older and my mother became more established in her career, she started letting us tag along on set.

As a kid I would brag to my friends about the celebrities I was about to meet and then completely clam up once I had the chance. Our exchanges usually consisted of my mother making the introduction, my face turning brick red, a weak handshake exchange with the star, and me skulking off, humiliated. It was kind of pathetic, but celebrities had always intimidated me.

I learned about sets from my father too. He was a set designer and would bring Ginny and I to work with him to check out whatever he was creating that month. His sets ranged from flashy game shows to sitcom living rooms and everything in between. He knew all the tricks when it came to color pops, perspective, lighting, and how to draw an audience in. He had visions of Ginny or me picking up the family trade, but design was never something that interested either one of us. In Ginny's case, work of any kind was unappealing.

While television sets were familiar to me, a pornography set was not. This type of production had not been in the repertoire of either of my parents or anyone I knew for that matter. I could now add "porn set" to the list of strange places my job had taken me. It joined ranks with places such as celebrity mansions, illegal drag races, jail, and my personal favorite: the Mexican border where I was nearly shot by border patrol.

One unpleasant aspect of my job, among many, was that I was often put in a position to witness things I preferred not to. For example, I worked on a television show where we had cameras rigged throughout a hotel that contestants were staying at. The contestants may have felt like they were alone when they didn't see any camera operators around, but of course they weren't. There were cameras mounted in plain sight in each of the bedrooms. After several beers and tequila shots, they tended to forget the cameras were there. The bedrooms were particularly active after hours and our cameras captured it all.

The editors used to pull up the footage of these unsuspecting fools having sex and watch it in their edit bay. It wasn't like watching a porn film, at least not to me. These were real people, having real experiences, and we were invading their privacy. I couldn't stand to watch the footage and I knew we didn't need to. This kind of thing would never air on TV. I would say to my editors, "We can't air this, why are we watching it?" But that never seemed to deter them. Those small edit bays could get mighty uncomfortable during those moments. In this business, sometimes you had to pretend to have a thicker skin than you really did. There was no HR handbook on harassment in reality TV. We were there to document the good, the bad, and the unsavory.

I wasn't a prude, but I did believe that certain things should be kept private. That might have sounded ironic, considering most of my hookups with Reid had been witnessed by other people. But that was an unintended result. I would have preferred to be intimate with him behind closed doors, but someone always seems to be opening them.

Stepping into the studio I found myself tensing up. Based on the wardrobe Rose was sporting, I wasn't sure what to expect inside. Would everyone be walking around naked? Was I walking into some weird orgy or something? Did they have a closed set or would they be filming a scene right before our very eyes? I didn't know the answers and I was nervous to find out.

Vinnie led us inside, with Reid, Foxy and Lou close to him and me and my crew trailing behind. Reid walked with confidence, seemingly comfortable in the environment. Of course, Reid usually worked cases involving dead hookers and pimps so this was probably pretty tame for him. As we walked, Foxy turned to me wide-eyed with a big smile and mouthed the words, "Here we go."

I felt my chest getting tight. We walked through a dark hallway past an office with a beaten up wooden door, closed from view. "That's my office," Vinnie told us as he continued to lead us through.

"Listen, a couple of my guys will be here in the next few minutes," Lou told Vinnie. "They're just coming off another job."

"Busy morning?" Foxy asked Lou.

"I'll say."

Mac pushed past the group and ran ahead, turning around and walking backwards so he could capture the men walking towards him. Manny and I jumped out of sight.

"Can you tell us about the victim?" Reid asked, now facing the camera.

"Yeah, sure," Vinnie answered. "Name was Lucky – Lucky Trevone. That might have been a stage name, I don't know. I hired him a couple weeks ago for this show. He had a good body, good face. That's the kind of thing we look for."

"Right," Reid continued. "And Rose discovered Lucky's body?"

"Yeah, she was screaming her head off."

"And what time was that?"

"Around nine-thirty. That's when people usually start showing up on set."

"How many people do you have working here?" Reid asked.

Vinnie counted on his fingers. "Uh, there's eleven. Or, there were eleven, now it's ten."

"And is everyone here now?"

"I think so. I really don't know. It's been a little hectic."

We continued down the hallway until we came to a corner. Around the corner, the lighting improved and the hallway became wider. On my right I saw a door with a small window in it to look inside. Above the door was a sign that said "Recording". The sign wasn't lit, which met the set wasn't hot at the moment. I peered through the glass, bracing myself for whatever might be going on inside. It was a small studio – maybe the size of a two-car garage, and it was decorated to look like outer space. There was a rocket ship in the middle of the room. On the left, the ship was covered with metal panels and circular windows. The right side was cut out exposing the interior of the ship. This was television, not film and so they needed views from both the outside and inside of the rocket available for the camera. The rocket was maybe fourteen feet high and ten feet wide, and the inside was painted silver and contained two captain's chairs. It wasn't impressive, but it wasn't terrible either. The galaxy and the stars were painted on the wall behind the rocket and the lighting was dark and moody.

Inside, there were some people milling around on set and a cameraman adjusting his camera which was mounted on a tripod. I didn't see any actors and everyone was wearing clothes.

Lou pulled out a roll of yellow police tape and started taping it across the hallway walls.

"Whoa, whoa, what are you doing there, pal?" Vinnie asked him.

"This is a crime scene," Lou said to him matter-of-factly.

"Yeah, but you can't block off our access. We're trying to get this show done by week's end," Vinnie explained.

"But now you've got a dead body on your hands," Foxy said.

"I know, but we still have to shoot. He died in the dressing room not the hallway. You don't need to be putting that tape up," Vinnie said, pulling it down. "I told you we only have this week to get this thing done plus now I have to rewrite half the show."

Foxy looked confused. "Won't the studio give you an extension?"

"Yeah right. Come on guys, I have a limited budget and I already paid for the studio time so we need to press on. You know what I'm saying?"

Foxy looked surprised. "Just let us do our job and then we'll be out of your way. There are certain procedures we have to follow, okay?"

"Yeah, I get it, but I don't want everyone freaking out around here over this."

"Do you know who killed the victim?" Reid asked Vinnie, switching gears.

Vinnie looked over at Reid and shook his head. "I have no idea."

"Were you the first one here this morning?" Reid asked.

"Yeah. I opened up around eight."

"Was Lucky here when you got here?"

"I don't know. I didn't check the dressing room. Rose found him. I told you that," Vinnie said. "Rose found him, she called me, and I called you."

We made a left into another area that appeared to be the final wing of the building. On my left there was another set, this one featuring the surface of the moon. The room was dark and the set was not in use. Next to it was an opening that looked like it led to a break room with two bathrooms next to that. On my right, there were two dressing rooms, and at the end of the hall was a control room, which doubled as an editing suite. There was an equipment storage closet next to the control room.

Rose was sitting in the first dressing room at a makeup table, while a young man, probably around twenty-two years old and chubby, applied powder to her cleavage. Mac turned and panned in to see Rose in her dressing room. All of the men in our group also looked in, their eyes seeming to linger for longer than necessary. Vinnie was the only one who didn't seem to find anything abnormal about the scene. In fact, he looked annoyed by it.

"Craig, quit fooling around and get on set before these guys shut us down," Vinnie ordered the man tending to Rose's boobs.

Craig rolled his eyes as he stood up and lumbered off to set, regarding us as he passed by.

"There are a lot of people walking around," Reid said to Foxy and Lou. "We need to round them up. I don't want anyone leaving."

Lou pulled his phone out his pocket and looked at a text message. "My guys just got here. I'll ask them to hold everyone outside."

When he reached the second dressing room, Vinnie stopped. The door was closed.

"He's in here," Vinnie announced.

Lou still had his yellow police tape in his hand and taped it across the top of the door. There was enough room beneath that we could still get inside, but Lou didn't want any unwanted visitors. Meanwhile, Lou, Foxy, and Reid all pulled on some rubber gloves.

I looked at my crew to ensure they were ready. Mac hung back to let the cops enter first. I nodded to Lou and he opened the door. Reid, Foxy, and Lou stepped inside, followed by Mac and Manny, and eventually me. The room was long and narrow. It consisted of a rack of lingerie and nighties hanging on the opposite wall and a makeup table mirror to our right next to the door. I didn't see the victim until I turned to my left to see the couch positioned against the side wall.

The couch itself was a green leather beaten-up love seat. Sitting on it was a man wearing a black and gold thong and a black mask on his head. He wore nothing else and looked relatively unscathed. There were a few smears of blood around his neck and chest, and a few drops of blood dripping from his neck.

"Did you touch the body at all?"

"No way, man," Vinnie answered.

"Do you know how he died?" Reid asked Vinnie.

"No, I just noticed he wasn't moving and we poked him and he didn't react so we knew he was dead."

"You just said you didn't touch him," Reid reminded him.

"Not with my hand. I poked him with a pen."

"What about the mask? Did you remove it?"

"No."

"What about Rose? Did she touch him?" Foxy asked.

"No!" Rose yelled from the next dressing room.

"Then how do you know this is Lucky?" Foxy asked.

Vinnie seemed amused by the question. "Look at those abs. I'd recognize them before I'd recognize his face."

My eyes moved from the man's thong – which I couldn't help but stare at, up to his abdominal muscles. Whoa. This guy had a hot body. Really hot. He must have spent hours in the gym every day to get a sculpt like that. I mean, if anyone could pull off a black and gold thong, it was this dude. I would have recognized those abs too.

Lou snapped dozens of pictures of the body with his camera. I stayed in the background, letting the police do their work. I noticed some blood on the victim's hands, like he was probably gripping his neck before he died. Yuck. Lou's team showed up and made quick work of collecting samples from the victim, the couch, and so on. They put fibers and hair samples in baggies. They took measurements and snapped more pictures.

After twenty minutes or so, two of Lou's men left the room to search the surrounding areas, while the other remained and continued to help. Lou turned to the cops. "I gotta take this thing off." Lou pulled on a fresh glove and in one swift motion pulled the mask off Lucky, exposing a lifeless face with a large puncture wound in the neck. The mask must have been holding the blood inside, because once it was removed it let out a cascade of dark red goo that poured down Lucky's chiseled chest. His eyes were opened and strained and his skin was pale and dead.

I felt myself starting to sweat. A moment ago I was enjoying looking at this man's package, and now suddenly, "Oh no!" I shouted before immediately vomiting on the floor.

"Oh, come on!" Lou shouted, throwing up his hands.

"I thought you were used to this by now!" Foxy snapped at me.

"Yeah with some warning!"

"I gave you warning!" Lou yelled at me. "I said, *I gotta take this off.* What the hell did you think I meant?"

"I didn't know you meant right away!" I felt like I was going to cry. I was embarrassed and wanted to crawl into my skin. I turned away for fear that looking at Lucky again might cause me to spew up the rest of my breakfast. "I'm sorry," I said.

"Hey man, are you okay?" Reid asked Vinnie who was starting to turn green as well.

"Get him out of here," Lou ordered. "Get her out, too."

Vinnie was more than happy to oblige and swiftly hustled out of the room. I remembered seeing a bathroom across the hall so I ran out to grab some paper towels to clean up my mess. I found some cleaning spray in there too, which I knew could help with the smell.

I avoided looking at Lucky as I reentered the room. "Let me just clean this up," I said, wiping the floor. I grabbed the cleaning spray and spritzed some on the brown carpet tiles.

"Don't do that!" Lou yelled at me. "Is that bleach? Honey, are you nuts? You're destroying my whole crime scene!"

I felt Reid's eyes on me and not in a loving way. As usual, I was interfering with his investigation. "Shit! I'm sorry!" I squealed, holding my hands up in the air. Lou's helper was staring at me, looking completely shocked by what I had just done.

"Just get out of here!" Lou moaned.

I quickly wiped up what was left of my regurgitated donuts and coffee. "I'll just wait outside," I whispered, leaving the cops and my crew inside the room. On my way out, Manny handed me a wireless headset so I could still listen to the conversation. I nodded at him gratefully.

I returned to the bathroom wearing my headset to wash my face and clean up my shirt. Why did this always happen to me? I probably should have prepared more for this job by hanging out at the morgue first.

"Nice girl you got there Reid," I heard Lou say through my headset. Of course, he didn't mean it. His voice was filled with sarcasm. "Is she your girlfriend or something?"

I had just splashed water on my face but froze for a moment, listening for Reid's answer. I heard some shuffling and some whispers and then someone clearing their throat. "What's the cause of death?" I heard Reid ask.

Damn. Manny probably told Reid that I was listening.

"Puncture wound to the neck," Lou answered. "Hard to say what it was. It doesn't look like a clean wound. If it was a knife, it was a dull one. The killer had good aim though – hit the artery right on. He didn't have a chance."

I dried off my face and walked back into the hallway, standing outside of the dressing room, leaning against the wall. I heard Lou clicking some more pictures through my headphones. In the hallway, a man walked by me who looked very familiar. He was wearing a pair of silk boxer shorts and a light-weight T-shirt. He was good looking with light brown hair and green eyes. He was movie-star good looking actually. He gave me a little smile then disappeared down the hallway.

It bothered me that I couldn't figure out where I had seen this guy before. I wasn't sure why it bothered me, I recognized people all the time that I couldn't place. I lived in Hollywood and probably half of the people walking around had been in some sort of movie or commercial or television show. But this guy was obviously an actor I had seen before. I didn't watch soft porn generally so why would I recognize him? Wait! It hit me like a flash. It was Kyle Belamy! Holy cow!

Kyle Belamy was probably one of the most famous porn stars of all time. He had been in hundreds of movies and was an international sensation. Wow, I was totally star struck! The even stranger thing was that I had just seen him a couple weeks ago while attending a concert at the Hollywood Bowl. Now here he was again. It was destiny!

"Guys let me have a little bit of time with him," Lou said in my headphones, snapping me back to reality.

"That's fine," Reid said. "We'll go talk to the witnesses."

A moment later, the door opened and the cops, Mac and Manny emerged.

Reid looked at me. "You okay now?"

"Yeah, sorry about that."

"Hey Sharpe if you want to change your shirt I saw some choice options for you in the dressing room back there," Foxy joked, slinging his thumb towards the door.

"Knock it off," Reid told his partner. "Let me go find Vinnie. I need to talk to everyone that's involved with this thing."

We nodded as Reid headed off to find him. Once Reid was out of sight, I grabbed Foxy's arm. "I just saw Kyle Belamy!"

Foxy turned to me, processing the name for a moment. "Wait, the porn star?"

"Uh-huh," I nodded, smiling. "He's here – he's working on this show."

"But this is boobs and butts," Foxy said and then laughed at the expression. "I'm never going to get tired of saying that."

"I know that, Foxy."

"Boobs and butts. Boobs and butts. But seriously, I thought Belamy only did the hard stuff."

"Maybe he's slowing down a bit. He was really hot!" I beamed.

"Well, the good news is that you'll probably get to see his butt. That should be rewarding for you, Sharpe," Foxy said and slapped my shoulder. "I'm glad to see you warming up to this place."

Indeed, I was. I was literally drooling over all the guys here, even the dead one. I probably spent a full minute staring at Lucky's package. What was it called when you wanted to have sex with dead people – necrophilia? Maybe vomiting was my body's way of punishing me for my dirty mind. I needed to get it together.

*****

The break room consisted of three circular tables, a little kitchenette and a craft service table filled with assorted fruits, sliced bagels, granola bars and coffee. It was customary in production to provide food on set because you didn't want people wandering off to grab lunch. This particular spread looked pretty good. Lou's colleague Tim had been holding the cast and crew together outside in order to keep an eye on them until the cops had a chance to speak with them. Reid asked Tim to move the group into the break room so he could address them all at once. The studio had lots of rooms and corners and Reid wanted to make sure no one was missed. It also provided a great opportunity for me to get release forms from everyone.

I stood in the back of the break room holding my clipboard with Mac and Manny standing next to me. We weren't filming yet, as we needed the group's consent first. I watched expectantly as different people filed in, looking for Kyle Belamy. Rose sauntered in with Craig and sat at a table in the front. Vinnie entered with another man by his side that looked very much like him. Both were Italian and a little overweight, however the other man was much taller than Vinnie. He carried a metal coffee thermos that he was sipping from.

Next came Kyle Belamy. He walked with a real confidence and had a certain swagger. I wondered what he was doing on a low-end production like this. Vinnie must have paid him a hefty salary. Kyle spotted me, gave me a wink, and sat down at a table alone. I was glowing. Kyle Belamy winked at me! I couldn't contain my excitement any longer. I pulled out my cell phone and texted my sister Ginny.

OMG, on a porn set right now with Kyle Belamy and he totally winked at me!

Two women walked in next. They were both pretty and thin and were probably actors. The taller of the two was a brunette with a pixie-style haircut, wearing a loose sun dress. The shorter woman had shoulder-length blonde hair and wore yoga pants and a sports bra. The sporty one looked like she was very upset, wiping tears from her eyes. The two ladies sat at the table with Kyle. Reid was standing at the front of the room, greeting people as they entered and guiding them to sit down. He reminded me of a funeral director welcoming guests to a wake.

"Hey, Enrique!" Manny said from behind me as a Hispanic man walked into the room. He was followed by a taller causation man who immediately walked over to the crying woman to comfort her.

I turned to see Manny putting down his equipment and walking over to high-five the man he called Enrique. The two of them exchanged some pleasantries in Spanish before breaking apart. Manny returned to his post by me and Enrique sat down at the final open table. The taller man also sat at the last table, but pulled his chair forward so he could be near the crying woman at the table in the front.

"You know that guy?" I asked Manny.

"It's a sound thing."

"So, he's the sound op?" I asked.

Manny nodded. "Pretty sweet job if you ask me. Except for the dead guy. That sucks. But he didn't do it – I can tell you that."

I scrunched my eyes. "Just like that? He's immediately not a suspect just because you know him?"

"The guy's got three kids and a wife. Why the hell is he gonna kill some dude in his underwear Sharpe?" Manny asked. He was speaking loud enough that it elicited a glare from Mac.

41

"Is that everyone?" Reid asked Vinnie from the front of the room.

"I'm here, I'm here," announced a twenty-something male with blonde hair and surfer-style good looks. He didn't look familiar to me but he definitely had an air of confidence about him. He was dressed in white-washed jeans, a white tank top, and a pair of flip flops. I could spot his type a mile away – total rich kid. Eye candy? Maybe, but he wasn't my type. I shifted my eyes to Reid. He was my type.

"That's everyone," Tim answered, walking in the room.

"Thanks, man," Reid said to him.

Tim, who was dressed in a police uniform, waved at Reid and then left the room in search of Lou.

"Okay guys, listen up," Reid began, addressing the group. "I know this is hard and you're upset about Lucky."

The crying actress let out a wail while the tall guy leaned forward to comfort her. I snapped to attention, nudging Mac to start filming. He swung his camera over his shoulder and pressed record. Manny held out his boom microphone to pick up the sound from the crowd. The cops were still wearing their mics and Manny had dropped some extra mics on the tables, so we had the room well covered.

"I have to ask for your cooperation as we go through our investigation. We need to speak to each of you one by one. Any information you have can be helpful to the case," Reid told them.

"Hey, what's with the cameras?" The tall guy wanted to know. "Vinnie man, what's this about?"

"They're filming a TV show called *Murder Live!*" Vinnie explained.

"What?" the exasperated crowd called out in unison.

"Lucky dies and you call a film crew Vinnie?" the crying woman asked.

"No, they just showed up," Vinnie tried to explain.

"Yeah right," someone shouted. "Anything for ratings, right Vin?"

Reid waved his hands. "Settle down everyone. The film crew is with us. They're following me and my partner and we just happened to land this case."

"I've heard of that show," the woman with the short hair said. "Wait, are we gonna be on that?"

"It looks that way," Reid answered.

The room started to buzz as their initial concern turned to chatter and excitement. It probably shouldn't have surprised me that a group of actors would be excited by the prospect of being on a TV show, even if the focus was on their dead friend.

"Okay, settle down everyone," Foxy interjected. "Sharpe – raise your hand."

From the back of the room I raised my hand while everyone turned around to look at me.

"Sharpe is the producer for the show and she'll have you sign a release form in a little while. If you sign the release you can be on the show. Right now we need your attention up here."

The group begrudgingly turned around and once again looked to the cops. "As I was saying," Reid continued, "we will need to speak to each of you to-"

Chirp! My cell phone buzzed. I looked down to see a text back from Ginny: *WHAATT?? Kyle Belamy?? OMG!*

"Uh, even the most seemingly insignificant detail can be important," Reid continued.

Chirp!

Why are you at a porn set?

Chirp!

I need details!

Chirp!

Can you send me a pic?

I felt my face growing red and hot as I fumbled around trying to silence my phone. "Sorry," I said to the group, who were once again craning their necks to look at me.

Reid looked at the floor, shaking his head, trying to remember what he was saying. "Anyway, we need cooperation from you all. I know that you may want to head home or mourn for Lucky somewhere else, but we need you to stick around for a while."

"Detective, we're still filming. We can't stop just because of Lucky," Vinnie interrupted.

Foxy shook his head. "Vinnie, with all due respect, you've got a dead guy in your dressing room."

"Screw you, Vinnie," the crying actress suddenly called out. "Lucky's dead. Does anyone even care?" The tall awkward man whispered something in her ear and rubbed her back.

"I care about him, Penny," Vinnie answered. "Shit, Lucky was great! His bod was unbelievable! Everyone knows that."

I looked around to see heads nodding in the crowd.

"But the show has to go on, darling," Vinnie continued. "Sweeps are just a few weeks away. We have to get this thing wrapped."

"But how are we going to finish without Lucky?" the crying woman named Penny asked. "He's a big part of the story."

"I'm rewriting it," Vinnie answered.

"You're cutting Lucky out?" Penny gasped, appalled.

"I might leave him in – I'm still trying to work it out."

"I'd like a bigger part," the blonde surfer-dude interjected. "I mean, I think it's only fair that I get more screen time."

"Ha!" Kyle blurted out. "That's rich. Give the no-name more air play."

"All right, all right, enough!" Reid said, losing his cool. "Jesus, can we focus here?"

"You'd better start taking this seriously," Foxy told the crowd. "This isn't a TV show, this is real life."

"I thought you said it was a TV show," the surfer dude commented.

"Wait, you said we were going to be on the show," the woman with the pixie haircut chimed in.

"No, it's a show. You are going to be on the show, I just meant that Lucky's murder isn't part of it," Foxy corrected. "Well, it is part of it. I just mean that Lucky really did die. That part isn't fake. That's the part you have to take seriously."

"We know that dude," the surfer guy told him. "We all went in there and looked."

"You all looked at Lucky in the dressing room?" Foxy asked.

"Of course we did," Kyle answered. "We thought it was a joke at first."

"Okay, so that's what I'm talking about. This isn't a joke, it's real," Foxy said.

"We know dude!" the surfer guy snapped, shaking his head.

"These guys are detectives?" Kyle asked, expressing skepticism.

"All right, listen up!" Foxy said, trying to regain control of the room. "We already know that the killer is sitting in this room, we just have to find him... or her."

The group collectively gasped and then glared at each other suspiciously. Reid nearly gasped too. He looked at Foxy like he was insane for making that type of accusation, but Foxy knew what he was doing. He had done it for the camera. It was the type of sound bite that would be featured in the promos of my show. Foxy was becoming a pro.

"What my partner meant to say," Reid announced, "is that we'd like to learn your names. My name is Detective Reid with the LAPD and I have been assigned to investigate this case. This is my partner, Detective Flanagan."

Foxy waved at the group.

"Now I'd like to go around the room and you can each tell me your name and your role with this production."

"This feels like an AA meeting," the man who walked in with Vinnie joked.

"How would you know?" Rose spat. "Just say your damn name so we can get on with this."

"Fine," the man said defiantly. "My name is Carmine Sputello and I'm the producer on this set."

Reid and Foxy held out their notepads and started writing down their names. I did the same.

"You his brother?" Foxy asked, pointing at Vinnie.

"Yeah," Carmine answered.

"Okay, next," Reid continued. "We already know Vinnie. You, say your name," he said, pointing at the Kyle.

"You've got to be kidding me," Kyle chuckled. He made a big show of standing up to address the detectives. "My name is Kyle Belamy – maybe you've heard of me? I'm an actor on this set."

"B-E-L-A-M-Y?" Reid asked.

Kyle laughed. "Is this guy for real?"

"Move on man. I've got him," Foxy whispered to his partner.

Reid looked up and motioned to Penny who was sitting next to Kyle.

"I'm Penny. I'm an actress too," Penny announced.

"Full name please."

"Penny Connors."

"Is that your real name?" Foxy wanted to know.

"Of course not. My real name is Marcia Kolowski. But don't you dare call me that." She turned around and looked at me. "I don't want that name used on TV."

I nodded, agreeing that I wouldn't. I would use her stage name.

Reid looked at the group, frustrated. "Okay, real names please."

"I'm Joy," the short-haired woman sitting next to Penny said. "Joy Evers. Real name Tammy Clover. I'm an actress too. I'm in this show but

I'm pretty new to this business. I'm more of a character actor."

The room collectively laughed. They had obviously heard this lie before. From my perspective, Joy didn't fit the bill for this type of role. Her hair was short and she was relatively flat-chested. She wasn't screaming "porn star" in my book.

"I'm Elroy Nichols and that's my real name. I don't think anyone would change their name to Elroy deliberately," the tall, skinny man said. He had moved away from Penny and returned to his seat at the table behind hers. "I'm the Director of Photography."

The room collectively laughed again.

"Fine, I'm the camera guy," Elroy corrected.

"Enrique Rodriguez. Sound," Enrique said holding a finger in the air. He was short and solid and spoke with a heavy accent. I got the sense that he knew enough English to get by, but not much more.

Reid and Foxy continued to nod and write down names in their notebooks. Next, it was the surfer-dude's turn. "Jason Niles," he announced. "Actor."

Kyle rolled his eyes grandly. "Boy, this group is being very creative with their titles today."

"I'm an actor Belamy," Jason told him.

"Sure you are," Kyle patronized.

Rose stood up from her table to ensure all eyes were on her as she spoke. "Rosario Ortez. That's my real name as you boys already know. I don't hide behind fake names, I know who I am."

"Don't act all high and mighty," Joy quipped. "If your name was Tammy Clover you would change your name too. That's a fat girl's name and I'm not fat!"

"Of course not," Rose said, gesturing with her finger down her throat, implying that Joy was bulimic.

"Knock it off you two," Vinnie ordered. "Come on, let's get this over with. Craig, you're next."

Craig, who was sitting next to Rose looked at the cops. "I'm Craig

Maddox. I'm… I guess you could call me a fluffer or at least that's how they sold it to me when they hired me." He glared at Carmine as he spoke. "Really it's more like a goffer or a personal bitch to the production. I do everything around here."

"Shut up asshole," Carmine jumped in. "I don't see you complaining when you're lubing the ladies up on set."

"Enough already!" Reid shouted. "Do you guys just bicker like school children all the time? Is that how things work around here?"

"Lucky just died," Penny answered. "We're on edge – can you blame us?"

"No," Reid answered, calming down.

"Thank you for those colorful introductions," Foxy said. "As I said before, the show's producer is in the back of the room. There's also her cameraman Mac and her sound operator Manny. They'll stay in the background but they will be filming. If you don't want to be filmed let Sharpe know. Otherwise she's gonna ask you to sign a release form."

"We're going to begin speaking with each of you one-on-one," Reid said. "Any information you can provide to us is important so don't hold anything back."

The group nodded and slowly stood up, heading towards me and my stack of releases. I had pre-populated some of the sections of the release, in particular the area that specified the length of time it covered. They were meant to be daily releases, but I had adjusted them to include filming for the next thirty days. I didn't expect to be filming that long, but I wanted to make sure my bases were covered. I didn't want an agreement to expire in the middle of filming only to have the subject tell me they were no longer willing to be part of the show. I had been burned by that in the past and learned to be much more careful.

Joy approached me first. She flashed me a smile and asked, "Where should I sign?" Working with actors was a breeze, at least when it came to agreeing to appear on camera. The fact that a second crew would be watching them in addition to the one on set, was like a dream scenario for these ego maniacs. Now their fans could learn everything about them both on and off set. A narcissist's fantasy.

Penny followed next and then Kyle. He gave me a wink and handed me his headshot. It was a color photo of him topless and grinning. On the back there were dozens of films and television shows listed. "Who should I make this out to?" he asked as he scribbled his name.

I shook my head. "I don't need your headshot. I just need you to sign a release to be on my show."

Kyle smiled. "I see. I'll have to ask my agent."

"Oh, that's fine. Give him a call," I instructed, handing him a copy and trying to act cool.

"I don't suppose you can email this to me, can you?"

"Sorry, I only have the hard copies," I lied. The last thing I wanted to do was email his agent the agreement so he could rip it to shreds. We didn't have time for that. "It's pretty standard language."

The language was standard but it certainly wasn't fair. It came just short of granting us possession of their first born. We could use a participant's image, their voice and their likeness in perpetuity. We could cut up their words, we could defame them, we could misrepresent them, and in return they waived all rights to sue us. "Maybe just take a photo and text it to your agent?" I suggested.

"Okay, I'll get back to you," Kyle said grabbing the agreement from my hand. "You can keep this," he said, tossing me his headshot. He turned and breezed out of the room so smoothly that I swore his shoes must have had wheels on them. I picked up the headshot and attached it to my clipboard.

"Do I have to sign this?" Craig asked me as he approached.

Before I could answer, Vinnie did. "Everyone should sign. This is good publicity for the show. Anyone that doesn't obviously has something to hide. You really want to be that guy, Craig?"

Craig shook his head and begrudgingly signed, as did Elroy and Carmine. Enrique scribbled his name too although he clearly had no idea what it said or why he was signing it.

Finally, Rose sauntered up to the table, her cleavage spilling out of her top, her red lips curling into a mischievous smile. "Softies. Every one of them. They should have played hard to get."

"Yeah Rose, they could really take a lesson from you on that," I told her.

"I saw the episode you did. Saw the way you made me look guilty."

"You were guilty. You went to jail, Rose. Albeit temporarily."

"I also gave you great ratings. If you want me back, it's gonna cost you."

Paying people off wasn't something I made a habit of, but sometimes people needed to be convinced to sign releases. I had bribed Rose the last time and it irked me that she was forcing me to do it again. She was good ratings and was also probably Lucky's killer so I knew I needed to, but I wasn't happy about it. I didn't like the idea of handing money to a woman that regularly hit on Reid right in front of me. She also loved shoving those big knockers in my face at any chance she got. And that accent she had – I couldn't bare it. Her Spanish drawl, the way she rolled her "r"s and those red lips. It was enough to make me want to tear her eyes out.

Rose was also a major distraction for my crew. I turned to look over at Manny who was in a trance, staring at her boobs. He wasn't even blinking.

I gritted my teeth and spoke softly. "I can give you… a hundred bucks."

"Ha!" Rose laughed. "Try a thousand. Cash."

My eyes opened wide. "You've got to be kidding me."

"Why not? Belamy is probably going to ask for way more than me. The way I see it, you're getting a bargain. No money, no release. Comprende?"

"I don't have that kind of cash on me. I have to talk to my boss."

"Okay." Rose smiled, turned on her heel, and charged off.

I shook my head. "Shit."

5.

The cops wanted to interview Vinnie first and that was okay by me. I would have to call Lenny about the bribe money before we could engage Rose and I wasn't in the mood for it. He would want to know all the details about this production down to the color underwear Rose was wearing. Plus, I knew he would cave as soon as I said Rose's name. Having a repeat character on this type of show was a novelty and he wouldn't want to miss out on it. Plus, the last time he had seen her, she was buck naked and spread eagle in my hotel room, an image that he had commented on more than once. I decided to hold off on calling Lenny for a while to let Rose sweat a bit. Besides, there were plenty of other people to interview in the meantime.

Mac looked around the studio and decided the extra set that wasn't being used was the best place to conduct the interview. It had overhead lighting and was sound proof, which made it a no-brainer. The room had a few different sets that were being stored in it. One was the sleeping quarters of the rocket ship, the other was a backdrop that looked like the surface of the moon. The ground was covered with a quilt-like material that was meant to look like gray craters. They were soft and pillowy, which meant it was easy to get your feet tangled up in them. While the moon might have seemed like an odd location to conduct important police interviews, I knew Mac would make it work.

Mac placed two chairs for the cops on the quilted surface and then one opposite them for Vinnie to sit in. Mac set his camera up on a tripod a few feet back from his subjects. He positioned the chairs about twelve feet away from the backdrop so he could rack his focus and allow the stars and the universe in the background to fall into soft focus. I had to admit I was impressed. Looking through that lens you would never have known you were on the surface of the moon. Instead, it looked like a glamorous backdrop with little stars and swatches of light twinkling in the background.

Manny mounted his boom microphone over the chair that Vinnie would sit in so he wouldn't have to hold it. These types of interviews were a cake walk for Mac and Manny. It took some time to get the shot just right with the boom out of sight, but once the shot was locked, they pressed record and sat back.

Mac had mounted a smaller camera on a tripod that would act as a second angle. It wasn't of the same quality as his ARRI video camera, but it provided the necessary cut-aways. Besides, these days even the lower end cameras still produced a quality product.

As the crew set up, Reid and Foxy chatted and compared notes. I tried to eavesdrop on the conversation. I wanted to get as much insight into the case as I could to understand where their heads were at and who we should be targeting.

"I don't know. It's pretty early for that," Reid was saying.

"I think we should consider it as an option," Foxy told him.

"Yeah, but this neighborhood isn't good. It could go horribly wrong."

"Reid, you need to take risks. If you don't, we could end up with nothing."

Reid thought about it, brooding for a bit. "I really feel like if we're getting hotdogs we should go to Pinks. I don't trust these local joints."

I frowned. So much for deep crime investigating!

"We're ready, Sharpe," Mac called out to me.

"Finally," Reid muttered.

"Do you want me to get Vinnie?" I asked.

"I'll get him," Foxy announced.

"I'll come with you," I told him.

We headed down the hallway to Vinnie's office. When we got there, Foxy knocked and entered before being invited in. Vinnie was sitting at his desk, typing madly on his laptop computer. His brother Carmine was sitting at a desk on the other side of the room sipping from his thermos and reading the newspaper.

"Vinnie, we're ready for you," Foxy told him.

Without answering, Vinnie held up a finger to Foxy in a "one moment" gesture. He continued banging away on his keyboard and smiling excitedly as he did so.

Foxy and I both stood in the room awkwardly waiting for Vinnie to finish up whatever he was doing. We stood there for a minute or two, shifting our weight from one foot to the other and looking around the room. Carmine said nothing. He seemed almost unaware that we were standing there as he paged through the paper.

"Hey I liked your last episode," Foxy told me, making small talk.

"Thanks," I answered.

"I heard you got poisoned."

"Occupational hazard," I told him, making light of the situation.

"How we doing Vinnie?" Foxy asked, looking to move this show along.

Vinnie looked up to see both Foxy and I glaring at him. "Ah, I'm sorry guys, I'm on a role here. I've got to get this script rewritten and the words are flowing right now. I feel like Shakespeare or something, it's pouring out of me. Why don't you talk to Carmine first? I can talk to you after."

Carmine looked up upon hearing his name. "Huh?"

"Talk to the cops," Vinnie told his brother. "They want to interview you about Lucky."

Carmine looked over at Foxy who shrugged and smiled. I knew they had to interview everyone anyway, so one brother was just as good as the next. They looked similar enough that I didn't think Mac would have to change the lighting or framing of the shot.

Carmine took another sip from his thermos and stood up, straightening out the wrinkled button-down shirt he was wearing over his jeans. "Sure, no problem."

Behind us, Joy entered the room. "Carmine, you okay? What's going on?"

"We're just gonna do an interview," Carmine answered.

"Do you want me to come with you?" Joy asked.

"That isn't an option," Foxy informed her. "We interview each of you separately."

Joy looked at Carmine with concern. There was a moment of silence between the two of them as they exchanged an almost imperceptible nod. "Ready?" Foxy asked Carmine.

"Yeah," Carmine answered.

The three of us walked out of the office in a tiny parade.

*****

The first moments of the interview were a little chaotic. "We got the other brother first," Foxy told his partner as we entered the room.

The room was dimly lit and it was difficult to see. The fake moon rock squished beneath our feet. Carmine's foot became tangled and he fell to the floor with a loud thud landing inches from Manny who was sitting on an apple box. The coffee thermos that Carmine was carrying went flying, exploding as it fell and splashing the contents onto Manny and his equipment.

"Ahh!" Manny screamed. "It burns!"

I rushed over to Manny, tripping over Carmine in the process and toppling on top of him. "Oh God!" I screamed as the wind got knocked out of me from the fall.

Meanwhile, Mac came to Manny's aide, ripping open his hacky sack. "Stay calm, Manny, I have salve."

"Hold on, it's cold," Manny said, touching the stains on his shirt. I was still sprawled across Carmine, but as I pushed up I noticed that the stains looked more like water than coffee.

Manny sniffed his shirt and frowned. "You drink this for breakfast, man?" he asked Carmine.

Carmine wasn't answering. He pushed himself up off the floor, slowly. "Did your equipment get wet?" he asked.

"It'll live," Manny said, wiping it off.

"Here," Mac said, handing him a handkerchief.

"Can we get started?" Reid asked. He hadn't bothered to stand up to help us and didn't seem amused by all the raucous.

"Yeah," I told him, standing up and stepping carefully towards Mac and Manny.

A few minutes later we were ready to start the interview.

"For the record, I'm not proud of all this," Carmine began. He was sitting in his interview chair with Reid and Foxy sitting to his right, angled awkwardly so everyone would appear in Mac's wide shot. Mac had his primary camera zoomed in to Carmine's face and locked off. "I got into this business because of my brother. I never wanted it."

"Why's that?" Reid asked.

"Are you kidding me? It's embarrassing. I can't even get a date. Once they find out what I do they're running the other way."

"What about the girls around here?' Foxy asked. "Joy seems like she cares about you."

Carmine wrinkled his nose as if the idea disgusted him. "I could never be with a woman who sells her body for money."

"I don't really give a damn about your love life," Reid snapped. "Who killed Lucky?"

Carmine shifted in his seat nervously. "I have no idea. I'm not saying that to give you guys more work, but I really don't know. I don't think he had any enemies around here."

"How did you meet Lucky?" Reid asked.

"We met at a meeting a couple weeks ago," Carmine whispered.

Everyone in the room knew what he meant by "a meeting," but Reid clarified for my camera. "An AA meeting, right?"

"Yeah. We started talking and I told him we were casting so he tried out. Vinnie does the casting though."

"How you doing with AA?" Foxy wanted to know. "Staying sober?"

Carmine looked at Manny who knew his thermos hadn't been filled with water.

"Trying to. Some days are harder than others."

"Like when someone you know gets killed?" Foxy offered.

"Yeah."

"And did you continue to go to meetings together after he started here?" Reid asked.

"No, he stopped going after that or maybe he switched locations. I don't know."

"Did you two see each other socially outside of work?" Reid continued.

Carmine shook his head. "No."

"What time did Lucky arrive at work today?" Reid asked, changing his line of questioning.

"I don't really know. Vinnie found him before I got here."

"And what time was that?"

"Uh…" Carmine looked at his watch and rubbed his head. "Maybe ten? They usually don't wait for me to start doing the shooting."

"What were you doing prior to arriving to work today?"

"Sleeping. I don't wake up so well in the morning."

"And what about the night before? When did you leave here and where did you go?"

"I left at probably around seven or eight. I went home after that," Carmine answered.

"Was anyone still here when you left?" Reid asked.

"Joy left a little before I did I think."

"So you were the last to leave. Did you lock up then?" Reid asked.

"I set the alarm, yeah."

"I'll need the name of your alarm company," Reid said.

"It's Protect It. They can pull the records for you," Carmine said.

"What exactly does a producer do?" Foxy asked him.

It was a decent question to ask. In Hollywood the term "producer" could mean a lot of things. It could mean the folks willing to put up the money for the project or it could mean the folks who found the folks to put up the money for the project. It could also mean the folks who found the actors to attach to the project to get the funding, and so on. There were producers who just had their names on the opening credits and there were producers who worked on set, overseeing the entire project and ensuring it flowed smoothly. As for me, I was a producer who drove results. I was a producer and a director really – I made things happen. That was probably one of the qualities Reid appreciated the least about me. Sometimes I was willing to bend the truth to get my story. As for Carmine, something told me he was more of a paycheck collecting producer than a results one.

"I handle the paperwork," Carmine answered. "I take care of the payroll, the insurance, hiring the crew. I make sure the show gets delivered to the network. Stuff like that."

I nodded in approval. This guy had some worth after all.

"Who discovered the body?" Reid asked.

"Rose did. Vinnie called me in the car and then he called you guys."

"This type of publicity could be good for your little production here," Reid said. "Don't you think?"

Carmine considered that. "Vinnie thinks it might. It's sweeps and we're filming a new television show."

"Do you think anyone would deliberately kill Lucky to drive up ratings?"

"If you're suggesting that my brother could have done this, you're way off," Carmine barked.

"And what about the show's producer?" Foxy asked.

Carmine's eyes widened and he looked momentarily stunned by the insinuation. "I don't care if this show gets picked up or not. As I told you, I don't like this business and I'd be happy to get rid of it."

"So why stay in it then? There are probably a hundred jobs out there you could get," Reid suggested.

"Yeah right, with *Sexy School Teacher* and *Sorority Sex-Up* on your resume? Give me a break. I can't get a producing job to save my life. Or are you suggesting I get a job as a banker or an accountant? That's even more unlikely. I'm a pornographer, a pervert, a weirdo. No one wants to hire me."

He sounded convincing but I knew better. No one in reality television would care if he had soft porn on his resume. Heck, Lenny would probably consider it a bonus! This guy was lazy. He had an easy job that paid the bills and he wasn't going to do anything to change that.

6.

We found the medical examiner in the dressing room exactly where we left him. I elected to hang back out of sight. Lou was probably still pissed at me for vomiting and I didn't want to risk throwing up again. I placed Manny's extra set of headphones on my ears and listened in as the cops and crew entered the scene.

"So, what did you come up with?" Foxy asked.

"I'm estimating the time of death to be between 6 and 8 a.m.," Lou told them.

"Okay so the guy either showed up really early this morning or he stayed late last night," Reid said.

"Right," Lou answered. "The puncture wound to the neck appears to be the cause of death. Like I said before, the weapon was dull, so it didn't go in clean."

"So, what does that mean?" Foxy asked.

"It means that either the knife was dull or they used something else. The shape of the wound is making me think it's a knife, but if this were premeditated they would have had a better weapon. Getting a dull blade through the neck takes effort and it looks like they only went through once."

"Do you think Rose would have the strength to do it?" Reid asked.

"Who?"

"Big boobs, stilettos," Foxy explained.

"If she was angry enough she could. I swabbed him for semen or vaginal fluid – I'll run that through the lab. It looks like he was in the middle of some sort of sex act."

"This seems to be the place for that kind of thing," Foxy added.

"I pulled some fingerprints and some hair samples too, but this is a dressing room. There's no telling how many people come and go in here. Who knows, maybe we'll get a hit on the fingerprints belonging to someone in the system."

If the fingerprints were found to be someone with a criminal record that wasn't associated with the production, it would be a big win. But something told me that was unlikely. Maybe it was just because Foxy had announced that the killer was among us, but I was starting to believe it. We'd already established that Carmine could have motive. Despite what he had said about hating his job and all that, Reid was right. It was sweeps and something like this was going to draw headlines. As they say: *All publicity is good publicity.*

"What's the timeline?" Reid was asking.

"Could be a couple days, could be a couple weeks," Lou answered.

My heart fell. A couple of weeks? We needed to solve the case *this* week. So much for forensic evidence. We'd have to solve this thing the old-fashioned way.

"Okay, we gotta notify the next of kin," Foxy said.

"His phone is locked," Lou answered. "I tried using his finger to unlock it but it didn't work."

"I'll call the station – see what they can dig up," Foxy offered.

"Anything else?" Reid asked.

"No. Give me another hour or so and I'll be done here," Lou answered.

With that I heard some shuffling and the sound cut out. Obviously without their fearless leader in the room, the guys had decided on their own to cut the shot.

"Mac, you got some good cut-aways, right? Nothing too gory?" I called out from the other side of the door.

"Doing that now, Sharpe," Mac answered, sounding annoyed.

Reid and Foxy stepped out of the room and looked at me. Manny was not far behind them. "So, what's next?" I asked.

"Let's grab Vinnie," Reid said. "No more excuses from him."

"Agreed," Foxy answered.

The two men started heading down the hallway but I stopped them. "Hang on guys, can you wait for Mac?"

I received an audible grumble from both Reid and Foxy, but they agreed to wait. When Mac finally stepped out of the dressing room, Reid and Foxy charged off and we went running behind them, camera rolling.

*****

We were heading towards Vinnie's office, but as we passed the door that led to the hot set, we stopped dead in our tracks.

Inside, Penny was being suspended in the air, held up by a pulley that Craig was gripping with both hands. She was dressed in a skimpy spacesuit, floating around, appearing to be weightless. Craig, meanwhile, was sweating profusely, trying to keep her in the air. The five of us gathered together, all peering in the small window.

Inside the spaceship, Joy and Kyle were making out while a seemingly oblivious Penny floated around in space. The kissing intensified and Kyle took off Joy's shirt exposing a lace bra. Instinctively, I covered Reid's eyes with my hand. He jumped when my hand touched his face.

"Arrrribba!" Manny called out rolling his "r"s in a high-pitched squeal so loudly everyone on set could hear him.

"Cut!" Vinnie screamed.

Craig lost control of the pulley and dropped Penny onto the floor much faster than he intended to. Penny landed with a thud. "Hey!" she screamed.

I slapped Manny on the arm before opening the door and walking onto set. The cops and my crew followed in behind me, piling inside. The room was smaller than I had thought and it was hot and stuffy.

Vinnie was holding a script and Elroy and Enrique were there operating the camera and sound respectively. Jason was sitting on a chair, probably annoyed he wasn't in the scene and Rose was nowhere to be found.

"Vinnie, is this for real?" Kyle barked, glaring at the director. "This is like amateur hour."

"I'm sorry, Kyle." Vinnie placated and then turned to look at Foxy and Reid. "I thought you guys weren't going to be disruptive!"

Reid elected to go on the offensive instead of apologizing. "We need to speak with you, Vinnie. Now."

I saw Craig run over to Penny to see if she was okay. She was sprawled out on the floor, rubbing her head. "Just get off of me!" she snapped, sitting up. "This whole show is cursed Vinnie. Lucky's dead and you guys just go on like usual."

"We called the cops, Penny," Vinnie fired back. "What the hell else do you want me to do? Solve the case myself?"

"You can start by talking to us," Reid answered. "That would help."

"Jesus, I've got a million things going on right now!" Vinnie shouted. "I can't deal with all this. I need to get this scene in the can!"

Manny turned to Reid. "I don't mind waiting. I mean, if they want to get this scene shot real quick."

I wasn't close enough to slap Manny on the back of the head, but Reid looked like he might.

"Maybe he's right," Foxy said. "I was just thinking it would be good research to understand how everyone interacts."

"Just let me get this one scene. Then I'm all yours," Vinnie pleaded.

Reid shook his head in frustration and threw up his hands. "Sure thing guys. Don't let me get in your way."

I felt my teeth clench. It was amazing how men could be reduced to children at the promise of seeing a woman's boobs. I was getting hot inside and not in a sexy way.

"Come on guys," I said with as much composure as I could muster. "This is a closed set."

In Hollywood when these types of scenes were shot, only the most essential crew members were allowed on set. It wasn't appropriate for everyone to stand around gawking.

"No, it's fine," Kyle said from the spaceship. "I don't mind."

"Okay, let's get set-up for another take," Vinnie announced. He turned and pointed a finger at Craig. "Don't drop her again."

Craig imitated Vinnie in a whiney voice, "Don't drop her again" and then hoisted Penny back in the air. She wasn't expecting it and gasped as the ropes pulled on her stomach.

"Craig, come on!" Penny yelled.

"Let's roll," Vinnie announced.

The heat in my body was getting to a boiling point. I expected this level of unprofessionalism from Foxy and Manny, but Mac and Reid? Did they really need to watch Kyle undressing Joy in order to solve the murder? I doubted it. They might want to watch this garbage but I wasn't going to. I turned on my heel and stormed off set.

*****

I stood out front, leaning against the building and getting some much-needed smoggy air. I took a deep breath, trying to relax as I watched the cars go by. The street was pretty busy, but there was almost no pedestrian traffic. LA was not a walking city. I had a 7-11 maybe eight hundred feet from my apartment and I still drove there when I needed a snack.

I needed to develop a thicker skin if I was going to successfully produce this particular story. I had to expect that there would be sexual innuendo. I had to expect that people might be "acting" out a sex scene while I was there. I had to expect that people might be having real sex on the set or in their dressing rooms or the bathroom. I already knew that Rose was a nymphomaniac – I had to assume that real sex was happening around here. The problem was, I didn't know how to act casual in this type of situation. I wanted to act like I was totally cool with this stuff, like it was just another day at the office for me, but it wasn't. Did I really cover Reid's eyes while they were shooting that scene? He probably thought I was crazy. I had acted like a jealous girlfriend without even knowing if Reid thought of me in that way. We'd never discussed it. We'd never agreed to be exclusive. We'd never even had sex.

I heard the front door open and turned to see Mac walking out. He walked over to me and leaned against the wall. "Not your ideal location shoot, right?"

I laughed. "Right."

"Me neither. I'd rather be shooting in the desert or the Everglades or pretty much anywhere other than this."

"You don't think Terry will approve?" I asked.

Mac smiled. "Not likely. How about Reid?"

"I don't know Mac, he seems quite at home."

"Maybe he is."

I turned and looked at Mac. "So you're saying he's a pervert?"

"Sharpe, knock that off. I meant this is his usual kind of case. This is probably pretty tame stuff for him compared to the dead sixteen year olds that were forced into prostitution, right?"

"Yeah, but Rose with her big boobs and red lips... I can't stand it Mac. I mean, what kind of a justice system do we really have if she's walking free?"

Mac shook his head. "There are a lot of sleaze balls in this world. Most of them work in our industry, in fact."

"We're not sleaze balls."

"No, we're not," Mac agreed. "Manny? Well it's questionable."

My phone vibrated in my pocket and I pulled it out. It was my boss Lenny calling in. "Speaking of sleaze balls," I said, holding out my phone.

Mac smiled. "I'll leave you alone."

"Thanks, friend," I told him. I was grateful I wasn't the only person who wasn't happy to be here. He nodded and gave me a wave as I picked up Lenny's call.

"Dead guy in a thong?" Lenny purred into my ear.

For a minute I didn't know how he got that information, but then I remembered the text I had sent him. I was excited at the time I had sent it, but the payoff had been a little less spectacular than I was hoping for. I needed to sound interested for Lenny so I tried to perk up as I told him the details.

"Yeah, it was pretty grisly," I explained. "His throat was stabbed."

"Sharpe, I left my phone in the john and didn't see your text until now. This thing has got me wet all over. Are you on the porn set right now?"

That thick skin I had been trying to develop was getting penetrated quickly. I was surrounded by perverts. "It's soft porn," I corrected. "It's all pretend with mild nudity." I could hear his heavy breathing in the phone. "It's one of the actors that died. Everyone is a suspect."

"No shit," Lenny squealed.

"And Rose is here." I braced myself for the reaction I knew was to come.

"Wait, the sexpot? The one who went to jail? She's involved?"

"The very one. She ended up getting the charges dropped."

"That's unbelievable!" Lenny was shouting now. "Holy shit – Damion, Avery – get in here. Sharpe's on a porn set with a dead guy, and Rose from the first episode is involved!" I heard a wave of excitement amongst the group through the phone.

"Yeah, but there's a catch," I added. "She wants a payout or she won't appear on camera."

"How much?" Lenny asked, not missing a beat.

"A thousand dollars," I told him, trying to make it sound like a huge amount of money. It was a huge amount of money to me and to Rose. To the show it was just a line item in the budget under "miscellaneous."

"Pay it," Lenny told me without hesitation. "If you need cash we have some in the office or I can send a runner."

I considered that for a moment. It was pretty tempting to take the long drive over to the office to give myself some space from this crime scene, but of course, I couldn't do that. It was my job to produce this show, and like it or not, I was going to do it. Besides, I needed to keep an eye on Reid.

"Yeah send a runner," I told him.

"Done," Lenny said.

I gave him the address and he asked me to keep him updated as the story unfolded. I agreed I would.

7.

Vinnie had done his best to push off his interview as long as he could, but now it was time to pay the piper. Reid had told him, in no uncertain terms, that he expected him to sit down for an interview in the next five minutes or be hauled down to the station to do it there. Vinnie said that he wanted to set a good example for his employees and so he finally agreed that he would talk.

We used the same set we had used for Carmine's interview, but Mac adjusted the lighting and changed the camera angle. His little tweaks made the tight shot of Vinnie's face look like it was filmed in an entirely different location. There were no twinkle lights in the background. Instead, the look was more dark and sinister. Mac and I had decided this guy seemed suspicious and Mac lit him accordingly.

When we were finally ready to roll it was after two o'clock. I was hungry and guessed my crew was too. Foxy was right, they should have gotten those hotdogs earlier! I knew how Reid worked – he would press on until they got their answers, but I was hungry now. I had vomited up my breakfast, so there was literally nothing in my stomach to sustain me. My head was starting to hurt.

Reid and Foxy began their line of questioning as the camera rolled.

"Do you know who killed Lucky?" Reid asked, using the same question he had asked him earlier.

Unlike his brother, Vinnie didn't flinch. "You already asked me that. My answer is still no."

"Did you kill Lucky?" Reid asked.

Vinnie acted shocked by the question, then realized they were actually looking for an answer. "No," he quickly said.

"You said you got here around eight. Was anyone else here when you arrived?" Foxy asked.

"No, I was the first."

"So Lucky wasn't here yet?" Reid asked.

"I told you, I don't know. I didn't see him walking around."

"Was his car in the parking lot?" Foxy asked.

"I've been parking out front on the street. We had some cars vandalized in our back lot. So, if Lucky's car was out there I didn't notice. As you know, my office is in the front of the building."

"Did you report this vandalism?" Reid asked.

Vinnie shrugged. "Probably somebody did. It was while ago and it wasn't my car."

"Whose car was it?"

"Joy's car. They broke her window and stole a few things."

"Okay. Tell me what you did when you arrived this morning," Foxy continued.

"Uh, I unlocked the front door, turned on the lights, went into my office."

"Did you disarm the alarm when you arrived?"

"I said I unlocked the front door so obviously yes. That's part of it," Vinnie explained rather sarcastically. "I put my key in the lock, I turn the key and then I type the code into the alarm."

"Which lights did you turn on?" Foxy asked.

"Jeez. You gotta be kidding me. The hallway lights and then my office."

"And then what?" Foxy asked.

"I went into my office and sat at my desk and opened my email."

"Anything interesting?" Foxy pressed.

"Just some emails from the network about our timeline. The same timeline that's getting blown every minute I sit here," Vinnie said narrowing his eyes.

"What else?" Reid pressed.

"In my emails? I don't know, a couple actresses looking for work, junk mail. I didn't get a note from Lucky's killer if that's what you're asking Detective."

Vinnie was getting antsy and agitated and we were just getting started. His frustration was good for TV, but annoying for Foxy and Reid.

"Then what?" Foxy continued.

"Then the cast and crew started filing in. My door was closed so I can't tell you who arrived when, I just know I heard the front door opening and closing a lot."

"Does everyone come in through the front door?" Foxy asked.

"No, I told you, we have a parking lot in the back. A lot of people still park there, but some park on the street. It depends if you can get a spot."

"Did you unlock the back door?" Foxy asked.

Vinnie thought about that. "No," he said finally. "Maybe someone else did."

"And what about your brother Carmine. When did he arrive?"

"Uh, I think a little before ten. I called him when we saw Lucky."

"Did you see Lucky alive today at all?" Reid asked.

Vinnie shook his head no.

"Do you think he was here when you arrived this morning or do you believe he was killed after you opened up the studio?" Reid asked.

"How the hell should I know?" Vinnie asked. "You're asking me questions like I'm the detective."

"Here's another detective question – did Lucky have any enemies that you knew of? Any debts owed?" Reid asked.

Vinnie shook his head. "He wasn't my friend, he was my employee. I'm not trying to sound like an asshole but I didn't know him that well. My brother was the one who brought him in. He had a great bod so I hired him. I think he may have been screwing one of the girls here. Maybe more than one. You know how these people are."

"Do you screw any of the girls here?" Reid asked, sounding crude.

Vinnie let a sly smile slide across his lips. "Sometimes."

I could pretty much guarantee he had slept with Rose. Hell, half the state of California probably had. That was probably how she got the part to begin with.

"Who was Lucky sleeping with?" Reid wanted to know.

"I don't know, man. Lots of people probably, with that body."

"How about Rose?" Foxy asked.

Vinnie got a goofy smile on his face. "Well, Rose is very… uninhibited. But they didn't like each other, so maybe not."

"Have you alerted the media yet?" Reid asked Vinnie.

Vinnie shook his head in confusion, pretending not to understand.

"This is big news, right? Wouldn't this boost your ratings?"

The side of Vinnie's lip twitched. "I don't know about that."

"Have you alerted the media? Yes or no?" Reid repeated.

I realized that in all my brooding I had forgotten to check. In years past, a dead porn star wouldn't have been important news, but lately the news outlets were struggling to provide the constant "breaking news" that their public wanted. A story like this would surely be picked up.

"I didn't personally, no."

Reid whipped out his smart phone and typed in Lucky's name. I could tell by his face that he found something. "Who did?"

Vinnie shrugged. "It's a set full of actors. It could have been any of them."

*****

"Are you freaking kidding me?" I said out loud as I stared down at my smart phone. The news story had broken about Lucky and not in a small way. It wasn't just a headline story, someone had actually been recording and streaming live from the inside. I watched a video clip of Reid and Foxy speaking to the group in the break room. I knew right away who had done this. A fame-hungry star with an ego the size of Texas.

I stormed onto the set, looking for Kyle. When I finally saw him, and was reminded of how handsome he was, I paused, but only for a second. A moment later I was storming over to him, demanding answers.

"You wouldn't sign my release, but you're streaming video of me and my crew?"

Kyle looked up at me and smiled. "I can see how that might not make a lot of sense."

"No, it makes sense Kyle, but you have to remember this is a crime scene and you have to let the cops do their job."

"Sharpe let me handle this," I heard Reid say from behind me.

"If you're recording me, I'm recording you, Pal," I continued. "So, you're going to sign my release, right?"

Kyle's eyes traveled from me over to Reid who was standing behind me. "She's feisty," he told Reid. "I have a call into my agent so I'll have to let you know."

I was about to argue when Reid placed a hand on my shoulder. "Sharpe, can you excuse us for a moment?"

"Sure," I agreed. I saw my crew walking around set with Foxy and Vinnie and decided to join them.

"They're in space and they've lost contact with Earth," Vinnie was explaining to Foxy. "They're doing what anyone else would do in that situation – making the most of it."

71

"What was Lucky's part?" Foxy asked.

"One of the astronauts. I'm trying to figure out if I should cut his scenes all together or have him killed by aliens. I feel like that's kind of a shitty ending for him though, considering he really did die. But maybe it's like a metaphor for his real life?"

Foxy raised an eyebrow. "I don't think it's a metaphor if he really died."

Vinnie considered that. "Yeah, that's true."

Reid walked over to us, having finished his conversation with Kyle. I would have liked to capture whatever they said on film, but I couldn't be everywhere and Reid did ask for privacy.

Lou approached us carrying his kit. "Okay guys, we're all done. We're taking the body now."

"That was fast," Foxy remarked.

"Yeah, it's nuts right now. We're short staffed and I just got another call," Lou explained. "Usually Fridays and Saturdays are my busy days, not Tuesdays."

"Let us know what you come up with," Reid told him, patting Lou on the shoulder.

*****

Mac and Manny filmed as Lou and his team dragged Lucky's body on a gurney out the front door. The rest of the cast and crew had also come outside to watch the scene. Mac panned to capture a few solemn faces as they watched Lou open the back doors of his truck, preparing to load the body inside.

A blue sedan pulled up and parked right next to the van, double parking on the street. Austin, the runner that Lenny had sent over, jumped out of the driver's seat, carrying an envelope.

"Get out of the shot, Austin!" I screamed as he nearly knocked over Penny and Joy who were sobbing and consoling each other.

"Oh Jesus, sorry Sharpe," Austin said as he ran over to me. "This is from Lenny."

I took the envelope of cash for Rose's payout and placed it into my purse. "Thanks."

"Can we get this car out of here?" Lou yelled at Austin.

"Sorry!" he announced. "I'm leaving."

Penny and Joy seemed momentarily distracted by Austin as he jumped back into the driver's seat and drove away. Meanwhile, Kyle was filming the whole thing on his smart phone. I made a mental note to request a copy of his video – it might make decent B-roll for the show.

8.

"Are you freaking crazy, man?"

Mac, Manny, and I were huddled together in the equipment storage closet shoving extra equipment onto the shelves and recharging the cameras batteries when we heard an argument beginning to brew. Foxy was in the bathroom and had been for the past twenty minutes, and Reid was standing outside the closet grunting and looking at his watch.

The commotion was coming from the dressing rooms and it didn't take more than a moment for Mac and Manny to spring into action and go running down the hall with camera and sound rolling.

Reid and I followed to find Craig and Vinnie standing in the room where Lucky had been murdered. Lucky was gone, but a pile of blood was left behind in the form of a deep red stain on the couch. There was blood on the floor too and a lot of it. The whole place was a mess.

I tried to imagine that the blood didn't belong to that chiseled, handsome stallion they called Lucky, but rather that it was fake blood staged for a scene in a movie. Unfortunately, those visualizations didn't prove effective. I started getting woozy looking at the red goo, so I turned my head, focusing on the argument instead.

"You're a PA, that's your job," Vinnie was telling him.

"To clean up freaking blood from a dead guy? Are you nuts, man?" Craig shot back. "You pay me seventy-five bucks a day and you think this is part of my job description? I was hired to lube up these women. I'm a fluffer damn it – not a cleaning lady!"

"Just do it!" Vinnie boomed before noticing all of us standing in the doorway filming. "What the hell are you looking at?" he yelled in our direction. "This doesn't concern your investigation. Mind your own business!"

Vinnie's face was growing red and hot. He had a temper, that was clear. Vinnie turned to Reid and glared at him. "Your fucking team leaves us with this mess?"

Reid took a breath and then answered calmly and professionally. "I can recommend a cleaning service. There are some that specialize in this sort of thing."

"I don't have the budget for that – that's why I have him!" Vinnie spat back, pointing at Craig.

"I'm not doing it, Vinnie," Craig asserted.

"Fine! I'll handle this myself."

"Good!" Aggravated, Craig stormed out of the dressing room.

Vinnie glared at me and my crew and then slammed the dressing room door in our collective faces. It was rude, yes, but it was also a great scene for my show. I made a note in my log: *Boss Vinnie is a hot head. Door-slamming shot. Good for transition scene.*

Reid followed Craig while Mac, Manny and I followed him. Reid caught up to Craig and placed a hand on his arm. "Hey, hold up a minute. I want to talk to you."

Craig turned to Reid, looking like he was on the verge of tears. I suddenly felt bad for the guy. He was just a kid and that was probably the first time he had stood up to his boss. Production Assistants had terrible jobs because they were basically required to do whatever was needed. That could mean running errands all over town, ordering lunch for the crew, emptying out the garbage cans in a production office and, in this case, even cleaning up blood. Here this poor kid was working this crappy job and garnering no respect in the process.

Reid looked over at me. "Sharpe, can we have a minute here?"

I hesitated for a moment. We were supposed to document everything. No exceptions. This was now the second time Reid had asked for privacy from me and my crew. But I also knew I had to be careful about stepping over the line too much. "Of course," I answered. I signaled the crew to give the guys some space, but privately asked them to keep the mics hot so we could record the audio. This was my usual trick. It allowed me to give them some privacy but also to capture the conversation. I was pretty sure Reid knew I would do this and so I felt okay about it.

We walked around the corner and Manny handed me my headphones so I could listen to the conversation.

"I'm so sick of doing the grunt work around here," Craig told Reid. "I moved out here to become a writer. My parents spent a hundred thousand dollars for me to go to film school and this is my job? I thought it would be cool. I mean, my friends think it's awesome, but there's a big difference between helping Rose into her costume and cleaning up blood. I'm getting screwed here, man."

"I understand," Reid assured him. "It sounds like this isn't what you signed up for."

"It's a freaking joke. I'm a joke. You think I want to be doing this?"

"No, it doesn't sound that way. What type of writing would you like to be doing?" Reid asked.

"This kind. Soft porn."

I stifled a laugh. The guy wanted to be a porn writer? I imagined the scripts to be about three pages long with dialogue like "Oh baby" and "Yeah, more." Craig wasn't the one getting screwed in this deal, his parents were.

"Oh," Reid finally answered.

"Vinnie told me he would let me help with rewrites. Now would have been the perfect time. With Lucky gone the whole thing needs to be redone. This could have been my shot. But no, he'd rather use my janitorial skills than my writing talents!"

"You're right. It sounds like this would have been a great opportunity. Were you close with Lucky?" Reid asked.

"We were friendly, I guess. The actors don't pay much attention to me. I'm just the hired help."

Manny and I could hear the conversation through the headphones clearly, but Mac wasn't wearing headphones. I looked over at him and noticed he seemed distracted. His attention was focused off to the side where he was staring at something. I followed his gaze and saw Penny sitting in the empty studio, legs crossed, hands resting on her knees. The door was open and she was in full view, although she seemed to be completely unaware of anything going on around her. She was meditating and completely still. I watched her chest rise and fall as she took deep cleansing breaths.

Suddenly, I felt a sharp pinch on my ass. My first instinct was to think it was Reid, but the rushing pain that accompanied it told me otherwise. When I couldn't take the pain anymore I squealed and turned to slap the person behind me.

I pulled off the headphones and faced Rose. "Don't touch me!" I snapped. I felt my pulse quickening and the anger in my belly growing. I knew this feeling. It was the feeling I seemed to get every time I was around the woman. I thought back to the time she confronted my mother at my sister's wedding, claiming she was having an affair with my father, which was completely untrue. Rose liked to play the same games with Reid, flirting with him incessantly just to get under my skin. I doubted she had any female friends.

"I see the way you look at me," Rose told me. "I thought I'd give you what you want for once. Wanna go to my dressing room?"

"Are you insane?" I asked her. I was so mad I felt like my head might explode. How dare she try to embarrass me in front of everyone! Did she expect me to take her up on the offer? I wasn't dumb enough to think she had any interest in me other than getting under my skin.

"Come on girl, you know you want me. Everyone does," Rose said, running her hand across my stomach.

I jumped back from her touch so quickly that I nearly knocked Mac over. "Get the hell away from me your crazy bitch!" I screamed. "Don't you dare put your hands on me ever again!" I was hysterical and out of control and I knew it.

By now I was mildly aware that Foxy and Reid had walked over. When I heard a man's voice whisper, "Cat fight," I was certain Foxy was near.

Mac put his arms around me and gave me a bear hug from behind. "Relax, Sharpe."

Rose's lips curled into a smile. "Another time then?" She ran her tongue over her lips and looked me up and down, then her eyes traveled over to Reid. A three-way could be fun."

"Get out of here!" I screamed at her. I had tears coming out of my eyes I was so angry. How dare she mess with me like this!

Out of nowhere, Penny appeared. Somehow, she had moved, catlike behind Rose. "Peace, Sister," she counseled, placing an arm around Rose and steering her away from the situation. Rose moved with her easily, acting like she was completely surprised and confused that I was upset. Acting like she was just trying to do me a favor, to give me what I had always wanted.

When they were out of sight, Mac placed his hands on my shoulders, rubbing them and telling me to calm down. I looked over at Reid, worried about his reaction to Mac massaging my shoulders.

"Are you going to be able to handle yourself on this case, Sharpe?" he snapped. "Rose is a damn murder suspect. What the hell are you doing getting tangled up with her again?"

I glared at him, my eyebrows bent into a solid V. "I'm fine and I can handle myself just fine."

"Oh obviously," Foxy smirked.

My glare shot over to him. "Why don't you go sit on the toilet for another hour, Foxy? I don't need your commentary."

"Whoa girl, whoa." Foxy smiled.

Penny returned with a serene look on her face. "Everything okay now?"

"Yeah, it's great," I answered, pulling away from Mac and shaking out my shoulders.

"I saw you meditating back there," Mac said to her.

Penny nodded. "I try to fill my spirit with love, especially now considering what happened to Lucky."

"Don't you find it hard with all the noise distractions?" Mac asked.

Penny shook her head. "Not really. But I've been practicing for a while. Do you meditate?"

Mac nodded. "Every night. But I like to do it at home, in a dark room, completely at peace."

"I like to do it that way too, but sometimes I end up putting myself to sleep." Penny giggled.

"This is murder investigation!" Reid snapped, annoyed by the lighthearted conversation in the midst of our argument. "This isn't yoga and friends! We have been here for hours and we've barely had a chance to interview anyone. I can't work like this!"

My heart tightened in my chest. This was the Reid I knew and didn't exactly love.

Penny turned to Reid and stared at his face intently. She stared so long that he started to get uncomfortable. "You are blocked emotionally," Penny finally told him.

I let out a little laugh while Reid rolled his eyes. "Thanks for the advice."

Penny turned to me. "You're blocked too." Her eyes traveled from me to Reid and back to me again. "You need to find a way to channel positivity. You both do." Penny nodded at Mac and walked away.

Reid and I exchanged an awkward glance. Of course we were blocked emotionally! We didn't know where our relationship stood. We didn't have the guts to talk about our feelings and we had never had sex. Any idiot could tell we were blocked. Considering we were already in a very uncomfortable environment for a new couple, Penny's revelation certainly didn't help things.

*****

"I'm freaking starving, man," Foxy told Reid.

It was six o'clock and Foxy's stomach was rumbling. The guys had discussed going to lunch earlier in the day but then things got busy and the opportunity never presented itself. Now we found ourselves starving with no leads and quickly running out of steam.

Reid seemed to pretend he didn't hear his partner's comment, focusing instead on what was going on around him. Vinnie had informed us that he had to end shooting for the day or else he might get stuck paying overtime. Mac filmed as the soft porn crew wrapped things up and the actors prepared to go home. I realized my production was soon going to have to pay OT to Mac and Manny too, but I didn't care all that much. It wasn't coming out of my wallet and we had a network show budget now.

I looked at Reid and could see the frustration growing inside of him. He was the type of guy who liked to grind and press on until the case was solved; meanwhile, everyone around him, including his partner, wanted to go home.

"I want to look around a little more first," Reid finally told Foxy.

"There's some food over there in crafty," Manny told Foxy, motioning towards the craft service set up in the kitchen.

"No shit. I've been grazing off that thing all day," Foxy grumbled. "I need a hot meal. Something with meat in it."

"Come on before they kick us out of here," Reid ordered his partner.

Begrudgingly, Foxy relented and followed behind Reid. I didn't have to ask my guys to follow along. They knew what to do.

Reid headed toward the dressing room where Lucky was killed. The blood was still there on the couch – nothing had changed since Craig and Vinnie had argued about it earlier.

Reid walked around the room slowly, surveying the scene. He checked the back of the door to see if there was a lock – there wasn't. He looked under the bloody couch for clues. The Medical Examiner had done this already and so had Reid and Foxy, but he wanted to check again.

Foxy walked over to the makeup table and opened the drawer. Inside he found some makeup and hairbrushes and a curling iron. There weren't any obvious clues, at least none that I could see. There wasn't a knife or the driver's license of the killer that they had accidentally left behind.

Reid walked out of the room and into the dressing room that was adjacent to the first one. It was the dressing room we had seen Craig and Rose in earlier. The room was empty now so the cops looked around. Reid made the same moves, looking under the couch, checking the door for any signs of forced entry.

Foxy walked over to the rack of sexy clothing and thumbed through it.

There were silk nightgowns, skimpy school teacher uniforms, and black leather dominatrix garb. Foxy stopped on a female cop costume and pulled it out. He looked towards me and raised an eyebrow. "A little role reversal maybe?"

I shook my head no, giving him a small smile.

Foxy continued to look. "I think I know Reid pretty well by now. This looks like more his speed." Foxy pulled out a leopard print teddy with pink lace lining around the bust and the bottom of the skirt. Reid looked over at the outfit Foxy was holding and I saw his eyebrows pop up.

Foxy walked over to me, holding the garment, still on the hanger. He held it up in front of me. "What do you think, partner?"

I posed for a moment, having fun, and then pushed the garment away after realizing Mac and Manny were staring at me. My eyes darted over to Reid who looked embarrassed as he fumbled around the room trying to act like he was looking for clues.

Satisfied that he had sufficiently embarrassed us both, Foxy went over to the makeup table and looked around. Inside the drawer he found similar items – a curling iron, some hairbrushes and makeup. There was, however, something in this drawer that wasn't in the other – a pair of scissors.

Foxy pulled on a rubber glove, lifted up the scissors and held them up to the Reid. "Check this out."

Reid examined them. "You didn't find a pair like that in the other room, right?"

"Nope," Foxy said, smiling.

Reid thought about it for a while. "It's possible. I'll talk to Lou. Let's bag it."

I understood that Reid meant that it was possible the killer used a similar pair of scissors that may have been in the dressing room where the crime occurred. He was implying that we potentially had identified the type of murder weapon used. Yet while I understood what he meant, my audience would not. This was reality TV. Moments of deep thought and reflection didn't work. Reid would have to describe what he was thinking. I would then have to add a graphic that said "possible murder weapon" to the show and maybe even make Foxy repeat it too. In reality TV you couldn't be subtle. You had to say exactly what you meant and often so that your audience could follow the storyline. This didn't mean our viewers were dumb, just that they were probably also looking at their smart phones or talking to each other while they were watching and wouldn't pick up on every nuance. We needed to make it easy for them.

I was about to ask Reid to articulate his thoughts when I heard the door to the other dressing room smash open.

"Cheap labor just isn't what it used to be," we heard Vinnie complain.

Foxy looked over at me and placed a finger over his lips indicating that we should be quiet and listen.

"Ugh, I'm gonna be sick," Carmine whined.

"Just shut up and do it," Vinnie shot back. "That little shit should be doing this. Kids these days are so damn lazy."

We listened and heard some grunting and heavy breathing but not much else. Finally, Vinnie spoke again. "Are you guys gonna spy on us all night? I know you're in the next room."

Foxy winced, obviously embarrassed we had been caught. He slipped the scissors he was holding into a bag and put it in his pocket. Reid didn't like to lose, so he puffed out his chest and strolled into the next dressing room. The crew and I followed behind him.

"We're not spying, we're investigating," Reid corrected. "We were looking for evidence around the other dressing room."

"Find any?" Carmine asked in a way that seemed like he was genuinely concerned that we did.

I walked over to see Carmine and Vinnie standing in front of the couch with a bucket of sudsy water. The two idiots were trying to get the blood out of the couch.

"Mac," I whispered to him. "Can you film this? Don't get the cops in the shot." I thought it would be a nice teaser to show these two thugs trying to clean up the crime scene. I needed Mac to frame the shot in a way that would imply they were doing this on their own, instead of with the two cops watching.

Carmine seemed to understand immediately what we were doing. "You enjoying this?" he said to Mac. "Watching the smut that goes on here?"

"Is cleaning up blood a usual occurrence on this production?" Foxy baited.

"I'm talking about the porn," Carmine said. "I see how you guys are looking at the talent – like they're meat. Like they're not real people. Like they're trash. I don't blame you if you do. We're smut peddlers here."

"Stop saying that!" Vinnie snapped. "You see we're on camera, don't you idiot? And this is SOFT PORN – you know that. What the hell is wrong with you?"

"Look at them," Carmine hissed. "They're all judging us. Every one of them. Especially the woman."

"Settle down," Reid boomed.

"Can you just get the hell out of here?" Vinnie asked. "We need to clean up this mess and I still have rewrites to do. I lost half the day dealing with you bozos."

Reid's eyes grew dark and hot as he leaned in. "You're cleaning up the blood of one of your employees. Unless you want to do the same for the next victim I suggest you let us do our job. I don't need to tell you that interfering with police work is a federal offense."

Vinnie looked angry but he didn't respond.

Reid turned and looked at Foxy, then my crew. "Okay, let's call it a day. We'll be back in the morning."

"What?" Vinnie gasped.

"We aren't done interviewing the suspects," Reid said coldly. "We will be back in the morning."

Vinnie and Carmine were pissed for a lot of reasons but I was feeling quite chipper. I had just captured a pretty compelling scene on camera and now we had the luxury of wrapping up for the day. It had been a day filled with discomfort and awkward moments and I was glad it was over. I needed time to mentally prepare to come back here tomorrow with a fresh attitude and fresh perspective. I knew that if I had some time to get used to the subject matter I would be able to handle it. I just needed some time away.

*****

I followed my crew to the kitchen where Foxy was stuffing his face with string cheese and crackers.

"What time should we meet here tomorrow?" I asked Reid.

Reid raised his eyebrows. "You're leaving?"

I crinkled my eyebrows, confused by his question. "Aren't you?"

"No. We're gonna wrap up here and then head over to the station. I want to do some research on Lucky."

I looked over at Foxy who gave me a sigh. I had been so excited to get away from this case that this news felt like a punch to the gut. The last cops I worked with rarely worked past five o'clock and honestly it was pretty enjoyable. Now I was back stuck in the trenches working twenty hours a day with a cop that wouldn't rest until the case was solved. Moments like this were the worst part of reality TV. When you were documenting someone else's life, it meant you lost your own. You followed them until they were ready to break, not until you were. Sometimes it really sucked.

"Okay," I told Reid absently, not wanting to argue.

Down the hall we noticed the cameraman Elroy walking towards the equipment closet carrying some heavy cables. I motioned to Mac to follow him. Mac carried his camera loosely dangling next to his hip, yet still rolling, as he casually approached the man to chat. I was impressed. Perhaps Mac had read my mind; this was exactly what I was hoping he would do. I strolled over to eavesdrop on the conversation. "Been doing this long?" Mac asked him.

Elroy was carefully placing the cords on a shelf, ensuring they were rolled up just right. "Long enough," he grunted.

"You like it?" Mac asked smiling.

Elroy stopped what he was doing and stared at Mac. "I'm trying to wrap up if you don't mind."

Mac put up his hands in a sign of surrender. "Just making small talk."

"Sure, you were," Elroy muttered and walked away.

Mac walked over to me. "Well, I'm no Victoria Sharpe."

I smiled. "Wow, Mac. That actually felt like a compliment."

9.

As we walked out into the smog-filled night air, I breathed a sigh of relief. I wasn't done with my shift for the day but at least I had gotten the hell out of that den of sin. Being around a corpse was one thing, but the cast of characters that worked there left me feeling like I needed to scrub my body with a Brillo pad.

"If we don't get some food I'm gonna freaking eat you," Foxy told Reid.

Reid nodded, knowing he had better heed his partner's warning.

"We can grab something," Manny offered. "In and Out?"

"Hell yeah!" Foxy said, suddenly cheering up. "Two burgers. Animal style."

The guys took everyone's orders and agreed to pick up the food while I headed with Reid and Foxy to the station. I had my small portable camera so I could capture some footage if I needed to.

On the way to the station I flipped the small camera on that Mac had mounted on the rearview mirror and started to fire out my questions. It was difficult to get these guys to stand still long enough to do talking head interviews, but now I had a captive audience.

"Can you guys talk to each other about the scissors you found back in the dressing room?" I asked.

"I'm too hungry, Sharpe," Foxy groaned.

"It'll take your mind off things," I offered.

"Fine," Foxy pouted. "Reid, do you think the scissor I found in the other dressing room could be the murder weapon?"

"A little less sarcasm please," I scolded.

"Okay," Foxy grumbled. "What do you think the chances are that the scissor I found back there is the murder weapon?"

"Probably about zero that the scissor *you* found is the weapon," Reid said, "But, it is possible there was a similar pair of scissors used on the victim."

"I looked in Lucky's dressing room and I didn't find any scissors in there. Maybe the killer grabbed them from the drawer, killed Lucky, and then ditched the scissors."

"Maybe. I can ask Lou if the size of the puncture wound is about right. He said the weapon was a dull knife. A scissor could fit that description."

"If it's a scissor, then we're probably talking manslaughter. Maybe something went wrong during sex like he lost his erection and the chick got pissed so she grabbed the scissors and killed him," Foxy offered.

"She'd probably stab him in the dick if that was what happened," I answered, forgetting I was supposed to be quiet.

Reid looked at me through the rearview mirror and raised an eyebrow.

*****

After parking the car at the station, Reid stepped out and slammed the door hard. He seemed annoyed. Maybe it was due to Foxy complaining incessantly about how hungry he was and how *we* should have picked up the food instead of letting the guys do it.

Foxy opened the back door for me and the three of us headed towards the station. It was getting dark now and the amount of cars in the parking lot had dwindled.

As we reached the door, Reid stopped. "I forgot something in the car. Foxy you can go up, I'll meet you."

Foxy nodded and headed inside. I followed behind but felt Reid's hand on my arm, pulling me towards him. Foxy entered the building, leaving Reid and I outside together alone. Reid took my hand and led me towards his car.

I felt a twinge of nerves as I braced myself for whatever tongue lashing he planned to give me about how I was interfering with his work. I was tired and stressed out and I wanted to go home. This guy was supposed to be my boyfriend and I felt like he was acting like an angry brut.

Reid opened the passenger's side door and asked me to get in. After I did he closed the door behind me, crossed the front of the car, and got into the driver's seat.

Once he closed the door he signed deeply. "Finally, we're alone." He leaned across the arm rest and covered my lips with his. It took a moment to register what was going on but soon butterflies were flying around in my stomach and my nipples were standing at attention.

"I nearly lost it today when Foxy held that nightie up in front of you in the dressing room," Reid whispered, hungrily kissing my lips.

"Wait, so you're not mad at me?" I asked between kisses.

"Mad?" Reid asked taking a moment to stop and look at me. "For what?"

I felt a wave of relief as my entire body began to tingle. Between us there was an arm rest and a parking break and police scanner and a GPS – all of which were in my way and getting annoying. I lifted up a leg and tried to move it over the equipment and onto Reid, but there was too much stuff in the way. "This isn't as easy as it looks," I told him as I struggled a few times to push my leg over it, cursing my lack of flexibility. "We probably should have sat in the back," I suggested, finally giving up and returning to my seat.

Reid laughed. "Sorry, I didn't think this out very well. I just knew I wanted to kiss you." He leaned over the center divider and placed his hands around my face, then moved them back into my hair, holding it in a ball, pulling me closer to him. His lips were hot and hungry and luscious. Now it was his turn to feel the GPS jabbing him in the rib, I hoped he could hold out. I remembered this guy. This was us. The case and the circumstances and Rose had made me forget for a moment.

"This is kind of painful," Reid said, pulling back and rubbing his ribs. "And this case sucks."

I smiled, leaning back in the seat. "Yeah, it's a little awkward, right?"

"Just a bit."

"Our cameras don't help matters."

"They're in the way, but I expected that. We just need to solve this thing fast."

"Agreed," I smiled.

*****

We found Foxy inside sitting at his desk, working on his computer. "Everything all right?" he asked as we walked in the room together. "You two look a little flushed."

"We're fine, dude," Reid grunted.

"Why did you have to go back to the car?" Foxy pressed, a sinister smile crossing his face.

"We went back to the car to make out, Foxy," I told him. "If the car wasn't so tight we might have done it right there in the parking lot." I looked over at Reid who was smiling, apparently amused at the possibility.

Foxy grew smug. "Thank you, Sharpe, I appreciate the honesty. If I could just get your boyfriend here to be more open about your sex life, then I wouldn't have to constantly pepper you with questions."

"I'll keep that in mind," I told him, pleased that Reid was being tight-lipped about our private life.

Reid walked over to his desk, logged into his computer, and started his research.

I had my B-camera with me and captured a bit of footage while we waited for Mac and Manny to arrive with the food. "What's taking them so long?" Foxy cried out at one point, followed by, "Did they ride their bicycles to the place?"

I tried to keep Foxy's mind off food by asking him to talk to Reid about what they were each finding on Lucky. They engaged in a conversation from their desks, pretending I wasn't there, while I tried to hold a steady shot on the camera.

"Lucky is his stage name," Foxy began. "Real name is Daniel Trevone." Foxy considered that for a moment. "That's not such a bad name really. Danny Trevone. He could have stuck with that one."

"Maybe he didn't want his parents to find out what he was doing," Reid offered.

Foxy continued to look through the various pages of information on his computer screen. "Looks like he tried to be legit for a while," Foxy explained. "A few decent day-player TV gigs and some theatre work. It looks like he did two other sex shows before this one. The guy was probably trying to play it straight but couldn't make ends meet."

"He lives in Van Nuys in a rental," Reid added. "Looks like his mother is the next of kin. Lives in, damn… Montana."

"We have to notify her," Foxy said.

"You can do it," Reid answered back. "You have that special touch."

Foxy frowned. In truth, I knew Foxy was terrible at delivering these types of messages. He just blurted the news out – no finesse. But, of course, no one wanted to have to make a call like this. Reid was probably happy to have his partner handle it.

"Foxy – maybe you should do it after you eat," I offered from behind my camera. "When you're in a better frame of mind." While my suggestion made logical sense, there was motive behind it. I wanted Mac and Manny here to capture that moment, not just me on my crappy backup camera with bad audio.

"Yeah, that makes sense," he answered.

"Food is here," Manny said as he entered the room carrying a bunch of In and Out bags.

"Did you guys come by way of Denver?" Foxy scolded. "Did you walk here? We've been waiting for over an hour!"

"You wanted the veggie burger, right Foxy?" Manny teased.

Foxy looked like a maniac as he snatched the bag out of Manny's hand, ready to chow down on whatever he found inside.

*****

With our bellies full and our brains now functional, Foxy set out to do the unpleasant task of calling Lucky's mother. Manny wired the phone so we could record the caller's voice and Mac set his main camera on a tripod in a locked-off shot. He used my little camera for some B-roll shots of the phone and various other objects we could cut away to in the edit.

It was nine o'clock mountain time in Montana. The phone rang a few times before a woman picked it up. "Hello?" her shallow voice asked into the phone.

"Mrs. Trevone?" Foxy asked.

"Yes?"

Foxy took a deep breath, glancing at the camera for dramatic effect. "This is Detective Flanagan of the LAPD. I'm calling with some information about your son, Daniel."

The woman audibly gasped and then there was a thud.

Foxy looked up at me. "I think she dropped the phone."

"Hello? Who is this?" A man spoke into the phone.

"This is Detective Flanagan of the LAPD. Is this Mr. Trevone?"

"Is something wrong with Danny?" the man asked.

"Yes, I'm afraid so sir," Foxy answered. "We found him unresponsive this morning – he was stabbed in the neck."

"Oh my God!" the woman gasped, obviously listening in on the call. "Is he alive?"

"No," Foxy answered flatly. "He didn't make it."

"No! Oh God no!" the woman called out, crying hysterically. "Not our boy, not our Danny!"

Foxy allowed the woman some time to cry and unleash her feelings. Mac was moving his camera between the phone and Foxy's hands which he was ringing in his lap. Behind him, Reid was working on his computer, divorcing himself from the situation. Manny and I were standing three feet away watching Foxy as he struggled to deliver the news. The whole situation felt very intimate and inappropriate. This woman was receiving the worst news of her life. This was the type of phone call every mother fears, and here I was, a Hollywood rat, capturing her pain, all in the name of ratings.

"Were you aware of the type of work your son did?" Foxy asked when she finally grew quiet.

"He was an actor," his father said. "He moved out to Hollywood to make it big. He was gonna be the next Brad Pitt."

"Right," Foxy agreed, not wanting to push it further. "We don't have a lot of leads right now. He was found this morning on the set of a production he was working on."

"This morning?" the mother screeched. "And you're telling me now?"

"Ma'am, what would really help is if you could let us know about anyone who you think could have done this. Did anyone want to harm your son?"

"No," Danny's mother said. "I mean, I don't know. He never said anything about that. We didn't really know his friends. We've never been out to Los Angeles. Danny said he wanted us to wait until he could fly us there on his private jet." She paused, reflecting on that thought. "I guess that's not going to happen now." She burst into tears again, stepping away from the phone.

"He has a roommate," the father offered. "George. Have you talked to him?"

"Not yet," Foxy told him. "He lived in Van Nuys, right? On Victory Boulevard?"

"Yes," the father answered.

"Okay, we'll speak to George next."

Foxy gave his contact information to the grieving parents and let them know he would keep them posted as the case progressed. They had some questions about Lucky's body and how they could transport it back to Montana for a proper funeral. Foxy provided them with Lou's contact information and explained that Lou was examining Lucky's body at the moment, but then could work with them to make arrangements to send Lucky back home. It was highly unlikely that the parents had been involved for a variety of reasons and the cops felt they could easily rule them out as suspects.

Foxy walked over to Reid who was sitting at his computer, looking at it intently.

"How'd it go?" Reid asked.

"I think I'm getting better at it," Foxy answered. "But the parents couldn't give us any leads. They don't know his friends here or his enemies. But he has a roommate that we should talk to."

"Okay we'll see him next," Reid answered.

"How about you?" Foxy asked. "Did you turn anything up?"

Reid pointed to his screen. "I looked up Carmine and Vinnie. Carmine has a couple DUIs and Vinnie has a few unpaid parking tickets."

Reid pulled up another screen and I was surprised to see that it showed their profiles on Facebook. "Looks like Carmine is a little tighter with Joy than he lets on," Reid explained as he pointed to some pictures of the two of them together at a barbeque. He pulled up Lucky's profile to show Foxy some posts of him standing in front of the Hollywood sign, posing for a selfie with Kyle Belamy and hanging out with some friends. His profile listed some of the shows he had worked on and listed Hollywood as his current place of residence.

Reid poked around and searched for other cast members as well. Most of them were the typical self-absorbed actor types, posting a ton of pictures of themselves on Facebook.

When Mac finally stopped rolling, I leaned in to ask Reid a question. "So the LAPD has access to people's Facebook accounts?"

"No," Reid said lightly. "I'm just looking at their public profiles. People don't realize how much stuff other people can see."

"I guess not," I agreed.

"Social media helps us track a lot down these days," Reid continued. "People posting their whereabouts or hate mail about someone who ends up dead. It's nuts. It doesn't usually help us too much for the types of crimes we get handed, but you never know what might turn up."

10.

Van Nuys was a city in the valley about ten minutes from where I lived. The population was mostly Hispanic but the reasonable rents also drew in a community of struggling actors.

It was nine o'clock and I was stifling a yawn. It was only my first day on the case and I had no reason to be tired, but I had gotten spoiled by my last team. Hollywood and Terry rarely worked past dinnertime. At the time I had criticized them for that, but now I was realizing there was something to be said for calling it quits come nightfall. Most of the world did that, right? Unfortunately, work-life balance wasn't something that generally existed in reality TV. It was either all work or all life (while looking for work) but never both. I didn't think Reid understood the concept either.

Lucky's apartment building was surrounded by large trees and partially hidden from view on the street. The building was brown stucco with dark brown trim, which contributed to the building's low-key profile. It was small, with only four units and two floors. I estimated it probably went for about eight hundred bucks a month.

We followed behind the cops, camera and sound rolling as they ascended an outdoor staircase on the side of the building. At the top of the landing sat Lucky's apartment – Apartment B.

"This is it," Reid told us.

We nodded and stepped back, giving the cops some space. Reid and Foxy stood at the front of the door, preparing to knock, while Mac held up his lens for the perfect shot. I held my clipboard and stood off to the side, capturing the date and time for my log.

Reid knocked on the front door and stepped back. Inside, we heard some clanging and shuffling around until finally the front door swung open. Inside, stood the closest thing to a Greek god I had ever seen.

George stood around six feet tall with black damp hair pulled back behind his ears. He wore a pair of grey sweat shorts and a pair of sneakers and nothing else. His torso was long and his chest was chiseled and marvelous with little beads of sweat dripping down it. He had a towel in his hand, which he used to wipe the sweat that had collected on his brow. He had clearly been working out and his body was glistening from it.

As I took in his body I also took in my breath, gasping at the sight of him. I didn't realize anyone could hear me until all of the guys turned around to look at me, including Reid.

George smiled, apparently used to this type of reaction. "What's going on?"

"We'd like to talk to you inside Sir. Can we come in?" Foxy asked.

"What's with the cameras?" George asked.

Reid grunted and gestured towards me. "She'll explain."

George nodded and the cops walked past him inside followed by Mac and Manny. I stayed back to speak with George. Wasn't I the lucky one?

"Hi, I'm Victoria," I began. "I'm working on a reality TV show where I follow these cops around."

"Oh really, which one?" George perked up.

"Um, it's a new one. They're still working on the title," I lied, not wanting to say *Murder Live!* and give away the news that the cops were about to deliver. I looked into his gorgeous, deep dark eyes and instantly became tongue tied. "Listen, I know you're very sweaty, I mean *busy*, but if you could just chest, I mean *attest* to the fact that you agree to be seen on television, I'd appreciate it." I felt my face turning red – I was blushing like a schoolgirl!

"Jesus Sharpe, pull yourself together," Foxy told me, embarrassing me thoroughly. "Dude, she's trying to ask you to sign the release. Just sign it, okay?" Foxy said impatiently.

I smiled sheepishly and held out the one-page release form. My face was still hot, I couldn't manage to calm my nerves down.

"Oh, sure," George said and gave me a wink. He seemed to be used to women being intimidated by him. George signed my form and stepped back, gesturing that I should enter the apartment with the others.

"Why don't you put your shirt on?" Reid said to George.

"I'd have him leave it off," Mac suggested to Reid. "Better ratings."

Reid stared at Mac for a moment and then answered slowly and deliberately. "He might be cold without a shirt."

"No, I'm not cold," George told him. "I'm actually pretty hot."

I'll say.

"Well, I don't want to look at your nipples the whole time," Reid argued.

George looked at Reid and leaned in. "I'm actually an aspiring actor, so if the camera guy thinks my shirt should be off, let's keep it off, okay? I mean, you saw how Victoria reacted, right?"

Reid glanced over at me. "Yes, I did see that."

Mac fired up the camera and George stood in front of the cops, muscles flexed, ready to hear what they wanted to tell him.

"Do you want to sit down?" Foxy asked.

"No, I'm good," George answered, his muscles flexing as he spoke. "What's up?"

"Is your roommate Lucky Trevone?" Foxy asked.

"Yeah, why?" George asked, his pecs twitching. He absently turned and glanced at me, giving the only girl in the room a little smile.

"Cause he's dead," Foxy answered with all the subtlety of a bulldozer.

I watched as George's flexed chest suddenly slacked and loosened. "Dead? I just saw him yesterday."

"Well, he's dead today."

George shook his head in disbelief. "This is how you're telling me? You're just blurting out he's dead? Is that how you guys do this?"

"We're supposed to break the news to you gently," Reid explained, "but it was hard to take you seriously half-naked. I asked you several times to put your shirt on."

"What, are you jealous?" George asked, getting angry.

I was half expecting Reid to take off his shirt to go muscle to muscle with George, but he didn't. He probably knew he would lose.

"Come on, let's sit down," Foxy said calmly, guiding George over to the couch.

Mac and Manny followed them over to the couch while I stayed where I was. George grabbed his T-shirt and pulled it over his head. Next, he pulled out his phone and started to scroll through it. He stopped on something and held the phone out to Foxy. "This is Lucky. Is this the guy you're talking about?"

Foxy leaned in to examine the photo on the phone then nodded. "Yeah, that's him. We found him this morning on set, stabbed in the neck."

"Someone stabbed him? In the neck?" George exclaimed. "Wait, was it part of the show? Did something go wrong?"

"No, it was in the morning before they began filming. We found him in his dressing room, wearing a pair of thong underwear and a mask."

"Thong underwear?" George repeated, shaking his head. "He didn't wear stuff like that. So, who did it?"

"We don't know. We were hoping we could ask you some questions."

"Yeah, of course."

"Can you tell me how long you lived together?" Reid began.

"About a year. We were getting ready to renew the lease on this place."

"And did you know each other prior to living together?"

"Not that well. I was looking for a roommate and a friend introduced us."

"And you're familiar with the type of work he does, right?" Foxy asked.

"Yeah, I know about it," George answered. "He's an actor – just like me. Well, I don't do the types of movies he does though. Oh shit – don't tell his mom! Oh man, it'll crush her."

"You don't want us to tell his mother that her son is dead?" Foxy asked.

"No, I just meant she doesn't know about the porn stuff."

"Did Lucky have any enemies you knew of? Did he have any unpaid debts?" Reid asked.

"No," George replied.

"How about his alcoholism? Did he make any enemies when he was on a bender?" Foxy asked.

George looked confused for a second. "Oh, you're talking about the AA meetings? That was just to get jobs. Most actors do it."

Foxy glanced over to me for validation. I nodded that it was a relatively common practice and a good way to potentially meet big Hollywood producers and agents. They weren't lying – they were acting!

"Okay – how about girlfriends?" Foxy asked. "Was he seeing anyone?"

"Oh yeah, he was dating this total sexpot," George said. "Super weird shit, you know."

I exchanged a look with Manny. We both knew who he was talking about. Why was Rose at the center of everything all the time?

"Big boobs, dark hair, Latina?" Foxy asked.

George shook his head no. "No, she had blonde hair – real skinny."

"Penny?" Foxy asked, sounding surprised.

"Yeah, that was her name."

"Really, she was a sexpot?"

"She's super flexible man. Lucky almost sprained his dick one time from her."

Foxy whipped out his phone and pulled up a picture. "Is this her?" he asked, holding out a picture of Penny he had snuck earlier.

"Yeah, that's her. Shit man, I can't believe Lucky's dead. This is like hitting me now!" George stood up and paced, running his hands through his hair. "He was twenty-three." George stood silent for a minute. "This is tough. I feel like this is the biggest acting challenge of my life right now, trying to keep it together in front of you guys."

"Why? Are you the killer?" Foxy asked.

"No, man. I just mean it's hard not to cry right now."

"Maybe you'll get an Emmy," Foxy offered, which seemed to give George some hope.

"Did Lucky come home last night after work?" Reid asked George.

"Yeah. He was here. We worked out together."

"Did you see him leave for work this morning?"

"No. He went out around eleven last night. He said he had somewhere to be. I didn't ask where. We didn't get into each other's business like that. I passed out watching the game and I didn't see him this morning."

"So, you don't know if he came home or not after that?"

"No."

"Tell us about your relationship with Lucky – your friendship," Reid asked.

"Yeah," George said and then pulled his shirt off again.

Reid looked agitated. "You're taking that off again?"

"Lucky and I were buds," George said. "We were in the business, you know. I didn't agree with his choice, you know the sex stuff, but he had bills to pay. Plus, that bod he had – I was so jealous of it. Everyone was. I guess he felt like the world needed to see it."

"You said he was struggling financially?" Foxy asked.

"That's the plight of the actor man. He wasn't getting big roles, so he found another avenue."

"Okay, so before this show I assume he spent a lot of time auditioning, right?"

George nodded. "He bartended too. He got a lot of chicks that way but he also got into fights a lot with the guys whose girlfriends he was hitting on." George smiled. "He got fired from like three different bars for that. Damn, what a freaking waste!"

I had to agree with George. Yes, he sounded like a total womanizer, but sometimes when a guy is that hot you don't really care that he's a womanizer. You just want a piece of the action. It's like an ego boost if a guy like that wants to have sex with you. Kind of like Kyle Belamy winking at me. If I slept with him, which I wouldn't, but if I did, I would know it was a one-time thing. It would be bragging rights for both of us. For him because he'd have another notch on his belt, and for me, it would be sleeping with a hot guy that was totally out of my league. Guys like that were good in bed too. They had a lot of practice.

"Did he ever default on rent payments because of his inability to hold a job?" Reid asked.

"A couple times, yeah. Actually, we got in an argument about that the other week. He even took a swing at me." George suddenly turned white and looked at the cops. "But I didn't kill him. Like, it wasn't that big of a deal. He was drunk."

"I thought you said he didn't have a drinking problem," Foxy said.

"I didn't say that. I said he wasn't really in AA. He did drink a lot, but when you bartend that's part of the job."

"Do you recognize this woman?" Foxy asked, holding out a photo of Rose on his phone.

"No, who is she?" George asked.

"Another one of the women on set," Foxy answered.

"Wow. I hope he hit that before he died," George said and then glanced over at me, realizing his crassness.

"We're quite sure that he did," Foxy confirmed.

After the interview concluded, Reid and Foxy asked if they could look around the place and George agreed. Mac, Manny, and I followed while Reid and Foxy explored.

We walked into Lucky's room and looked around. The room was pretty sparse and consisted of a bed with no headboard, a beat-up old dresser, and a sheet covering up the window with a few thumb tacks. It was a regular seduction lounge. On the dresser was a pile of headshots of Lucky. The eight by ten photos were black and white featuring Lucky wearing a white tank top. He looked good. If I were a producer I would ask him to sit on my casting couch.

Foxy opened a drawer in Lucky's nightstand and pulled out some bills. "Yeah, this guy was in debt. This credit card bill is close to eight grand. It looks like a bunch of cash advances and then clothing purchases, bar tabs, and that sort of thing. Lucky liked to party."

Next, Foxy pulled out a box of condoms from the drawer and examined it. The box marked "extra-large" was nearly empty. "Do you think guys are actually extra-large or do they just buy these to show off?"

"Showing off," Reid answered immediately.

"Wouldn't it fall off during sex then?" Foxy asked.

"It could," Reid said.

"I don't think women are looking at the size listed on the condom box," I commented. "They probably don't even see it. They just tell the guy to put it on. But, if the guy was extra-large the woman would be able to tell. She wouldn't need it written on a box."

Reid stared at me. "Thanks Sharpe for explaining that to us."

"I wonder if he had to special order those," I said. "Can you buy them in store?"

"Yeah they sell 'em," Foxy said, then cleared his throat. "I mean, of course I could wear them, but I prefer a tighter fit."

"Of course," I smirked.

*****

I grabbed one last peek at George's shirtless physique before we closed the door to his apartment and stepped out into the night air. It felt cool and helped to soothe the burning I was still feeling in my cheeks.

"Let's call it a night," Reid announced. "We can meet back on the set tomorrow morning."

"Nine o'clock," Foxy told us then turned to head down the steps. The cops got into their car and took off without much fanfare.

I jumped in the front seat of the rented SUV with Mac in the driver's seat and Manny in the back.

"They took off kind of abruptly, huh?" I said when we started driving. "Do you think they're sick of us already?"

"I think they were sick of us before we started," Mac said, "But that's not why they took off like that."

"Then why?"

"Come on Chica, what are you doing to that guy?" Manny asked.

"What guy? George?"

"You're tying him up in knots baby."

I turned to Mac. "Who?"

"He's talking about Reid," Mac told me. "Look, I understand that these people objectify themselves for a living, but that doesn't give you an open license to treat them like meat. That guy, George, had a face you know. Did you look at it once?"

"I certainly did," I mused, picturing him in my mind.

"There she goes again!" Manny said, slapping the back of my chair. "You gotta keep it in your pants girl. Your boy is getting jealous."

"He is?" I asked, surprised by the idea.

"You can't talk about dick size like that," Mac told me. "Guys don't like it."

"I wasn't talking about Reid's size. I was just commenting on the size George wore."

"Right and that Reid is smaller than that," Manny said.

"I was just answering Foxy's question!"

"Girls can tell – we don't need a condom package to know if they're extra-large," Mac mimicked.

"Oh my God! I wasn't talking about Reid. We haven't even had sex! I was just offering the woman's perspective on the matter."

"Qué? No sex yet, Chica?"

"And how about that Kyle Belamy winking at you all day?" Mac continued.

"Now you're starting to sound like a jealous boyfriend, Mac," I told him.

Mac shook his hand. "Not jealous, just observant. You're acting like a kid in a candy store on this porn set and your boyfriend doesn't like it."

"You know this is such a double standard! You assholes stand around googly eyed all day at these women. You can't pass by the set once without craning your necks so hard that they might snap just to see if someone might be topless."

"That's true," Manny agreed. "I like looking in there. But I wouldn't do it if my girlfriend was standing next to me."

He had a point there. I had been feeling terribly uncomfortable all day on set, seething at how easily men could turn to mush at the sight of a naked woman. I was feeling sleazy and uncomfortable and objectified just because of my gender. Yet somehow, I had managed to turn the tables and make Reid feel jealous instead? A smile crept across my face as I thought that through. He was jealous of me? Ha! Good.

11.

"Start your day with positivity!" I awoke to the sound of a woman proclaiming these words while talking to a newscaster on television. I slowly opened my eyes to look over at the TV, which I had left on overnight. The show's guest was a bubbly brunette wearing a pink mini dress. "You must start the day by saying, *Yes I Can*!" she told the audience. "If you put yourself in a positive space, it will radiate out to those around you and good things will come. I guarantee it!"

I listened for a while as the woman talked about how the power of positivity had affected her life and how it was now filled with love and happiness. It made me think about my own life and the conversation I had with Mac and Manny in our SUV the night before.

Mac telling me that I had been objectifying the men on set was actually a comforting concept. It meant I had just as much power as the guys did. I didn't have to feel uncomfortable or ashamed to be there. I should embrace it!

While the idea of making Reid jealous was appealing, I knew it wasn't right. I knew how angry I felt whenever Rose tried to flirt with Reid, so imagine if he was flirting back? I had to make a conscious effort not to get swooped up in the environment. I needed to focus on being the ruthless producer I was known to be. We had a murder here and the victim was gorgeous. America deserved to see him and he deserved justice. How dare someone take a specimen like that away from us?

I decided the perky brunette was right. Today, I would let positivity be my guide. I took my morning shower then cleared the steam from the mirror with my hand. As I stared at my reflection, I recited aloud, "Today is going to be a good day!" and, "Yes I can!" Over and over.

I drove my Miata to the set with the roof down. It was about eight-thirty in the morning and it was hot, but not scorching yet. I wore my usual work clothes, which consisted of a pair of jeans and a T-shirt and my hair pulled back into a ponytail. I was still thinking happy thoughts when my car starting lurching forward and backwards. "What the hell?" The car started to drive slower and slower, despite the fact I was pushing the gas pedal to the floor. I managed to pull my car to the side of the road before it completely died.

I took the user manual out of the glove compartment and flipped through it, trying to figure out what had happened. The table of contents didn't have headers like "Car Died" so it was hard for me to figure out what went wrong. I flipped to the trouble shooting section and my heart sank. I looked at my gas gauge and realized my stupidity. Yep – out of gas.

I needed to keep a positive outlook. After all, today was going to be a great day! I pulled up my roof, locked the car, and headed to the office on foot. I was only a few blocks away and the exercise would do me good. How's that for positivity?

As I walked, I debated who I should call for help. Should I call Reid or should I call my Dad? Reid was closer – he was probably already on set. My dad lived all the way in Venice beach and it would probably take him an hour to get here. Then again, my dad was retired and this would give him something to do. My dad would come with no questions asked. Reid would ask a lot of questions. Ultimately, I decided my dad was the right choice.

"Hey sweetie. What's going on?" my dad said into the phone.

"We're shooting in Burbank and my car just ran out of gas."

"Do you need me to come get you?"

"No, I'm walking to the set but I left my car parked on the side of the road. I was thinking that if you were maybe gonna be in the neighborhood…"

"Yeah, I was planning to be in Burbank today actually," my dad told me. I knew he was lying, of course. People who lived on the west side did not come to the valley. Why would they? To visit our local Target store? They had everything they needed on their side of the mountains, including the cooler weather.

I started to feel guilty. "You know, Dad, it's okay, I can see if one of the guys here can help me out."

"No, no Honey, I don't mind. I'll come by in a couple hours – would that be okay?"

"Thanks, Dad."

"Tell me about your latest case. Anything good?"

I hesitated, not exactly sure what to say. After all, I was speaking to my father. My mom would eat this kind of thing up, but with my dad things were a little more PG. "Uh, I'm on set at Happy Day Studios. One of the actors was killed during a shoot."

"Happy Day studios. I think I've heard of them. They're on the Warner Brothers lot, right?"

"No. They're a bit smaller," I told him cryptically.

"Well, the story sounds great. Another big show for you, Honey. Give me the address where your car is at and I'll take care of it."

I told him where I had parked my car and then realized I would need to leave my keys for him. I turned around and walked two blocks back to hide them above one of the tires where he could find them. Twenty minutes later I was at the studio, huffing and puffing at the front door, my back drenched in sweat. It wasn't that strenuous of a walk, but it was hot out there!

I looked around and was surprised when I realized that the cops hadn't arrived yet. I found Mac on the set that we had been using for interviews – the one that looked like the surface of the moon. He was sitting in the dark, legs crossed in a deep state of meditation. Penny was sitting across from him in the same pose.

Normally I would have balked at the effort, saying something like, "Who has time for meditation?" or, "I'm too busy to relax." But today I had a new outlook. I was proud of these two for finding their inner peace!

As much as I admired their efforts, I wasn't ready to get my Namaste on just yet. Instead, I headed over to the other set to see what was going on. The actors were mulling about while Elroy and Enrique readied their equipment. Kyle was sitting on a directors' chair reading a script, presumably for the next part he had been offered. Joy was flirting with Carmine, and Craig was running around the set, ensuring all the props were in the right spots. After his blowup the day before I wasn't sure he was even going to show up today.

I saw Manny helping Enrique with some cables and waved hello to him, then I walked over to Vinnie who was going through the latest version of his script.

"Good morning, Vinnie," I said with a smile.

"Back again," Vinnie mumbled.

"What are you shooting today?" I asked.

Vinnie seemed frustrated that I was interrupting his concentration, but managed to put on a phony smile and look up at me. "Today we're finishing the space scene that we didn't finish yesterday and then we move on to shoot a bedroom scene between Rose and Kyle."

"Is the bedroom in the spaceship?"

"No, it's a fantasy scene so it's just in a regular bedroom. We don't have the budget to have them floating around in a rocket ship while they're banging."

"Right," I said, smiling politely. "I was curious why you went with the space theme to begin with. Isn't the weightlessness thing an issue?"

Vinnie looked at me like I was an idiot. "The sets were already built. Do you think we made these? Sweetie, you have a lot to learn about this business."

"We're ready boss," Elroy said to Vinnie.

"Excellent," Vinnie said, standing. "Craig – can you call Penny and Rose in here? We're ready to go."

"I can get Penny, boss," Elroy said. "I'm headed that way anyway."

I didn't feel like smelling Vinnie's cologne anymore, so I followed Elroy off set towards the studio where I knew Penny and Mac were sitting.

When we arrived, the lights were still off and the duo appeared to be in a deep trance. Elroy quietly entered the room and whispered Penny's name. When she didn't respond, he stepped inside to get her. I decided to hang back, not wanting to startle anyone.

I watched through the glass as Elroy placed a gentle hand on Penny's shoulder to let her know it was time to move to the set. Penny roused slowly, lifting her head up as if she was a machine, in a slow and smooth movement. It was clear how much Elroy cared for Penny but I didn't know if the feelings were being reciprocated, especially now we knew she and Lucky were an item. No wonder she was so hysterical about the whole thing.

The door of the studio opened and Penny breezed past me. Elroy followed behind her like a lost puppy and then Mac emerged.

"Wow, she's amazing," Mac told me.

"Are your chakras in order now?" I asked him.

"Yup," Mac smiled. "All seven of them."

"Great."

To my right, I saw Reid and Foxy walking towards me, having just arrived. My breath caught as I remembered how the two had left last night without saying a word, not even goodbye. The sneaks had probably gone back to the precinct to do some real work while we weren't around.

"Morning," I said, in my most convincing and cheery voice.

"What's going on?" Reid said.

"They're getting ready to start shooting now on set. I was just coming out here to get Mac."

"Morning," Mac said to the cops.

"Sorry man, I didn't get one for you," Reid said to Mac as he handed me a coffee. "You like milk and one sugar, right?"

I melted. "Yeah, that's right. Wow. I can't believe you remembered!" I gushed all over Reid as I took the coffee from his hand. I was still feeling hot and sweaty from my morning walk, but that didn't matter. I planned to enjoy this hot coffee anyway. "Are you gonna interview Penny today?" I asked hopefully.

"Her and everyone else," Reid told me. "Why?"

"I was just curious about her and Lucky. Maybe she had a motive."

"Leave the detective work to us, Sharpe," Foxy told me, trying to sound like a tough guy but coming off more like an asshole.

"Now Foxy, I could never do that," I teased.

*****

I managed to convince Reid and Foxy to do a talking head interview quickly before we began filming for the day. I pulled the guys outside of the studio for an interview, but Manny said the noise from the cars on the street would cause too many sound issues. We moved to the back parking lot where things were a little quieter. When we got there, Foxy starting talking right away.

"That's Lucky's car," he told me, pointing to a green two-door hatchback. "Lou checked it out. The engine was cold so he thinks the car was sitting there for a while. So maybe Lucky came here after he left his apartment Monday night. Maybe he was meeting up with his killer."

"What the hell are you doing?" I snapped at Foxy. "We're not even filming yet! Don't be spewing out gold like that before my guys are ready!"

"Wow." Foxy smiled and raised his hands up in defense. "Sorry."

Mac threw the camera over his shoulder while Manny threaded the lavaliere microphones down the cops' shirts and clipped the microphone packs to the backs of their jeans. When we were ready I asked Mac to frame the two cops in a medium shot, showing them from the waist up with Lucky's car behind them.

Foxy was wearing an oversized green polo shirt while Reid was dressed in a gray, short sleeved dress shirt. Foxy repeated what he had just told me about the car and how the Medical Examiner believed it had been sitting there for some time.

"He also could have left with someone in their car and then they dropped him back at the studio later. We don't have enough information at this point," Foxy elaborated.

"Do you have any suspects?" I asked.

"Everyone is a suspect right now," Foxy told me. "Today, we have to spend some observing the cast and crew and seeing how they interact."

Reid glanced over at Foxy and smiled, shaking his head. "I know what you want to observe," Reid smiled.

"Can you take this seriously dude?" Foxy retorted. "A man was killed."

"What about George?" I asked. "Is he a suspect?"

"Sharpe, have you been listening?" Foxy asked me. "I literally just said everyone is a suspect. So yeah, your boyfriend George is too."

Ouch. I guess Mac and Manny weren't the only ones who noticed my apparent interest in that gorgeous Greek.

*****

On set, the day's shoot was already underway. Between takes we snuck inside to capture some of the action. This gave Foxy his chance to "observe" and me a chance to get some decent footage. The scene was a non-sexual one, which meant I could actually air parts of it on *Murder Live!*

Penny and Joy were sitting inside the makeshift rocket talking about aliens. Both were dressed in skimpy attire and sitting on metallic chairs. This must have been a magic rocket ship as the two didn't seem to have the usual issues with weightlessness that most astronauts had. That or Vinnie just forgot to ask Craig to hoist them up.

"They're out there," Penny said as she looked out the circular window of the space shuttle into space.

"I'm scared," Joy said, doing her best to look frightened.

Next, Rose entered the scene wearing a black and red lace nightie. "What you talkin' about?" Rose asked in her thick Spanish accent.

"The aliens," Joy answered. "They're going to come for us."

"Don't worry, the guys will protect us," Penny told them. "I got a good look at TJ's muscles last night." She giggled.

Rose shook her head back and forth. "They didn't protect Johnny. He was killed!" Rose raised a hand to her chest and took a deep breath in an exaggerated motion. "Johnny, I'll miss you!" Rose threw herself on the nearby bed and pretended to cry, her huge breasts heaving up and down in the process.

Johnny had been the character Lucky had played. Vinnie had decided death in the real world wasn't enough for Lucky – he would kill him in the script too.

"Cut!" Vinnie screamed. "Rose, don't add lines to my script. I don't see nothing in this script about you missing Johnny."

"I should though," Rose defended. "It makes it better. Craig told me so."

"What would make it better is if you could act like you were actually scared of aliens. Come on Rose!"

"Why do you even have her?" Joy complained about Rose. "She can't act."

Rose turned and shot Joy a sharp look.

"Cause she's got big boobs," Vinnie told Joy. "If I wanted flat-chested babes who *could* act, I would have hired three of you."

"Hey!" Carmine jumped in. "Show some respect."

"This is such bullshit, Vinnie," Penny interjected. "Do you really think Lucky would have been killed by aliens? I feel like you're just killing him off to take the easy way out of the script."

"He's dead, Penny. He can't be in any more scenes unless you want me to use his corpse. So, I have to kill him off. Understand?"

"Well if he has to be dead we should at least act like we care."

"This is soft porn!" Vinnie shot back. "Should everyone be crying over this or something? Are you trying to get an Oscar nomination?"

"Your brother's right. You have no respect, Vin!" Penny shouted back.

The drama when the cameras were not rolling sure beat the "acting" Rose, Joy, and Penny were attempting to do. Perhaps Foxy was right, this was a great way to observe how people interacted, who had motive and who didn't. I was glad Mac was filming it.

I had experienced people like Vinnie before; LA was filled with them. He was completely self-centered and thoughtless. In some ways I wished he was the killer so he could get locked up for his crassness, but I didn't think he was. It would take a real psychopath to be so blatantly careless about a murder if they had actually committed it.

12.

Rose sat across from Reid and Foxy, still wearing her black and red lace teddy. It would have been very easy for her to throw on a robe to cover up, but that wasn't her style. I had asked the crew to use the dressing room where Lucky was murdered as the location for the interview. We all had our suspicions about Rose so placing her in the scene of the crime might subconsciously convince the audience of the same thing.

Manny was arranging the boom microphone on a stand above Rose's head. "You really don't remember me baby?" he asked Rose.

Rose looked up at him. "Oh, I do mi amor. Don't worry." She patted him on the hip and then looked at me. "Where's my money?" I walked over to get my bag and pulled out the money.

Rose held out her hand, eager to grab the cash. I counted out five hundred dollars and handed it to her. "Five now, five later – if you cooperate," I told her.

Rose considered my offer for a moment then shrugged. She had no reason to say no. She snatched up the cash and smiled brightly, now ready to be interviewed.

The vibe in the room was subdued. Despite the fact that Rose was visual eye candy, no one seemed to want to play her games. She had lied to us last time and would probably lie to us again.

"Let's start with your whereabouts," Reid began after Rose was situated and the cameras were rolling. "What time did you leave work on Monday night?"

Rose looked up and ran her tongue across her lips, thinking. "Maybe around seven?"

"Okay and then what did you do?"

Rose smiled mischievously. "I went to the gas station. I met a guy and we hooked up in the bathroom. Then I went home."

"Should I assume you didn't catch the name of the guy you were with?" Foxy asked.

Rose shrugged.

"Did you look at his face? Could you identify him if you saw him?"

Rose shrugged again, not sure.

"That may be your only alibi, honey," Foxy scolded her. "You'd better pull on that memory bank of yours. What did you do after you got home?"

"I took a shower," Rose answered.

"I'm glad to hear it," Foxy said. "Gas stations are dirty places, especially the bathrooms." He shook his head. "Do you realize how unhygienic a place like that is?"

Reid looked disappointed. "You had all day and night to come up with your story, Rose. I was expecting something better."

Rose leaned in, her big red lips parting. "It's not a story."

"Did anyone see you when you got home?" Reid asked.

"I live alone," Rose answered.

"When did you arrive to work yesterday?"

"Around nine," Rose answered in her thick Spanish accent. "I walked into the dressing room and I saw Lucky – he was lying on the couch in a mask. At first, I thought he was being an asshole like he always was, but then I poked him and he wasn't moving. Then I started screaming and Vinnie came in."

"It sounds like you didn't like him," Foxy said.

"He was a little prick," Rose spat. "Stupid and arrogant – he thought this job would give him opportunities. I'm not a dreamer, I am realistic."

"Were you two sleeping together?"

"No."

"Okay. Were you sleeping with anyone else here? And I'm not talking about Manny."

"Who?" Rose asked.

"Me, Chica!" Manny whined.

"Oh right. Manny." Rose nodded and repeated, "Manny" as if training herself to remember his name.

"Yes, his name is Manny," Foxy confirmed. "That guy over there who you had sex with twice is named Manny. Got that? Now, who else here have you slept with?" Rose's eyes scanned curiously from Reid to Foxy and then over to Mac. "I'm not talking about us, Rose! I'm talking about the other people that work here!"

Rose smiled at her mistake, then adjusted her boobs before answering. The tops of her nipples were peeking out behind her lace teddy and it was pissing me off. "As you know I have a compulsion."

"Then why not Lucky?"

Rose stiffened. "Do I have to have a reason?"

"Was it out of respect for Penny?"

"No. I told you, I didn't like him."

"So, who around here did you *like*?" Reid asked.

Rose turned and looked at me. "Give me another hundred dollars."

"Knock it off or I'll haul you down to the station right now," Reid told her.

"Fine. There was Kyle Belamy of course. The PA... what's his name? Craig? Elroy and then Vinnie. I'm not proud of that last one."

"How about Jason?" Foxy asked.

Rose nodded. "Oh yeah, him too."

"What about Carmine?" Reid asked.

Rose seemed to be racking her brain, unsure. "I don't remember. But not Enrique. I know his wife. I didn't with him."

Foxy laughed. "Of course not. That would be unethical!" Foxy turned to look at Manny. "You really need to get tested, man."

"I'm tested," Rose asserted. "You have to be in this business."

"There's no way you're not carrying around at least five diseases," Foxy told her. He seemed to have lost his professionalism early in the interview process this time. But how professional could you be talking to a woman in a teddy about her *compulsions*?

"I don't usually get complaints," Rose told him, leaning forward. As she leaned in, the shoulder strap of her top fell down her arm, exposing her right breast.

"Oy Mommy!" Manny blurted out.

"Put your top up," I scolded. "We can't show that on TV."

"Oops." Rose smiled, adjusting the straps and covering herself up. "I know you guys want me to be the one who did it, but I have news for you – I'm not."

"Who do you think did?" Reid asked her.

Before she could answer, the door behind me opened and light flooded the room. "Oh, I'm sorry, I didn't know you were taping," I heard my Dad's voice say.

My eyes popped open wide. This was not the best moment for my father to show up on set. Why had I called him and not Reid? What was I thinking?

"This is your Daddy, right?" Rose asked, looking at the tall slender man dressed in chinos and a cardigan. "Aww, does he always visit you at work?"

"Hey I'm sorry kid," my Dad said to me. "They told me you were in here. I should have knocked first."

Before I could ask him to leave, Rose stretched out her hand towards him, still sitting in her interview chair. "It is so nice to meet you. I'm Rosario."

My Dad looked slightly paralyzed, taking in the sight of this nearly naked Latina beauty in from of him. "She's a murder suspect," I snapped.

"Oh," my Dad said, not knowing what to do next. "Uh, well good luck with all that."

As Rose leaned closer to my father, her top fell down once again, exposing her breast in the process.

"Oy Mommy!" Manny repeated.

"Cover up!" I spat at her.

Rose looked down at her huge breasts, pretending she had no idea they were showing again. I couldn't bare the sight for a moment longer. I grabbed a robe from the wardrobe rack and threw it at her. "Show some decency for God's sake!"

My Dad looked horribly embarrassed. "This is my fault. I'll just get out of your way."

"No Dad, it's her fault." I was so angry, I was shaking. I felt absolutely humiliated. "Rose, you apologize or give me the five hundred dollars back!"

Rose took the money that was still rolled up in her hand and stuffed it in her underwear. "Come and get it."

That was it! I wasn't having it any more with this woman – her time had come. I gathered a spit ball in my mouth and shot it right into her face. Bullseye!

"Punta!" Rose screamed before lunging at me. As she moved, she knocked over Mac's tripod and I saw him dive to save the equipment.

I felt her hands pull my hair hard. It hurt. I realized like a flash that I had no idea what I was doing. I wasn't a fighter, I was a television show producer. A wave of panic washed over me. Was it too late to call a truce?

My dad was the first to come to my aide. He grabbed Rose's shoulders shouting, "Don't touch my daughter!"

Then Reid grabbed us each by the shoulders, pulling us to opposite sides of the room with Herculean strength. "Knock it off!" he boomed.

I was panting and humiliated. I looked around to see everyone staring at me. My father looked worried, my crew looked surprised, and Reid looked pissed. There was at least one thing that was clear to me at this moment – this interview was over.

*****

My father had filled my car with gas and parked the Miata out front. We stood outside, leaning against the brick building staring at the car and saying nothing. I looked like a disheveled mess. My father had been so proud of me lately. He had just gotten a cold, hard look at what really went on behind the scenes. Fancy editing couldn't cover up what he had seen live and with his own eyes. He knew the truth and I felt like a fool.

"That was really something back there," my dad finally said.

"Dad listen, I've never been in a fight in my life. That woman, she just – she's the same one from the first episode. Do you remember?"

"I know who she is. I don't like you hanging around dangerous people like this. Honey, I'm old but I'm not stupid." His voice grew quiet. "This is a porn set. Victoria, what have you gotten yourself into?"

"Dad, I'm investigating a murder that just happens to take place at a porn set. And it's not porn – it's soft core – it's like rated NC-17. Probably the stuff Mom likes to watch."

My dad raised his eyebrows. "Sometimes I worry that your mother's lifestyle is going to wear off on you girls. I think my fears were just realized."

"Dad! I'm not like Mom, don't even say that. I can't control who dies or where they die. I just document it."

He smiled and looked at me. "Well, that was certainly more exciting than my usual routine. I have a good story to tell."

"Please don't tell this story, Dad. Seriously."

My dad shook his head. "I'll just tell Mom."

I smiled. "Thanks for fixing the car."

"That's what dads are for. Well, I'd better get back inside."

"Aren't you leaving?"

"Not just yet. I offered to help out Vinnie for a little while on the set design. It's no big deal."

"You got a job here?"

"No of course not. I'm retired. This is pro bono work. I thought of a couple easy tricks to make it look realistic. It won't take me long and I'll stay out of your way." My Dad kissed my cheek before heading back inside.

*****

As I walked back into the building, Reid was waiting. His put his arm around me and not-so-subtly pulled me down the hall to a secluded spot. "Do I need to pull you off this case, Sharpe?"

"I'm not a cop Reid and you're not my boss," I snapped. After being humiliated in front of my father, I certainly didn't need a lecture from him.

"I can't have you attacking our suspects."

"She attacked me."

"You spit in her face."

"She did that first. Remember at the hotel at Ginny's wedding?"

"That was weeks ago! Don't be childish, please. This woman has been involved now in multiple murders and I don't want her coming after you next."

I rolled my eyes and shrugged. "Fine. I'm okay by the way. I didn't hear you asking about that."

Reid just shook his head. "What's with your dad? I just saw him walk onto the set carrying a can of paint."

"He's an opportunist."

I left Reid and went in search of my crew. I found them sitting in the front office chatting with Vinnie, Carmine, and Joy. Carmine was sitting at his desk while Joy stood behind him, rubbing his shoulders. Vinnie was leaning against the wall, holding the call sheet for the day.

Mac was holding court, telling everyone a story. "The iced tea was so sweet. I never drink stuff like that. I should have known something was up, but she used it to cover the taste of the poison."

"Bro, I've done a lot of drugs in my life," Manny explained to Carmine, "but nothing like that."

"Wow," Carmine said, shaking his head in disbelief.

"That was the closest I've ever been to death," Mac told them. "Well that and when I jumped out of an airplane and the parachute failed."

I smiled and rolled my eyes. Mac and his stories of heroism. Carmine and Vinnie seemed to be eating it up, but Joy wanted to get back to business.

"Great story guys but we have to get focused here," Joy said. "Who's in the next scene?"

Vinnie looked down at the call sheet. "We got Rose, Belamy, Penny, and Richie Rich next."

"Who's Richie Rich?" Mac asked.

"Jason," Vinnie answered. "His dad bank-rolled half the production."

"Oh really?" I asked, joining the conversation.

"He bought the part for him when his kid said he wanted to get into show business." Vinnie laughed a throaty laugh. "I jacked up the price too. Poor schmuck didn't realize he was funding this!"

"So that's how you got Belamy, right?" Mac asked.

"Of course," Vinnie answered. "Half our budget is going into his pocket, but he's worth every penny."

"Vinnie, why didn't you mention this earlier when the cops were interviewing you?" I asked.

Vinnie guffawed. "It's not my job to investigate this thing – it's theirs. Besides I didn't think of it at the time. Hell, they're supposed to draw information out of us, aren't they?" Vinnie turned to Mac and Manny. "I'm not impressed with these cops. Why the hell isn't this thing solved yet?"

"They're working on it," I assured him.

Vinnie stared at me, examining my face. "What the hell happened to you? You have scratches on your cheek. Did you get attacked by a cat?"

"More like a Rose," I answered.

"Well those things have thorns on them," Vinnie continued.

Mac walked over to me, pulling a tube of ointment out of his hacky-sack. "Use this salve. It's good stuff. I got it in Africa."

Mac had a salve for everything. I took the tube and examined the label, half-hoping I would see "Walgreens" printed on the side. I didn't. I squeezed the tube and rubbed the cream into my skin.

Vinnie looked around. "Where the hell are the cops now? Eating all of my craft service probably! We're not filming. *This* would be the right time to interview people. Should I run their shoot too? Go tell them to talk to Joy next. She's not in the next scene – talk to her."

Joy looked up at the mention of her name.

"Do you think Joy is a suspect?" I probed, knowing she could hear me.

Vinnie looked at her and then back to me. "Could be."

I saw Joy tense up at the suggestion.

13.

"Maybe Lucky had it coming," Joy told us from her interview chair in the break room.

We were trying to move the interviews around to get different backgrounds and settings. The break room wasn't totally private but we set up in the back corner and put a sign up that said "Quiet Please." In retrospect it wasn't my smartest move. People were walking into the break room to snag food from the craft service table and then lingering for a while, trying to eavesdrop.

I examined Joy as she sat in the chair. With her flat chest and her short hair, she didn't look like the stereotypical soft porn star. When I thought about the way Rose looked and then compared her to Joy, they were like polar opposites.

"Maybe we all have it coming," she continued, with an air of arrogance in her tone. "Working in this business. It's all garbage and smut."

"Carmine said something similar to that," Reid told her.

Joy nodded and seemed pleased that their perspectives were similar. "He's right. The people around here are disgusting. I call them incestuous. I mean they're not actually related to each other, but people are sleeping around with multiple partners. It's gross. I wouldn't engage in anything like that unless it was on camera, and neither would Carmine."

"I don't think you can speak for Carmine," Foxy said.

"What are you talking about?"

"We asked Rose about him earlier. There may be some history there. She couldn't remember."

Joy glared at Foxy for a moment. "Do you think I'm stupid?"

Foxy shrugged.

"Why do you do this then?" Reid asked. "If you think this industry is so disgusting, why are you a part of it?"

"For Carmine. To support him. His brother roped him into this business and he can't get out. He's like a slave to the sex trade. An unwilling one."

"As someone who has seen real slaves in the sex trade and prosecuted their captors, I don't appreciate your reference," Reid told her. "Carmine doesn't have to work here. Unless you're saying that his brother is blackmailing him?"

Joy flushed. "Oh, I don't know anything about that."

"You don't know anything about it or don't want to say anything about it?"

Joy shook her head. "You're confusing me. Carmine is someone I respect and look up to. I'm here to help him in any way that I can."

"Even if that means lying for him?" Reid asked.

"No. Carmine wouldn't ask me to lie."

"Are you and Carmine dating?" Foxy asked.

Joy looked embarrassed again. "Oh no. I mean, not officially. We're just good friends."

"Okay, so if he and Rose were sleeping together, you wouldn't have any claims over him, right?"

Joy narrowed his eyes. "Carmine isn't sleeping with Rose. Stop saying that."

"How do you know?" Foxy asked.

"I just know," Joy told him.

"Okay so you and Carmine are not dating, got it. Do you ever kiss?" Foxy asked.

"We have. What does this have to do with Lucky anyway?"

"We're just trying to understand the relationship dynamics here on set," Foxy explained.

Dating or not, it was obvious that Joy had a big crush on Carmine. I thought about how silly that was. Carmine said he hated this industry, especially the actors in it. By being one she was virtually guaranteeing he wouldn't have any interest in her.

"How did you and Carmine meet?" Foxy asked.

"When I auditioned for *Sorority Sex-Up* last year. That was another show the brothers produced." She smiled. "I got the part and then when this project came up I asked Carmine to consider using me again. Of course, he agreed."

"How did you get into this business?" Foxy asked.

"Oh, I used to be a prostitute," Joy said nonchalantly. "So, this seemed like the natural next step." When she saw Reid and Foxy raise their eyebrows, she clarified. "Not like a street walker, more like an escort."

"So, you had sex with people for money?" Foxy asked.

"Am I going to get in trouble here? I feel like I shouldn't be announcing this to the police. I don't do that stuff anymore. Not for at least a year."

"So you haven't had sex with anyone on this production for money, right?" Reid asked.

"Well, I have fake sex for money as part of this job."

Reid shook his head, frustrated. "I'm talking about real sex."

"Oh. No," Joy answered.

I thought back to Carmine's interview. Hadn't he said he could never be with a woman who sold her body for money? Then why was he kissing Joy?

"Did you arrive here yesterday before or after Lucky's body was found?"

"After," Joy said, looking down.

"Who do you think killed him?" Reid asked.

Joy's eyes widened, then she looked up in the air, thinking. "Well Carmine didn't. That's for sure. I mean, they were in AA together. Carmine and Lucky were friends."

"Did Carmine leave around eight when you did?"

Joy had to think again. "Oh, I'm sure he did. I left and I'm sure he was right behind me."

"But you didn't walk out to the parking lot together?" Foxy asked.

"No."

"So you don't know for sure that he left after you did?"

"Carmine didn't kill Lucky," Joy asserted. "End of story."

"Did you?" Reid asked, surprising her with the question.

Joy's eyes widened. "No! Of course not. You know who I bet it was? Jason. He was always making a big deal about scenes he wasn't in. He felt like he should have had more lines and more scenes. He probably did it."

As a producer, I liked that she was assigning blame to someone specifically. I made a mental note that we needed to get more people to do that. If they were all blaming each other, it would make for a compelling edit.

*****

While the cops went to grab Penny for an interview, I walked over to the hot set to check out what was going on. Inside, I saw was my father holding a paint can, adding detail and contour to the outside of the space ship.

"Are we gonna have continuity problems?" Vinnie barked at my dad. "I can't have this thing looking totally different mid-shoot."

"I'm making it more realistic, Vin. Have your guy grab some shots of it when I'm done and insert them in," my dad told him.

"Looking good," I told my dad, walking over to him.

He put down his paintbrush and wiped his hands with a rag he had hanging over his shoulder. He had paint splattered all over him and looked like he was having fun. "This reminds me of when I first started out in the business," my dad cooed. "No budget, no time and we just had to make it work. Check this out." My dad led me over to the interior of the rocket ship and pointed to the control panel. "See this? They just painted the buttons on. It was completely unrealistic." He laughed. "I used one of the phones from the control room and lit up the buttons using some twinkle lights I found. Doesn't it look great?"

I had to admit that it did.

"And look at the side here. You see how I darkened it to make it look more like metal?"

I smiled. "I'm glad to see you're having fun, Dad."

Watching my dad in his element reminded me of when he used to bring me and Ginny to set as a kid. My best memory was of a show he did called *Consequences*. It was a game show where kids competed against their parents. If a parent answered a question incorrectly, the "consequence" was usually something humiliating. Ginny and I used to help my dad on set, testing the props to make sure they worked. We dunked the crew into tanks of slime, we threw pies in our Dad's face and we dressed men up in women's attire. It was a blast and we were the envy of all our friends. Thinking about my youth and how much fun we used to have brought a smile to my face.

"We need some oil for Belamy's butt cheeks Craig!" Vinnie called out.

His grumpy voice and crass way of speaking broke the spell, pulling me out of my happy memory and back into reality.

"Sounds like they're getting ready to start shooting again," I said.

"I'm gonna get out of here soon, kiddo. I'm almost done. Your mom is ordering take-out from Marios. After all this hard labor, pasta sounds really good."

I smiled at my Dad and gave him a kiss on the cheek. He was the kind of guy who could make lemonade out of lemons any day of the week. I envied that.

*****

The cops were getting antsy so we agreed to let them interview Penny in the break room. We were already set up there so it was faster than finding another spot. Mac made some camera adjustments to make the scene look a little different for the viewers. We couldn't have different people sitting in front of the same backdrop and it couldn't look like a kitchen. The background had to be soft and blurry and moody.

Penny stood in the break room, watching Mac set up. Her right leg was bent and resting on her left inner thigh, balancing in a yoga pose. Mac was working quickly but seemed distracted by her. "How are you not falling over?" he asked her. "I see your eyes following us – how do you keep your balance?"

"Lots of practice," Penny said, remaining still.

"Can you sit in the chair so I can check the lighting against your skin tone?" Mac asked her. Reid and Foxy were already sitting in their chairs quietly, comparing notes.

Penny walked over to the chair, but instead of sitting on it, she climbed on top, balancing on the balls of her feet in a squat.

"Is that how you plan to sit?" Mac asked her. "I'll have to adjust my shot."

Penny nodded. "I try to push my muscles whenever I can. Anytime I can search for balance, I do. It keeps me strong, both in here." She pointed to her head, "And here." She pointed to her legs.

Mac nodded and tilted his shot up. "I could learn from you."

"You're not going to start ribbiting, are you?" Foxy asked Penny, noticing she was in a frog squat.

Penny ignored him. She was slender and lean from all of her yoga. Her hair was long and blonde with dyed brown tips. Her eyes were chocolate brown and matched the bottom of her hair. She had changed into a white tank top with the word, "Breathe" written on it and neon green leggings.

When Mac and Manny were finally ready, I asked them to roll and Reid and Foxy began asking Penny questions.

"So tell me about yourself," Foxy smiled.

"Sure. As I told you, I go by the name Penny Connors and I'm an actress on this pilot. As you may have noticed, I'm pretty flexible and know how to use my body so that was appealing to the brothers."

"Have you been doing this type of work long?" Foxy asked.

"Not too long. Maybe two years now. I'm saving up to buy my own yoga studio. I teach on the side between gigs, but this kind of thing pays more. I figure it's worth it if it gets me towards my goal. Yoga is all about setting intentions and my intention is to open my own studio."

"How close are you?"

"About six months away. I already know the name of my studio. Do you want to know what it is? It's going to be called the Meditation Station. Isn't that cute? Yoga isn't just about doing poses you know."

"Yes, I saw you doing some meditation earlier," Foxy told her.

"I meditate for an hour every morning. I use the moon walk set. I like the peace and serenity in there."

"Wow," Mac mouthed to me. I could tell he was really impressed with this woman. If he hadn't already been dating Terry, I might have suggested that Penny could be Mac's soulmate. The only obstacle was her profession. Mac wouldn't appreciate that.

"I'm a healer too. I tried to work on Carmine but he wouldn't let me. I'm going to incorporate healing into my yoga studio too."

"Is that why you said my partner was blocked? Because you're a healer?"

Penny nodded. "His root chakra is blocked. That represents his sex organs."

Foxy let out of laugh. "So you can cure that for him?"

Penny nodded. "I can."

"How would you do that exactly?"

"I would dance with him. I'd have him walk around barefoot. And I'd ask him to see the color red."

Foxy looked over at his partner who didn't seem to appreciate the conversation. "He may be seeing red right now Penny," Foxy joked.

Reid straightened up in his chair. "Okay, let's get focused here. You said you meditate every morning. Were you here meditating the morning Lucky was killed?"

"Yes, I was here. I arrived in the morning and went to the studio like I always do. So, I didn't notice Lucky…was…" Penny's voice trailed off as she stared at Reid intensely. Then her eyes began to fill with tears.

"It's okay, take your time," Reid told her.

Penny, still squatting, placed her hands together palm to palm and slowly raised her hands up in the air, joined together. She breathed in and out deeply and slowly. She closed her eyes and went inward. She seemed like she was meditating.

We sat there for an uncomfortable two minutes until she slowly opened her eyes and lowered her hands back down. "There we go."

"Okay." Foxy let out a laugh. "So what happened after your meditation?"

"It wasn't after, it was during. I heard Rose screaming for Vinnie. I don't know how long she was screaming or what time it was – I was very deep into my core by then. Usually at the twenty-one minute mark I really get in the zone. I lose perception of time and space. I become the light of my soul. Anyway, when I finally came out of the spell, I centered myself and walked towards the sound of Vinnie and Rose's voices. Rose was telling him to call the police. I walked in and saw, well, I saw…"

Penny's eyes began to well up again. This time she sat down on the chair, folding her legs into a cross-legged position. She closed her eyes, opened her hands, and reached them into the sky. Mac looked over at me, pointing to the camera lens, silently communicating that she had messed up his shot. Now we were seeing the top of her head and her arms, instead of her face. He had asked her if she planned to stay in her frog position throughout the interview and she had said yes. Now she was six inches lower.

Another two minutes later Penny came back to earth and opened her eyes once more. "I saw Lucky, and well, you know everything after that."

"You can't keep doing that," Foxy told her. "We'll be here all day!"

Reid leaned in. "Were you and Lucky dating?"

Penny smiled. "Just kind of hanging out. I don't know if I'd say dating. I guess we were."

"Were you having sexual relations?"

"Yes," Penny answered.

"Was he having sexual relations with anyone else that you were aware of?" Reid asked.

"No, he was not," Penny said matter-of-factly. "But I'm a free spirit and so was he. We didn't put restrictions around our relationship."

"Were you in love with Lucky?" Reid asked her.

"The only person I can truly love is myself. But I cared about him deeply. He was a good man. He was... I'm sorry." As the tears began to surface, Penny once again crossed her legs, placed her palms together, and reached towards the sky.

*****

We managed to get a little more information out of Penny before her interview concluded. She didn't know who might want to kill Lucky but she knew he and Rose didn't like each other. She told us that Rose had hit on Lucky at one point and he had turned her down. That type of rejection was not something Rose was used to or appreciated. After that, Rose found reasons to bicker with Lucky about almost anything. She said that others in the cast had witnessed it, but it had never gotten violent. It was more just Rose yelling at him in Spanish and Lucky flipping his middle finger at her and walking away.

Penny described Lucky as a man who didn't know the bounds of his own sexuality. She said that people could appreciate his striking good looks and physique, but it was more than that. He exuded a sexual quality like she had never seen. She said his aura glowed red. She knew he would make it big in this industry and the others did as well. He was a rising star with a life cut too short.

My cell phone rang and the area code 310 came up. I figured it was someone from the office calling so I answered on the second ring. "Sharpe here."

"Victoria Sharpe, I have Richard Lazarus for you," a man said into the phone.

"Who?" I asked.

"From Artists and Agencies. He represents Kyle Belamy."

"Oh, okay," I said. "Put him through."

My heart sank. All I needed was some greedy talent agent to get involved and screw things up for me. He wasn't going to let Belamy sign the release, I knew it.

The assistant switched my call over and a man with an Australian accent greeted me. "Hello Victoria. Richard Lazarus here."

"Hi Richard," I said pleasantly.

"Victoria, let's cut to the chase. I need to know why my client hasn't been interviewed by your cameras yet. As I'm sure you are aware, Kyle Belamy is the biggest star on that set by a long shot. I would like to understand why a day and a half has passed and no one has spoken to him."

"Well," I stumbled, "I was actually waiting for your client to sign our release form. He said he was going to send it to you."

"I told him he can sign that. Bring him a fresh copy and he'll sign straight away. Bring him a pen too. Leave nothing to chance."

"Okay! Thank you, Richard, I'll make sure he's next on the interview list."

"Do that," Richard instructed me, his tone growing dark. "I'm very busy and I don't appreciate having to make calls like this. Belamy is the star over there and don't you or your little cable show forget that."

"Oh, we're not cable. We're network now," I corrected.

"How nice."

"You said Artists and Agencies, right? My mother Evelyn Sharpe is represented by Rex Reid."

"Oh wonderful!" Richard exclaimed, his tone brightening. "Yes, I know Rex well. Victoria, it was an absolute pleasure to speak with you. Good bye."

I grabbed Reid and pulled him aside. "Kyle's agent works with your dad at Artists and Agencies."

"How do you know?" Reid asked.

"I just got a call from Richard Lazarus demanding we interview Kyle next."

Reid rolled his eyes. "I can't stand actors."

*****

We found Kyle sitting in his dressing room looking at his smart phone. He was dressed in a pair of ripped jeans that probably cost two hundred dollars and a T-shirt depicting a logo that I didn't recognize. Reid and Foxy approached him with me and my crew alongside them.

"Kyle, your agent said you'd be willing to sign the release," I said jumping in and handing him the paper and a pen.

Kyle continued to fiddle around with his phone and didn't look up when I spoke. He scribbled his name on the release form and then looked up at me with a crooked smile. I took the signed form and attached it to my clipboard.

I glanced over at Mac. "What are you doing?" I asked, noticing he was standing on one foot.

Mac shrugged. "Working on strength and balance. Penny said I should do it every chance I get."

I shook my head. "Okay, we can start shooting. On two feet please. I don't want a wobbly shot."

"It wouldn't be wobbly," Mac protested, as he put his second foot on the floor and started rolling.

Reid looked down at Kyle's phone to see that he was posting on social media. "I thought I told you we were trying to keep this thing contained."

Kyle looked up, un-phased. "I didn't think you even knew I was here. I guess I'm not very suspicious compared to the others."

"Mr. Belamy, we have numerous suspects in this case and a lot of interviews to conduct. I don't appreciate your agent getting involved in our process," Reid scolded.

My phone vibrated as I got the notification on social media of Kyle's post. I had followed him on Twitter earlier in the day. I discretely pulled my phone out of my pocket and took a look. *Everyone is a suspect. They have us on lockdown.*

Well, that would get people's attention! I shared the message with Lenny and all my other followers too, adding the hashtag *#MurderLive*. I knew the cops wouldn't like it, but it was good publicity for our show.

I was about to put my phone away when it vibrated again. I looked to see that Kyle had just tweeted: *The producer of Murder Live is hot!*

Instantly I blushed and looked at Kyle who was staring at me, smiling. Sensing something was going on, Reid walked over to me and took my phone out of my hand. He read the tweet and then glanced over to me. I didn't know what to say. I mean, I didn't ask Kyle to write it. But I was totally going to re-tweet it as soon as I got my phone back.

Foxy grabbed the phone, read it, and laughed. He looked at Kyle. "Well, I guess you're not famous for your brains."

"Are you saying she's not hot?" Belamy asked, pointing at me.

Everyone turned and looked at me while I stared at Foxy, waiting for his answer.

"I meant you're stupid to mess with his girl," Foxy said, pointing to Reid.

"Oh," Kyle said, leaning back in his chair. "I didn't realize you two were an item."

"Knock it off," Reid yelled at Kyle. "No more tweeting or I'll throw you in jail for interfering with a police investigation." He shoved my phone back in my hands without so much as glancing in my direction.

"Okay look, we'd like to ask you a few questions, Kyle," Foxy told him.

"Like hell you are," Kyle barked. He looked over at Mac. "Turn that thing off."

Foxy looked at him sideways. "Dude, are you high or something? Did you mix up your meds? You just signed the television release form."

"I refuse to be interviewed here. The lighting is atrocious," Kyle spat, sounding every bit like a drama queen.

"It's a damn television set," Foxy reminded him. "The lighting is fine!"

"I can make the lighting beautiful," Mac offered.

"I'm sure you can, but I simply cannot do this here. It's not private. It's not intimate."

"What did you have in mind?" Reid asked through gritted teeth.

Kyle placed his finger to his chin, thinking. "Hmm, where to do it? Where to do it? Well, I'm having a party at my house tonight. Why don't we do it there? It's just a small gathering of friends. Nothing too wild I assure you."

"You want to be interviewed about your possible involvement in a murder at a party at your house?" Foxy asked.

"Well, it's not like I'm guilty!" Kyle laughed. "Come on, you guys seem like you could use a change of scenery. I have a room downstairs already pre-lit. I'll answer any questions you want."

"Should we handcuff you after the interview and drag you out in front of your guests?" Foxy asked.

Kyle smiled. "They'd probably get a kick out of that."

"This is a murder investigation not a television show!" Reid exploded.

Kyle's eyes traveled to me and my crew, not understanding Reid's point.

"It is a television show, but it's not a joke like everyone here seems to think it is. We're trying to solve a murder, not put on a show for your vapid, strung-out friends." Reid looked at Foxy. "You know what? Get me away from this guy." Reid threw up his hands before storming out of the room.

"If you want me to talk, we do it at my place," Kyle told Foxy.

Glances darted around the room between Foxy, me and my crew. No one was going to say it out loud, but inside I knew we all wanted to go to the party. It would bring some great production value to our show and would expose our audience to the private life of a Hollywood porn star.

Not to mention that it meant bragging rights with all our friends.

"I'll talk to him," Foxy told Kyle. "Give me your address."

14.

I let the water hit my face in a cool burst, washing the day away. I thought about the television show I had watched earlier suggesting I start my day with positivity. The morning began with my car running out of gas and me dissolving into a pile of sweat walking to the office. Then I spit in the face of a murder suspect and had her lunge at me and scratch my cheek in return. My father witnessed me at one of my lowest points and then my boyfriend got mad at me. But, the day was finally turning around. Foxy had managed to convince Reid that the interview at Kyle's place was a good idea. He said it would give us a glimpse into Kyle's personal life and would allow us to assess if Kyle was involved in the murder or not. Reid was reluctant but finally agreed.

At the studio, after the conversation between Reid and Kyle, Foxy decided it was better that we left the set for the day. He wanted to give everyone a chance to settle down. It also gave us time to get ready for the party. I certainly couldn't show up to an industry party wearing my grubby sweat-soaked clothes. Technically I was there to work, but I still wanted to look good. This wasn't the type of party I was invited to often and I was racking my brain trying to figure out what to wear.

My cell phone announced, "You have a visitor." It was sitting on the vanity in the bathroom close enough for me to hear but, but far enough that I couldn't reach it. "Shit!" I said from the shower. My mother had gotten me an app on my phone that allowed me to hear and see who was at my front door. I wasn't home often and my mother worried that a burglar would rob my apartment while I was away. The app allowed me to see anyone who was standing at my front door. I could also speak to them through my phone.

I stumbled out of the shower and pressed the "answer" button on the app. "Who is it?" I asked, dripping wet.

"Vic – it's Kelly. Are you in there?" I heard my neighbor ask through my phone.

"I'm in the shower," I answered. "Give me a minute." I grabbed a towel off the rack and threw it around my body.

Kelly lived a few doors down from me and over the years she had become a good friend. She worked in development for one of the biggest producers in Hollywood so she was home as rarely as I was. Her latest project was a script that was given to her by Hollywood, the cop I worked with on my last episode.

"I saw your car in the garage. I couldn't believe you were actually home," Kelly told me as I let her in.

"Yeah, I'm here, but not for long," I explained, ushering her into my apartment so I could close the door and throw on a robe. "I'm getting ready for a party tonight."

"Do you need a plus-one?" Kelly asked, plopping herself on my couch.

"It's for work, so I can't bring guests." I had left Kyle Belamy's headshot on my kitchen counter and I picked up to show Kelly. "Guess whose house it's at?" I grinned, flashing her his picture.

"No way!" Kelly exclaimed. "We just saw him at the Hollywood Bowl. Do you remember?"

"Of course I do," I said, tossing her the headshot and then disappearing into my room to throw on a robe. "I saw your project mentioned in the *Daily Buzz* yesterday." I called from the other room. "Pretty cool, Kel."

"Thanks," she called back.

Once I was covered I walked over to the kitchen and pulled a bottle of wine out of the fridge and two jelly jars to pour the wine in. I handed a jar to Kelly with a generous amount of wine in it and then poured one for myself. "I shouldn't be drinking while I'm working, but I have to get rid of my nerves."

"How did you get hooked up with Kyle Belamy?" Kelly raised an eyebrow and looked at me. "Victoria, are you working in porn now?"

"No. Why does everyone keep asking me that? My latest murder case is on a porn set. It's a soft porn. It's just boobs and butts. No penetration."

Kelly's eyebrow raised even higher. "Boobs and butts? Did you really just say that?"

I shrugged. "I've been on set for two days and I'm already becoming desensitized." I sat down on the couch next to her. "Kyle invited us to his house tonight for the party. We're there to interview him."

"OMG – are you sure I can't be your plus-one?" Kelly asked.

"And look at this," I told her grabbing my cell phone. "Kyle's been tweeting about me."

Kelly looked at the tweet saying I was hot. "Holy shit. Wait, you're not interested in this guy, are you? He's probably got a ton of diseases."

"No, he doesn't," I assured her. "They test them before each production."

"Okay," Kelly said, shaking her head. "Well, I can think of about a thousand more reasons you shouldn't get involved with him. Do you want me to name them?"

I blushed. "I'm not interested. Well, not that much at least. It's just cool for a movie star to take an interest in me. You know?"

"Oh my God, you're like a horny teenager right now."

"I know. And it's not just with Belamy. The victim's roommate is really hot too."

"Victoria!"

"I know. Mac actually told me I was objectifying the men on set and that I needed to calm down."

Kelly let out a laugh. "Are you acting like this in front of Reid?"

"I'm trying not to, but do you know how awkward this case has been? Reid and I are on a porn set together. We're literally watching people get naked and do what I don't have the guts to do with him. It's like a cruel joke."

"What are you afraid of?"

"That I'm out of practice, I guess. Or that once it's over he'll stop calling me. I haven't had sex in a while, Kelly."

"That's normal," Kelly assured me. "We're working girls. It's hard to find time to date. But you don't need to worry about sex or your abilities. You have a hole that he can stick himself in – that's all guys want."

I burst out laughing. "You make it sound so special."

"Listen, you're a beautiful woman and he's lucky to have you. Plus, you've been dating for a couple weeks now. If he was going to walk away, he would have done it already. But honey, people don't wait for love anymore when it comes to sex. You know that, right?"

I took a deep breath and gave that some thought. "I'm probably making an already uncomfortable situation even worse by flirting with Kyle... and George. I've been so worried that Reid would be interested in the women on the set, that I've been overcompensating and flirting with the men instead."

"And how is Reid responding?"

"Not well. I mean he practically choked Kyle after he sent out that tweet."

Kelly looked at me and smiled. "He really cares about you."

I knew she was right. Reid was this amazing guy and I was taking him for granted. We needed some time together alone. Maybe working together wasn't the best thing for our relationship.

"And Reid's damn hot! You're like a magnet for hot guys lately. I don't know what you're doing girl, but I want in."

*****

Whether I was interested in Kyle or not, I still wanted to look good at this party. After going through my entire closet and Kelly's, I realized I had absolutely nothing to wear.

In an act of desperation, I called my mother. The thought that my 60-

year-old mother would have something sexier in her closet than I did was kind of pathetic, but it was also the reality. My mother was in her sexual prime, dating any guy that glanced in her direction. Her wardrobe had become risqué while mine was conservative and boring. I needed to look fierce and my mom could help me do it.

On my way to the west side I texted my sister Ginny and let her know I needed to primp and prep for a party at Kyle Belamy's house. She promised to meet me at my mother's house within the hour. The party was in Malibu so it wasn't totally crazy that I was driving all the way to the west side for a hot dress.

*****

Ginny lived closer to my parents' house than I did so she was already there when I arrived. My father's car was there too, having finished up his work on set for the day. When I arrived, I went straight up to my mother's room, skipping the visit to my dad's study to say hello. My parents were divorced and had been for years, but lived together anyway. They liked each other, they just weren't in love anymore. At first, they remained in the same house for the kids, but then the arrangement became permanent. My father turned my old bedroom into his, while my mother kept the master suite. They usually went their own ways during the day, but came together for dinner and an occasional brandy out on the back deck. They lived on the Venice Canals and enjoyed sitting outside at the sunset and watching the boats.

My mother's closet was larger than my bedroom with built-in shelving to accommodate her shoes, her gowns, her leisure wear, and her numerous drawers of jewelry. When I arrived, I saw that she and Ginny had pre-selected some outfits for me and had them lying on the settee.

"Is this like a sex party? Like an S&M kind of thing?" my mother wanted to know. "Because I have something you could wear to that."

"No Mom," I said quickly, but then thought about the question. "Well actually, I don't know. I hope it's not like that."

"Are people going to be walking around naked?" Ginny asked. "Is it like the Playboy mansion where the girls walk around in their underwear and all the servers are wearing thongs?"

I shook my head. "I have no idea. I guess I should have asked. He said it was a party for a few friends."

"Honey, that's movie star talk," my mom explained. "When I have a party for a *few* friends – how many would you say that is?"

I looked at her, understanding the point. "Usually at least a hundred."

"Exactly. Otherwise he would have called it an intimate affair. Darling, you know how insecure celebrities are – we have to surround ourselves with people who adore us."

She was right and also oddly self-aware. I started to panic. "What the hell did I get myself into? I'm not gonna fit in. I'm going to make a fool of myself!"

"Okay, okay, calm down," my mother said, sitting me in a chair. She opened up a cabinet that was hidden in the corner and pulled out a snifter of brandy. She poured a glass and handed it to me. "Here, this will take the edge off." I took a gulp feeling the burn as it traveled down my throat. My mother poured another for herself and one more for Ginny. "I keep a supply in here so I don't have to go all the way downstairs if I'm feeling anxious," she explained. "We all get nervous going to parties Victoria. It's natural."

The brandy was helping. That combined with the wine I had earlier.

"So what's Kyle Belamy like?" Ginny asked me. "Is he really hot?"

I smiled and nodded. "Pretty much."

"Oh, I almost forgot!" my mother announced. "I got something for the occasion." She jumped up and grabbed the remote control to a television she had mounted on the wall.

"Is there anything you don't have in here mother?" Ginny asked. "Is this also a bomb shelter?"

My mom pushed a few buttons and then Kyle Belamy appeared on the screen wearing a pair of tighty-whities and nothing else. He was walking towards a woman who was naked on the bed.

"Mom! Come on!" I yelled at her.

"What?" she asked innocently. "I wasn't familiar with his work. Don't you think I should learn more about the people my daughter works with?"

"Oh, wow!" Ginny called out as Kyle dropped his undies and faced the camera commando-style.

We all turned and stood there mesmerized for a moment, staring at all of Kyle Belamy.

"Holy shit," my mother said.

"Turn this off!" I yelled, finally snapping out of the trance.

It was a few more moments before my mother managed to regain her faculties and reach for the remote.

Ginny looked at me expectantly. "Do you think Bob and I could come with you tonight?"

"No," I told her. "This is work. I can't bring guests."

"All you have to do is get us in the door. If we show up with you they'll let us in. Then we can split up and you can do your work. Bob and I really want to go."

The thought of my brother-in-law accompanying me at this weird sex-party was reason enough to say no. "Sorry, Ginny," I told her.

My mother gave me a number of wardrobe options, including a yellow cat suit, a royal blue mini dress, and a black one-piece jumper with a plunging neck line. The black jumper was the winner – sexy and yet demure. Ginny grabbed a necklace to hang down between my cleavage and a pair of strappy heels for my feet.

My mother found a pair of pasties and before I could stop her, she pulled my top to the side and slapped one on my nipple. "Mother!" I screamed. "I can do that myself, thank you!" I grabbed the other pastie out of her hand. I couldn't get the sticky backing off so my mother ended up putting on the second one anyway.

At the makeup table my mother applied eyeliner on my lids. "Your father told me about the set you're working on. I know what it's like to be the only woman on set surrounded by all those sexed-up men."

Ginny laughed. "Mom, that's like your dream."

"Well, that's because I know how to handle those types of things, but for your sister it may be hard. Honey I don't want you to let those men make you feel like anything less than the intelligent and driven woman that you are."

"I'm trying not to, Mom."

"Good. Daddy had quite a lot to say about his day today. I don't think he's said that many words to me in a row since the divorce."

I laughed. "Glad I could be a topic of conversation."

"You usually are, honey. But we're encouraged now that you're dating Reid. Daddy said he's very protective of you."

"Yeah, he's a good guy."

"I'm glad things are progressing with you two. Then I can have both of my daughters married off. Not that I want to be a grandma or anything." She turned to Ginny. "I'm too young to be a grandmother. You understand?"

"I wouldn't worry about that, mother," Ginny told her. "Bob is so busy at the office we barely even have sex."

"What!?" My mother exclaimed. "But you're newlyweds!"

"That's why we need to come to this party, Victoria. This kind of kinky sex stuff is exactly the kick-start we need. Come on, take us with you."

I looked at my image in the mirror. I was wearing a lot of makeup and my hair was combed back and straight with a slick of oil to keep it in place. I didn't look like myself, but I did look good. I actually looked really good and I knew Reid would like it. Ginny had played a big part in helping me look this way. How could I say no?

*****

I drove north to Malibu alone in my beat-up Miata while Ginny and her husband Bob followed behind in their new Mercedes. I was fashionably late – literally late because of fashion, and was now speeding as a result of it. I knew the guys were already there and I didn't want to make them wait. Especially because I was technically going to this party to work.

Malibu was where Reid had grown up and where his parents still lived. I had never been to their home but I knew it was facing the ocean. Houses in Malibu were expensive and airy, covered in windows. Reid had grown up living next door to some pretty famous celebrities so I assumed his childhood home was pretty amazing. Reid had texted me that he was going to stop at their house for dinner before the party, but didn't invite me to join him. Even though dining with them would have put even more stress on the evening, I was still a little hurt that I wasn't invited. I had met his parents before so inviting me over wouldn't have been that out of the ordinary. I didn't want to push so I just responded to his text with: *Sounds good.*

At the bottom of Topanga Canyon, I made a right and drove along the Pacific Coast Highway. I looked around, taking in the city and the ocean. The sun was setting and the waves were crashing on the sand. Each house was more spectacular than the next, sitting on stunning views of the high surf and sandy beaches. I could get used to living around here.

The GPS on my phone told me I was nearing my destination so I slowed down and tried to read the street signs. It was nearly dark by now and most of the homes consisted of a mailbox near the street and then a long driveway leading to a house on the beach. When I reached number sixty-nine, my GPS told me I had arrived at my destination. Sixty-nine was the perfect address for Kyle.

As I pulled into the long driveway I saw a large two-story house with glass and windows everywhere. The house was built in the contemporary style that was once popular in the eighties. It had rounded columns, triangle-shaped windows, and gray paneling positioned at a 45-degree angle. Yet despite the eighties influence, I could tell Kyle had also done a lot to modernize it. The roof had been redone in wood shingles and most of the original windows looked to have been replaced with larger versions. The lighting was bright and the colors were beachy and cool. I could see lots of people gathered inside on the second floor, in what I assumed was the main living space.

Parking was limited, but Kyle had two young and gorgeous male valets standing in the driveway to take our cars. This was supposed to be a small gathering of friends, but as my mother correctly predicted, for celebrities, the term was relative.

I stepped out of the car, exposing the pastie covering my left nipple in the process. The valet's eyes went wide and directly to my chest alerting me that I was exposed. I readjusted my top, turning red with embarrassment. I wasn't used to dressing like this. I needed to slow down and move more carefully.

Behind me, Ginny and Bob stepped out of their car. Ginny ended up having to borrow something from my mother as well given the time crunch and was dressed in the sparkly blue mini dress my mother had suggested for me. She was younger than me and perkier and her body looked amazing. But you know what? So did mine.

Ginny had called Bob and told him to wear something hip. Bob was an entertainment attorney and a bit of a dud. There was nothing hip about him so he decided to wear a black suit. He might have been overdressed but he looked better than he would have dressed casually. Some guys didn't look good in jeans.

"Hi Bob," I said to him, eyeballing his suit. Despite the fact that he wore suits to work every day, he looked uncomfortable. The jacket must have been too small as it seemed to be squeezing and inflating the size of his head.

"This place is amazing!" Ginny cooed looking towards the house. "Oh honey, I'm so glad you agreed to come." Ginny snaked her arm through Bob's, leaning into him.

Bob looked at me and offered an explanation. "I figured it'd be a good story for the guys at work."

"Just head down that way," the valet told us, pointing towards the beach. "The entrance is around back."

The gravel under our feet turned to sand as we got closer to the back of the house. There were lots of people hanging out on the beach and some people even surfing in the waves. There was a large bonfire lit and party-goers were drinking beers and tossing alcohol into the fire to watch it blaze. There was music playing too. It was the new age style that I knew Kyle liked after spotting him at a Hollywood Bowl concert weeks before. The music was loud, but was mostly drowned out by the din of chatter from inside the house.

"Don't embarrass me and don't act like you're crashing this party," I warned Bob. "I'm here for work and I don't want anything to distract from that."

Bob looked me up and down. "This is how you dress for work?"

"When I'm visiting the home of a porn star, yes it is," I answered confidently. As I led them to the back door of Kyle's house, I was nervous. In my mind, I was being transported back to when I used to try to sneak into night clubs underage as a kid. I would be terrified that the bouncers would know I was only seventeen and not let me inside. It was as if my

145

entire life would fall apart if the bouncer turned me away. I used to get myself so worked up that my friends could feel the nervous energy emanating from my body. But I didn't need to worry about that now. I was invited. I was supposed to be here. And if someone found out Ginny and Bob shouldn't be, well, that was their problem.

At the door, I was relieved to see that no one was checking names off a list. I opened it and felt a wash of warm air come over me. The great room was huge with cathedral ceilings and windows all the way up the wall. There was seating for probably fifty people on a variety of modern sofas, swings mounted from the ceiling, and an assortment of over-priced bean bag chairs.

A bar was set up in the corner and hors d'oeuvres were being passed around by servers dressed in purple leather corsets, black fishnet stockings and purple thongs.

"Holy cow, look at this place!" Ginny squealed.

I turned to my sister, anxious to shake her and Bob loose. "Gin, I'm gonna go find my crew. You guys have fun tonight."

I moved to the corner of the room, next to a large painted picture of a penis to try to survey the scene. I noticed lots of erotic art hanging on the walls and sculptures on the floor. The guests were dressed in sexy club-like attire, but nothing lude or vulgar. I had to give my mother props. She got my outfit just right.

I was about to text Mac when I saw Reid approaching me. He was alone and wearing a pair of dark blue jeans and a black short-sleeved button-down shirt that was pulled tight around his biceps. I compared his look to Bob's and got a little chuckle out of the comparison. I wasn't competing with Ginny, but if I was, my guy was way hotter.

Reid's hair was gelled back and as he got closer I got a whiff of his cologne. He smelled amazing. As he neared I felt every part of my body stand at attention, including my nipples, which turned out to be pretty painful thanks to my mother's pasties.

Reid tilted his head sideways as he looked me up and down. "Wow," he said and he leaned in to kiss the side of my neck. "You look amazing."

"You *smell* amazing," I told him, placing a hand on his broad shoulder and squeezing.

"It's my Dad's cologne."

"Oh." I frowned, feeling like that just sucked the sexiness right out of it.

"Where are the rest of the guys?" I asked.

Reid shrugged. "Who cares?" Reid placed his hands on my hips and looked me up and down. "I don't know if it's the makeup or the outfit, but this is really doing it for me."

I decided not to tell him that I'd gotten the clothes from my mother. Instead, I smiled, feeling a rush of adrenaline course through my body. Reid leaned in, covering my lips with his, locking them in a deep and passionate kiss. I leaned back against the wall behind me for support. I was keenly aware of the large penis painting that I was standing next to and how this may have looked, but I didn't really care. Yes, I was working, but so was Reid and he seemed to be okay with this display of affection. Who was I to say no?

I wrapped my arms around Reid's neck and let the kiss deepen. He moved his hand from my waist to inside the fold of my top. With keen precision he navigated past my garment and to the pastie-covered breast below.

"Oh God, you're killing me," Reid whispered in my ear.

The truth was, he was killing me right back. I was glad my mother's wardrobe was doing it for him just like his father's cologne was doing it for me. We had been existing in a sexed-up environment for the past two days and now we found ourselves at a party filled with phalluses and naked art. Being entwined with this gorgeous man who was stirring up every female desire I had was making it nearly impossible to say no anymore. This was the type of party that had rooms available for couples needing to take the edge off. It wouldn't be romantic, but it would make both of us feel a hell of a lot better.

I ran my fingers over the muscles in Reid's chest, squeezing hard while he kissed me in a way that took my breath away. My body, which was already warm from the night air, was starting to get really hot.

"I don't know if I'm gonna make it through this case," Reid whispered.

"That makes two of us," Foxy said from behind Reid. We both froze at the sound of his voice.

"Just be quiet and he'll go away," Reid suggested, but as I opened my eyes I could see the big goofy grin on Foxy's face. He wasn't planning on going anywhere.

"This case is really getting you two worked up!" Foxy joked. "I'm starting to wonder if I should have brought Sherry along."

Foxy had two kids at home, so the idea of bringing his wife to this party was probably a pipe dream. Sherry tended to get very possessive of her husband, too. She was even convinced Reid had a crush on him.

"Maybe you should give her a call," Reid suggested.

"Nah, too late to get a babysitter. Unless you two are interested in watching the kids."

"Sure. Do you mind if we use your bedroom while we're there?" Reid teased.

"My bed? My actual bed?" Foxy considered that for a moment. "Nope, I'm fine with it."

"Are Mac and Manny here?" I asked, changing the subject.

"We're right here, Sharpe," Mac told me from my right. "We've been standing here for a few minutes now."

I flushed and straightened out my clothes as best I could. "Well, I hope you all enjoyed the show."

"We did, Chica. We did," Manny confirmed.

"My television crew is here!" We heard a voice boom from across the room. The room grew quiet as Kyle Belamy appeared, dressed in a pair of khaki shorts and a white unbuttoned shirt. Any non-movie star would have looked like a slob dressed the way Kyle was, but his chiseled abs and dreamy smile totally made up for it.

The crowd seemed to part as Kyle moved across the room towards us. "Welcome to my humble abode."

"It's beautiful. Thank you for having us," I responded.

Kyle looked over at me. "Hubba hubba. Wow miss producer – you look good enough to eat."

Protectively, Reid held his hand up, covering my exposed cleavage. He liked looking at it, he just didn't want anyone else to. My heart swelled.

"He's right, Sharpe." Manny agreed. "You look smoking hot baby." I tried to play it cool but a big smile spread across my face.

"You said we could talk," Reid said to Kyle, stepping in front of me, blocking me from sight. "Is there someplace we can do that privately?"

"Patience, my friend," Kyle smiled. "It's a party. Enjoy yourselves for a while."

"Mr. Belamy, we're here because you agreed to be interviewed," Reid said.

"Okay, I'll tell you what. Give me one hour and then I'll meet you downstairs in my bedroom."

"Can you show us where it is?" Mac asked. "We can start getting our equipment set up."

"Of course," Kyle told him.

"And can you sign this location release for your house?" I asked, pushing Reid aside so I could hand Kyle the paperwork.

"Of course. What's mine is yours," Kyle told me, smiling.

*****

Mac and Manny went downstairs to set up while Foxy, Reid, and I stayed behind. "I'm not really that interested in what Belamy has to say anyway," Reid told us. "I'm more interested to see the other cast members and how they act around each other."

"Are they here?" I asked.

"I saw Carmine and Vinnie before," Foxy said.

"I saw that kid Craig too," Reid added. "Let's split up and keep an eye on them."

"Okay great, Sharpe you come with me," Foxy said, playfully grabbing my arm.

"Nice try, pal," Reid said and pulled me away from Foxy and back over to him.

I noticed that Reid seemed to be warming up to the idea of public affection, which was really sweet. Just when I was starting to get scared about where our relationship stood, he was giving me every reassurance. Maybe it was a cop thing. Reid always seemed to sense how I was feeling and give me exactly what I needed.

"I'm guessing that doing it in the bedroom of a porn star's house isn't how you pictured our first time, right?" Reid asked me when we were alone.

I smiled. "You're so good at reading my thoughts sometimes."

"So you did think about it?"

I demurred. "I may have considered it."

"Interesting," Reid smiled. "Let's see what else. Are you worried that with all this build up, when we finally do it, it could be anti-climactic?"

"Not for me," I said. "Maybe for you."

Reid shook his head. "No chance."

"Like you said, having sex in a porn-star's house isn't really how I want to explain the story of our first time."

"You girls talk about that stuff, right?"

"It'll be the first question my mother will ask," I admitted. "Then my sister will ask, then my neighbor, and so on. I'd prefer to be able to say something like: *At Reid's house.*"

"You could lie," Reid offered.

I laughed. Clearly I had come to a turning point in our relationship, where I had decided that sex was inevitable and I had to succumb to my body's cravings.

"You can't dress like this anymore," Reid whined. "And the makeup. You know how I get when you wear makeup like that."

I grinned. Yes, I knew how he got when I wore this much makeup. The last time was at a local bar that Manny had taken us to. Some women offered to do my makeup and when Reid saw how I looked, he practically ate me whole.

"Okay," I promised. "I'll try not to be so desirable."

Without another word, Reid pulled me in for a kiss that nearly made my knees give out. This guy was the real deal and I was falling for him, hard.

15.

Kyle Belamy's bedroom was exactly what one might expect. A large, expansive room with a white bear skin rug, a California-King sized bed, and of course, mirrors on the ceiling. I looked at the mirrors over the bed and wondered if the mirrors were for Kyle to look at his partner or for Kyle to look at himself.

"I use them as motivation to do better," Kyle said, noticing me staring at the mirrors. "It's like watching a performance. I can study myself – the expression on my face, how my body looks as it moves. No legitimate actor should be without a mirror above his bed."

I nodded. "Right, of course." I sipped on an orange colored cocktail that I had grabbed from upstairs as I looked around.

"Are you freaking kidding me, Mac?" Foxy said when he saw the set-up. Mac had set his shot so that Kyle was sitting in front of the bed, with the ceiling mirror onscreen above him. Chairs for Foxy and Reid had been placed next to him. "It looks like I'm sitting in bed with the dude!"

"This is a great backdrop," Mac argued. "It tells you everything about Kyle in one shot."

"Look, I'm normally a reasonable guy, but I have to draw the line here. My friends will never let me live it down," Foxy whined.

"How about in front of the closet?" I offered.

Foxy looked at the closet, which was open. Inside there was a full assortment of men's and women's lingerie and shelves filled with every type of condom you could imagine. Foxy grew red in the face. "No."

"Foxy, come on," Mac protested.

"No! Just do one of your usual shots where everything in the back is blurry. I'm not having my wife and kids see this."

"Fine!" Mac spat, annoyed and frustrated. He racked the focus on the camera, readjusted the lights, and in a few minutes was ready to go. Foxy insisted on checking the shot before he sat in his assigned seat. Once he was finally satisfied, he gave Mac the okay.

"I'll need to have a look as well," Kyle piped in.

Mac and Reid threw their hands in the air at the exact same time, both growing increasingly frustrated at how long this set-up was taking.

"This is your fault, Foxy!" Mac scolded. "You started this!" Mac connected a monitor to his camera and handed it to me.

"Kyle, sit down and I'll show you how you look on the monitor," I offered. Kyle sat down while I spun the monitor around so he could see what he looked like.

"I need a softer filter," Kyle told Mac.

Mac glared at Kyle. Normally Mac was a mellow guy but the constant critique from everyone involved seemed to really be getting under his skin. Without a word, he pulled a light filter that looked much like a piece of parchment paper from his case and attached it to one of the lights using a clothespin.

"Much better," Kyle said, looking at his image in the monitor. "We can get started."

Once Reid and Foxy were seated, Kyle handed them each a piece of paper. "Just some warm up questions for you."

I nudged Mac and Manny to start rolling while Foxy let out a laugh. "Is this our script?"

"I always give questions to the person interviewing me. Just some easy ones to get the conversation going." Kyle smiled.

Foxy looked down at the paper. "I understand your childhood was challenging. How did you go from rags to riches?" Foxy read the words in a monotone voice showcasing a severe lack of acting chops.

Reid glanced over at his partner and then let out a laugh. "We're going along with this?"

Foxy smiled. "Sure, why not?"

"Okay, I've got one here," Reid said, smiling. He lifted his left arm in the air and grandly said, "Tell me what inspired you to be an actor."

While the cops were making a joke of it all, Kyle answered the question seriously. "My motto in life has always been: Never Stop and Never Settle. I've chosen acting as my craft because it allows me to constantly perfect what I do. Sometimes I cringe at the first films I starred in. I was so amateur, so unpolished. But I never gave up and I never quit. I constantly practice over and over until I get things perfectly."

Foxy looked confused. "You're talking about your porn acting, right? Don't you just have sex with people?"

Kyle shook his head, appalled by Foxy's ignorance. "Pornography is a type of film and films require acting. Not everything can be reality TV." He pointed at Mac's camera disapprovingly.

"So how do you practice then? Do you have sex with a lot of people?" Foxy continued, curious.

"Actually, I participate in an improvisation group once a month. I also study with one of the finest thespians in the city. And yes, I also have sex a lot." As he said the words, his tongue unfolded from his mouth and he left it hanging there, exposed. He stayed like that, with his tongue extended, for what seemed like a long time. We sat in an uncomfortable, tongue-filled silence before he finally pulled it back in.

I looked over at Manny who had his eyebrows raised high into his forehead. I covered my face, trying to stifle a smile. This guy was certainly a character.

"Were you having sex with anyone on set?" Reid asked, breaking from the script Kyle had provided him.

"I have a personal goal of bedding one hundred women annually. I keep a journal with all of their names. Does that surprise you?"

"The part about you knowing their names does," Reid muttered.

"The goal is aggressive. It means one woman every three days. But sometimes I can knock out several in a weekend or even in a night. Tonight, for example, I have already enjoyed one woman. Well, she enjoyed it. It was a little sloppy for my taste. But it still counts!"

I looked over at Mac who seemed to be the only person not finding some comic relief in this interview. He was still reeling from the criticism he had received over his shot.

"To answer your question, of course I was sleeping with some of the women on set. As I told you before, I never stop and I never settle – especially when I've set a goal for myself."

"So who specifically were you having sexual relations with?" Foxy asked.

"Well, Rose of course. I tried with Penny – she's a limber one! But we didn't get past third base. And I wasn't interested in Joy."

"So does Penny count towards your goal or no?" Foxy asked. "Do you mark that as three quarters in your journal?"

Kyle looked astonished by Foxy's ignorance. "Third base doesn't count. If the goal is sex, three quarters of the way isn't good enough. Didn't your friends tell you that in high school?"

"Pal, I was happy with whatever I could get," Foxy told him.

"What about men? Do you *bed* men too?" Reid inquired.

"Not intentionally. Sometimes group sex can get confusing though." Kyle laughed. "You're not sure where you're sticking your dick!"

I couldn't help it – I burst out laughing. This guy could do stand-up!

"Sharpe, shut up!" Mac snapped at me. "What the hell is wrong with you?"

I looked at Mac, shocked. "Sorry," I whispered, not sure what had gotten stuck in his bonnet.

"Aren't you worried about catching an STD?" Foxy wanted to know. This interview had taken a weird turn, seeming to have nothing to do with Lucky's death.

"I'm very careful. But like I said, I need to keep up with the craft. Sex changes, you know. People aren't doing the same things today that they were two years ago. You have to stay sharp."

"I didn't know that!" Foxy exclaimed. "I've been married for twelve years and nothing has changed. It's always the same with us." Foxy froze, suddenly remembering he was on camera. "Oops – Sharpe don't play that on the show, okay?"

I nodded to him that I wouldn't, but motioned that they should continue. This topic certainly had my attention. I hadn't had sex in a while and now I was hearing that whatever I was doing back then was not what they were doing now. Yikes!

"What exactly has changed in the past two years?" Reid asked. "Can you give us an example? I mean, for Foxy's sake."

Foxy punched Reid on the arm looking embarrassed. Reid caught my eye and suddenly he looked embarrassed too. How had Kyle managed to take control of this interview?

"Sex has trends and fads just like fashion does," Kyle explained. "For a while S&M was really popular, especially when those books came out. But people don't like that stuff anymore – now they crave danger. Sex in a car or an elevator or on a plane – anywhere that poses a risk for getting caught. In the water is a good one too. There are probably a dozen people out there right now doing the nasty. Danger is really trending right now."

Two years ago, I wasn't doing S&M and I certainly didn't have an interest in having sex in some dirty airplane bathroom. If I was out of touch then, I was really out of touch now.

"Lingerie is big too. It always has been, but it continues to be popular. Men are visual creatures and we need to see something that gets us excited! A naked woman just isn't good enough." Kyle leaned in, looking at Reid. "Sometimes women get too complacent. They wear their hair in pony tails and stop putting on makeup. They wear jeans and a T-shirt to work." He glanced over at me and then back to Reid. "They have to remember how visual we men are. We can't imagine how they would look in something sexy, so they have to show us. Like tonight. A low-cut jumpsuit and a little makeup can change everything."

My eyes went wide. During the first part of the interview, I found myself amused by Kyle. He was quirky and funny – a regular comedian. But now I wasn't laughing. Now I was hanging on his every word, listening to him dispense advice like he was Oprah. It made me think about the reaction Reid had when he first saw me tonight. He was all over me – he couldn't get enough. On set I was surrounded by actresses with their boobs hanging out and their makeup applied perfectly. They were literally porn stars and I was standing around my boyfriend dressed like a tomboy. Of course, he wasn't paying me much mind – why would he? I needed to get a clue here. If I wanted to keep Reid around, I was going to have to step it up.

"What the hell does this have to do with Lucky's murder?" Mac snapped. "And quit talking about how Sharpe dresses at work – she looks fine!"

Everyone turned and looked at Mac.

"Bro, you all right?" Manny asked.

"Yeah I'm great," Mac snapped. "Let's keep talking about sex. Let's do nothing but talk about sex all night, okay?"

"Mac, what's going on?" I whispered. "Is everything okay with you and Terry?"

"Yeah… she has her period," Mac whispered.

"Oh," the group collectively mumbled.

"Can we just get on with this?" Mac asked. "You're supposed to be asking about Lucky. You know, the dead guy?"

"I was just following my script!" Foxy joked, waving the piece of paper at Mac.

It was clear that Kyle seemed like an unlikely suspect for the murder, but we still had to find out what he knew. Foxy and Reid fell into their usual line of questioning asking Kyle where he was at the time of the murder, his relationship with Lucky and so on.

Kyle explained that he and Lucky were co-workers and that their relationship hadn't extended outside of the production studio. He hadn't worked with him before, and while he liked him, he felt he needed more practice. He told us he was on social media the morning that Lucky died and had been posting pictures of himself wearing boxer briefs in varying colors. He told us how important it was to keep his fans engaged and that social media was a big part of that.

He had arrived at the studio around eleven that morning after we had already arrived. He wasn't in the first scene and the night before he was "bedding" a woman after midnight so he came in late. He didn't recall what her name was, but after consulting his sex journal he was reminded that her name was Rachel. "Rachel, last name, unknown" to be exact.

"It's ironic that this all happened during pilot season," Kyle told the cops. "I mean, something like this can definitely boost ratings. It's boosting my followers for sure – that's why I keep posting about it."

"And did you post that we were coming to your party tonight?" Reid asked him."

"Yeah, of course. I even posted a pic of you and Miss Jumpsuit over there going at it," Kyle told Reid.

Reid's eye widened as he turned to look at me. I whipped out my phone to see that I had several alerts. "You son of a bitch!" I screamed then read off his tweet. "Sexually repressed producer and cop go at it." I looked at Kyle. "That's what you posted?"

"What the hell?" Reid jumped up, grabbing the phone out of my hand. The picture featured Reid and me kissing against the wall next to the penis painting. "You take this down! Take it down now!" Reid shouted at Kyle.

Kyle smiled deviously.

Reid wasn't fooling around. He grabbed Kyle by the collar and lifted him up in the air. Mac stopped recording and spun the camera away from the action. "Take that down now!" Reid yelled.

"Okay, okay. Just having a little fun with you," Kyle whined as Reid placed him back in his chair. He clicked around on his phone for a minute and deleted the post.

"Just because I don't have sex with a hundred people a year doesn't mean I'm sexually repressed," I told him.

"Honey, I saw the two of you down there," Kyle told me. "If you two were actually doing the nasty, there's no way you'd be going at each other like that."

Reid glared at Kyle and pointed a finger in his face. "You post anything involving any of us again and you'll be sorry. You hear me?"

"Loud and clear."

*****

It was ironic that a man being interviewed about his perverse and sordid sex-life had managed to turn the tables and humiliate almost all of us for our lack of experience in the area. I think Manny was the only one left unscathed.

After the interview concluded, Foxy and Reid decided to stick around for a while longer to watch the cast members interact. I thought it would be a good idea as well and asked Mac and Manny to film the party as part of the show. It would offer some great production value.

There were a handful of B-list celebrities at the party but they were irrelevant to our storyline so I didn't bother trying to get them to sign releases. I already had releases on the cast and crew from the production and they were who we were focused on.

We found Elroy upstairs in the kitchen snacking on some carrots and drinking a beer.

"Hey man, how you doing?" Mac said to him, trying to engage him once again.

"Hey," Elroy answered, seeming uninterested.

"Is Penny here?" Foxy asked him.

"She is?" Elroy said, suddenly straightening.

"No man, I asked if she *was* here," Foxy told him.

"Oh. I don't think so."

"You were hoping she was, right?"

Elroy shrugged and walked away without saying another word.

"That guy is a great conversationalist," Foxy said to us. "Don't you think?"

Next, we found Joy and Carmine sitting next to each other on a couch in the living room. Carmine was drinking a bottle of water, and Joy, in a sign of solidarity, was doing the same. She was whispering something in his ear and he was laughing. His arm was resting on the couch behind her. It wasn't quite resting on her shoulder, but it was near it. They seemed pretty cozy.

I signaled the crew to hold back so we could film the two of them unnoticed. They didn't seem to be interacting with anyone at the party except each other. Joy took a swig of her water and then laughed grandly. "Good stuff," she appeared to be saying.

We filmed them for a few moments more until we were spotted. Carmine glared at us and Joy frowned. Carmine stood up and walked out of our sight, with Joy running behind him.

On the back deck we found Craig who was hitting on a woman probably twenty years his senior. She had fake boobs, fake lips and fake hair, and she seemed to be entranced by her energetic young suitor. "I could get you in. I just have to talk to my boss. He's always looking for new talent," Craig was telling the woman. "Trust me, I have a lot of pull."

I smiled as I listened to this desperate young kid trying to weasel his way into the pants of an older woman. This party certainly had a sexual charge to it.

Craig noticed me watching him from behind the camera and gave me a quick up and down. "Whoa, holy shit!" he said to me. "You look sexy!"

Despite the fact that Craig was young and kind of an idiot, I still smiled at the compliment.

"This is my TV crew," Craig told his lady-friend.

"No, this is *my* TV crew," Foxy interjected, coming into view. "You're a potential suspect in a murder trial."

Craig grew pale, but his lady-friend seemed intrigued. "You're not gonna kill me, are you?" she demurred.

We weren't interested in socializing with these two. We were just there to watch. We pushed past Craig and the woman so they could get back to their conversation.

Once we were away from them, Foxy whispered in my ear, "Maybe Belamy was right about danger. That woman seemed to like it. It spices up the romance, right?"

I smiled. "So they say."

"I'm thinking of seducing Sherry in our car when I get home," Foxy continued.

I looked at Foxy's large waistband and sizeable rear end. "Do you think that would be comfortable? What kind of car do you have?"

"It's a minivan. The kids will be sleeping and the neighbors might see us. Is that dangerous or what?" Foxy's eyes lit up and he gave me a sly smile.

"Oh yeah, Foxy. Totally dangerous."

As we walked outside on the beach towards the ocean I spotted a man and woman kissing in front of the bonfire. The woman was dressed in a bra and short skirt and the man was topless. They both fell onto the beach in an embrace while several spectators watched the show.

As we approached I realized who the stars of this performance were. Kyle Belamy and Rose Ortez. "Oh, give me a break!" I blurted out, tired of seeing Rose half-naked.

"She's already in your journal," Foxy called out. "This doesn't count Belamy!"

Kyle pulled his mouth off Rose's and looked over at us. "Oh, sorry. I guess we got carried away."

Rose stood up and adjusted the huge breasts that were spilling out of her bra. "Oh, they don't mind. Some of these guys like to watch."

Manny enthusiastically nodded his head, but Rose wasn't talking about him. She was glaring at Reid.

"No, we don't," Reid corrected.

"That's the danger I was telling you about," Kyle whispered to Foxy. "Women eat it up."

Foxy nodded, taking the information in.

"We're leaving now," Reid announced, putting an arm on my shoulder.

"Great idea," Rose said, her eyes flashing. "Let's get out of here. I know of a place."

"There you are!" Ginny said from behind me. "Oh my God – are you Kyle Belamy?!" Ginny gasped, holding her hand out to him.

Bob was trailing behind her on the beach, holding his shoes and socks in his hand, looking totally out of place in a business suit.

Kyle extended a hand. "A pleasure, miss…"

"Darden. Ginny Darden. I'm Victoria's sister."

"Victoria?" Kyle said, looking at me. "Is that your real name?"

"Ginny, we were just heading out," I told her.

"Yes, to the next party," Rose added.

Kyle slapped his hands together and smiled. "I have a fantastic idea. Why don't we all go to the party? You guys come too and film the whole thing. It'll be like a day in the life of me!"

"I don't think so," Reid scoffed.

"Excuse us for a second," Foxy told Kyle, pulling Reid aside.

Ginny looked at Rose. "I recognize you. Weren't you on Vicky's show before?"

"Yes, I'm a famous character." Rose smiled.

Meanwhile, Bob had been staring at Rose's breasts for the past few minutes. He was so fixated on them he didn't realize that he shouldn't be looking. He probably wasn't used to seeing shirtless women at the law firm. Unfortunately for me, naked people were quite common at my job.

After a brief huddle Reid and Foxy returned to the group. "Okay, we're coming with you," Foxy told Rose. "Where is this party?"

*****

Mac suggested it might be easier if we all drove together as opposed to taking separate cars. Rose and Kyle drove separately, but the rest of us, including Ginny and Bob, piled into our rented SUV.

Reid agreed to drive given that Mac wanted to hang out the window of the passenger's side to get some shots of Kyle and Rose driving in his sports car. I sat in the second row with Foxy while Ginny, Bob, and Manny sat in the far back row.

Mac filmed Kyle as he pulled a bright red Porsche convertible out of his driveway, while Rose kneeled on the passenger's seat facing backwards. She was waving her arms in the air so everyone could see her barely-there bra and huge breasts. I had thought Kyle had taken her shirt off during their make-out session on the beach, but I was mistaken. It seemed that Rose's bra was doing double duty as both a shirt and a brassiere. Why leave anything to the imagination, right? After all, as Kyle said, men are visual!

"I hope he hits a pothole," I muttered, imagining Rose being thrown into the air and onto the pavement. As Kyle pulled onto Route 1, I was disappointed to see Rose sit down in her seat and buckle herself in. Reid pulled our SUV out of the driveway, carefully following behind Kyle.

"I can't believe he's leaving his own party," I said to Foxy. "Isn't he worried they'll trash his place or rob him?"

"Danger," Foxy whispered to me, smiling.

"Is this guy kidding me?" Reid said as he struggled to keep pace with Kyle.

"He's got a Porsche, man," Mac told him. "You can't expect to keep up with that."

"I expect him to follow the speed limit when he knows he's being followed by the police."

"True. That is pretty dumb," Mac agreed before lifting his camera to his eye again, trying to get a steady shot.

"Are you gonna give him a ticket?" I asked Foxy.

Foxy shook his head no. "I thought about it, but he's my partner. I feel like it could damage our relationship."

I smirked. "Very funny."

"That was some party!" Manny announced from the back seat. I heard the familiar sound of a cigarette lighter clicking and then the car was filled with Manny's favorite type of smoke.

"What the hell is going on here?" Reid blurted out. "We're police officers. You're sitting in a car with two police officers, Manny!"

"What? It's legal. I got to unwind, man," Manny cooed. "That party was off the hook. Did you see the chicks in there?"

"You're not supposed to smoke it while someone is driving, Manny," Reid told him.

I turned around to look at Ginny who was sitting next to Manny, looking slightly amused. Bob, on the other hand, looked terrified. "Open the window Bob, come on!" I yelled at him. "Reid's gonna get high and crash this van into a wall."

"I've smoked weed before, Victoria," Reid told me from the front.

"What?" I shrieked. "You just totally blew my image of you. You're not as wholesome as I thought."

"Danger," Foxy whispered to me.

"Okay, you need to stop saying that Foxy."

"Slow down!" Reid yelled at Kyle, honking his horn. We were almost going ninety now.

Manny exhaled then passed the joint to Ginny. "This show has got me wound up tighter than a spring," he told us. "I'm banging Rose tonight – mark my words."

"I think Kyle's doing that," Foxy told him.

Ginny took in a deep puff of smoke then breathed it out. "Manny, that woman is nasty. Come on, you don't want to be with someone like that."

"Like hell I don't."

Foxy turned around and looked at Manny. "If you do that you're picking up cooties from Belamy, that creepy camera dude, Craig, Vinnie and maybe Carmine, she can't remember. That's gross, man. Think about that."

"I slept with her first," Manny reasoned. "So those guys already slept with me. I'm just returning the favor."

I crinkled my nose, repulsed by the conversation. Were all men this weak?

"All I know is Sherry is going to get a little surprise when I get home," Foxy announced. "Well, a big surprise. It's a very big surprise."

"Terry too," Mac announced from the front. "Period or not, I'm going in."

"Bob too," Ginny giggled from the back seat and leaned over to kiss him. The image of the two of them kissing was enough to make me wish for blindness.

I knew sexual tension was in the air and it was obvious everyone felt it, but did we have to talk about it constantly? Even worse, did those that were already doing it need to brag to the rest of us about it?

I saw Reid glance at me in the rearview mirror. Was he waiting for me to announce that he and I would also be having sex tonight? I wasn't sure what this party had in store for us, but I was suddenly feeling very unsettled.

16.

"You made it, Grandpa," Kyle teased Reid as he got out of the car.

"You see what I'm driving, right?" Reid countered. "The whole thing was rattling like a tin can."

We piled out of the SUV and looked up at an old warehouse. It had several loading docks with steel gates that were partially opened at the bottom exposing the feet of the patrons inside. The music featured a deep base track which pumped and pounded, rattling the building around it. The parking lot was old and crumbling. This was an underground club if ever there was one. I was sure some very illegal things were going on inside.

Mac already had his camera running while Manny adjusted the mic pack that Kyle was still wearing and tested it for sound. Rose didn't bother to wait for the rest of us; she ran ahead towards the club.

"Do you think the van will get stolen?" I asked.

"Maybe. But they'll probably steal Kyle's car before yours," Reid assured me.

"So, what is this place?" Bob asked Kyle, sounding intrigued.

"It's a place for fantasy," Kyle told him with a grin. He was still dressed in his khaki shorts and white button down, which looked strange, but he was a celebrity and could do what he wanted.

Bob pulled out his cell phone and starting snapping pictures. "The guys at work are never gonna believe this," he told Ginny.

Ginny squealed with delight, squeezing her husband's arm in the process.

We followed Kyle to the door where two large bouncers were standing. "Are they checking IDs?" I asked, realizing I had left my purse in the car. I was thirty years old and not used to being carded anymore.

Kyle turned to me with a laugh. "They don't serve alcohol here, honey. They're here for security. We need to keep the riff-raff out." Kyle gave the two bouncers a subtle nod and gestured that we were with him.

"Wait," the bouncer said to Mac upon seeing the camera. He was a big burly guy wearing a leather jacket, a black beany and a gold chain. "No cameras."

"This is my film crew," Kyle told the bouncer through clenched teeth. He shook the bouncer's hand, passing him a wad of cash. "Dante knows – they're fine."

The bouncer looked unsure, but finally nodded and lifted the rope to let us inside.

As we stepped into the building the din of music washed over us as the bass vibrated the floor. It was smoky and dark and hard to see much. We were walking through a narrow corridor to the warehouse on the other side.

"Kyle, do you think you could ask Dante to sign a location release?" I screamed into Kyle's ear as we walked.

"What?" Kyle screamed back.

"A location release. To film here. Would Dante sign it?"

"Who the hell is Dante? I just made that up." Kyle smiled and squeezed my arm.

"Oh." Wow, I couldn't be less cool if I tried.

Reid came up behind me and put an arm around me. "Are you gonna be okay?" he asked in my ear.

"Yeah, why?"

"There's gonna be some weird shit in this place. I need you to stay where I can see you." Reid looked down at my exposed cleavage.

"Definitely stay where I can see you."

I smiled as he took my hand and pulled me to the end of the hallway. We pushed through a set of double doors and looked up in awe at the spectacle that was in front of us. The club was expansive and filled with party-goers. There were large wooden crates turned on their sides and women dressed in leather thongs posing on top of them. The lights were white and flashing, highlighting pools of smoke and crowds of people dancing.

The music had an industrial beat and thumped and reverberated throughout the warehouse. There were no bars to get a drink or areas to check your coat – just a raw space with a very shadowy vibe. I looked around, amazed. I had heard about places like this, of course, but had never actually been to one. How did people find places like this? How did the people organizing it pull it off? There were some couches and chairs lying about, probably left over from when the warehouse was in use. Some people were lounging on them, but mostly people seemed to be there for the dancing and the music.

The majority of the patrons were dressed in black and most of them were scantily clad. While my outfit probably cost more than the weekly income of most of the people in the place, I otherwise fit in. It was hard to remember that I was on duty as I bobbed my head and stood in awe at all there was to see.

I was expecting to see some weird bondage stuff going on, but then I remembered that Kyle said that was out of style. Instead, people were uninhibited, kissing and grabbing each other, even stripping off their clothes.

"Exhibitionism," Kyle said in my ear. "With that bod, you should try it." He slapped me hard on the ass and then disappeared into the club.

I looked over at Reid and was relieved he didn't see what Kyle had just done. "It's too damn dark in here," Mac complained. "I can't pick up anything on this camera."

"And I can't hear shit," Manny agreed. "Hey Sharpe, maybe we should call it a night and just hang out."

"No," I told him. "Come on, we have to see what Rose is up to. She knows something – she always does."

Bob pulled out his smart phone and began recording a video of the club. "I can't believe I'm here!" he screamed. "I can't believe we're at a place like this!" Ginny seemed equally excited and the two jumped in the air for a while, giddy with excitement.

"There's Rose," Foxy called out. She was dancing on one of the crates with another woman. She seemed to be competing with the woman more than dancing with her, resorting to taking off her bra to expose her breasts when she realized she couldn't dance as well as her competitor.

I motioned to Mac that he should record her, which he did, but he could only see her every half-second when the white lights flashed. The edit would be a disaster.

Mac pulled out a small light from his hacky sack and mounted it on the camera. He turned it on and cast a large floodlight across the room and onto Rose. Some of the club goers glared at Mac, annoyed, but he just shrugged it off.

"Look!" Foxy pointed again, as Kyle climbed up the wooden crate to meet Rose. Mac's floodlight was helping us to see better at least. Now there were three people on the rickety platform and Kyle quickly shooed the other woman away by pointing to the floor and ordering her to get down. The woman seemed annoyed, but did as he said.

Once the two of them were "alone" Kyle placed his hands on her huge breasts and kisses her madly. As Kyle's lips moved to Rose's neck, she turned to look at Reid and smiled.

I felt a rush of anger come over me and without thinking I grabbed Reid's arm and led him away from her. Mac and Manny could handle this; I needed some distance from that woman.

Reid didn't protest. Instead, he charged ahead of me, leading me into a corner and pressing me against the wall. It was dark and I couldn't see much, but when I felt his lips on my neck I became keenly aware of what was going on.

His lips parted and his tongue dragged from the bottom of my neck up to my jawline, which he nipped and kissed. I felt every pore in my body come to life as tingles ran up my spine. Reid's fingers spread wide as he placed them on my hips and squeezed, pulling me into him. I felt my body both melt and come to life in the same moment. I grabbed the muscles of his upper arms and squeezed as I moved my mouth to meet his.

The kiss was powerful and hungry, like we were starving and we each were the very thing we had been craving. Reid moved one of his hands to the back of my head and gripped my hair as he pushed closer, devouring me with his mouth.

I felt so lost in his kiss that I forgot everything that was going on around me. Where were we? Why were we here? None of it mattered. I was drunk off his scent and mesmerized by his touch. The music became an indistinguishable hum, the lights and the crowds barely noticeable. I was completely in tune with his body and with mine. It was as if we were dancing in perfect synchronicity.

"I'm not too proud to take you right here," Reid whispered in my ear.

His words sent a feeling of exhilaration through my body, knowing he wanted me as badly as he did. The danger of doing it in a nightclub added an extra thrill.

"This outfit, your hair – how do you not have guys crawling all over you?" Reid wanted to know.

I smiled. "Pretty sure I do."

"I can't hold back anymore, this is torture."

"I know," I told him letting my hands move down his back to rest on his hips.

We kissed again, even more deeply, which seemed almost impossible. I felt my body warming down below, signaling to me that it was ready, willing and able.

"Maybe we should get out of here," I told him. "Manny and Mac can do the work – they don't need me."

I couldn't see much in the darkness but I was pretty sure Reid was smiling. He kissed me hard, pressing his tongue against mine.

I felt a hand on my shoulder that felt different from Reid's. Reid pulled away and when my eyes came into focus, I saw Foxy standing next to us.

"What the hell are you doing, man?" he asked his partner. "You're practically mauling her."

Reid didn't say anything; he just stared at Foxy wide-eyed. I wiped my mouth, looking like a schoolgirl who had just been caught by her parents making-out with her boyfriend in the car.

"You might want to fix your top," Foxy told me in a disapproving tone.

I looked down and saw that one of my boobs had completely come out. The only thing giving me any form of privacy was the little pastie that was hanging on for its life. I looked at Reid embarrassed as I adjusted myself.

"Rose is on the move," Foxy announced in a tone that seemed to be meant to remind us we were there on business. It was odd to be lectured by a guy who was usually the life of the party, but for whatever reason he didn't seem amused by what he was seeing. "Come on, let's go."

I looked at Reid and without a word we both nodded and followed Foxy as he led us away from our corner.

As we followed Foxy, I caught a glimpse of Ginny and Bob awkwardly dancing on the dancefloor. They looked like they were trying to "dirty dance" but neither of them knew how to do it. Ginny turned her back to Bob to rub her body against his, while Bob spun around nearly knocking her over in the process. They were a disaster, but equally matched.

Foxy pointed at Rose who was now dancing with a new man towards the center of the dancefloor. In contrast to Ginny and Bob, Rose and this new guy were perfectly in sync.

Mac was already there recording the scene as Rose placed a hand on the gentleman's shoulder, bent at the waist and swung her hair against his crotch.

"This lighting sucks!" Mac complained. "I don't care what these assholes say, I need this light on!" Mac flipped the spotlight on once again to the gasps and annoyed glares of the dancers on the floor. "Sorry," Mac said, not meaning it. "I need to be able to do my job here!"

With the light now beaming towards Rose and her partner, I could clearly see the face of the man she was dancing with. Before I could say anything, Foxy blurted it out. "Holy shit, that's George!"

George was wearing a black shirt and jeans, which was probably why I didn't recognize him initially. I was used to seeing him topless.

"That son of a bitch said he didn't know her!" Foxy yelped.

Rose moved her head up to George's mouth and they kissed. We all groaned in disgust. How many men could the woman be with?

"I wonder if he can taste Belamy on her lips," Foxy commented.

"Hey man, turn that shit off!" an angry patron said, putting a hand over Mac's light. He was lined with thick muscles and an angry snarl and I didn't think Mac would want to mess with him. Mac complied and turned off the light.

"See if you can hold the aperture open on the camera to get the shot," I suggested to Mac.

"This isn't a still camera, Sharpe!" Mac barked. "It's digital and I can't do anything about these lights."

"We need this shot!" I told him, panicked. "This could blow the case right open."

"What the hell do you want me to do? Punch that guy out?"

"You're MacGyver, figure it out!" I yelled back.

The DJ switched up the music and turned off the strobes in favor of green and pink lights flashing across the crowd.

"Okay, I can work with this," Mac assured me. He pulled a small green gel out of his hacky sack and put it over his spotlight and then lit it up again. With the green gel overtop, the light was far less distracting and actually kind of matched the scene. "I'm good," he assured me.

It was pretty irritating to have to watch yet another Rose make-out scene, especially on the same night. Maybe that was how Foxy felt about me and Reid. George and Rose seemed oblivious to Mac's green light shining on them as they continued to rub their hands all over each other. After a few minutes Rose whispered something in George's ear, then took his hand and snuck away.

"Should we follow them?" Foxy asked his partner.

"No," Reid said. "She knows we're here and she knows we're watching. We can question her in the morning."

"You sure?" Mac asked, not wanting to miss out on a good old-fashioned camera chase.

"Yeah, let's go home," Reid told us.

This night had gone sideways quickly and so I wasn't exactly disappointed to hear we were wrapping. We had all driven together, which meant we would all have to leave together. I looked around the club. Where the hell was Manny?

*****

We found our trusted sound man sitting on a busted leather coach with a woman straddling him. His hands were on her hips and his lips were on her collar bone.

"Jesus," Foxy muttered. "Is everyone on ecstasy or something?"

"Maybe you should break them up," I suggested. "You have a knack for that."

Foxy glared at me then walked over to the woman and pulled her off Manny. "Hey lovebirds, party's over. We're leaving."

"Yo man, you serious?" Manny asked.

"Let's go," Foxy ordered.

"Hey, if we're done for tonight just leave me here. I'll find my way home."

"I wouldn't do that," Foxy warned. "There are drugs everywhere. I already called it in. The PD will be here any minute now."

For a guy that was usually very chill, Manny suddenly looked really pissed. He stood up and got right in Foxy's face. "What the hell you doing to me, man?!"

"Saving your butt," Foxy shot back.

"Like hell!" Manny shouted giving Foxy a firm push on his shoulders. "You bring me here, then you hold me back from closing the deal?"

"I'm doing you a damn favor!" Foxy roared.

It was looking like these two were seriously going to come to blows. Mac handed me his camera before jumping in-between them. Reid was right behind him.

"Calm down!" Reid screamed. "Calm the hell down!"

Reid pulled Foxy back while Mac took hold of Manny. "I don't work for you!" Manny was shouting to Foxy. "I don't have to do what you say!"

"Come on guys, we have to get out of here," I pleaded. Out of the corner of my eye I saw Ginny and Bob "freaking" on the dance floor. I knew Mac and Reid had the situation under control so I took the opportunity to run over to grab them.

I tapped Ginny on the shoulder but she was transfixed by her own dance moves and didn't notice me. I waved my hands in the air to try to get Ginny and Bob's attention and then wedged myself between their bodies to pry them apart. This place certainly affected people! I would have to try to find out when the next party was.

"Come on guys, the cops are coming to break this party up. We gotta go!"

I grabbed Ginny by the arm and led her and Bob towards the rest of our group. We hustled to the front door of the club and winced as the light of morning dawn filled our eyes. I hadn't been out this late in a very long time. I wasn't even drunk!

We made our way to the van. "Son of a bitch!" Mac called out as the SUV came into view. The side door had been vandalized with a pink penis spray-painted on it. On the front hood the culprits had written "Cock Hunters" in big black letters. I looked over at Kyle's red Porsche which sat completely untouched.

Mac got behind the wheel of our newly named *Cock Hunters* vehicle, with Manny sitting next to him in the front passenger seat.

Foxy, Reid, and I sat in the back row while Ginny and Bob sat in the middle row. Mac put the SUV in drive and we silently pulled out of the lot. We sat quietly for a few minutes, each one of us having our own reason to be angry. Finally, Ginny broke the silence. "That was freaking amazing."

"I took some pictures on my phone," Bob added. "The guys at work are never going to believe this."

"You can't show those pictures at work, Bob," I told him. "That was like a drug and sex club. You'll get fired."

Bob looked at me like I was a fool. "Vicky, I'm an entertainment lawyer. Every guy I work with is on drugs. It's a known vice of our industry."

"Then how do you read the contracts and stuff? Doesn't that require concentration?" I asked.

"That's why I am the top at my firm. I'm the guy everyone can count on."

"But not tonight!" Ginny cheered and leaned in to kiss him. "Oh Vicky, this is exactly what me and Bob needed. You have to take us to another one. Hey, I wonder what happened to Kyle. I hope the cops didn't arrest him."

"Were you the first one to report the disturbance?" Reid asked Foxy.

Foxy looked away, not saying anything.

"You didn't call, did you?" Reid asked him.

"Are you kidding me, man?" Manny yelled from the front seat. "You have something against me getting laid?"

"You know how many germs that girl probably had?" Foxy shot back.

"Dude, you have a wife at home. You can get laid. Don't mess with another man's mojo – you hear me?"

"I have two kids too! Don't forget that!" Foxy yelled back, looking embarrassed.

"They're probably sleeping right now," I offered. "You can wake Sherry up when you get home."

"It's five in the morning, Sharpe. Do you really think she'd appreciate that kind of a wake up?" Foxy shook his head and looked out the window.

Wow, this assignment was messing with all of us. I had been so focused on my own discomfort that I failed to realize that it was affecting everyone. No wonder the whole cast of *Babes in Space* was sleeping together – what choice did they have?

Suddenly I felt extremely tired. I leaned in to Reid who was sitting to my left and rested my head on his shoulder. Next to me he felt distant and stiff.

"I'm sorry about before," Reid said to me in a hushed whisper.

I looked up at him. "Sorry for what?"

Reid shook his head. "Don't make me feel like more of an asshole than I already do, okay?"

"I'm not trying to."

"When's call time?" Mac asked from the front. "We all need to get some sleep."

I wasn't sure how to answer. I was confused by Reid and tired and my brain wasn't working very well at the moment. "Uh, well we still have to get home from Malibu and that's gonna take a while." I looked at Reid and Foxy. "What do you guys think?"

"Let's do a late start. Maybe I can get with Sherry after the kids go to school. How about noon?"

"You'd better not be hitting that!" Manny yelled from the front seat. "No way are you hitting that. Eight a.m. call time Sharpe. Say it."

"Let's compromise on eleven, okay?" I offered.

Everyone seemed to agree with that, even though it meant we would still only get a small amount of sleep.

I looked up at Reid who didn't seem to want to make eye contact. Anyone who said women were confusing needed to date a man for five minutes. They were way worse! I decided I was too tired to pursue the conversation, especially with everyone else listening. Instead, I looked out the window, reconstructing the events of the evening and wondering what the hell went wrong.

17.

I woke up the next morning wishing my brain had an on/off switch. I made a mental note to ask Penny about her meditation rituals. Maybe they would help!

Kyle's words from the night before still rang in my head. *Sometimes women get too complacent. They wear their hair in pony tails and stop putting on makeup.* Even though I was frustrated with the way Reid shut me out, I still wanted to make sure I had his attention. In fact, I wanted to get him right back in that heated state he was in last night, unable to resist me!

I still wore jeans, but I opted for a more form-fitting pair and I wore a shirt with a low V-neck as opposed to my typical gender-neutral T-shirts. I spent some time in front of the mirror too, putting on makeup and mascara. I had gotten about four hours of sleep so it took some time to cover the bags under my eyes, but in the end I was satisfied with how I looked.

*****

All my primping, combined with the fact that I was moving kind of slowly this morning, caused me to arrive to set later than call time. I found the cops interviewing Jason in the break room. Fortunately, Mac and Manny were there recording the scene. Quietly, I grabbed a seat next to Manny and listened in as the conversation continued. Manny shook his head and wagged his finger at me, disapproving of my tardiness.

Jason sat in a chair wearing a pair of black jeans that were ripped at the knees and a coral colored tank top with a faded design on the front. He had blonde messy hair that looked like it had been washed in the ocean

177

waves. He was leaning back in his seat, with arms resting comfortably on his stomach, looking pleased with how the conversation was going so far. Considering the fact that Jason's wealthy father had unknowingly footed the bill for this production it occurred to me that his ripped-up jeans probably cost a fortune. The rest of the cast and crew were otherwise preoccupied on set shooting a scene, so we had Jason all to ourselves.

"That dude never paid attention to me. I was a checked box, a notch on his belt. That was it," Jason explained, talking about his father. "That dumbass is gonna be so surprised when he finds out he's the executive producer on this thing!"

"What do you mean?" Foxy asked, sounding confused. It suddenly occurred to me that I knew something the cops didn't. Vinnie had told me, Mac and Manny about Jason's upbringing, but we forgot to tell the cops. Well, there was no point in mentioning it now! Better to let the cops think they uncovered something new. My job was just to observe anyway.

"That's how it works," Jason said. "You pay your way into a movie and you get EP credit. It's pretty standard. I told my dad I needed him to fund this movie I wanted to be in." Jason laughed. "I told him it was a sexy thriller. That's sorta true."

"So your dad just cut you a check? No questions asked?" Foxy asked.

"A hundred grand," Jason explained. "All of which probably landed in Belamy's pocket."

"So you have a lot of animosity towards your father," Reid suggested.

"You could say that," Jason confirmed.

"What's gonna happen when he finds out?" Foxy asked.

Jason thought for a minute. "He'll yell at me, I guess. My shrink says I'm craving attention, even if it's bad. I'll tell him it was a call for help or some such BS. He'll get over it."

"Aren't you worried he'll cut you off?" Foxy asked.

Jason considered that too. "I guess I'm not."

"Tell us about the victim – Lucky. Did you know him well?" Reid asked.

Jason shifted in his seat. His eyes glanced over at me briefly, noticing the new person in the room. "Not that well. This was the first time we'd met."

"Did you get along?"

"We got along fine, I guess." Jason gave us a sly smile. "I didn't kill him if that's what you're asking."

"Who did?" Reid countered.

Jason let out a laugh. "You're direct. I like that. Listen, if I knew who did it I'd have told you two days ago. Obviously I'm not very high on your list of suspects. Does it normally take you this long to interview everyone?"

"No," Reid answered bitterly. "Have you ever thought about killing your father?"

The words struck Jason like a slap across the face and he sat there looking stunned. "How am I supposed to answer that?"

"Truthfully would be good," Reid pressed.

Jason looked uncomfortable. "Yeah, I mean, who hasn't, right?"

"Right. Did you ever try to act on your impulses?"

Jason looked over at my crew and then back to Reid. He laughed almost manically and then grew serious. "No, man. Why would I do that?"

Reid cocked his head and looked at Jason. "I was just thinking that Lucky could have been some good practice before the main event."

The room was dead silent with everyone hanging on his next response. "Dude, you're freaking me out!" Jason exclaimed. "I didn't kill Lucky and I don't want to kill my dad! I mean, are you serious right now?"

"I'm glad to know that man," Reid told him. "And where were you the morning of the murder?"

"I was at the beach. Surfing. I could give you the names of like a dozen witnesses if you want."

"Okay, give me those names."

"What now? Um, Johnny was there, Rebone, MacKenzie."

"Do these people have last names or phone numbers?" Foxy interjected.

"I'm sure they do. Look, they're just friends of mine that I surf with. I don't know them that well, but they could definitely tell you I was there. Maybe tomorrow you could come with me to the beach? You could ask them yourself."

"All right, we'll do that," Reid told him, glancing at Foxy to take over the questioning. As he turned his head, Reid's eyes caught mine for a brief moment. I raised my eyebrows by way of greeting, but it was too late. He was already turning back around to face Jason.

"Do you think Lucky's death will boost ratings for your show?" Foxy asked Jason.

"Yeah, I think so," Jason said, grateful to change the subject. "Belamy's social media has been blowing up and they covered us in the trades yesterday."

Wow. I had been so pre-occupied I hadn't even bothered to check the *Daily Buzz* for the latest developments. I realized I should also probably text Lenny with an update.

"Would anyone have wanted to kill Lucky for that reason? To get the show picked up?" Foxy asked.

"Are you talking about Vinnie?" Jason asked. "He is kind of a prick I guess. Maybe. Listen guys, like I said before, if I knew who did this I'd tell you, I swear."

"What time do you surf in the morning?" Reid asked him.

"Waves are best at six, but I usually get there late."

"When will you be there tomorrow?"

"Um, is eight okay?" Jason asked. "Zuma beach. I can meet you in the parking lot."

"We'll be there."

*****

As Manny removed the microphone from Jason's shirt I sensed someone behind me. I turned and jumped to see Kyle had pulled up a chair and was grinning at me.

"You scared me," I told him.

"I wasn't sure you'd make it in this morning. You don't seem like the kind of girl who can hold her liquor well," Kyle said to me, still grinning.

"I can hold my liquor fine. Besides, I barely had any. There were too many… other things going on." I glanced to the side to look at Reid. He had been sitting in a chair talking with Foxy but looked over when he saw me with Kyle.

"Did you have fun last night?" Kyle wanted to know.

"It was an experience," I told him, trying to downplay the evening. "But I've been to parties like that before."

"Uh-huh," Kyle smiled. "I liked what you were wearing."

I heard the sharp scrape of a chair sliding across linoleum. I turned to see Reid walking out of the room. The sound brought me back to reality. Kyle was just trying to mess with Reid. Just like Rose was trying to get at me through Reid, Kyle was trying to get at Reid through me. Reid was someone I cared for deeply. He was the one who should be getting my attention. I needed to avoid getting sucked into the charm of a man who had a mirror on his bedroom ceiling and a closet full of condoms. Not worth it.

"Excuse me please," I said to Kyle and stood up to follow behind Reid.

I caught a glimpse of Reid's back as he walked into Vinnie's office. I followed him inside.

"Hi," I said to him once I got inside the office. It was empty except for the two of us. "Were you looking for someone?"

"Yeah, Rose. I thought she might be in here," Reid answered barely making eye contact with me. "She hasn't shown up to set today yet."

He moved over to Carmine's desk, noticing he had left his coffee thermos on top of it. Reid picked it up and removed the top. He took a big whiff and then replaced it on the desk.

"A little early for this stuff," he said to me.

"They say it helps dull the pain," I offered.

"Maybe I should give it try it. This case is getting to all of us," Reid said with a faint smile.

I smiled back. "Agreed. Listen I wanted to get some talking heads with you and Foxy – are you up for it?"

Reid sighed heavily but then relented. "Sure. If Rose doesn't show up soon I want to go after her. She needs to explain why she claimed not to know George."

*****

We grabbed a private corner on the unused moon walk set to film Foxy and Reid's talking head interviews. Foxy had worn his cop uniform today and looked quite dashing. Reid opted for his usual look: blue jeans, a white undershirt, and a white button-down shirt over top. He looked dashing too.

"We haven't been able to find any signs of forced entry or any information that anyone other than the cast and crew were present during the murder or any time the night before," Reid explained to the camera. "I called the alarm company and I got lucky. The kid on the line was willing to talk."

"What do you mean by that?" I asked.

"Sometimes detectives have to try a few different approaches to get information. Alarm companies don't have to turn over their records without a subpoena. But if you're aggressive and you get someone new, you can usually get what you need," Reid explained.

"And what did they tell you?" I asked.

"That the alarm wasn't turned on that night at all," Reid explained. "Carmine told us he set the alarm that night on his way out. But he didn't. No one did."

"So that means anyone could have walked in that night," Foxy continued. "Anyone at all. And we don't know what time Lucky came back to the studio or even if he left."

"If Vinnie typed in the alarm code in the morning it wouldn't have mattered. The alarm wasn't armed," Reid explained to the camera. "The other outstanding item is Rose. She and George, Lucky's roommate, claimed they didn't know each other, but we saw them together last night and it didn't seem like the first time they'd met. There's a possibility that George is involved, especially because he's been caught in a lie."

"Is that a good indicator of guilt?" I asked.

Foxy placed a hand on Reid's shoulder indicating that he would like to answer the question. "People act strangely around cops sometimes. They might tell us every bad thing they've ever done or they might start lying about things they don't need to lie about because they believe it will somehow implicate them in the crime. Being caught in a lie doesn't necessarily mean George is guilty, but we need to understand why he lied and if he or someone else has something to hide. It isn't much, but it's a small break in the case. At this point we just want to get this damn thing put to bed… no pun intended."

I heard the door open behind me and turned to see Craig standing in the doorway. "Rose is here," he announced.

"Thanks." Reid looked over at me. "Are we done here?"

"Sure," I agreed and let the cops charge out of the room to find Rose.

*****

We found Rose in her dressing room rushing to get her makeup applied. She had already changed into her costume for the day, which consisted of a white set of silk pajamas that exposed her midriff. Total astronaut gear.

"We need to talk," Reid told her.

"Like hell," Vinnie said from behind Reid.

Mac and Manny were there to record, while I hung back and watched.

"Excuse me?" Reid said, turning to glare at Vinnie.

"I need her on set. She's two hours late!"

"No shit, I've been waiting to talk to her all morning," Reid barked.

"Boys, you don't have to fight over me," Rose teased. "There's plenty of me to go around."

Neither Vinnie nor Reid looked amused.

"Get to set," Vinnie snapped, glaring at her.

Rose nodded as she quickly finished applying her lipstick. She stood up and walked towards the door. On her way out, she brushed past Reid and placed a hand on his chest. "If you want to talk to me, your girlfriend over there had better be willing to pay up. Otherwise, my lips are sealed."

Rose sashayed off to set with Vinnie following behind her while Reid exploded. He threw his notepad across the room, smashing it into the wall.

I decided to give Reid some space and motioned for the guys to stop filming and to head to set. Foxy stayed behind to talk with his partner. I knew it was best that I didn't interfere so I decided to slip out too.

Down the hallway I caught a glimpse of Penny and Elroy talking. She was standing with her back against the wall while Elroy leaned in towards her. I was probably fifty feet away, but even from where I was standing I could read their body language. Whatever Elroy was saying, Penny looked completely disinterested. In fact, she looked a little uncomfortable being cornered like she was. I decided to casually walk past them to eavesdrop on the conversation.

"Have you ever thought about it?" Elroy was asking. He stiffened up as I walked past.

"It's not something I'm used to," Penny answered. "I prefer vinyasa."

So much for my body language reading skills. They were just talking about yoga. As I approached the door to the set, I found Manny and the sound guy Enrique chatting in Spanish.

"What's going on?" I asked the guys who suddenly both wore guilty looks on their faces.

"Nothing, Sharpe. Just waiting for shooting to start," Manny said.

I narrowed my eyes. "What were you guys talking about?"

"Guy stuff, Chica."

"Where the hell is my camera and sound?" Vinnie boomed from set.

Enrique snapped to attention. "Elroy!" Enrique called before hustling onto set. I saw Elroy break away from Penny and go running past me towards Vinnie's beckoning voice. Manny followed the men inside, slamming the large sound-proof door behind him. I stood there alone in silence.

Penny walked towards me slowly and deliberately. "Are we having fun yet?"

I smiled, not sure what I was supposed to say.

Penny opened the big door and stepped onto set leaving me alone in the quiet once more. I stood there for a moment, completely still. My job was chaotic, which meant my life was chaotic. It was go-go-go all the time. Sometimes I had a rare moment like this one where I could be alone with myself. A single moment where all the madness going on around me stopped and I could breathe. It didn't last long, maybe thirty seconds or so, but I enjoyed it.

I sighed deeply then turned towards the door, ready to face the music once more. Inside, I felt the rush of cold air and the sounds of crew members firing off orders. It was show time.

18.

Kyle was the hero as he shielded the three defenseless women, Rose, Penny and Joy from Jason who was now playing a deranged astronaut who couldn't handle being in space anymore. There were words and shouts exchanged between the men as the three women cowered behind Kyle dressed in their nighties. Apparently, the fight broke out just before bed.

The acting was mediocre at best with Rose being the worst of the group by far. Even her huge boobs unsupported and falling out the bottom of her half-top didn't cover up her melodramatic cries of, "Oh no!" and "Don't hurt us!" As she spoke her lines she gestured dramatically, laying a hand across her chest and puckering her red lips.

After two more takes, I felt bored. We weren't going to solve the crime doing this anyway so I decided to step off set and snoop around. I didn't know where Reid and Foxy were – perhaps they were doing the same thing.

In preparation for my spy mission I decided to stop at the ladies room. I had learned the hard way that an empty bladder was essential when going undercover. When I entered the bathroom, my lip began to twitch as I thought about the many communicable diseases that might be lurking on those toilet seats. I knew I couldn't sit on the seat, I would have to squat. I started off strong, but towards the end my thighs were shaking like crazy under the weight of my body. Squats were not an exercise I practiced regularly and my legs nearly buckled under the strain. I placed my hand on the top of the toilet paper dispenser to keep from losing my balance completely. When I finally finished I felt like I had been through one of Penny's yoga routines. I made my way over to the sink and washed my hands vigorously. I wasn't normally a germ person, but these circumstances were bringing out my inner OCD.

I pulled out my phone to check what day it was. When you work seven days a week it is easy to lose track. It was Thursday, which was day three of this investigation and we were no farther along than when we started. I knew the case was good for *Murder Live!*, but I couldn't help but wonder if anyone else had been murdered recently? Perhaps we could solve another case instead? I worried that the audience at home wouldn't have any sympathy for Lucky and therefore wouldn't be invested in us solving the case. I would have to edit this thing just right.

As I contemplated how best to start pulling the show together, my cell phone buzzed. I looked down to see my boss Lenny calling me, as if on cue. I knew I was supposed to play up the story and tell him how great it was coming along, but I couldn't bring myself to do it. Instead, I tried a different approach.

"Your girlfriend is demanding more money," I answered.

"How much did you give her so far?" Lenny wanted to know.

"A thousand," I lied. Lenny had approved me to give her a thousand but I had only given her half thus far.

"Give her another five," Lenny told me. "Is it good stuff?"

"Maybe," I told him. "We followed her last night and found her partying with Lucky's roommate even though the roommate claimed he had never met her before. After I pay her she said she'll answer our questions."

"Wow, that girl is naughty. Hey, I was thinking about stopping by the set," Lenny continued. "Maybe in an hour?"

And there it was. Maybe subconsciously this was the very reason I had been avoiding Lenny. First, I had the pleasure of my dad visiting me on set and now my sleaze ball boss wanted to make an appearance. I had to think fast. "Oh, I don't think that's such a good idea. The cops are really on edge and I don't think they want any more TV people here. The interviews have been going slower than they would have liked."

"I don't care what the cops think. I'm paying them, aren't I?"

He had a point there. The cops actually did receive a stipend from the show for their participation. We didn't advertise it widely, but it was fairly common in the industry. The fact that participants were going above and beyond their regular day job meant they deserved to be compensated. The stipend was a lump sum of money that we paid the participants weekly. Guys like Vinnie or Kyle didn't get it, but Foxy and Reid did. It wasn't enough to retire on, but Reid and Foxy were getting about eight hundred a week from us while still taking home their normal paycheck from the precinct. Lenny wasn't completely incorrect to suggest that Reid and Foxy were on his payroll, but I knew the cops didn't see it that way.

"Well we might be wrapping shooting for the day soon," I explained. "You're coming from the west side so it will take a while to get here."

"Just give me the address, Sharpe," Lenny ordered.

I took a deep breath and recited the address to him. This idiot showing up on set was the last thing we needed.

*****

In an effort to clear my head I grabbed my trusty handheld camera and captured some B-roll. It gave me the opportunity to capture some cutaways that I could use during my edit and the opportunity to snoop around a bit.

I walked into one of the dressing rooms and grabbed some shots of the makeup laying on the makeup table, the large light bulbs encasing the mirror, and the cardboard cutout of a star on the outside of the door. I moved over to the costume rack and starting pulling out some of the outfits to get better shots.

I came across a pink and black corset with matching garter belts and a pink feather hair piece. It was the type of thing someone in a movie would wear, but no one in real life would ever consider purchasing.

"That's your color," I heard a voice tell me.

I looked up from my camera to see Reid standing in the doorway. He was leaning against the door jam with the top few buttons of his dress shirt unbuttoned exposing the T-shirt underneath. I smiled and put the outfit back on the rack. I placed my camera on a small table behind me and continued to thumb through the outfits.

"What are you doing in here?" Reid wanted to know.

I shrugged. "I was just capturing some footage. Sometimes I need it during the edit."

"It's not looking like this thing is getting solved anytime soon," Reid admitted. "No one seems to give a damn around here."

I pulled another garment off the rack and looked at it. This one was a green sequined oversized bra with a matching cheerleader skirt. I held it against my body and turned to Reid. "Too much?"

Reid smiled and stepped inside the room, closing the door behind him. He walked over and stood alongside me as I continued to thumb through the rack. I stopped on a black option and pulled it out.

Reid shook his head. "I didn't like when Foxy held that lacey thing up against you last time. I don't like guys thinking about you like that."

"Even though you do?" I asked him.

Reid took the black lace outfit from the rack and examined it. He turned to me with a sly smile. "I think about you like *that* all the time. I can't stop. This place is making me act crazy. I practically forced myself on you last night," Reid said looking like he hated himself.

"No, you didn't," I assured him. "Well, I mean, I was a willing participant."

"I'm not like that, Sharpe, I'm not. It's just been so long since I've done it and now I have this hot, sexy, amazing woman driving me crazy and I can't have her."

Reid put the dress back on the rack and plopped himself on the new couch that Vinnie had put in the room to replace of the one Lucky was killed on.

"I know I've been making you wait," I told him walking over to sit down next to him. "And I also know that my decision had more to do with my fears than anything else."

Reid looked at me, brushing a piece of hair behind my ear. "Honey, I'm not going anywhere."

"I know. And I also know that resisting you at this point isn't serving either one of us. We both need the release."

I saw a slight smile creep across Reid's face as he ran his finger through my hair and pulled me in for a kiss. I felt the warmth of his lips and wetness of his tongue and my body surged. I was tired of waiting, tired of holding back. My body was literally throbbing everywhere, begging me to give in. I threw myself over him, straddling my legs over his and kissed him deeply. I ran my fingers over his face as his hands traveled to my hips and squeezed.

I moved my hips back and forth over his growing manhood as the kisses intensified. I was caught in the moment, lost in his touch, his caress. Were we really going to have sex for the first time on a porn set, in the dressing room where a guy was murdered? It seemed that way. I didn't plan to stop it and I didn't think Reid did either.

Reid moved his lips down to my neck as he liked to do. I felt tingles all over my body from the base of my spine to the top of my neck. I arched my back and opened my eyes, staring up at the ceiling. As I looked up, I noticed a vent in the ceiling with a tiny red light flashing from inside. I squinted my eyes to make sure I was seeing it correctly. What the hell was that? A security camera? What was it doing in the dressing room?

"Reid," I said looking down, breathing into his ear.

"Oh yeah." Reid said, not getting the message.

No Reid, hold on," I said, pushing him off.

Reid let out a big sigh. "Sharpe, come on. Are you seriously trying to kill me?"

"No," I told him. "Look up there." I pointed at the ceiling vent.

Reid sat up and turned around to look up at the ceiling. He stared up for a moment, squinting his eyes. "What the hell?"

"Looks like a camera, right?" I said to him.

Reid pushed me off his lap and stood on the couch, getting a closer look inside the vent. He pulled at the grate until it came off. "Holy shit. Why the hell didn't Vinnie mention this?"

"Good question," I told him.

Reid replaced the grate and stepped down off the couch. I was standing up now and he stood in front of me. "Okay – this is happening," Reid told me waving his finger from me back to him. "You and I are happening, just not here."

I nodded smiling. "Tonight?"

Reid smiled from ear to ear. "Tonight." He kissed me on the lips, savoring the moment for a little bit longer. "Come on, we've got some questions we need answered."

*****

As we opened the door from the dressing room to the hallway, Reid nearly collided with Rose. She had just finished her scene on set and was returning to the dressing room to relax. "Dios mio!" Rose screamed as she jumped back in response.

She wasn't the person we were looking for, but I knew Reid wanted to ask her questions about last night. "I need to talk to you," he said.

Rose shifted her gaze towards me and moved her fingers back and forth, indicating I would have to pay up if I wanted her to cooperate.

"I have the cash. Let me get my crew," I told her.

Reid seemed frustrated. I wasn't sure if it was because I was paying her or because grabbing my crew would further delay him. I hustled to get Mac, Manny and Foxy and quickly returned back to the dressing room with the guys in tow. Inside Rose was sitting on the new couch and Reid was standing across from her. I realized now why Reid was frustrated. He had been stuck in the same room with Rose standing in silence waiting for us. It must have been awkward. We all stepped inside the room while I pulled five hundred dollars from my wallet and handed it over to Rose.

She counted the money and then stuffed it into her bra. She made herself comfortable on the couch that Reid and I had just practically screwed on. She looked at us expectantly. Foxy stood next to his partner, while my crew and I stepped inside the room and closed the door. Rose's eyes traveled from Reid and then over to me. Under her stare I shifted my weigh uncomfortably, leaning on one leg and then the next. She looked at my hair, which was probably a mess. Reid tended to comb his hands through it when we were intimate. Rose raised up her finger and pointed from Reid over to me. "What were you two doing in here before?"

My eyes grew wide and my cheeks flushed as Mac, Manny, and Foxy turned to look over at me.

"Mac, are you rolling?" Reid asked in a huff.

Mac shook his head no. "I can't get a good shot with you guys standing and Rose sitting. Can you sit down?"

Reid gave Mac his usual glare and then grabbed the chair from the makeup table, turned it around, and sat down, resting his arms on top of the back of the chair. I couldn't help but notice how hot he looked in that position. His strong arms were flexing and his biceps curling. Was he doing this just to drive me wild?

There weren't any other chairs available so Foxy plopped himself down on the couch next to Rose, shifting his fat ass back and forth and knocking her over to the right side of the couch. Now she had Reid on her left, Foxy on her right and me and my crew filming her from the center. We had her cornered. Mac pressed the record button and signaled that the cops could begin.

"We saw you with Lucky's roommate last night at the club. Why didn't you tell us you knew him?" Reid demanded of Rose.

Rose looked confused by the question. "You didn't ask."

"We asked him," Reid pounced. "And he said he didn't know you. But he sure as hell seemed to know you last night."

Rose squared her eyes. "We just met last night."

"Bullshit!" Reid snapped at her. "Tell me the truth. When did you first meet him?"

"I said last night," Rose demanded. "We met at Kyle's house and I told him to meet me at the club."

"I didn't see him at the party," Reid countered. "If he was there I would have recognized him."

"Maybe you had your eyes on something else," Rose answered glancing over at me.

"Did you sleep with him?"

"Of course," Rose answered matter-of-factly.

"Where?" Foxy asked.

"His car," Rose answered. "In the parking lot."

"You know what I think?" Reid told her, applying the pressure. "I think you and George have known each other a long time and last night you were celebrating your victory in getting away with Lucky's murder."

Rose rolled her eyes. "Try again cop."

"Lucky liked to sleep around, but he wasn't interested in you Rose, which is ironic because of how easy you are. But Lucky didn't want to be with you, he hated you. He couldn't even stand to be in a scene with you."

"That's not true," Rose retorted.

"Sure, it is. It's in every interview we've conducted," Reid lied. "Lucky thought you were disgusting. You couldn't handle that. You couldn't handle a man willing to resist you. That's why you went after his roommate. When that didn't bother him, you decided to go after Lucky directly. Admit it, Rose. This thing has your name all over it."

"Lucky was an asshole. I hated that piece of shit and I'm glad he's dead. But I didn't kill him. Sorry cops, you're going to have to find someone else to blame."

That was a great line. I wrote the timecode down on my notepad. Too bad she used so many profanities.

Rose took a deep breath. "Are we done here?"

"For five hundred dollars?" Reid asked. "We're just getting started."

Reid and Foxy spent the next hour hammering Rose with questions. They had her describe every move she made for the last few days. Where she went, who she saw, what she ate, when she slept. It was meant to torture her, but it ended up being torture for everyone involved.

Rose was rude and difficult to deal with, but she held her ground and didn't give up much. She was insistent that she didn't know George and that they had just met that night. We all wanted to solve this thing and we all really wanted Rose to be the killer, but by the end of the interview we didn't have much more than we started with. I was starting to wonder if maybe Rose was innocent. When the cops were finally finished, she stormed out of the room and back onto set.

Reid looked at Foxy and pointed at the ceiling vent. "Check this out." Once again Reid stepped onto the couch and removed the grate. This time Mac was recording him as he did it. He pointed to the camera mounted inside.

Foxy squinted as he looked up. "Are you shitting me? There's a damn security camera at the scene of the crime?"

"Apparently," Reid confirmed. "And neither Vinnie or Carmine said anything about it."

"I wonder if these are all around, or just in here. Did the alarm company say anything to you about cameras?"

Reid shook his head. "They said there weren't any."

"Maybe we should look around first before we talk to Vinnie."

Reid agreed and the two headed into the hallway to take a look while the others were preoccupied on set. Mac followed behind the cops, camera rolling, capturing the search.

The guys looked around the hallway and in the ceiling vents, but didn't see any more red flashing lights. We looked in the kitchen, in the second dressing room, in the supply closets, and in Vinnie and Carmine's office. Nothing. The only camera that seemed to exist happened to be in the very room Lucky had been murdered in.

"Did Penny use this dressing room too?" Foxy asked his partner when we returned to the first dressing room.

"Yes, all the girls did. Belamy usually monopolized the other one."

"I wonder if the camera guy knew anything about this. He certainly had a thing for Penny," Foxy offered.

Reid nodded. "That's true. Maybe he was spying on her."

"Maybe the reason Vinnie didn't tell us about the camera was because he didn't know," Foxy offered.

"Let's talk to Elroy next," Reid suggested.

Reid looked over at Mac who was still filming. "Maybe we should try a different approach. Mac, what would you say about cozying up to Elroy? See if he tells you anything."

Mac put his camera down and stopped filming. "Well, I don't know how we would document that in the show."

"To hell with the show!" Reid snapped. "I... WE need to get this thing solved so we can get the hell out of here. We don't seem to be making much progress at all so far; we need to try something new."

Mac shrugged. "I've tried talking to him a couple times already. But if you want, I can try again."

I smiled, looking at Mac, like a proud mother. Sometimes I tended to take the vigilante route to help get these cases solved. It wasn't because I cared about justice. It was because I was on a time schedule. Mac wouldn't admit it, but down deep I knew he was always jealous that he didn't get to go undercover. Now was his time to shine.

"Take a look and tell us what you think," Reid said to Mac, gesturing at the ceiling vent.

Mac placed his camera down and jumped up on the couch so he could get a closer look at the camera hidden in the vent. He pulled a small screw driver from his trusty fanny pack and removed the camera from its mount.

"No wires," Mac confirmed. "It's probably hooked to a wireless receiver. Maybe I can sneak in the control room while they're still filming to see what I can find."

"Sounds good," Reid confirmed.

Mac turned the camera over in his hands. "This is consumer grade. Nothing fancy. It probably cost a few hundred bucks." Mac opened a door on the camera. "There's no chip in here so it must be feeding somewhere else."

Mac handed the security camera to Reid and then jumped down from the couch. "Wish me luck," he said as he headed down the hall to the control room. Reid and Foxy followed while I stayed back to answer my phone, which was vibrating in my pocket.

"Hello?" I answered.

"Last night was amazing," Ginny said into the phone.

"Was it good for you too?" I teased.

"Bob and I couldn't stop talking about it. And we had sex too!"

"Did he cry?" I teased, knowing a little more about their weird sex life than most. He usually wept after sex, but we were not exactly sure why.

"No, he didn't!" Ginny exclaimed gleefully. "It was like totally normal sex! Oh Victoria, this was exactly what we needed. I asked for your help and you totally delivered!"

I couldn't help but smile. I wasn't used to getting compliments from my sister so this was especially nice. "Well, I'm glad you two had a good time."

"You have to take us to the next one. No Victoria, I'm not even joking. You have to."

"I don't know if there will be a next one, but if there is, I promise I will."

"How do we find that underground club again? Maybe Reid remembers the address?" Ginny asked hopefully.

I shrugged. "I don't think they usually have those parties at the same places. I think they move around."

"Can you ask Kyle? Honestly, Bob was dying over it. He called me three times today from work with guys from the office so that I could confirm that we really did go to an underground sex club. He was super stoked!"

I laughed to myself. Entertainment lawyers were a strange breed. Who brags about going to a sex club to their highly educated, law-abiding business colleagues?

"Did you and Reid finally hook up?" Ginny wanted to know.

"No," I frowned. "He got a little carried away on the dancefloor and then shamed himself into not closing the deal. But, tonight is the night. We're really going for it."

"It's about time. Wear sexy underwear tonight. And shave your legs. Good luck!"

I thanked her and hung up. I felt a pang of anxiety in my chest. Why was Ginny wishing me luck? Did I need it?

19.

I was heading outside to get a few breaths of fresh air when I heard voices coming from Vinnie's office. The door was slightly ajar and I peered in to see Carmine on the phone with Joy sitting on the corner of his desk. The caller was on speaker and Joy seemed to be giving Carmine guidance as to what he should say next.

"Yes, we're still continuing the filming despite the unfortunate incident with Lucky," Carmine was telling the caller.

Joy pressed the mute button on the phone and looked at Carmine. "Tell them how you think this will increase ratings – but don't sound like a jerk about it."

Carmine unmuted the phone and spoke towards it. "I think Lucky's death will help increase our ratings," Carmine recited.

Joy slapped his arm and whispered. "Sound sad!"

Carmine cleared his throat. "Um, I mean we feel terrible about what happened but it's bringing some media attention to our production over here. I believe it'll do very well in sweeps."

I watched the two of them from the doorway unnoticed. Joy's legs were crossed as she sat on the desk while Carmine was hunched over the phone. These two had a strange relationship – I still couldn't figure out who was in charge of it.

"How's the rewrite coming?" the person on the phone wanted to know.

Joy muted the phone again. "Make sure you tell him we're keeping Lucky in."

"Hello?" the person on the phone asked.

"Yeah, I'm here," Carmine confirmed. "Um, we've decided to keep Lucky in the show, you know to honor his memory, so we're just changing the script a little to say he got killed in space."

"No, no! You can't have him killed off. That won't work. Have him abducted by aliens or go back to Earth or something. No death, Carmine. That's too close to home."

Joy was nodding furiously while looking at Carmine. "Yes, you're right. I'll go talk to Vinnie right now. I'll talk to you later, Roger."

"Ciao."

Carmine ended the call and sprung up from his chair. I turned and ran, desperate not to get caught snooping outside his office. I fled into the kitchen where I came face to face with Elroy.

"What's the rush?" he asked me as I nearly knocked him over.

"Oh, they're filming and I didn't want to be seen in the shot," I lied. "I'm always getting in the way. You understand, you're in the industry."

"Yeah," Elroy agreed.

"So, um, what other types of camera work do you do?" I asked. I wasn't sure if Mac had made any progress in his investigation so I figured I might as well see what I could dig up.

"Mostly commercials. Some photography," Elroy answered.

"The cameras you use here are really big," I commented, sounding like a total bimbo. "We have to use small ones. Sometimes even really small ones mounted in the car dashboard. Do you ever use any like that?"

"Not for this type of work," Elroy answered. "The quality on those things is pretty low."

"Oh yeah? Like black and white or something?"

"No," Elroy corrected. "They can get a decent image, but not broadcast quality. Well, I guess your show thinks they're okay, but I wouldn't use them."

"Would you have any recommendations for cameras we should try?" I asked.

"Why don't you ask your cameraman? He was asking me these same kinds of questions a minute ago. Don't you guys even know anything about equipment?"

I frowned, feeling stupid. "Of course we do. I was just trying to make conversation, okay?"

Elroy threw up his hands and shrugged. "Whatever."

"Hey, Sharpe?" I heard Vinnie's voice call out from around the corner. "You've got a visitor."

Vinnie walked into the kitchen with Lenny in tow.

"Lenny, hi. What great timing," I said through clenched teeth. "Vinnie, this is my boss, Lenny."

"Yeah, we met obviously," Lenny told me. "He showed me around a little too. Quite an operation you've got here, Vinnie."

Vinnie smiled at the flattery. "Thanks. We try to do our best."

"The story about Lucky is big news," Lenny continued. "After Sharpe is done with the edit, it's going to be even bigger. Keep an eye on this girl. She may not look like much, but she can find a story."

"Uh, Lenny this is Elroy," I said, realizing he was still standing next to me. "He's the camera operator."

"Are you the killer?" Lenny joked. He was wearing a black short-sleeved polo shirt that looked like it had been worn a few times without being washed, and a pair of wrinkled khaki pants held up by a brown braided leather belt.

"I might be," Elroy answered. "These guys tell us the killer is among us."

I smiled. "Yeah, that's true. But we probably shouldn't discuss the case in front of Vinnie and Elroy, right Lenny?"

"Oh, sure." Lenny smiled. "I know the drill."

I led Lenny out of the room and over to the control room where the cops and my crew were huddled together. The room was small and crowded so we left the door open. "Guys, you know Lenny," I announced to Reid and Foxy.

"Hi guys, how's it going?" Lenny asked.

"There's that little pervert who likes to look at me," Rose said from outside the control room door. We all turned to see her staring at Lenny. She was referring to an incident in a hotel room at my sister's wedding where Lenny and I walked in on her lying nude on the hotel bed.

"Hummina-Hummina!" Lenny cooed as he stared at her. He walked over and extended a hand out to hers.

Rose didn't take the bait. Her standards in men were low, extremely low, but Lenny was too nasty for her to mess with. "I hope you appreciated the financial compensation we provided you," Lenny began. "There's more where that came from."

Reid shook his head in disbelief. "Did you just proposition her, man?"

Lenny seemed startled and confused. He said stupid things all the time, but he wasn't used to being called out for it. "Uh, I…"

"Prostitution isn't legal in this state," Reid continued. "I'd better not be witnessing you trying to solicit sex from this woman."

Rose looked up at Reid, smiling at his heroism in saving her from this evil pervert. In truth, Reid didn't give a damn about Rose or what she did with her body. Reid knew how much I disliked my boss, so he was taking the opportunity to put a scare into him.

"Um," Lenny continued to stumble, looking at Rose. "I didn't mean sex when I said that. I just meant that we appreciate your cooperation on the show."

Rose raised an eyebrow. "I deserve the money. A body like this will get great ratings for your show and you know it." She flaunted her boobs, pressing them together with both hands until a nipple sprouted out from the top like a little mouse peeking out from its hole.

"Huh." Lenny inhaled, barely able to maintain his breath at the sight.

Rose straightened up her body and tucked her nipple back into her top. Her gaze moved over to Reid. She gave him a wink and then turned to walk down the hallway.

Every encounter with that woman seemed to give me a visceral reaction. This one was no exception.

*****

Mac and I shared the details of our failed attempts at cozying up to Elroy. Foxy was squinting his eyes and staring at us intently. I wasn't sure if he was really listening or just holding in a fart.

Both Mac and I confirmed that Elroy wasn't giving up much information and that our exchanges with him had served only to paint us as complete incompetents.

We were standing outside of the empty control room gathered in an obvious huddle. "I want to take another look at that camera," Mac said. The dressing room was empty so Mac slipped inside. Instinctively, we all huddled closer now that one of the members of the circle had broken off.

"Maybe you guys should sneak in overnight to look around. You know when the rest of these people aren't here," Lenny suggested.

"We need a warrant for that," Foxy reprimanded. "We have to do this by the book. We're on TV after all."

"You said there aren't security cameras anywhere except the dressing room," Lenny said, sounding confused.

"Not that kind of TV, dude," Foxy said. "Your show. Your TV show."

"Are you guys talking about the cameras in the dressing rooms?" a voice from behind us asked.

We turned to see Craig standing there.

"Actually yeah," Foxy admitted.

"They're Vinnie's," Craig told us. "Sick shit likes to watch. Guess watching them on set isn't enough."

"You said cameras. There's more than one?" Foxy asked.

"He has two. But lately he just uses the one in the girl's dressing

201

room. Kyle has been hogging the other one and Vinnie doesn't like watching guys."

"Do the girls know about the cameras?" Foxy asked.

"Yeah, everybody knows. Vinnie isn't shy about his fetishes."

Lenny nodded. "A man after my own heart."

*****

We burst into Vinnie's office, cameras blazing, ready to demand answers. We found him hunched over his computer screen typing, while Carmine sat at his desk, nursing his thermos and reading the newspaper.

"You've got some explaining to do, Vinnie," Reid told him with Foxy right behind him.

Vinnie looked up, shocked at the interruption. "What are you talking about?"

"You failed to mention the camera you have running in the room where Lucky was murdered," Reid chided. "Don't you think that detail would have been helpful to our investigation?"

Vinnie looked sheepish. "Uh, yeah, you're right. But that was an accident. I haven't looked at those tapes in a while. I guess I forgot."

"Where are they?" Reid demanded.

"Where are what?"

"The tapes, jerk," Reid barked.

Vinnie looked confused. "What are you talking about, tapes? What are you, in 1980 or something?"

"You said tapes," Reid told him sounding frustrated. "You just said you haven't looked at the *tapes* in a while."

"That's a figure of speech," Vinnie informed him.

"The source!" Foxy yelled. "Where does the footage feed to?"

"Oh." Vinnie swiveled his chair around to look at a large bookcase that was directly behind his desk. He fumbled around, removing some books until a safe was revealed. Vinnie popped open the safe and inside we saw a small monitor. The screen was black. "Did you turn the camera off?" Vinnie asked.

"Yeah, we turned it off," Foxy answered, holding the camera out in his hand to show Vinnie.

"Okay, well, when it's turned on I get a feed in here," Vinnie explained. "It's motion-detected so it only turns on if someone is moving around."

Foxy pressed the power button on the camera and we soon saw an image of us in the monitor, standing in Vinnie's office. Foxy waved his hand in front of the camera to make sure it was live – it was.

"Were you watching your monitor the night Lucky was murdered?" Reid asked.

"No!" Vinnie shot back. "I told you, I wasn't even here."

"Were the tapes rolling?"

"They're not tapes!" Vinnie insisted. "Do you see your camera guy switching out tapes? No! It records to a chip."

Reid grabbed the security camera out of Foxy's hand. "How do you play the *chip*?"

"You want to watch this now?" Vinnie asked. "The network just gave me a bunch of rewrites to do."

"Now!" Reid boomed.

Vinnie leaned over and popped a chip from a box that was attached to the monitor. He opened the camera door and placed the chip inside. Reid pressed play on the camera and we all leaned in, but the screen was way too tiny for all of us to see.

"Hang on," Lenny interrupted. "Mac, can you plug into this thing? We need a better image for our edit."

Reid shook his head. I knew exactly what he was thinking. *Damn television producers.* Lenny was possibly even more annoying than I was.

"Sometimes I go in the control room to watch," Vinnie shared, glancing at his brother. "It's a little more private."

We all exited Vinnie's office and marched down the hall towards the control room.

Lenny didn't seem to know what to do with himself, so he stuck to my side. "Is Vinnie wearing a mic?" Lenny whispered in my ear.

I shook my head and pointed to the boom that Manny was holding in the air.

"We really need clean sound here. This could be a big breakthrough," he whispered.

I tried not to let him see my frustration, but it was hard to miss. I placed my finger over my lips signaling Lenny to be quiet. When we reached the control room, we all piled in, closing the door behind us. Vinnie sat down and began hooking up the camera to the big monitor. "You can really see a lot of detail this way," he smirked.

"How often do you watch these tapes?" Foxy wanted to know.

Vinnie shrugged. "Usually once a week, on Fridays when everyone goes home."

"You said you haven't watched them in a while," Reid countered.

Vinnie shrugged. "I just said that for Carmine's sake. He doesn't like this stuff."

I looked at the chair Vinnie was sitting in and then the garbage can below his legs. Were there used tissues in there? I shuddered to think what he did in this room.

"How much footage can this thing hold?" Foxy asked.

"A few days. Just depends on how much motion is in there."

"And then what happens?" Foxy asked.

"I usually wipe it clean on Fridays, after my... session. And then I record again. If it runs out of space before the next week it doesn't really matter. There's usually plenty to look at."

"Play it," Foxy ordered.

Vinnie fired up the camera and skipped back in time for a bit. As he scanned he saw a blurry image of two people kissing on the couch. "Is that

Lucky?" Foxy asked hopefully. Vinnie stopped rewinding and pressed play. A green and grainy image played on the big screen.

Instantly my cheeks flushed as I realized we were watching Reid and I kissing madly on the couch. I was straddled over his lap rubbing myself all over him. I gasped sharply while Reid placed his hand over the screen.

"Jesus Christ. Can we ever get some privacy?" Reid snapped.

It was true. Nearly every near-sexual encounter Reid and I had was either captured on video or witnessed by someone live. Tonight we would have to remember to double lock the doors.

"Keep going!" Reid scolded. "This was from today. Go back further!"

Vinnie raised an eyebrow and looked over at me. "Well, well."

"Just rewind it!" Reid yelled.

I knew Lenny was staring at me, but I refused to make eye contact. If he gave me another speech about how participants were not our friends I was going to scream.

Vinnie scanned back further. There was timecode embedded on the visual so it was pretty easy to try to pinpoint the exact day and time. There was no audio on the camera, just video. Vinnie scrolled back to the afternoon of the crime and we saw the usual hustle and bustle of actresses and actors coming in and out, undressing and dressing. Lucky was among them and it was eerie to watch him joking around with the girls and flexing his stomach muscles in the mirror, knowing he was going to die that night. I looked over at Lenny. We both knew this was going to make for an amazing edit.

At around six-thirty, Lucky left the dressing room and turned off the lights. We sat attentively, waiting for what would come next. We were about to see Lucky get killed and I needed to brace myself for it. There was black for a minute or two and then the camera went into hibernation mode, conserving memory in the absence of motion.

The next image that came on was the lights flicking on in the room and Lucky lying dead on the couch, just as we had found him. There was no audio, but by the way Rose was jumping and shaking it was obvious she was screaming. Next, we saw Vinnie run in and start screaming as well.

Vinnie looked up a Reid, alarmed.

Reid pressed pause on the camera. "Well, isn't that convenient. Seems the camera didn't record during the entire murder. Are you telling me there was no motion in the room that whole time?"

There was sweat beading on Vinnie's forehead and he looked like he was going to faint. He shook his head in disbelief. "I don't know what could have happened."

"Oh, save it," Reid barked.

Vinnie looked over at Foxy, then at the crew, and then me. "No, I'm serious. I swear I don't know anything about this. I didn't do anything to that footage, I swear!"

"You erased it, didn't you? After you murdered Lucky to boost your ratings!" Reid screamed. The control room was small and hot and the sounds of raised voices were amplified in the space.

"No, that isn't true! Please, you have to believe me. I know how bad this looks, but I didn't do this. Come on, do you really think I'd be stupid enough to leave the camera in there if I knew it recorded the murder?"

"Maybe that's why you never told us about it," Foxy chimed in.

"No, I have a lot on my mind. I just didn't think of it. I forgot about. I really did."

"You're a liar!" Reid screamed.

Vinnie gripped his chest. "Oh my God, I think I'm having a heart attack."

I raised my eyebrows and looked at Manny. This was a first.

"All right, calm down, calm down!" Foxy told him. He turned to us. "Everybody out, give him some space."

"No way, buddy. This is too good," Lenny told him.

"Out!" Reid bellowed, pointing his finger at the door.

Mac placed his camera on a table behind the three men and turned on the camera's microphone. Then we all shuffled out to give the men some "privacy."

*****

Twenty minutes later, the door opened and Vinnie emerged, a flustered and sweaty mess. Reid and Foxy stayed behind in the control room while Vinnie shuffled past us towards the set, avoiding eye contact.

Reid stood in the doorway. "Mac, can you come in here for a minute?"

Mac nodded and did as he was told and the rest of us filed in after him. Lenny, my constant shadow stood six inches away from me as we listened to Reid and Mac talk. I could smell Lenny's body odor – a mixture of heavy perfume and rancid eggs.

"Do you think you can tell if this thing was tampered with?" Reid wanted to know.

"Yeah," Mac confirmed, sitting down to take a look.

"Mac, you'd better give your hands a good wash after this," I told him.

Mac looked up at me and smiled, then pulled a wet wipe out of the fanny pack wrapped around his waist. "I've got it covered, Sharpe," he assured me.

Mac toggled back and forth on the video, watching the time code, looking for jumps. I reached for Mac's camera and knowing it was still recording, picked it up and filmed the screen over his shoulder. "We should have this digitized," Mac said. "There might be a hit here, but I can't tell."

"What do you mean a hit?" Foxy asked.

"A digital hit – a glitch where someone erased the tape. On this crappy camera I can't toggle very well, but if we load it into our editing software we can get down to a fraction of a second."

Suddenly I had a great idea. "Lenny, you have to go back to the office, right? Maybe you could bring this tape with you?"

"Yeah, the sooner the better," Reid added. "This could crack this case wide open."

Lenny beamed, thrilled at the chance to actually do something useful. "Yeah, I could do that. I can put my best editor on it."

"Thanks man," Reid said, handing Lenny the camera.

We all stood together quietly staring at Lenny, waiting for him to leave. "Oh, now?"

Reid nodded. "That's what I meant when I said *the sooner, the better.* But thanks for stopping by."

"Sharpe, maybe you should take it and I can keep things under control around here," Lenny suggested.

"But I live in the Valley and you live right by the office. It's on your way, but for me it's like an hour out of my way."

I could see the wheels turning in Lenny's brain as he searched for some reason to stay. This was like an adult playground for him, complete with Rose and her nipples. But alas his small mind didn't return any good ideas. "Okay then. See you later," Lenny announced, before turning and exiting the control room.

"Mac, maybe we can do a quick interview?" I suggested.

"Yeah," Mac said, grabbing the camera from me and pointing it at Reid and Foxy who were both sitting in chairs in front of the monitor. They swiveled their seats so we could see their faces and Manny held his boom up overhead.

"Can you tell me what happened after we left the room?" I asked.

Foxy raised his hand, signaling that he would answer the question. "Vinnie was showing a lot of signs of stress. He was sweating and breathing heavy and threatening that his heart was attacking him."

"His heart was attacking him?" Reid asked.

"Sharpe, let me try that again," Foxy said. "Okay. Vinnie is certainly a possible suspect at this time. The tape he showed us appears to have been tampered with, and the fact he was sweating and very nervous is a possible sign that he knows more than he is letting on."

"Do you think Vinnie had motive?"

"Vinnie's possible motive was television ratings. But there could have been something else going in beneath the surface that we don't know yet."

"Did anyone else know about the camera?" I asked.

Foxy looked over at Reid, letting him take this one.

"Vinnie claims that no one knew about the camera, but of course we know that isn't true. Craig, the production assistant knew about it and he indicated that others did as well. Plus, Carmine obviously knew about it. If that footage was erased, and it seems like it was, then there are a number of people that may have known to do it."

"Would they know how?" I asked.

"That's a good question," Reid conceded. "I wouldn't know how to erase a portion of a chip, just the whole thing. It's probably not that hard but we should consider who had the right skills. Elroy, for example, would certainly know how."

"What about Enrique, the sound guy?" I asked.

"Come on, Sharpe," Manny said to me. "Get real."

"We should be considering everyone," Reid offered.

"And what about Rose?" Foxy said to his partner. "She's late for everything, yet on the morning of the murder she's one of the first to show up on set?"

Reid nodded. "Fair point. Plus, there's the lie she's feeding us about George, which doesn't add up. I'm not buying that she met him at the club for the first time."

"So, who's next?" I asked the cops.

"Elroy," they answered in unison.

20.

The cops were running out of unique ways to approach Elroy so they decided to go with the "gotcha" approach. Elroy was in his favorite place – the kitchen, getting a cup of coffee when Reid and Foxy charged in with me and my crew trailing behind them.

"Were you aware that there were hidden cameras in the dressing rooms?" Reid demanded.

Elroy choked on his coffee as he turned to face the barrage of people now confronting him. "Uh, hi, Elroy, how are you today? Maybe try that approach first?"

Reid smirked. "I don't need tips from you on how to do my job. Did you know about the camera or not?"

Elroy looked away. "Yes, I did. But Vinnie liked to pretend no one knew."

"You had cameras rolling during a murder. Don't you think that would be important to mention?" Reid snapped.

Elroy looked from Reid to Foxy. "I fully intended to tell you about the camera when you came to talk to me."

"Have you already watched the tape?" Foxy wanted to know.

Elroy scrunched his eyebrows. "Of course not. And what do you mean by tape?"

"Chip, digital video, whatever!" Foxy corrected. "Well, we watched it. We saw everything, including the portions that were erased."

"What's that supposed to mean?" Elroy wanted to know.

Foxy smiled. "Sometimes it helps to have friends in the film biz. My crew here knows how to recover footage that has been tampered with."

Elroy smiled, almost looking sorry for the cops. "Are you talking about these two? I'm sorry to burst your bubble but they don't know their ass from their elbows when it comes to equipment. They were asking me for tips!"

"Hey!" I snapped, breaking the invisible wall, as usual. "We were just saying that to see if you would slip up."

"Oh, so now you have a TV crew doing your police work?" Elroy asked Foxy.

"Why don't you tell us your whereabouts the night before Lucky was killed?" Reid said.

Elroy leaned against the countertop of the kitchenette and settled in, ready to talk. He took a slow sip on his coffee before he answered. I looked over at Mac who was racking focus on Elroy's face. Something told me this footage would come in handy later. We might have to analyze it for obvious "tells" in his mannerisms. It could help us determine if he was lying. "I cleaned up my equipment on Monday night like I usually do and then headed home."

"Was anyone here when you left?" Foxy asked.

Elroy thought about that. "I don't think so. I'm usually the last to leave, unless Vinnie is sticking around to watch his tapes, but that's usually just on Fridays."

"So, Vinnie wasn't here that night?"

"No, he left after we wrapped."

"What about Carmine or Joy? Were they here?" Foxy asked.

"No, I was the last one."

"What time did you leave?"

"Maybe like seven-thirty?"

"When you went to your car in the parking lot, were there any other cars there?" Foxy asked.

"No," Elroy confirmed.

"And you have a key to lock up?" Reid asked.

Elroy scratched his neck for a while until it was red and irritated. "You don't need a key. Just the alarm code. You lock the door from the inside and pull it shut."

"Who else has the code?" Reid asked.

Elroy raised his eyebrows. "The code is 1-2-3-4. I think any idiot can remember that. Even Vinnie."

"And did you set the alarm when you left?"

"Yes," Elroy confirmed.

"You know we can check if the alarm was armed or not. In fact, we did check and it wasn't turned on. Are you sure you set it?" Reid asked.

Elroy shrugged. "Maybe I forgot."

"Do you agree with your employer's decision to film women as they change in their dressing room?" Reid asked.

"No, I don't."

"Have you ever watched the tapes?" Foxy wanted to know.

"Sure," Elroy admitted. "The first time I walked in on Vinnie in the control room I saw what he was watching."

"And how did he react when you caught him?"

"He offered me a hundred bucks to keep my mouth shut. Then he asked me if I wanted to watch too. I said yes to both."

"And what did you see on the video?"

"Rose getting undressed. The stupid thing was that Vinnie gave me the hundred bucks not to tell her, but she already knew. The way she was playing to the camera, she totally knew."

"Was this before or after you had sex with Rose?" Reid asked directly.

Elroy looked caught off guard and began scratching his neck again. "Before," he finally answered.

"And was this before or after you and Penny slept together?" Reid asked.

Elroy looked confused. "Who told you that? Penny and I aren't sleeping together."

"You're not? The way you follow her around, I just assumed you two were an item," Reid challenged.

Elroy's eyes narrowed. "If I follow her around it's because I'm protective of her. Lucky was her boyfriend and now he's dead. I'm just trying to be a friend."

"Okay, you're not sleeping with Penny. Would you like to be?"

Elroy tried to step backwards but he was literally backed into a corner in the tiny kitchenette. "Penny is a beautiful woman, inside and out. I enjoy her company very much."

"So then yes is the answer?" Foxy asked.

Elroy shook his head. "If Penny wanted to pursue a relationship with me I'd be open to it."

"Where did you go after you left on Monday night?" Reid asked.

"I went home. There's a series on the History channel that I like, so I got some Chinese food and went home to watch it."

"Where do you get your Chinese?" Foxy asked.

"Manchu Kitchen. It's in Studio City."

"Yeah, that place is good. What did you order?"

"The General Tso's chicken."

"Yeah, that's a nice choice. I like their sesame beef," Foxy said.

Elroy stared blankly at him, not caring. What a poker face he had!

"Don't let Penny know you eat like that, Roy," Foxy offered. "She's a health nut."

"It's Elroy. Not Roy."

"Can anyone verify you were home that night? Do you have a roommate?" Reid asked.

"Nope. You'll just have to trust me. Maybe a neighbor saw me or something. I live in an apartment complex."

"Write down your address for me," Foxy said, handing him a pad.

"Has Vinnie ever asked for your help erasing the chips on the hidden cameras? It seems like it'd be a hard thing for him to figure out."

"If you or your *crew* knew anything about cameras you could figure it out. You just hit erase data. It's the same on a digital camera. I don't know if he erased them or just put in a new chip each week. You'd have to ask Vinnie."

"And what were you doing the morning Lucky was found dead?"

"Sleeping, I guess. I came to the set around nine and started prepping the equipment."

"So, when you got here he was already dead. You didn't go in the dressing room?"

"The women's dressing room? Why would I?"

"I guess there's no reason if you have a camera rolling in there anyway, right?" Foxy commented.

Elroy narrowed his eyes. "You'd have to ask Vinnie about that."

*****

"I heard you talking about me." Penny said from around the corner of the break room when we finally let Elroy get back to work. "You think Elroy and I are an item. Don't you?"

"Are you?" Foxy asked.

We were all still mulling around the kitchen so it was easy for Mac to whip his camera around to record Penny.

"No," Penny said with conviction. "I have no interest in Elroy. I've tried to make that very clear to him. As you know, Lucky and I were involved. He was my sole focus."

"But you weren't his sole focus, were you?" Reid asked.

A flash of anger crossed Penny's face. "I know you think that everyone here is promiscuous because we work in this business, but that simply isn't true. I'd suggest you stop judging us from the surface."

"Kyle told us he got to third base with you," Reid countered. "That's the oral sex one, right?"

Penny glared at Reid. "If you need me to explain to you what third base is, then you have bigger problems than I thought."

"I'll take that as a yes to you and Belamy. What about Lucky and Joy? Were they seeing each other too?"

"I'm not stupid, detective. I know what you're trying to do."

"What's that?"

"You're trying to craft some story about how I was jealous of Lucky having other relationships so I killed him."

"It does fit pretty well. It's usually the wife that kills the husband anyway, right?"

"Sorry to disappoint you. Kyle and I got together way before Lucky and I did."

"Way before? Haven't you been filming for like a week?"

"We've been doing this for three weeks actually. Days in production are like years in the real world. Ask your girlfriend over there – she can tell you. There's a different kind of bond and intimacy that happens on set." She glared at Reid. "Know what I mean, detective?"

*****

"These guys are getting pretty aggressive with us," Foxy commented to Reid when it was all over.

"I think we're wearing out our welcome," Reid agreed.

"Vinnie is probably getting in their ears too. We should have solved this by now. Instead, we're just spinning in circles."

We were all sitting around a table in the break room plotting our next steps while everyone else was filming on set. Foxy had a notepad out on the table and he was writing down the various times that different actions occurred. I asked Mac and Manny to roll while I stepped back and the guys talked.

"Okay, the night of the murder," Foxy began. "We've got Joy saying she left around seven, Carmine saying he left after her and that he was the last to leave."

"And he said that he put the alarm on, which he didn't," Reid added.

Foxy nodded, writing down the times and suspects. "Then we have Elroy who claims he was the last person to leave around seven-thirty, and he also claims he set the alarm."

"And Vinnie said he disabled the alarm Tuesday morning. There's something weird about this alarm thing," Reid said. "Let's go check it out."

We followed the cops as they walked out the front door of the building and onto the sidewalk. Reid turned to his partner. "Elroy said it was 1-2-3-4, right?"

"Yeah," Foxy agreed.

Reid punched the code into the alarm panel while we stood back filming and watching. He turned the door knob and the door opened. "That didn't work," Reid said. "Let me try again." He tried again and once more the door opened easily with no alarm going off. Reid lifted up the alarm panel and found that it easily pulled from the nail that was holding it against the wall. He examined it.

"One of the wires is cut," he told us as Mac rushed in to get a shot of the cut wire. "They may have thought they were setting the alarm, but they weren't." He frowned.

I looked over at Mac who was filming the scene standing on one foot again, trying to maintain a steady balance.

Foxy walked over and looked at the cut wire. "Yeah, this thing's busted all right." Foxy pulled out his notepad again. "So, the alarm stays off all night. The timecode on the video stops around 6.30 p.m. and then doesn't restart until the next morning. So, we know the murder happened after 6.30 at night. Lou gave the time of death between 6 and 8 a.m."

"Then we have Rose discovering the body at 9.30 in the morning," Reid added. "Elroy said he arrived around nine. Vinnie got in closer to eight. Penny said she got there around that time too, but didn't check the dressing room. She was meditating."

"I think we should pay George another visit," Foxy offered. "I think he knows more than he's letting on."

"That's a good idea," Reid told Foxy. "Let's do that tomorrow."

"Okay," Foxy said, confused. "Then who do you want to talk to next?"

Reid looked at his watch. "I don't know. I'm thinking we should call it a day. Last night was a late one and the crew has to catch up on their hours off anyway."

My crew was still filming but looked pleased by Reid's suggestion.

Foxy scrunched his eyebrows together. "Dude, it's not even five o'clock."

"Yeah, I know, but I want to give Vinnie a little space here. Like you said, we're wearing out our welcome. Maybe we give them a break."

"Give them a break? They're cracking. This is the time to put on the pressure, Reid."

Reid shrugged. "I think we can put the pressure on tomorrow."

"Okay, so why not go to George's house then?" Foxy asked. Reid was the type to work all night and this behavior wasn't normal.

I tried to hide a smile as I listened to Reid try to convince his partner that breaking early tonight was the right thing to do. I knew why he was doing it. "I just feel like I need some time to regroup. Get my head together, you know?"

Foxy looked at his partner and then over at me. I was trying to suppress my grin. Suddenly Foxy broke into a big smile. "Get your head together, huh? Which head we talking about?"

Reid turned to look at my crew and clapped his hands together. "Okay guys, let's meet back here tomorrow at nine, okay?"

No one was going to argue. We all broke off, heading back inside to clean up, leaving Foxy standing alone, dumbfounded.

Inside, as I collected my things, I saw Manny talking to Rose in the hallway. She was leaning against the wall, flirting with him, and Manny was whispering to her in Spanish. I smiled. At least he was persistent.

I walked to my car out front with Reid following behind me. His ugly black Mustang was parked right behind my car. I felt Reid's hand reach for mine, pulling my back towards him. He leaned in, pressing his chest against my back and mouth against my ear. "Are we still on for tonight?"

I smiled, not facing him. "I don't know," I teased. "There's this show on the History channel I really wanted to watch. Elroy told me about it." I turned to face him, smiling.

Reid placed his arms around me, bringing me closer to him in an embrace. "Well, I was planning to clean my air conditioning vents. But if you came over, maybe you could convince me to do something else."

I smiled. "I can try. Let me go home and get changed first. I want to wear something more conducive to *vent cleaning*."

"Honey, you don't need to worry about clothes. I prefer to clean naked."

I blushed. "Just give me a chance to freshen up. The musty smell of this place is sticking to me. I'll meet you at your place in an hour?"

Reid kissed my neck and I felt goose bumps everywhere. "I'll be waiting."

I stood there for a moment, having trouble disengaging. Finally, I took a deep breath. "I'll see you soon."

*****

My hand felt a little shaky as I knocked on Reid's door. It had been a long time since I had been with a guy and even though Reid and I had come close many times, the finality of the situation was giving me nervous knots.

Reid opened the door after the first knock and stood in front of me wearing jeans and a black T-shirt. He smiled at me. "Hi."

"Hi," I smiled back.

Reid stepped back out of the doorway to make room for me to enter. "Come in."

I dropped my purse on the side table next to one of his couch, having been to his place many times before. I was wearing a simple black dress that was loose against my body and wouldn't leave any unflattering indentations on my skin.

"Are you hungry?" Reid asked, heading towards the kitchen. I followed him as he opened his fridge. "I have some leftovers in here."

"No, I'm not hungry," I told him.

"How about a beer?" Reid asked, pulling one out of the fridge for me and unscrewing the top.

I shook my head. "Nah, I'm good."

Reid looked down at the beer he had just popped open and placed it on the counter, untouched. He looked over at me, examining my dress. "You look pretty. Beautiful I mean." Reid smiled awkwardly. "We're in our thirties so we have to use adult words, right?"

I took in a deep breath, trying to calm my nerves.

"I told Foxy not to call me tonight. If anything happens he has to handle it on his own. And I turned my phone off." Reid smiled.

"Mine is in my purse," I said, motioning to my bag on the side table. "On vibrate. What about the front door? Did you lock it?"

Reid nodded. "I used the deadbolt."

"Then I guess we're all alone."

"No interruptions." Reid took my hand and led me quietly down the hallway and into his bedroom. I half expected him to throw me against the wall in a blind display of passion, but he didn't. I wouldn't have minded, but instead he moved with me to the bed and we sat, side-by-side.

Reid leaned towards me and placed his hand on my cheek and pulled me in to meet his lips. His kiss was slow, tender, and soft. I was still feeling the jitters, until he moved his lips over mine, taking my whole mouth inside of his. I felt his tongue tickle my lips and then slip inside my mouth for a long deep kiss. I felt a surge of heat rush through me as he kissed me. I felt myself wanting to fall back onto the bed, but he held me still, placing his other hand behind my head to keep me steady. He kissed me over and over again until my head was swirling and all the nerves had disappeared. I ran my fingers through his hair and over his chest all while he continued to kiss me in a way that made me feel dizzy.

I couldn't think about work, or my family or even what day it was. I was barely aware of where I was. All I could focus on was the rush of emotions I felt cycling through me. I wanted to be with him, I wanted him to be with me, but I felt immobile, like I had forgotten how to move. I was putty in his hands with his spell cast over me.

Reid gently guided me down to the bed and I fell down on my back with Reid lying next to me, perched on his side, looking down at me. I kicked off my shoes while he fumbled with the buttons on my dress. It was one of those dresses with buttons all the way down the front – easy access.

After unbuttoning me, Reid pushed the dress to the side, revealing a black lace bra I had worn for the occasion. He barely acknowledged the bra, instead pushing it aside to access my breast hidden below. He took it in his mouth and as his tongue began to dance around my nipple my back arched.

"I finally have you where I want you," he murmured as he pecked and nipped at my breast. His hand came across me and down to my buttocks where he pulled me towards him, taking more and more of me in his mouth.

I reached for his shirt, helping him to pull it up over his head, revealing that hard and solid body that I had grown so accustomed to. It was mine for the taking. He was mine. This gorgeous sexy man was in bed with me, lusting after me, desiring me. It was enough to make me swoon.

I ran my fingers across his chest and over the muscles in his upper arms. They were strong, reliable, and trustworthy. They were a part of exactly the kind of man I had been searching for.

Reid moved his hands down to my panties and expertly pulled them down my legs. I reached over to his pants and unbuttoned his jeans, then pulled down the zipper. Now the only thing separating us was his cotton boxers and my bra which was half-off already.

We laid on our sides and let our bodies touch, my breasts pushing against his pectorals, his erection pushing against my flesh. We kissed again. We kissed as if we couldn't get enough of each other. As if this kiss was the last one we would ever have. Our bodies were talking to each other, sending a strong message, but we stayed with lips locked, enjoying the pleasure we were experiencing. I felt as if we had forever. As if I could kiss him like this all night and not mind at all. The phones were off – the distractions were away and we were taking our time and savoring the moment.

I reached down to pull off Reid's boxer shorts and take hold of his swollen member. I didn't feel scared or shy; I felt like I wanted to do everything I could to make this man happy. As I moved my hand across him Reid cried out almost in a whimper, a sound I had never heard him make before. He pulled back from me and stared at me looking bashful.

"Victoria, you've had me on edge for a while now. I don't think I can let you do that right now or I may explode."

I looked down at my hand on him and smiled. "Okay, so what should we do then?"

Reid smiled and pushed me on my back. He pulled off my bra and kissed me all over, starting with my breasts and then working his way down to my stomach and then lower. My eyes opened wide as I felt his tongue slip inside of me. "I can't touch you, but you can do this to me?" I asked him breathlessly.

I heard Reid laugh as he licked and stroked and brought me to climax. When he was finished I heard him fumbling around in his side drawer looking for a condom while I laid on my back, legs spread, ready for more.

As he entered me I felt a rush through my entire body. A surge of energy and pulse and pleasure. I cried out and Reid did as well, enjoying the sensation. We had wanted this for so long and now it was happening I wondered why I had ever bothered to wait.

Reid moved slowly inside of me, trying to keep his body under control from releasing too soon. He filled me well and felt amazing every time he moved back and forth inside of me. I gripped my arms around his shoulders, feeling another rush of heat as he moved faster and harder until my teeth were clenched and I could barely see.

"Honey, I can't hold out any longer," Reid told me.

"Neither can I," I assured him as he thrust himself in me, letting out a huge gasp of relief.

As his body let go, my body shuttered from the aftershocks. My eyes were closed and I saw visions of sunlight and stars in my eyes as they pulsed and exalted from his energy. I felt Reid's body go limp over mine and I wrapped my arms around him.

He found a comfortable spot in the crook of my neck and rested his head on me, breathing heavily and deeply. "Aw honey, I love you."

With the words, my eyes snapped open, suddenly bringing my full attention and awareness to the present moment. Did he just say what I thought he said?

Reid kissed my neck. "That was amazing."

I smiled. "Yes, it was," I said truthfully.

Reid pulled his head up, looked at me, and smiled. "Ready for round two?"

21.

I woke up lying on the right side of Reid's bed, hugging the edge of the mattress. My sister used to tease me that no matter how big the bed was, I was always hanging off the side. As my eyes fluttered open, the memories of where I was came flooding back. I looked at the wall, which was white and shadowed by the blinds that were closed over the windows. There was a small amount of light streaming in telling me it was morning, but whether that meant 6 a.m. or 10 a.m. I wasn't sure.

I listened for a while, not moving, trying to figure out if Reid was awake or not. It wasn't like this was a one-night stand or anything but the morning-after still had the potential of being awkward. Last night we had learned so much about each other. He had been inside of me. I had touched him everywhere. We were different now. Plus, there were those three words he uttered that were sticking in my brain.

Was it possible that he was in love with me? Was it possible that I was in love with him? If I thought about what we did the night before, I didn't think I would call it "sex." "Making love" was probably a more accurate description. I did feel a strong connection to him last night. I expected there to be passion between us, as it had been building up for weeks, but that wasn't what it turned out to be. The passion was there, of course, but what I didn't expect was the tenderness. Last night when I walked in the door, I expected him to tear my clothes off. And I would have been okay with that, as I was ready for it. But Reid seemed to have a different type of evening in mind. He was careful, he was gentle, and he wasn't in a rush. He turned what was supposed to be a night of animalistic sex, into a night of passionate love. Maybe that's why Reid said what he said. Not because he was in-love with me, but because he was swept up in the moment.

I felt Reid's strong arm flop over me and then pull me by the waist across the bed towards him. "You always sleep that far away?" he asked me, nibbling at my neck.

"Yes actually," I smiled. "Don't take it personally. I like living on the edge."

"So I've noticed."

I turned around to look at my sleepy-eyed boyfriend. He had a goofy grin and a relaxed look on his face that made me feel like I must have done something right.

"How did you sleep?" I asked him.

"Like a baby. Best sleep since I've been dating you." Reid smiled. "Most nights I can't sleep because I'm too busy thinking about you. But last night I found you in my dreams."

I smiled demurely. "Did the reality live up to the fantasy?"

"Oh yeah." Reid nodded then leaned in to kiss me. "Did you enjoy yourself?" Reid asked, pulling back and looking into my eyes.

"Couldn't you tell?" I smiled.

"It has been way too long since I've done that," Reid laughed. "But it was worth the wait."

"Did you read a text book on the right things to say the morning after?" I asked him.

"Why am I doing well?"

"I'd say pretty close to perfect. Now you just have to talk about my body and how you've never been with a sexier woman in your life," I smiled. "Even if that's a lie, you should say it."

"I've never been with a sexier woman in my life," Reid repeated. "You've ruined me. I can't be with anyone other than you now."

Honestly, I liked the sound of that. I smiled and leaned in and gave him a kiss. "What time is it anyway?" I asked.

Reid sighed deeply. "It's eight-thirty. We told the crew we'd be in around nine."

"Oh, then we'd better get up!" I said, jumping up.

"We can save time if we shower together," Reid said with a sinister grin. "Have you ever done it in the shower before?"

"Of course I have," I replied. "I'm not a prude, you know. I was just waiting for the right moment with you, until the feelings were real." As I said the words I wished I could pull them back in. I wasn't ready for a conversation about feelings right now. I smiled. "But I've never done it in the shower with you."

Reid smiled and pointed towards his bedroom door. "Lead the way."

*****

There was something about a new relationship coupled with some good sex that made me smile. I should have been tired as we were up most of the night. But this morning I was feeling grand. The only thing gnawing at me were those three little words that Reid had said to me. Why did he have to say them? I should have been basking in the glow of my many orgasms, not trying to psycho-analyze Reid.

We drove to the set in different cars and arrived only slightly late at ten o'clock. Reid had been wrong about how showering together would make things go faster. It actually had the opposite effect.

We arrived within seconds of each other, both electing to park our cars out front behind Mac's *Cock Hunters* rental SUV. As I walked towards the building Reid grabbed my hand and pulled me back towards him for a quick kiss on the neck. "I'm gonna be thinking about you all day," he whispered in my ear. "But we have to play it cool."

"I know," I told him. In reality, the entire crew totally knew what we did last night. Reid had told Foxy not to call him, we were both arriving on set late at the same time, plus we were in very good moods.

As we entered the building we walked by Vinnie and Carmine's office. Carmine was sitting in his chair with Joy sitting on the corner of the desk attending to him.

We popped inside to say hello. "Morning," Reid said to them.

Joy was hunched over towards Carmine, but she straightened up when we entered. "Oh good, you're here again," she said sarcastically. "You know this investigation is starting to become a nuisance."

"Yeah, it's a real pain when someone you work with is murdered on the job. Totally gets in the way, right?" Reid goaded.

Joy squared her eyes at him. "You know what I mean. We're against tight deadlines here and poor Carmine is stressed beyond belief."

I looked over at Carmine who was nursing his all-too-familiar thermos. Why this guy who did basically nothing all day was stressed, was beyond me.

"Perhaps if people started cooperating with this investigation we could expedite things," Reid chastised.

"We've cooperated," Carmine snapped.

"Oh yeah? What about the camera in the dressing rooms. Did you forget about that detail? Your brother sure did," Reid asked.

Reid looked at Carmine's face and then Joy's, trying to read their reactions. Joy reacted first by scrunching her nose. "What cameras?"

The dialogue going back and forth was good and I was frustrated that my crew wasn't there to capture it. I debated pulling out my smartphone to do some recording but the quality would be too low and it would be weird.

"Vinnie was recording you girls in the dressing room and then masturbating to the footage every Friday night." Reid smiled as he dropped that piece of information like a bomb on the table.

Joy's eyes shot open in surprise while Carmine didn't even flinch.

Behind us Craig walked in. "Joy, they need you on set."

"Oh. Yeah, sure," Joy said and walked past us and out of the room.

I couldn't tell if Joy was finding out about these cameras for the first time now or if she was delivering her finest acting performance. Craig had said everyone knew about the cameras. Joy wasn't doing herself any favors by lying to us.

*****

"I missed you at the beach this morning," Foxy said to us when we found him on set.

"Huh?" Reid asked absently.

"We were supposed to meet at the beach to check out Jason's alibi. I would have called you but you told me not to."

Reid shook his head. "I totally forgot. I'm sorry, man."

Foxy smiled. "It's okay. I talked to his buddies who corroborated his story. So, did you two have a nice time last night?" Foxy asked with a big grin.

"Knock it off," Reid shot back, but not in his usual way. He was trying to suppress a smile, which was really cute.

"Come on, just give me a nibble. Give me something. Sharpe, you can never keep a secret. Was it good? It must have been to make my partner's brain go to mush."

I looked down, trying to hide my smile.

"That'll do. I'll take that!" Foxy laughed. "Good job, partner," he said patting Reid on the back.

Reid laughed. "Glad to have your support, Foxy."

Reid was acting differently this morning for sure. He wasn't doing his usual tough-cop modus operandi. He was relaxed and easy. I wanted to go over to him and wrap my arms around him, but I couldn't.

Penny and Kyle were engaged in a "weightless" love-making scene, which was going horribly wrong. Penny was flexible but even she was struggling to contort and mold to Kyle's body while being suspended from a wire "floating" in a rocket ship.

I shook my head. "This plot is really dumb. Does that matter to you guys or is it all about the sex?"

"It's the sex, Chica," Manny confirmed, smiling. I looked at Manny as if noticing for the first time that he had the same type of glow that Reid and I did. In fact, as I looked from Manny to Mac to Foxy, everyone seemed to be feeling much better this morning.

"Did you and Rose have some fun last night?" I asked my sound man.

Manny beamed. "She won't forget that one. I made sure of it."

Reid, who was listening in, let out a laugh while I continued to eye Mac and Foxy suspiciously.

"We all enjoyed the night off," Foxy said to me, beaming. "Mac, too. It was a good night for the cast and crew of *Murder Live!*"

Reid let out a louder laugh and I joined him. "Okay then," he said, placing an arm over my shoulder. Reid's cell phone chirped and he pulled it out of his pocket. "It's Lou."

"Mac." I nudged, indicating that he should start filming. Mac swung his camera over his shoulder to capture the phone call.

Reid put the phone to his ear while heading out of the studio to a more private location. "Reid," he answered.

We followed Reid out into the hallway and back towards the control room that was quickly becoming our meeting place. We knew there were probably some bodily fluids from Vinnie in the room but at least it was quiet.

"Wow, really?" Reid said to Lou on the phone. "Interesting. Okay thanks, I appreciate it." Reid hung up the phone and looked at Foxy. The camera was rolling now so me and my crew were hanging back to stay out of the scene.

"What did he say?" Foxy asked.

"He said the scissor you found matched the size of the puncture wound in Lucky's neck."

Foxy's eyes widened. "That's great!"

"Yeah, he's having it analyzed just in case it was the actual murder weapon. And listen to this," Reid continued. "The blood he found on Lucky – not all of it was real."

Foxy's face dropped as he tried to understand what this revelation meant. "Fake? Wait, did they use any fake blood for the show?"

"I don't think so. It's just astronauts having sex in space. No gore. Why would Lucky have fake blood on him?"

"Maybe it was some weird kinky sex that went wrong?" Foxy suggested. "Like they were pretending to kill each other and then someone got excited and did it for real?"

Reid raised his eyebrows. "Weirder things have happened."

Manny tapped me on the shoulder and I turned to him. He whispered, "Can I say something?"

I shook my head no.

"Guys?" Manny said, completely ignoring my orders. "I'm not trying to mess with your work, but there's something you should think about."

"Spill it," Foxy ordered.

"There's these movies they make on the black market – called snuff films. People kill other people for real on them and they record it."

"We know what snuff films are, Manny," Reid told him.

"I was just thinking maybe they were making one of those? Like a sex movie on the side where they kill somebody?"

Foxy and Reid considered that for a moment. "It's certainly possible," Reid conceded. "I like your thinking, Manny."

"We've got to get through these interviews and I mean today," Foxy said. "There are still people we need to talk to and this is taking too long. No more being nice; we need to crank through these and get this thing solved."

"Agreed," Reid smiled.

*****

Having Manny around had proved to be beneficial, especially during our interview with Enrique, the Spanish-speaking sound operator. The man could speak very little English and so the interview consisted of Reid and Foxy asking their questions to Manny who then translated them for Enrique. I don't think any of us were expecting much from this interview but we had to go through the motions. As we listened to Manny ask Enrique about his whereabouts on the night of the murder and if he thought there was anyone in particular that we should be investigating, Enrique suddenly became quite animated.

He held up two fingers to his ears and then pointed those same fingers out, moving them across all of us. It was as if he was warning us that he was listening.

"He says that his job is to do sound and that means he's always listening," Manny translated. "He says that there's lots of whispering and conversations and people don't think he's listening, but he is."

"What has he heard?" Foxy asked, leaning in.

Manny asked Enrique the question and we all stared at Enrique as he answered in Spanish.

"He says he can't understand much English," Manny translated. "So when people are whispering he doesn't know what they're saying."

"Is this guy freaking kidding me?" Foxy asked Manny.

"Ask him who he sees whispering," Reid said to Manny.

Manny asked Enrique who said, "Joy y Carmine. Penny y Elroy. Rose y, ay carumba, Rosa y todo el mundo!"

"What did he say about Rose?" Foxy asked.

"He said, Rose and everyone are whispering."

Foxy shook his head. "Wow, that's a great insight. I think we're done here."

22.

By now, we had exhausted most of our options for locations to interview suspects in. For Craig, we chose to use the supply closet as our setting. The closet itself wasn't big enough for us to fit in so we opened the door and put a chair in front of it for Craig to sit on. The rest of us were stationed in the hallway facing him. It wasn't private, but we encouraged the rubber-neckers that were passing by to keep moving.

"I wish you could have put me in a cooler setting," Craig began. "My friends are super jealous of me right now, but this is messing with my vibe."

Reid and Foxy were sitting across from Craig while Manny and I were sitting behind them. Mac had his camera mounted on a tripod and took the opportunity to once again work on his balance by squatting on the balls of his feet. "Keep it up," Penny said to Mac from the hallway as she passed by. ""I'm impressed." He smiled, proud of himself.

Mac had framed some of Reid's shoulder in the shot so that the audience would know that Craig was talking to the cops. Mac also set up our second support camera in a wide shot that captured the two cops and Craig from the side. This would give us more choices in the edit.

"Why are they jealous?" Foxy wanted to know.

"I'm being interviewed by you guys. I mean, how many people can say they were a suspect in a murder. Right? I mean, you saw what happened with that chick at Belamy's party. She was totally turned on!"

"Yeah, super cool," Foxy said sarcastically. "Kid, there are lots of people in this town that are murder suspects. I wouldn't go posting it on your Facebook page."

Craig squinted. "Whoops, too late on that one."

"It might be wise to take this seriously," Reid warned.

Craig straightened in his chair. "Oh, I do, I do. But I didn't do anything. I have nothing to hide – that's why I'm not worried."

"Oh well, then I guess we're done here," Foxy said.

"Really?" Craig asked.

"No, not really. Why don't you tell us about your relationship with Lucky?"

Suddenly Craig looked upset. "Who told you? Was it Rose? She's such a jerk sometimes. Look, I don't get to pick and choose. I have to take care of everyone. It doesn't mean I'm gay or anything."

"Pick and choose what?" Reid tried to clarify.

"Who I fluff."

"What exactly do you do man?" Foxy asked.

"I get the talent camera-ready. That means making them shiny where they need to be shiny and powdered where they need to be matte."

"And which spots are those?" Foxy wanted to know.

"Forehead and face should be matte," Craig explained. "They do their own makeup but on set I may come in and touch them up if I see shine. It reads like sweat, which we don't want unless the scene calls for it. In those cases, I spray them with water for the sweat."

"And the shiny spots?" Foxy asked.

"Legs, buns, boobs."

"Okay and that's for men and women. That's what you meant about your relationship with Lucky?"

Craig shook his head, taking a moment to remember the man. "That guy had abs for days. He used to give me tips on working out. I didn't want to be an actor or anything, but I could use a little help in the area.

The ladies don't really take me seriously." Craig looked over at Foxy. "You know what I mean."

Foxy squinted his eyebrows at the apparent insult. "No, I don't know what you mean. I'm a happily married man."

"Oh, good for you."

"So you and Lucky were friends," Reid stated.

"I guess you could say that. I mean, I felt like we were, but a guy like Lucky is kind of out of my league."

Foxy and Reid exchanged another glance, clearly having trouble understanding what Craig was trying to say. "You said your relationship with Lucky wasn't gay, but did you guys ever kiss or touch each other or anything like that?" Reid asked.

Craig looked horrified by the question and instantly held up his hand in front of the camera. "Hell, no! Are you guys trying to make me look like a chump in front of my friends? I took this job for the ladies, okay? Jesus, I'm sorry I said this interview was cool. I totally regret saying that now!"

"Okay, calm down. We ask these questions to everyone," Reid assured him.

"You ask everyone if they're gay?" Craig wanted to confirm.

Reid nodded. "Standard police procedure."

Craig's face had become red and hot but upon hearing that everyone had been accused of having an affair with Lucky, he seemed to calm down.

"What time did you leave the studio on Monday night?" Reid continued.

"Like maybe six-thirty? It was a few days ago."

"And tell us what you did after you left."

Craig thought about it. "I just went home. Got drunk with my roommates."

"We'd like to get information from your roommates to confirm your alibi," Reid explained.

"Oh yeah, they'd love that!" Craig said, then straightened up, trying to be serious again. "Do you want to call them now?"

"In a few minutes. How about the next morning? Tell me what you did before getting to work."

Craig thought for a minute. "I'm pretty sure I threw up in the morning. Maybe it was during the night, I don't totally remember, but there was some spew on the shower curtain that I had to clean up. Then I took a shower. I didn't have breakfast that day I don't think. No coffee for sure. And then I came to work."

"And what time was that?" Reid asked.

"Call time. I don't arrive before call time. You can check the sheets. I think it was ten that day."

"When was the last time you saw Lucky alive?"

"The day before, I guess. I think he was still here when I left."

"Do you think anyone had motive to kill your friend, Lucky?" Foxy asked.

Craig nodded his head. "I've been thinking about it and there are lots of people. I mean Vinnie could have done it for ratings. Maybe he and Carmine did it together? Elroy had a thing for Penny so maybe he knocked Lucky off. Or what about Rose? He's probably the one guy around here she didn't bang. He warned me about her, but I didn't take his advice on that one. I mean, I have to get something good out of this job. The money sure doesn't cut it."

"Anyone else?" Foxy asked, not really meaning it.

"Pretty much anyone could have done it. Anyone other than me."

"What about Enrique?" Foxy asked.

Craig shook his head. "Oh no, not him. That dude can't even speak English. He wouldn't have done it."

*****

Reid decided to try calling George on the phone rather than going over to his apartment again. While they made the call, I left the crew filming and stepped out into the back parking lot of the studio. I had been waiting for a free moment all day and this was finally my opportunity.

I pulled up my phone directory to speed-dial my sister. It was true that she often got on my nerves, but deep down she was my best friend and I needed to talk to her.

"Victoria, I'm at the nail salon. In a minute I'm going to have to give the woman my other hand. What's up?" Ginny said into the phone.

"Reid told me he loved me last night."

"What?! Oh my God! Ma'am, I'm so sorry," she said to her manicurist. "No, I have to take this call. Just take a break or something. We can finish the fingers after... What? Yes, a ten minute massage would be fine. Victoria, tell me everything."

"Well I don't know if this is a happy story."

"Oh my God, did he dump you?"

"No. Last night we had sex, finally. And it was amazing. He was, I don't know, a gentle lover I guess they say? A kind lover? Anyway, it was really special but after we finished he was lying on top of me and said, 'I love you.'"

Ginny was silent for a moment. "Did he look you in the eyes when he said this?"

"No. his face was buried in my neck."

"What did you say?"

"Nothing. I didn't know if he was just saying like, I love you, meaning the sex was good or if that was something he normally says to girls after sex. Some guys do that I think."

"That's true. I knew a girl who had a one-night stand and the guy said he loved her during sex. Obviously he didn't, it was just like his sex talk track."

"Right, so I don't know if he meant it like that or for real."

"What happened after you didn't say anything?"

"He asked if I wanted to have sex again and I said yes. And he hasn't mentioned it since last night. Maybe he forgot he said it?"

"Seems like a pretty hard thing to forget. Yikes, I don't know, Victoria. And this is extra weird because you're in love with him. Why didn't you say it back?"

"I was surprised! I wasn't expecting it, Ginny. And don't say I'm in love with him. I've never told you that."

"Yeah, but I think you are, Vic. It's okay, he's a good guy. Was he there when you woke up this morning?"

"It was his house."

"Okay but was he like, present or in the shower?"

"He was there. Then we had sex again, in the shower actually."

"Oh, you lucky girl! Okay, so he's sticking around. Wow, this poor guy. He's doing everything for you and you still can't give him an inch. I mean he waited forever for sex with you-"

"It was like three weeks!"

"For men that's a lot. And now he's telling you he loves you and you don't say anything back? I think you need to take a minute to think about how YOU really feel Victoria."

"Yeah but even if I do... love him... how do I bring it up? This is so awkward now."

"Maybe just be honest about it. Tell him you heard him last night and you were caught off guard and didn't know what to say. Just have a real conversation with the guy."

Ginny was right. For maybe the first time in her life she was giving me some really good advice. I knew I had to take it. "Thanks, Gin."

"Any time."

*****

I caught up with Mac and Manny as they followed behind the cops towards the rocket ship set. "Did they get a hold of George on the phone?" I asked Mac.

Mac looked at me and smiled. "Yeah. George really did meet Rose for the first time that night. After he saw her picture on Foxy's phone, he sought her out."

"Oh, that's kind of funny," I smiled.

Reid and Foxy pushed open the set door and we followed them inside. We found Joy sitting on one of the director's chairs, rehearsing her two lines for the next scene. She was dressed in a space suit with her short hair held back with silver metallic space clips. Reid approached her first with Foxy at his side. I hung back as my crew filmed the interaction.

"Joy, we'd like to speak with you again," Reid told her.

Joy looked up from her script with an annoyed expression. "You're kidding, right? I'm working here."

"We've been working our way through all the staff members and there are a few more questions we want to ask you," Reid told her.

"I'm cast. I'm a cast member, not a *staff* member detective. There's a difference."

"Not to us. Let's talk in the other room."

"You know you and your chubby friend couldn't solve your way out of a paper box," Joy challenged.

Foxy raised his eyebrows, seeming to take offense. First, he had been accused of not being able to attract the opposite sex and now he was being called chubby.

"We have a show to produce here you know," Joy continued. "In fact, the executives from the Lush network are stopping by today. We invited them thinking this *investigation* would be over by now."

"Sorry to disappoint you," Reid told her. "But it's important that we speak to all *staff* before drawing any conclusions. Now, we'd like to re-interview you in the other room. Now."

Joy looked annoyed. "Fine."

She skulked past Reid and Foxy and off towards the other studio where we had set up our camera equipment. Mac filmed her as she walked off while I stole glances at Reid, trying to see if I could read his thoughts. Was he all business right now or was he thinking about me and last night?

He said he would be. I hadn't stopped thinking about him.

I requested that Joy remain in her spacewoman jumpsuit during the interview. I thought the contrast of the ridiculous silver costume juxtaposed against some serious questions about a murder, might provide an ironic contrast for my viewers.

Joy looked at her watch. "Let's make this quick. They'll be here in less than an hour. And I don't want you guys hanging around when they get here either."

Foxy shook his head in disbelief and smiled. "Lady, you don't call the shots around here. We do. We're the police. Did you see our badges?"

"You're harassing innocent people, Sir. That's not what police are supposed to do."

"Sure, it is." Foxy smiled. "Besides, we don't know that you're innocent. You haven't given us any reason to believe you are. Are you innocent, Joy?"

Joy narrowed her eyes. "Of course I am."

"You seem like you call the shots around here. Is that correct?" Reid asked her.

Joy softened a little bit at that. "You could say that."

"He did say that!" Foxy joked. "Would you?"

"Yes, I would say that. Carmine has learned to rely on me to be his eyes and ears around here. I help with the network too. Sometimes he gets… overwhelmed. I help out."

"You mean drunk, right?" Reid asked.

Joy looked at the cops suspiciously. "He's currently in AA."

"I know that, but he still gets drunk, right Joy?" Reid pressed.

Joy looked down and shook her head. "Sometimes, yes."

"Do you ever get his coffee for him, Joy? The special way that he likes it? Ever help him out if he's in a bind?"

Joy's eyes widened. "Of course not."

"Maybe sometimes right, Joy?" Reid asked.

"Maybe," Joy relented.

I looked over at Mac to ensure he was getting all this. He was.

"So, you enabled his addiction and in exchange he let you take on more responsibility on set. Do I have that right?" Reid asked.

Joy stammered. "I wouldn't say it like that. Look, Carmine needed help and I care about him so I was there for him."

"Are you two sleeping together?" Reid asked her.

Joy's eyes widened again. "I already told you before, we're good friends."

Foxy laughed. "Come on. We see how you fawn all over him. We saw you at Kyle's party too. You can admit it."

"Admit what? There is nothing going on," Joy snapped.

"Oh, it's a case of unrequited love then, eh?" Reid asked her.

"No, not really."

"When one party is in love and the other isn't, that makes for a difficult situation, doesn't it, Joy?" Reid pressed.

I looked over at Reid. He was asking the question to Joy, but was he really asking the question to me? Was Reid feeling like his love was unrequited?

"I'm not in love with him. God, you men are so stupid. The man has a drinking problem. Why would I want to get mixed up with someone like that?"

"Okay, talk to us about the network. It sounds like you arranged the meeting with the executives, is that right?"

"Yes, you have *that* right. Which reminds me that we need to move this conversation along."

"What does the network think about Lucky's death? Are they planning to pull the show?" Foxy asked.

"They can't pull something they haven't picked up yet, genius. Plus, Lucky's death is a good thing... for them at least. It's giving us some good publicity."

"Have you ever been in a production where a cast member died before?" Foxy asked.

"Once, yes. It was an older gentleman. He was playing a dying man in a hospital scene and then that night he went home and really did die. It was weird."

"And how did the network react in that situation?" Foxy asked.

Joy leaned in. "I know what you're trying to do here but it isn't going to work. In that situation no one cared that he died because he was a day player. It didn't boost ratings and it didn't give me any ideas about killing anyone else I was working with."

"If you did have the idea to kill Lucky, who would you ask to do it?" Foxy asked.

"A hitman, I guess," Joy answered, sounding confused. "Look I didn't kill Lucky and neither did Carmine."

"But you admit that his death will help ratings, right?"
"Yes, that's why the executives are coming here."

"Then why do you want us to leave? Wouldn't that make things even more real for the executives?"

"I just don't want anyone to feel uncomfortable," Joy answered.

"You know I don't think her love for Carmine is unrequited, Reid," Foxy said aloud to his partner. "Do you remember what Carmine said about Joy?"

"Oh yeah," Reid said, playing along. "Like how she was the kind of girl that would take a bullet for her man. And that he would trust her until the end."

I was becoming convinced that these detectives were learning from my style. This was textbook reality TV producing right here. The question was, would it work on Joy?

"Well that's very sweet of him," Joy said.

"Yeah, he seemed to think that you were very good at keeping secrets. Do you know what he meant by that Joy?" Foxy asked her.

"Oh, it's probably just about the drinking, I guess. I was pretty good with that secret."

"Who do you think could have killed Lucky?" Reid asked her.

"I already told you, I don't know. Did you talk to Jason? What about Rose? She has a record, doesn't she?"

"Did you know that Vinnie was recording you in your dressing room?" Reid asked.

"I already told you that I didn't know that. Is there something wrong with your memory?"

"No, I just think you did know. I see how often you're in Vinnie and Carmine's office. And Craig said everyone knew," Reid explained.

Joy shrugged. "I guess I don't pay attention to gossip."

"The tape was erased anyway. But don't worry, we're having the tape analyzed to see if we can recover the lost footage. I think we can."

"Great, then your mystery will be solved and we can move on with our lives," Joy said.

The door to the studio opened and Carmine appeared. "Joy, the network is here."

"Oh!" Joy said, jumping up from the hot seat. "I'll be right there. Detectives, please excuse me."

Reid stood up as did Foxy. "We'll come with you," he said with a wide grin.

Joy straightened her space suit. "Great."

23.

I found myself staring at Reid's rear end as I followed him, Joy, Foxy, and my crew to meet the executives. I smiled inwardly, feeling like Reid and I had a secret. I knew what was under those jeans he was wearing. I knew every inch of his body and I couldn't wait to see it again.

We found two men and a woman standing in Vinnie's office, mulling around. One of the men was tall and thin while the other was shorter and rounder. He was built like Vinnie actually. The taller man was in a suit while the shorter wore jeans and a blazer. The woman who was with them wore a cardigan and khaki pants.

Mac and Manny weren't recording yet and kept their gear in their hands and pointed down. I had asked them not to start recording until I had a chance to get release forms signed.

Vinnie and Carmine were in their office already with the executives but seemed to be waiting for Joy to get things started. Joy walked in with confidence, extending her hand out to the shorter man. "Roger, so good to see you again."

"Joy, hello!" Roger said, taking her hand. "I see you dressed for the occasion."

Joy looked down at her spacesuit and smiled. "I suppose my work clothes are different from most."

Everyone had a laugh over that one. "Let me introduce you to Detectives Reid and Flanagan of the LAPD. They're investigating Lucky's death. Detectives, this is Roger Bramson, his associate Ryan Slater, and their assistant Tracy."

Reid stepped forward and extended a hand to Roger first, understanding the pecking order from Joy's introduction. "Nice to meet you."

"How's the investigation going?" Roger wanted to know.

"Well," Foxy chimed in, "I think we're closing in on a suspect."

"Wow, that's great. Anyone in this room?" Roger joked.

"Could be!" Foxy joked back.

It didn't seem like Joy intended to acknowledge me to the execs so I stepped forward to introduce myself. "And I'm Victoria Sharpe. I'm with the show *Murder Live!*"

"We feel like the *Murder Live!* show can help boost our ratings when we do air," Vinnie explained, cutting me off. "They're covering Lucky's death, plus with the media blitz we've been getting, it's a lot of good press all around."

"Not to mention the social media Belamy has been putting out," Ryan Slater added, pulling out his phone. "Ha! He's live streaming right now."

We all crowded around Ryan's phone to take a look. Kyle was sitting in the hallway talking to the camera.

"The network execs just arrived and they're meeting with the cops right now," Kyle was saying. "I heard one of the cops say they're zeroing in on a suspect."

"What the hell?" Reid and I said at the same time.

Reid looked out the office door to see Belamy standing in the hallway talking to the camera on his phone. "Are you nuts?" Reid said, swiping Belamy's phone out of his hand.

"Ha! Now the cop is on!" Ryan announced. We looked at his phone to see Reid pulling the phone out of Kyle's hand and then fumbling around with it, trying to turn it off. "Hey, there's us!" Ryan announced as Reid held the phone up in the air, inadvertently pointing it at us. Finally, he switched it off.

"This is an official police investigation," Foxy told Kyle. "It may not seem like it, but it is. We could arrest you for obstructing justice."

"Yeah, yeah. You keep threatening but you can't really do anything," Kyle shot back.

Reid slipped Belamy's phone into his pocket. "Don't push me, pal. If I catch you broadcasting again I'm going to handcuff you to the wall."

"Kinky," Belamy teased. "Now give me my phone."

"No," Reid said with a smile. "You can have it when this investigation is done."

We all stepped back into Vinnie's office and closed the door, leaving a bewildered Kyle Belamy standing in the hallway looking like he just lost his puppy.

"We need to know when you'll be ready for air," Roger said to Carmine who was sitting slumped at his desk, only partially engaged in the conversation.

"Soon, right Vinnie?" Joy answered.

"I'm done with my rewrites and we should have everything in the can by tomorrow night. Then I need a week to edit."

"You changed the script, right? Lucky doesn't die?" Roger urged.

"Yeah, yeah. I made him take a booster rocket back to Earth. He sneaks out in the middle of the night."

"Good," Roger said. "I don't want bad press. Only good press."

"When does your show air?" Ryan asked me.

"Well, we have to find the killer first otherwise it's not going to air at all," I cautioned. "Audiences don't like unanswered questions. Then I have to edit, which takes around three days."

"When are you gonna solve this thing?" Ryan asked, looking at Reid.

Reid crinkled his eyebrows. "To be honest, it'd have been solved by now if we had more cooperation from the production."

"I had to rewrite the whole script and reshoot half the scenes!" Vinnie protested. "I gave you plenty of access to my people. Don't blame me for the fact that you can't figure this thing out."

"You withheld evidence and blocked us from interviewing your staff," Reid blasted back. "Come on Vinnie, let's get real here."

"Okay, okay, okay!" Roger interrupted, holding up his hands. "Look, there's a lot of buzz right now and we have to get this thing on air. Joy, I need you to send me some footage so we can start putting teasers on air. Vinnie, I need you to work with these cops. We need a murderer. Understand? Anything you know you have to tell them."

I nudged Mac that he should start filming. Roger seemed committed to the cause, which I interpreted as providing me with his consent. I would get the official release forms from these guys afterwards. Mac slung his camera over his shoulder and pressed record.

"Roger, should we start thinking about episode two at this point?" Joy asked. "I know we're just shooting a pilot right now but we could lose the studio space if we don't lock it in soon."

Roger and Ryan exchanged a glance while Vinnie, Joy, and Carmine held their breath. "I think that would be wise," Roger confirmed.

Joy and Vinnie both audibly gasped with relief. A big smile climbed across both their faces.

"We've got momentum right now so let's pull this off," Roger told them. "You might even want to think about using some footage of Lucky in future episodes. Keep his spirit alive."

"Great idea!" Vinnie cheered.

"Okay. Now why don't you show us around?"

Carmine stood up and pushed past Joy towards the door. "Follow me. I'll handle this."

Roger and Ryan nodded as Carmine led the two of them and their assistant Tracy out of the room. On their way out, Ryan placed a hand on Mac's arm and said, "We don't want to be on the show. You'll cut us out, right?"

"Yeah, sure." Mac nodded as he swung his camera around at Vinnie instead.

I was discouraged but not defeated. I would find a way to get them released. Once they were gone Vinnie and Joy clasped hands and squeezed. "Yes!" Joy said, smiling.

"This is everything we could have ever wanted!" Vinnie told her as they both hugged.

Mac was still filming the exchange although I didn't think Vinnie or Joy realized that. They were too caught up in the excitement. I pulled out my log and noted the timecode and what was happening. I would have some fun editing this footage. Cut in the right way, these two would look guilty as hell.

I grabbed Tracy in the hallway and innocently asked her if her bosses would sign my release form, even though Ryan had already said no. She looked a bit uncomfortable and out of her element. "Are you okay?" I asked her.

"Carmine just toured us around the dressing rooms and we walked in on Kyle Belamy and a Spanish woman...doing it." Her face was white as she told the story and she looked extremely uncomfortable.

"That's our Rose for you. How did Roger and Ryan take it?"

Tracy looked annoyed. "Fine. They thought it was great actually. So did Kyle; he started laughing when he saw us. He wasn't embarrassed at all. You know, I thought getting a job for studio executives was going to be rewarding."

"Most men in this business are slime," I told her.

"I think I'm going to quit or talk to HR."

"Well, before you do that, can you get Roger and Ryan to sign a release? It states they consent to appear on the show."

Tracy shook her head. "They won't sign that. They don't want to be on the show."

I frowned. Roger walked over to Tracy with a big smile on his face. "Tracy, you look like you've seen a ghost. I hope you didn't burn your eyes back there." Roger looked at me and laughed. "I swear this girl belongs in a convent. Loosen up, am I right? What's a little T&A every once in a while? Am I right?"

"Sure." I smiled brightly. He seemed satisfied enough with my response and walked past us. "That was pretty inappropriate," I told Tracy. "If my boss did that to me I'd teach him a lesson. You know what I mean?"

"Give me the releases," Tracy said. "I'll sign for them."

"Great," I said with a smile.

*****

I decided that I wanted to spend some time with my editor tonight. I had a lot of footage and interviews and I wanted to start pulling the story together. Lenny would need to start running some trailers too. The media knew we were covering the story – we needed to start to deliver. I was lying earlier when I said that the show wouldn't air unless the case was solved. This story was too big already. I didn't need a murderer, just a suspect. Much like the justice system, all I needed to do was to cast reasonable doubt. I just needed to decide who I would cast my shadow upon. I liked the idea of Rose being the prime suspect as she was a reoccurring character on the show, but Vinnie also had a lot of motive. In fact, most of the people on set seemed to have motive to kill him.

I gave Lenny a quick call to see if he could arrange for my editor to stay late tonight so I could work with him. I filled him in on the progress we had made as well as the unanswered questions we still had. He offered to come back to the set to help me out, but I quickly shot him down.

I was sitting in the break room writing in my log book and trying to piece the story together when Kyle Belamy entered the room. "Hey gorgeous," he said to me.

"Hey," I said, looking up. "I heard the network execs caught you with your pants down."

Kyle smiled. "Yeah, that was a little embarrassing. But I didn't have my phone, you know? I had to find something to do."

Kyle sat down at the table in front of me. "I like that dress you're wearing."

I looked down at the button-down dress that I had worn the night before over to Reid's house. I hadn't had time to go home to change and it may have been a little dressy for work.

"So you and that cop are screwing, right?" he asked me, leaning back in his chair and crossing his arms. He closed his lips and let his tongue peek out as he waited for my answer.

"I don't think that's any of your business."

He squinted his pretty green eyes at me. "I saw the two of you at my house and at the club. Pretty sexy stuff." He placed a hand on my arm. "I know you're a little light on experience. I can tell."

I felt myself freeze up. Why was he saying this to me?

"I'd like to offer my services to you. I'd like to think I'm a professional in this area."

My eyes grew wide. Was this guy propositioning me? A few days ago I would have been flattered, but he literally just had sex with Rose. Like five minutes ago. This guy was gross.

"What's going on here?" Reid said from the doorway.

My face was flushed and Kyle's hand was still on my arm. Kyle turned to look at Reid with a sly smile, keeping his hand where it was. "Just talking. She seemed to be interested in what I was offering."

I pulled my arm away. "No, I wasn't."

Reid moved over to Kyle and grabbed him by his shirt. He pulled him up from his chair and threw him up against the wall, knocking the chair over in the process. "Reid!" I screamed, shocked by how he was behaving.

Reid held Kyle against his wall and stared him down. "Stay away from her, you understand?"

Kyle was flustered but tried to play it cool. "You have something I want, so I'm taking something you want."

"What are you talking about?" Reid demanded.

"Give me my damn phone!"

Reid smiled, taking his hands off Kyle's shirt and straightening it out for him.

"Wait, were you just hitting on me so you could get your phone back?" I asked.

Kyle shrugged. "I'm a celebrity. I have to stay connected."

"You're an asshole," I told him. "And for your information my answer would have been no."

Kyle smiled but didn't say anything.

Reid pulled Kyle's phone out of his pocket and handed it over. "Stay away from her."

"Thanks," Kyle said, taking the phone and skipping out of the break room. "Catch you later, girl."

Reid picked up the chair that had fallen over and sat down on it next to me. "I'm sorry. I shouldn't have done that."

"I've never been with a guy that beat up other guys for me," I told him.

"I didn't beat him up. I just scared him a little," Reid said, running his finger from my shoulder down to my elbow. I felt a chill run throughout my entire body. "I'm a cop. We're not supposed to abuse our power. But with you I get… protective."

Without thinking I leaned in and kissed him. His lips tasted so good. I didn't like violence but the way he threw Kyle against that wall – it was pretty irresistible. I wrapped both of my hands around one of his biceps, feeling the strength and power of this man.

"I don't think we should do this here," Reid told me.

"I know," I told him, leaning in again for another taste. My head was filled with him. I wanted to curl up inside his body.

Reid laughed, pulling back again. "Come on Sharpe, stop."

I pulled back knowing he was right.

"Am I going to see you tonight?" Reid asked me.

I frowned. "I'm going to the office to work on the edit. Rob's staying late."

Mac walked in the room, interrupting us, holding his camera with Manny walking behind him. "Do you want us to trail the network guys?" Mac asked me.

I leaned away from Reid, trying to look natural. "Yeah. I got them released so they're okay. Just try not to be too obvious about it. They don't exactly know they signed the releases."

24.

I sat behind my usual editor Rob on a couch in the edit bay. Rob sat at the Avid, which was the computer editing system we used to piece together the show. He was dressed in gray sweatpants and a T-shirt – prepared for a long night. He swiveled around in his comfy ergonomic chair to talk to me. "Kyle Belamy? Are you serious right now?"

I smiled. "Don't believe the hype. He's kind of a scumbag."

"Well yeah, I assumed he was a scumbag. And I saw the interview. The guy's got goals at least."

I laughed. "I guess so."

"I had the assistants put together the assembly edit last night. There's some good stuff here," he told me.

"Yeah, but we don't know the punchline yet. That makes it hard."

"My money is on Rose," he said. "I couldn't believe it when I saw her. How could you not text me?"

"Sorry, I've been a little distracted. But you're right, she's a magnet for trouble. We're well past the 48-hour mark and this case is getting cold. We may just need to paint her as the villain."

"You're the boss."

Rob played me the assembly, which was essentially a string of all the footage pieced together. It was almost two hours in length. Normally an editor wouldn't show their producer a cut so long, but without any direction on who to focus on, he had to include everything and everyone.

"We could have some fun with this many suspects," Rob told me. "So many of them have a motive."

"What did you have in mind?" I asked him.

"Maybe some fun with graphics. Like a freeze frame on each with their motives?"

"I like it," I said, leaning in. "Let's go through the motives. This could be a good exercise for me anyway. Then I can grab some more talking heads with the cops tomorrow and get them to say the same thing."

Rob pulled up some video of Rose and froze it on screen. He added a translucent red box below her face and used a police-like font to list out her motives.

"Previous track record," he said regarding Rose's motives.

"Hated Lucky," I added. "He rejected her sexually."

"Anything else?" Rob asked.

I shrugged. "Not really."

"Not that strong on motive," Rob commented.

I knew he was right. "Okay let's talk about Vinnie."

"Okay, Vinnie." Rob scrolled through the footage on the Avid looking for an image of his face. All the footage we had produced so far had been digitized and uploaded into the system so he could easily retrieve it.

"For Vinnie it's all about the ratings," I said. "A murder like this is getting him lots of press. He spent big bucks to get Kyle Belamy on the show and he needs it to pay off."

Rob nodded and typed *PR* and then added *General Sleaze Bag* to the list of reasons. I got a laugh out of that.

For Carmine, we listed the same reasons as Vinnie but also noted there could be some sort of AA connection. After all, Lucky had lied about being an alcoholic, so maybe this was some sort of revenge on Carmine's behalf.

Joy also had the PR motive but not much else. Penny was Lucky's lover. Maybe there was a quarrel or something that she wasn't telling us about? Kyle had an interest in the ratings and also seemed to enjoy living on the edge. Would this type of thing be the next sexual risk he was willing to take?

Elroy had a crush on Penny so he had motive to get rid of her current boyfriend. I didn't think Enrique was worth considering but Craig was. He seemed to have an obsession of sorts with Lucky and a level of jealousy. Maybe it got out of control? After all, Lucky was almost naked when we found him. He was certainly involved in some sort of sexual activity. But with whom? And did he normally wear a thong like that? It didn't seem like something a normal woman would find to be a turn on. Maybe Lucky and Craig were having some fluffing fun?

The last suspect was Jason. Was he doing this as a practice exercise before killing his dad? Was he trying to get Lucky out of the way so he would have more screen time?

We worked for the next few hours editing down the content. Though we didn't know the ending it almost helped us to develop the story. Everyone truly was a suspect as we had no idea who did it.

At around nine o'clock, Keith, one of the assistant editors appeared in the doorway. "Hey, Sharpe. How's the edit going?"

"It's going," I told him. I was getting tired and hungry. "Rob, maybe we should call it a night."

"You saw that email I sent you, right?" Keith asked me. "About the footage?"

I looked up at him with a blank stare. We had to use our personal emails for work and between all the spam and junk mail I received, sometimes emails got lost. "Uh, can you tell me what it said?" I smiled.

Keith smiled back. "I figured you didn't see it! I couldn't believe you didn't reply."

"Well you have my interest now. What did the email say?" I asked. Rob was interested too.

"Someone definitely recorded over the murder. I slowed it down to a single frame and I can see three people in the room."

I sat straight up in my chair. "Is Lucky one of them?"

Keith nodded.

"Wait, are you sure? Are you sure it's him?" I asked.

"Yeah I'm sure. I digitized all your footage. I've been staring at that dead guy for days. Wanna see for yourself?"

"Yes!" Rob and I both said in unison.

"Come on then." Keith waived his arm and we eagerly followed him to the "cave" as we called it, where the assistant editors worked uploading and downloading footage from the servers.

Keith had the footage ready to go and as he slowed it down and froze it, I gasped. "I knew it!" I rubbed my eyes, thinking hard about the best approach. "Okay, I need to call Reid. He has to come down here. I'm gonna call Mac too. We need to get this on camera."

*****

Twenty minutes later, I had Reid, Foxy, Mac, Manny, and Keith gathered in the lobby of the production office. "Okay, I know this is crossing the line between cast and crew, but in this case we have no choice," I told them. "I already got Keith to sign a release and he agreed to be on the show."

"Hi," Keith said with a wave and a smile. Like Rob, Keith was dressed down in a jogging suit and a baseball hat. It was late and he hadn't expected to be on TV. Luckily, he was a guy and didn't care much about how he looked on camera.

"He'll lead you to the cave and show you what he found," I told the cops.

"What about you, Sharpe? Shouldn't you be in the shot too?" Reid teased.

"I've had enough fun on this show already after being poisoned last time. I'm good."

"Come on already, let's do this. I want to see what you found," Foxy complained.

"All right Mac, let's roll."

Mac swung his camera over his shoulder and I cued Keith to start talking.

"Hey, I'm Keith, nice to meet you," he said, giving Reid and Foxy a loose handshake. "Come on, I'll show you what I found."

Keith led the way with Foxy and Reid in tow, followed by me and the crew. They walked into the cave where Keith already had the footage loaded up on the screen. The computer was frozen on a shot that looked like a fuzzy screen glitch where the recording had been spliced.

Keith sat in front of the computer and addressed the cops. "So, you sent me this footage to look at. Sharpe told me, er, um... I understand that you believe the recording has been tampered with. As you know these cameras record at thirty frames per second. I was able to isolate it to a few frames that survived before they edited out and recorded over the rest. Would you like to see?"

"Hells yes!" Foxy told him.

Keith worked the controls until he stopped on the first frame in question. The image was grainy but we could clearly see Lucky sitting on the couch, topless. Straddling his lap was a woman with long dark hair.

"Son of a bitch! I knew it!" Foxy proclaimed. I smiled, having had the same reaction.

"Hang on, there's more," Keith said. He toggled the footage slightly forward and another woman appeared on screen. It was difficult to make her out, as you could only see a fraction of her in the corner frame, but the haircut gave her away.

"Is that Joy?" Reid asked.

Keith nodded. "We think it is. And the other woman is Rose. For sure. You can see that Lucky isn't wearing that mask that he was found with. I can't tell if he's naked or wearing those thong underwear because Rose is on top of him, but this is definitely from the night in question. See the timecode? It was three-thirty in the morning."

"Son of a bitch! That old pervert solved the mystery after all!" Foxy smiled, referring to Vinnie.

"Now look at this," Keith demonstrated. "If I rewind the footage back before this scene, the timecode jumps into the future."

"I'm not following," Foxy confessed.

"This means that someone, after realizing the scene was recorded, rewound the footage to record over it. So the timecode before this actually occurred afterwards. But the camera was motion controlled, so at a certain point it would have stopped recording. So it shut off and we got to see some of the footage recorded beneath before it started recording again. Essentially it glitched and we got Lucky."

"Okay so hold on," Reid cautioned. "This proves that Lucky was with Rose and Joy the night he was murdered, but it doesn't prove that either one of them killed him."

"Yeah, but both of them lied about being with him that night. Why would they lie if they weren't in on it?" Foxy asked. "Plus, Rose has a track record here."

Reid shook his head, thinking. "Why were both women there? Were they all having sex or was Joy watching or something?"

"And what about the fake blood?" Foxy asked. "Maybe Manny was right. Could they have been filming a movie? Like something afterhours?"

"If Joy was involved there's a good chance," Reid agreed. "She seemed to be pretty chummy with those network guys. Maybe they had a side deal going on."

Foxy flipped through his pocket notebook. "Lou said the time of death was between six and eight in the morning. But that time isn't exact. This is close to the timeframe he quoted." Foxy smiled wide and patted Keith on his back. "This is a game changer, man. Great work."

Keith beamed.

*****

I stood at the counter of my favorite Chinese take-out place in Venice Beach waiting for the wacky chicken salad I had ordered. I felt my phone vibrate in my purse and I pulled it out to take a look. Reid had texted me: *Where did you go?*

Whoops. I was so hungry that I ran out of the office with nothing more than a wave in his direction. In fact, I was still very hungry and growing angry at how long it was taking for them to make my salad. They weren't cooking anything, so what was the issue?

Sorry, I was starving. I texted him back. *I'm getting take-out.*

I saw three dots in the text box of my phone, indicating that he was writing me back. *Can I join you?*

Sure, I typed back. I looked around for an address. "Excuse me," I said to the person in the back. "What's the address here?" I felt a hand on my shoulder and I turned around to see Reid standing behind me. "Oh!" I said, surprised to see him.

"Here's your salad," the clerk said to me in a Chinese accent.

I turned to grab the white Styrofoam box from the counter and looked back at Reid. "Do you want to order something? I can't share with you – I'm too hungry."

Reid looked at me and a smile crept across his face. "Not a food sharer. Good to know."

"If you order another salad I can share this one with you now," I offered.

Reid smiled. "Honey, it's almost eleven at night. I ate dinner hours ago."

I was too hungry to flirt with him. I grabbed some plastic utensils and sat down at a table. Reid followed me and sat down across from me.

I opened the box and poured the candied ginger dressing all over the salad. Yes, a salad seemed like a strange choice for someone who was starving but this salad was sweet and crunchy and delicious. I dug in, shoveling the food into my mouth. After I had managed to swallow a few bites I started to feel like I could carry on a conversation. I looked over at Reid. "Did you follow me?"

"I like to keep an eye on you."

I raised an eyebrow then shoved some more food into my mouth. "I thought you'd be tired."

"Because of last night? I'm actually quite energized," Reid said with a smile.

I blushed and looked down at my food, smiling. "I was curious…" I began. "When you usually have sex with a woman…"

Reid leaned in smiling. "Yes."

"What's your usual routine?"

"Excuse me?"

"Like, after it's over. Do you usually, like, say anything?"

Reid smiled. "Like what?"

I shifted in my chair. "Oh, I don't know. Like some guys have certain lines they like to say I think. I mean, I've heard that."

Reid held out his hand and placed it over mine stopping me mid-bite. "You mean like, *I love you?*"

I blushed and looked away. "Yeah, I mean. Is that like your thing that you say?"

"No," Reid said, staring at me.

"Oh okay, me neither," I told him. "I thought I heard you say something like that last night."

Reid sat back, looking frustrated. "It slipped out. I didn't intend to say it and it's not my *line.*"

I suddenly got the feeling Reid was going to walk out. I panicked at the thought, knowing I had approached this all wrong. This guy had said something really special to me and I was treating it like it meant nothing to me and nothing to him. I reached across the table and put my hand over his.

Reid looked hurt and I shook my head, trying to get a handle on my thoughts. "I didn't mean to imply I didn't like hearing it. I was just surprised."

Reid settled a little, softening his resolve. "It surprised me too."

I felt a dip in my heart, like it was literally melting in my chest. I looked at him. "Honestly, I was half-expecting you to be gone in the morning."

"Well, it was my house."

"I'm well aware of that. That was part of the plan," I told him honestly.

Reid smiled as he thought to himself. "So you were expecting me to bolt and instead I went in… another direction."

I smiled back at him. "Pretty much."

"Oh-my-God!" I heard a woman's voice cry out. I turned to see a twenty-something blonde wearing pink yoga pants and a black sports bra charging towards our table. Reid and I exchanged a glance, wondering which one of us knew her.

"You're from that show. *Murder Live!* right? You're that hot cop!" She squealed looking at Reid. "OMG, can I get a picture with you? My friends would die!" She pulled her cell phone out of her purse.

"Um, sure," Reid said, looking uncomfortable.

"That episode where you beat up the bad guys after they were attacking your partner. That was so hot." She tilted her head next to his and snapped a selfie on her camera. "What's your next case about?"

"Um, well that's confidential right now. This is my producer," he said, pointing at me.

The woman turned as if just noticing me for the first time. She gave me a half smile. "Are you two working right now?"

I nodded. "Yeah, so if you don't mind, we really need to get back to our conversation."

The woman curled her upper lip into a snarl and glared at me. Apparently, I had offended her. I didn't care. She was insulting me by drooling all over my boyfriend. She turned and looked at Reid one more time. "You're older than I thought you were. Interesting. Thanks for the pic." With that, she turned on her heel and walked over to the counter to pick up her take out.

Reid looked at me and smiled. "So, I'm old now?"

"I still think you're cute."

Reid glanced down at the little bit of lettuce that was left on my plate.

259

"Feeling better?"

I nodded yes for several reasons.

"Can I follow you home?" he asked me.

I smiled at the prospect of spending another night with him. "Yes."

*****

The sex was different this time. The tenderness was still there but the passion was too. Now we knew what it felt like, we knew how good it could be and so we craved it. We lusted after it. I felt like my body had been awakened from a long nap. I felt energized and excited, like I had this new friend to play with. I couldn't get enough of Reid. I knew that no matter how many times our bodies came together, I would always want more.

He lay on top of me, kissing my lips and running his hand through my hair. We were both naked, our most intimate parts touching each other. We had waited, I had made him wait, but now I couldn't get enough. I felt like I wanted to stay in bed with him for weeks, exploring every inch of him. Instead, we would have to find quiet moments in our busy schedules to come together. Tonight that quiet time came after midnight. We should have been exhausted, we hadn't slept in days, but the adrenaline of the relationship was keeping us going.

As I reflected on other relationships I had been in, this pattern was familiar. At the start we discovered that we really liked each other and wanted to spend every moment together. I could survive on three or four hours of sleep and most of my waking thoughts were of my new partner and when I would see him next. Some of those relationships lasted years while others were more short-term. I had been in love before and knowing that, I couldn't deny that my feelings for Reid were real. As his lips moved down my neck and down to my breasts, I realized that something had changed for me. Had I been holding out for love? I didn't think so. I wasn't trying to make him love me, just to commit to me. I realized I got that in spades. This man, this glorious, gorgeous, amazing man loved me and I felt like the luckiest girl alive.

After we climaxed, Reid fell down on top of me, breathing heavily, just as he had done the night before. Reid sighed deeply and spoke into the curve of my neck once again. "I love… sex." He lifted up his head with a silly smile, looking for my reaction.

I smiled knowing he was teasing me and grabbed a pillow to swing at him. My initial swat turned into a full-fledged pillow fight, ending with the two of us laughing and rolling off the bed together clinging to each other in a naked embrace.

*****

Reid and I drove together to the set in his Mustang. I didn't like the car and I wasn't shy about telling him that. Yes, it was roomier and more powerful than my Miata, and yes it had working air conditioning. But I still didn't like it.

"I got a call from the captain last night," Reid said. "The cases are piling up and the other detectives are stretched. She wants us to move on from this case."

I looked over at him. "But we're so close."

"The footage from last night helped a lot. But it doesn't prove that either Rose or Joy killed him."

"But they lied about being with him," I offered.

"Yes, so we have to figure out why. Of course, this isn't the first time Rose has lied to us about a murder that she had all the answers to. History may be repeating itself here."

"So now what?" I asked.

Reid looked at me. "I need you to make me a promise."

"What is it?"

"I don't normally go by my gut. I like facts. I like to know that I'm right. But we're out of time and something is telling me that only way I'm going to solve this thing is to take a risk."

"So, what's the promise?"

"If I'm wrong," Reid began, "don't make me look like a total asshole on TV."

"Reid, you're my boyfriend." I said, choking on the word and feeling like a teenager. "If I make you look dumb, then I look dumb too."

Reid looked over at me. "Yeah, but I know how ruthless you can be when you're chasing a story."

I placed my hand on his knee. "Rob and I already cut the episode to cast suspicion on Rose. Even if you don't solve the case, I think the episode will be okay."

Reid nodded, looking out the front window.

"Is it Rose?" I asked.

Reid looked at me and smiled. "I guess you'll have to tune in to find out."

25.

I grabbed the talking head shots with Foxy and Reid that my edit desperately needed. I had them recount the various steps they had taken and talk through why each of the different suspects might have motive. The exercise would help to fill in the gaps of my storyline and also to validate the assumptions that Rob and I had made.

Foxy was frustrated that he had to talk to me and my crew for nearly an hour, but Reid didn't seem to care. He answered the questions somewhat cheerfully and without objection. I thought back to what a jerk he had been when we first met a few weeks ago. It turned out he just needed to get laid to turn his mood around.

Foxy and Reid talked about the footage we discovered last night and that their approach would be to interview Rose and Joy separately. This was pretty standard. They would lie to each of them about what the other had said and hope one of them cracked.

Reid and Foxy decided they would split up to speak to the women simultaneously. Reid would take Joy and Foxy would take Rose. The arrangement made sense as Rose usually wasted a lot of time flirting with Reid. Her usual tricks wouldn't be necessary with Foxy. She wasn't interested and neither was he.

I followed Reid using the secondary camera while Mac and Manny followed Foxy to find Rose. We all had a suspicion that Rose was the killer and we wanted to make sure to nab her on the good camera.

Joy was sitting at her usual perch on the side of Carmine's desk in his office. Carmine was sipping his thermos of booze and she was leaning over him, looking at his computer screen. Vinnie was at his desk typing on his computer.

"Joy, I need to speak with you," Reid told her. I was standing behind him holding the camera as steady as I could.

Joy was wearing a pink silk teddy with a robe over the top and looked up, startled. "Right now?"

"Yes, outside please."

"Are you serious?" Joy barked, clearly annoyed. "How many times are you gonna want to talk to me?"

"As many as it takes," Reid answered. "Please." He gestured towards the door.

"No!" Joy insisted. "I'm busy right now."

"Vinnie, the network asked for your full cooperation here," Reid reminded him.

"Go ahead, Joy," Vinnie told her. "It's all right."

Joy stood up and straightened her outfit, then walked past Reid and out the door. He followed her with me trailing behind, camera rolling. We agreed to speak on the second set where we would have complete privacy.

As soon as the door closed, Reid got right to the point. I focused my camera on Joy, occasionally panning over to Reid for cut-aways. "We have you on tape," he told her.

Joy's eyes went wide, but she didn't say anything.

"You told me that you didn't know Vinnie was recording the dressing rooms. But when we asked around, everyone knew. I don't believe that you didn't know about it."

Joy took a deep breath in. "I guess I didn't want to believe it. That Vinnie would actually do that."

"That camera caught you on tape, with Lucky on the night of the murder."

Joy's eyes widened further, but she remained quiet.

"Someone tried to erase the tape, but we had it analyzed and we could clearly see you with him that night. You and Rose were both there, weren't you?"

Joy looked down, shaking her head and shrugged. "So what? That doesn't prove anything."

Reid laughed aloud. "Doesn't prove anything? You lied to us. Do you know why people lie in an investigation, Joy? It's because they have something to hide."

"So what?" Joy repeated. "Yeah, we were with him that night. That doesn't mean we killed him."

"Then why did you lie about it?"

"Because…" Joy was getting backed into a corner and she was starting to struggle.

"Why did you lie about it?" Reid screamed at her. "If you're trying to protect your friend Rose, I wouldn't waste your breath. This isn't the first murder she's gotten herself mixed up in. In fact, she just spilled her guts to my partner in the other room. She said everything was your idea."

"So what if it was my idea? She went along with it!" Joy cried out.

Holy shit. Was Joy confessing? I held my shot steady.

"We have the equipment here – so why the hell not?" Joy continued. "Carmine knew about it too. He was fine with it."

"What did you have to gain from it?" Reid asked her.

"Money, obviously. We all have to pay the bills. Look, those films are only illegal if you actually kill the person, which we didn't. We just made it look like we did."

"But he was killed," Reid corrected.

Joy shook her head. "Not by me. He was alive when I left."

"And what time was that?"

"Six in the morning. Maybe seven. I don't remember."

"And when you left did Rose go with you?"

Joy nodded. "Maybe a few minutes after, but around the same time, yes."

"So Rose and Lucky were together when you left?"

Joy nodded.

"Joy, who erased Vinnie's tape?"

She shrugged. "I thought Lucky did."

*****

I entered the girl's dressing room and saw Rose speaking with Foxy while Mac and Manny recorded the conversation. Reid was behind me and we entered quietly mid-conversation.

"It's all for show," Rose was saying. "The blood was fake." She regarded Reid and I as we walked in.

"What were you going to do with the footage?" Foxy asked her.

"It was for a movie. People like it. You know?"

"Who was the buyer?" Reid asked, chiming in.

Rose shrugged. "Joy was handling that."

"What was your cut?" Reid asked.

"We were dividing it by three," Rose answered.

"So now it's two," Foxy added.

"Now it's nothing. We didn't finish it."

"Who has the footage?" Foxy asked.

"Joy has it," she answered. This was true. Reid had convinced Joy to hand over the footage to him before we concluded her interview.

"So when did things get out of hand?" Foxy asked.

"They didn't," Rose shot back. "He was fine when we left him."

"Joy said she left first and you stayed behind, Rose," Reid told her.

Rose thought about that. "Maybe a few minutes."

"So you and Lucky had sex after she left?" Foxy asked.

"I take longer than a few minutes cop! No. The stuff with Lucky was for the camera. I didn't like that son of a bitch."

"So, to be clear, you didn't have sex with Lucky after Joy left?" Foxy asked. "Be careful Rose, we've already done the forensic tests."

Rose looked at Foxy with venom in her eyes. "I said no."

"What happened to Lucky, Rose?" Reid demanded, leaning in. "Don't bullshit us. We know this pattern from you. You know something."

"Maybe I do, but unless you're ready to arrest me, we're done talking."

*****

We sat in the control room at the studio, loading up the footage that Joy, Lucky, and Rose had filmed. "It was just like I said," Manny beamed. "They were filming a smut film after hours. I totally called it guys!"

"Indeed, you did, Manuel," Foxy said, patting him on the back.

"But it was a fake," Manny continued. "They used fake blood to make it look like he was dead."

It seemed obvious to me that even if they didn't really kill Lucky in the snuff film, that they would have to kill him eventually in order to claim their movie was legitimate. Lucky was somewhat recognizable and viewers would realize he was still alive after they saw him on TV. The way I saw it, they probably filmed the scene using the fake blood and then killed him afterwards. It seemed entirely logical.

Mac set up the video monitor so that everything was cued up. The cops gathered around the monitor to watch, while my crew and I stood behind them, filming. Foxy pressed play and we watched Joy's footage.

Joy was operating the camera so we didn't see her on screen, just Rose and Lucky. He was sitting on the couch alone, wearing a pair of jeans and no shirt when there was a knock at the door. Lucky stood up, opened the door, and let Rose inside. She was dressed in a black lace negligée, which quickly came off as things escalated.

I rolled my eyes, growing increasingly tired of watching this kind of crap. In the past few weeks I had seen entirely too much. Reid seemed to read my thoughts and pressed the fast forward button on the controls. He stopped at the moment Rose was pulling out a knife from behind her back. She was straddling Lucky and he was topless but wasn't wearing the black mask. Rose raised the blade in the air and without much delay plunged it into his neck.

"Huh!" I gasped then slapped my hand over my mouth.

Lucky grabbed his neck and made a loud gasp and gurgling sound. Then blood started oozing from beneath his hands.

We all sat there in silence, wondering if this was real. It sure looked that way.

"Cut!" We heard Joy say and the camera switched off.

"Wait, is that it?" Foxy asked. "Is that the end of the tape?"

"It seems so," Reid confirmed.

"Was that real or fake?" Foxy demanded, sounding frustrated.

"Hang on, let me pull it back," Mac offered, jumping into the scene. He handed me the camera and moved over to the controls. He rewound the footage then jumped back behind me and grabbed the camera. We watched again, this time slower. After Joy called cut, Lucky seemed to open his eyes.

"Is he moving there?" Reid asked.

"He's moving but it's hard to tell if it's because the scene is over or because he's taking his last breath," Foxy answered.

"If he was stabbed for real he would have been more surprised," Reid commented.

"Let's look at the stabbing-part again," Foxy suggested.

We ran through the footage several more times trying to figure out if Lucky was actually killed or was just acting for the camera. While I understood why this type of detail mattered to the cops, I didn't care one way or the other. Rose appeared to have killed him and that was good enough for me! This footage was the money shot for my viewers! Lenny was going to freak.

"I can't tell if this is real or not," Foxy said, throwing up his hands. "This is like a joke, right? We have a case where we have footage of the victim being killed and we still don't know who the murderer is!"

That was true. It was also a great line for the trailer of this episode. I made a note in my log book. Rob would want to use this.

*****

While the cops brooded and tried to figure out their next steps, I took the chance to sneak out back to call Ginny on my cell phone again. I had been dying to talk to her about my conversation with Reid and now seemed like as good a time as any.

I pressed Ginny's name in my phone directory to call my sister. It occurred to me that Reid was pretty low on my speed-dial list. Ginny was number two and Reid was number nine. Now that he was in love with me I mused, I should probably move him up.

"Vic?" Ginny answered.

"We had the talk."

"You did?" Ginny said into the phone.

"Last night," I told her. I stepped off the back stairway and down a few steps to a quiet corner of the parking lot. I didn't want to risk Reid overhearing me. Behind me the back door opened and I saw Rose emerge from the building. I quickly backed into a corner behind a garbage can and hung up on Ginny. I silenced my phone so she couldn't call me back.

I could hear Rose whispering to someone. It was another woman. "Don't lie to me," Rose hissed.

"Lie to you?" the voice said. "How can I trust a thing you say?"

It was Joy's voice, I knew it. I looked down at my phone and saw Ginny calling me back, but this was too important. I switched to the camera on my phone and turned on the video recording. I wasn't going to risk them seeing me by trying to get a shot of them, but I thought I might be able to capture some audio at least.

"Those stupid cops. They're trying to turn us against each other. They don't know anything," Rose told Joy.

"They know about the tape. They know we lied to them," Joy replied.

269

"Doesn't matter," Rose consoled. "I didn't kill him."

"Why should I believe you?" Joy asked.

"I don't care what you think," Rose told her. "I know what I didn't do."

"And I know what I didn't do. Don't you dare try to pin this thing on me, Rose. You understand?"

It sounded like there was a bit of a scuffle and then the door opened and closed. When I was sure they were gone I stopped the recording feature on my phone. They hadn't confessed to anything, but the cops were rattling them. That was for sure.

*****

I found the cops right where I had left them, in the control room watching the tape again.

"I have something," I told them, holding up my phone.

We staged the event so that it seemed like the audio had been recorded on Foxy's cell phone and not mine. I let Foxy listen first without Reid so that Reid would be hearing it for the first time on camera. His acting skills weren't great so this approach would allow him the element of surprise. Reid wasn't thrilled with the approach, but he was grateful for any information that would help close this case.

Mac recorded and Manny rolled sound while Foxy played the recording for Reid. This was the second time I had made Foxy look like a hero on this show. The first time was when Mac saved Reid from getting attacked by a perp and I edited it to look like Foxy had saved him.

Reid listened to the audio on the phone while we watched for his reaction. "Neither one of them are taking the fall," Reid told his partner.

"Maybe neither of them are guilty," Foxy said with a frown. "Okay, let's go through it." He pulled out his notepad and pencil and started to jot some notes down. "After hours, Lucky, Joy, and Rose stay behind. Their goal is to film a snuff film for sale on the black market. They want to make it look like Lucky is dying, but use fake blood instead of killing him for real."

Foxy wrote down the names: Lucky, Rose, and Joy on the paper.

"Rose told me they finished up around six in the morning. They killed Lucky onscreen, but we don't know for certain if it was real or fake. Even if it was real they threw some fake blood on him at some point."

"Okay, so they finish shooting, then someone realizes Vinnie's tape is rolling and goes to erase it," Reid noted. "Joy said Lucky did it. Remember what Keith from the production office said? Lucky probably wound back the footage but then when there wasn't any motion for a while so the recording stopped."

"So then the girls leave and Lucky stays behind. Why?" Foxy asked.

"I just told you – to erase the tape."

Foxy nodded. "He wasn't wearing that mask during the filming and when we found him his body was pretty clean. Maybe he also cleaned himself up?"

"Yeah, if he was alive he would have."

"Or maybe Lucky never erased it because he was dead so Rose came back in to erase it. She's late every day and yet she was one of the first to arrive that morning to find him?" Foxy said.

"What about Vinnie? He got here early that day too. Maybe he grabbed the tape to watch it then freaked out when he saw the murder and erased it. If Rose and Joy killed Lucky it would ruin the production. Vinnie would have known that." Reid shook his head and placed it in his hands. Finally, he looked up. "I have an idea. It's a risk, but I want to try. I talked to Sharpe about it earlier. If it doesn't go right she'll dump the footage."

Foxy looked at his partner and raised an eyebrow.

26.

"You're kidding me, right?" Foxy asked his partner.

At Reid's request we were not filming while he strategized with Foxy how best to close out this case.

Reid shrugged. "Why not?"

Foxy looked over at me and then back at Reid. "I think your girlfriend is rubbing off on you. This isn't how we operate."

"Yeah, but what if it pays off?" Reid asked. "What's the harm?"

"The harm is that we never solve this case. Even if we do manage to point the finger at a suspect, the courts will throw it out for improper police work."

"No, they won't."

"Reid, I've been thinking about this and maybe it isn't such a good idea," I said. "Last time I did something like this I was almost killed. In fact, my bright idea almost got four people killed. I don't want anything to happen to you."

Reid walked over to me and placed a hand on my cheek. "Honey, that's not going to happen."

"Can we break up this tender moment please?" Foxy chided.

"I like the idea," Mac chimed in.

Foxy threw up his hands. "Of course you do."

"No, it'll have real theatrical impact. It's like that movie *Clue*. The audience will love it."

Foxy spoke to Mac as if he was a child. "I know how important viewers are to you guys, but we're talking about a real case here. Lucky was murdered in cold blood. Don't you think he deserves our best effort?"

"This is our best effort," Reid countered. "Come on, I can't keep talking to these people. We're just spinning our wheels. We need to solve this thing and then get the hell out."

"I'm not in such a rush," Foxy said. "This place is doing wonders for my sex life."

"Captain Harris told me she's going to pull us from the case anyway. There are too many others piling up. Listen, I can do the talking. This whole thing will be my idea," Reid offered.

"Ha! So then if it works you look like the hero."

"Would you two shut up already!" Manny cried out. "Sharpe told me we have enough footage to cut this thing together anyway. You're not doing this for us. We don't need you to solve it. Do it for yourselves – take the risk!"

I raised my eyebrows. Go, Manny.

"Fine," Foxy said. "I'll ask Vinnie to call everyone together."

*****

We gathered on the rocket ship set. We chose it because it was the largest room in the building and was best equipped to hold everyone. Plus, it was a cool backdrop for Mac's shot and had good lighting. Mac had mounted the secondary camera to a tripod to allow for a second angle and left it rolling. He held his camera over his shoulder and signaled to the cops that he was ready. Manny had already mic'd up the cops and placed some extra microphones loose around the room to pick up sound. He held his boom in his hand prepared to jump around to anyone who elected to speak.

Vinnie had been instructed to gather everyone up. Slowly the cast and crew filed in. "Gather around me," Reid told everyone as they entered the room. Anyone who wanted to sit was asked to pull their chair over so they could sit in a big semi-circle. Vinnie and Carmine sat in the director's chairs, as did Kyle Belamy. Craig grabbed a folding chair to sit on as did Enrique. Elroy, Rose, Joy, Penny, and Jason all chose to stand. The cops and my crew chose to stand as well.

Mac and Penny waved at each other while Manny looked at Rose. "Hey, baby," Manny said. Rose looked completely disinterested, ignoring his greeting and looking instead to the cops.

"What's the story guys?" Kyle asked. "Did you finally solve this thing?" He was holding his phone up and aiming it at Reid.

"You're not that stupid, are you?" Reid asked him.

"Just kidding," Kyle said, placing his phone back in his pocket.

Reid looked at the group and spoke. "When we first gathered like this we told you that the killer was among us. Do you remember that?"

The group nodded collectively.

"I can now confirm that our suspicion was correct."

Mac panned with his camera to the crowd. Joy shifted her feet while Rose stood stone cold. I don't even think she was blinking. The only way I could tell she was alive was by looking at her maracas which were heaving up and down.

Vinnie started rubbing his chin, trying to feign interest while Carmine took a big hard swig from his thermos. Penny took a deep breath and lifted her right leg to her left inner thigh. She held her hands in prayer and closed her eyes, standing silently in the yoga tree pose.

Reid pursed his lips. "Our first hint of foul play was an altered recording of the crime. As I believe all of you are aware, Vinnie has a camera mounted in the dressing rooms to record the actors getting undressed."

Penny opened an eye at that and then frowned before closing her eyes again. Craig looked over at Vinnie who was looking down, pretending as best he could, that he wasn't there.

"Vinnie records these tapes to masturbate to, which he does in the control room every Friday night. Sometimes Elroy joins him," Reid continued.

Elroy shot Reid a dirty look while Vinnie sunk lower and lower into his seat.

"The camera is motion activated and was switched on the night that Lucky was murdered," Reid continued.

"We were able to examine the video and determine that the content had been tampered with," Foxy explained, taking over. "This means that the camera did record Lucky being killed, but that someone erased over it."

"This led us to understand that whoever committed this crime knew about the camera," Reid explained. "Raise your hand if you knew about the camera in that dressing room."

Reid stared at the group who seemed shocked that they were being asked this question openly. Reluctantly, everyone raised their hand with the exception of Enrique who seemed to have no idea what anyone was talking about. When he saw everyone else raising their hands, he raised his hand too. I watched Mac rack focus on Vinnie's face. He looked totally humiliated.

"It's just for fun," Vinnie managed to mutter.

Penny's eye was opened again and it was glaring at Vinnie.

"But," Foxy continued, "the killer was sloppy. They didn't erase all of the footage. During one of the starts and stops we were able to isolate a few frames to see Lucky in the room that night and he wasn't alone."

Kyle leaned in. "Man, this is getting interesting. Who was on the tape?" Kyle had his smart phone in his hand again and was touching the screen. I felt my phone vibrate in my pocket and pulled it out to see a social media alert: *Kyle Belamy is broadcasting live.*

"Man, will you ever learn?" Reid asked, ripping Kyle's phone out of his hand and throwing it hard against the wall. Kyle instantly slouched back in his chair and sulked. "You're still on TV, man," Reid assured him. "There are cameras all around." Kyle seemed to perk up at that reminder. His presence at this moment would still be memorialized.

"We actually saw several people in that room with Lucky throughout the night," Reid continued. He was pacing back and forth, grandstanding now. He walked over to Carmine. "They were filming another production here, a snuff film."

Penny placed her second leg down on the floor. "A what?"

"It's when people kill each other, for real, on camera while having sex," Foxy explained. "They're sold on the black market."

Penny shook her head. "No way, that can't be real. Lucky didn't even like Rose."

Rose sneered at that. "Why are you listening to these stupid cops? They know nothing."

Vinnie looked over at his brother. "Did you know about this?"

"No," Carmine said defensively. "I didn't know anything about it."

"Joy told us you did know, Carmine," Reid countered.

Now Joy looked uncomfortable. "Maybe you were drinking the night I told you?" she suggested.

Carmine looked angry. "What are you talking about? I'm sober."

With that comment the group let out a collective laugh. Apparently, Carmine wasn't fooling anyone.

"So we've got a pervert and a drunk at the helm." Kyle narrated. "Classic."

Penny's neck was starting to get red and she began scratching at it vigorously. She turned to look at Rose and Joy. "So, you were making a sex movie with Lucky and then you... killed him?" As she spoke the words, tears filled her eyes and Elroy rushed to her side.

"Penny, are you okay?" he asked her, placing an arm around her.

"No," Rose told her. "That isn't what happened."

"Why don't you tell us what did happen, Rose!" Elroy demanded, protecting Penny.

"We were doing it for some extra money," Rose began. "Joy set it up."

"With who?" Vinnie asked Joy.

Joy hesitated but then blurted it out. "The network. Roger connected me with someone who was interested."

Vinnie stood up from his chair. "You did this under my nose? You tried to turn a profit under my roof, using my equipment? And you!" he said turning to his brother. "I told you that you shouldn't get involved with her. You idiot, she's not even sexy. I should have never let her on this show!"

"Hey!" Joy shouted back.

"Do you think I like learning that Lucky was murdered for profit in my shop?" Vinnie spat.

"We didn't murder him!" Joy snapped.

"We have video that shows otherwise," Reid shot back. "You actually gave it to us, remember?"

"That was fake, I told you that!" Joy countered, sounding desperate.

"Then why isn't there a single frame of Lucky alive after Rose plunged a knife into his throat?" Reid asked.

"GRRR!" Penny thundered, throwing Elroy's arm off her and lunging at Rose. "I'll kill you!" Penny leapt up in the air and in one swift move, body-slammed Rose to the ground. When they landed with a thud, Rose put her hands to her face, trying to protect herself, while Penny clawed at them like a cat.

Reid and Foxy sprang into action with Foxy grabbing Penny by the waist and pulling her off Rose. Reid helped Rose to her feet but kept his fist clenched tightly around her arm in case she planned to retaliate. Mac was recording everything, getting dangerously close to the fray, while capturing some really good footage.

"I didn't kill him!" Rose screamed at Penny. "It was a trick. We used fake blood!"

"Lucky hated you!" Penny continued. "He would have never had sex with you willingly. You tricked him and then you killed him!"

"No, I didn't!" Rose called out. She sounded desperate and afraid, like I had never seen her before.

"He wanted the money," Joy offered. "It wasn't about sex for him."

"We didn't have sex!" Rose pleaded, dropping to her knees. "It was pretend for the cameras! It was all pretend! Penny, I swear! His underwear was on the whole time. On my life, I swear to you, Penny!"

Penny's expression moved from shock to complete horror as her eyes grew wide. She looked around at the faces of everyone else in the room and then cried out at the top of her lungs in a primordial scream, "No!" We all jumped at the sound and watched Penny collapse to the floor. She banged her fists on the ground, hard, wailing with grief.

Reid let go of Rose's arm and walked over to Penny, placing his hand on her shoulder. "You believed Rose and Lucky were having an affair, didn't you?"

Penny looked up at Reid with tears in her eyes. "I heard them in the dressing room that morning when I got there. How was I supposed to know they were just acting?"

"You couldn't have known."

Rose was staring, wide-eyed, listening.

"I waited for Rose to leave, then I went inside the dressing room. I didn't even notice the blood. Didn't see it. How could I have not seen it?" Penny asked.

"We wiped it off," Rose said, still on her knees.

Penny thought about that for a while, processing the information. Reid stood there stoically, listening to her, not speaking. No one spoke, not even Kyle Belamy. No one knew what was going to happen next. Finally, when it looked like Penny wasn't going to say anything else, Reid egged her on. "You felt betrayed, so you entered the room and you saw the scissor on the table. So you grabbed it."

Penny looked over at Reid, her eyes vacant, as if they were lost in thought. "Sometimes when I meditate I can get into this state where nothing seems real, you know? Like I'm all powerful and all knowing. Do you know what I mean?"

Reid nodded.

"We liked to use masks. It was fun for us. It was part of the fantasy. It made it easier to feel outside of myself, like I wasn't looking at someone who actually had a soul. Like I was just pretending. I felt like I was in that state. Like I was in a deep meditation, looking down at my life." Penny's eyes drifted off again, but then returned to Reid's. "From the clouds I imagine my life to be so complete. A job that pays the bills, my own yoga studio in the works, and a boyfriend who cares about me. That's what I see from the clouds. But here on Earth, when I look at the truth, I realize that I'm a step away from being a prostitute and in love with a man who was fucking another woman."

I looked around the room at the faces of everyone. Their hearts went out to her, I knew they did.

"You were in love with that jerk?" Elroy blurted out. "After all I did for you, you were in love with that bastard?"

Penny looked over at Elroy, annoyed. Her tone was stern. "How stupid are you? How many fucking hints can I give you before you get the fucking message?"

"Well if you don't fucking care then maybe I should tell these cops here that I erased that footage for you. How about that?" Elroy snapped.

Joy raised her eyebrows. "You were the one who erased it?"

Penny stood up and spread her arms wide. "Who fucking cares, Elroy? I just told them that I killed Lucky. You think I care if you tell them you erased the tape?"

Bingo! I tried to hide my pleasure, but damn it, that confession was amazing! I looked over at Mac who looked utterly destroyed that his yoga teacher was a cold-hearted killer. Manny had his mouth hanging wide open. "Wow," he mouthed to me.

I looked over at Reid feeling so proud. He had a hunch. A hunch that if we brought this group together and started to turn them against each other, that the truth would come out. He had a hunch and he was right.

27.

On any other day I would have grabbed the footage from Mac, ran back to meet Rob in the edit bay, and worked all night on the episode. The cops brought Penny back to the station to book her and Mac and Manny tagged along. Elroy seemed completely surprised to learn that his admission about erasing the tapes for Penny would get him arrested as well.

While the footage at the police station was important to close out my story, it wasn't essential that I was there. We had a confession on camera and we knew who did it. This case was closed. I really wanted Rose to be the killer, but the plot twist with Penny was pretty satisfying.

I gave Lenny a call and explained to him what had unfolded. He offered to have Rob stay for the night shift but I told him it could wait for the morning. I had texted Rob earlier to tell him Penny was our girl and he was already shaping the narrative in that direction. Mac agreed to drop the footage off so that one of assistant editors could get it loaded into the Avid overnight. Rob and I would work together the next morning when we were fresh and rested. Honestly, it wasn't even that late, the sun was still shining, but mentally I felt like I needed a break.

It wasn't the murder or the location or the situation that was weighing on me, but rather the pretty heavy conversation that Reid and I had the night before. I needed time to sort out my feelings for him and I needed to do it alone. I headed back to my apartment, poured a glass of wine, and sat out on my balcony.

As I sat there I thought about my past relationships and when I knew I was in love. Reid seemed to know how he felt about me, but I needed to decide how I felt about him. Shouldn't it be obvious? How had I handled these conversations in the past? I was thirty years old, this wasn't the first time I had feelings like this, but something was different. Maybe it was my age. In your twenties, an "I love you" doesn't necessarily mean forever. But now that I was thirty, it held a different meaning. If I loved this guy, that could lead to marriage and kids. Was I ready for all that?

I needed to remember that Reid could be a jerk. The first time I met him he was beyond rude and he could still get annoyed relatively easy. Did I want to get involved with a hothead like this? On the other hand, he was stable, he owned his own home, and he was handy. He even installed his own kitchen. He was strong and would protect me through thick and thin. He was the real deal and I knew it. From the depths of my soul I knew it. I also knew what I had to do next.

*****

I sat on Reid's front step for probably an hour before he arrived home. I didn't mind. This was another rare moment of peace and I was enjoying it.

Reid had a big smile on his face as he stepped out of his car. "This is a nice surprise," he said as he walked towards me.

I stood and greeted him with a kiss on the lips and a hug.

"I thought you'd be at the production office."

"Tomorrow," I told him. "Rob has what he needs for now. I wanted to see you."

Out back Reid had a fire pit with some chairs around it so we grabbed some beers and headed outside for a chat. Reid snuggled against me on a chair built for two. "I was kind of hoping this was a booty call," he told me.

I laughed. "Why, you don't like talking to me?"

"Depends what we're talking about."

"It's about us," I told him.

Reid frowned. "I figured."

I pulled away from Reid and sat up straight in the chair, turning to look him in the eyes. "Listen, I'd love to just go into your room right now and be with you all night."

"Oh, okay," Reid said, grabbing my hand to lead me inside.

I smiled and held my ground. "Come on, I want to say this."

Reid settled in his chair and looked at me, listening.

"This isn't a conversation I wanted to have, but you forced it with what you said the other night. I've been thinking a lot about us and how I feel about you." I felt my face starting to flush. "I just, I never even thought you'd like me. Hell, I didn't like you when we first met. And you're so good looking. I mean you're seriously hot, Reid. You are."

Reid placed a hand on my knee. "You're pretty hot yourself, Victoria."

My heart melted. "Honestly, I feel like I'm still in disbelief about this whole thing, you know? It's hard to explain."

Reid looked at me. "Sharpe, I know you and I are a strange couple and I know we didn't get along very well in the beginning. I didn't expect to feel like this about you either. But I'm not sure why you have this notion that I'm somehow out of your league. Honey, if anything you are out of *my* league. I'm not sure how you don't know that. You're smart, you're sexy, and you're tough as nails."

I smiled, trying to find my words.

"You seem to forget that I read people for a living," Reid continued. "I know what you're thinking before you say it. So no more excuses, say what you want to say. I already know what it's going to be."

I took a deep breath and tried to be brave. "I love you too," I said, feeling really stupid.

"Oh thank God!" Reid said, placing a hand on his heart in apparent relief.

"I thought you said you could read my thoughts?" I yelled at him.

"I was bluffing," Reid smiled. "I have no idea what goes on in that head of yours!"

I smiled and punched him playfully. Reid kissed me deeply. I wrapped my arms around him, hugging him tightly. Through our kiss I felt a sense of surrender. I was his now and he was mine.

"Can we go to my room now?" Reid asked.

I giggled, feeling a huge weight off my shoulders. "Yes, we can."

*****

I sat on the couch behind Rob watching him work. Reid was onscreen doing a talking head interview. It was hard for my thoughts not to drift to him considering I had literally been watching him on screen all day.

Rob was editing excitedly, barely stopping to eat or drink. "Some of this footage is really shaky. What the hell was Mac doing?" Rob asked.

I grinned. "He was standing on one leg most of the time. Penny suggested it."

Rob frowned. "Tell him not to do that again please."

"I think he learned his lesson."

"Do you think I should lose this shot of Penny?" Rob turned to ask me. "I don't want the viewers to suspect her."

I thought for a moment. Now that we knew the outcome it was hard for us to truly evaluate if it would be obvious to the viewer at home who the true murderer really was. It was almost easier to edit when we didn't know the killer. "Yeah, lose it," I told him. "We probably need someone unfamiliar with the case to watch the cut when we're done."

As if by magic, Missy my producer colleague and arch-nemesis popped her head into the edit suite. "Did I hear you say you needed a second set of eyes?" She smiled. Her long skinny neck pushed her pointy chin in the air giving the distinct and accurate impression that she was stuck up.

"Yeah, that would be great." Rob smiled giving me a little wink. "Come back in an hour okay?"

"Sure," Missy smiled. "I just finished my edit with Dylan so I have some time."

Missy was either trying to brag to me that her edit was done or to bait me to ask to see her edit. I had no intention of asking. I could care less. Rob continued to sift through the footage and sighed. "We're gonna have to cut these words up," he told me. "These interviews with the cops aren't working."

"I'm sorry, I suck," I told him.

He swiveled around in his chair and looked at me, crinkling his nose. "It's not your best work."

I knew he was right. There were so many suspects that we had to interview that I didn't focus enough on talking head interviews with the cops. These types of interviews were the connective glue that helped to tell the story but my glue was more like Jell-O in this case.

Normally I didn't think twice about franken-biting a participant's words. It was a pretty easy process where we took some words from one interview and spliced them with another. So, for example, if a cop said, "Joy is coming in for questioning" in one interview and, "Everyone is a suspect" in another interview, we could piece those words together to say, "Joy is a suspect." We did it all the time to tell the story we needed to tell. It was no big deal but I did feel a little guilty doing it to Reid.

Rob pulled Reid's words together to make him say, "We worked all night interviewing the suspects." Reid didn't actually say that, but we needed to make it seem like he was working around the clock instead of clocking out at five and then banging the show's producer. Reid would probably never notice something this small, but it still felt a little deceptive to literally be putting words in his mouth.

*****

Nine hours later we were ready for notes. Missy had already come and gone and provided her feedback and now it was time for Lenny to come in. Missy was pretty helpful, pointing out some moments in the edit where we tended to point to Penny as a suspect too soon. I admitted that her feedback was helpful and thanked her for it.

Lenny showed up at our edit suite carrying an assortment of gourmet tacos and a case of Mexican beer. This was LA after all. Showing up with pizza didn't always cut it. Not when we had some of the best Mexican food north of the border.

"Wow, thanks boss," Rob told him.

Lenny laid out the food on a side table that was next to the couch and we dug in. I sifted through the options and decided to go with a fish taco that seemed to be calling my name. I didn't realize how hungry I was until I started eating. I also didn't realize it was already seven o'clock. I hadn't been in touch with Reid all day, but I was okay with that. He was probably busy at work and so was I. We had been single for a long time with jobs that utilized most of our time and it was hard to change that. I knew we would find our groove eventually.

"So, how's it looking?" Lenny asked me.

"Good I think," I told him. "Missy was pretty complimentary."

"Give me a minute and I'll play it," Rob told us, biting into his taco.

Reviewing an edit with Lenny was not just a matter of hitting play. He would stop Rob constantly to give him notes and changes. For the easy ones, Rob would make them right away, but for larger changes both Rob and I would write them down and work on them later.

We sat in that room for another two hours while Lenny poked and prodded, getting the edit really tight. Sometimes these notes sessions could be frustrating, but I knew in the end the edit would be better for it.

When we were finished, Lenny stood up and said, "Good work guys. When can I see the edits?"

"Tomorrow. Around noon," Rob said, subtly indicating to Lenny that he didn't plan to stay and edit all night.

Lenny stood there for a moment, sizing Rob up before nodding his head. "Noon it is. This show has to deliver in two days. I'm already running the ads. Okay?"

"Okay," Rob said.

"The Lush network isn't airing *Babes in Space*, Lenny," I told him, offering some gossip. "Kyle Belamy is pissed. I guess broadcasting a show with a known murderer and her victim is too low for even those guys to sink."

"Yeah, I heard," Lenny said. "Vinnie and I have kept in touch."

It didn't surprise me that those two had exchanged numbers. They were two of a kind.

"Hey Sharpe, can I talk to you privately?" Lenny asked me.

"Sure," I answered, confused about what he might want. I stood up and followed him outside. It was late and almost no one was around so we had plenty of privacy standing in the hall.

Lenny turned and looked at me. "There's something I want to talk to you about. It's about your job performance."

Immediately I felt my stomach drop. Had I done something wrong? Was this because I hadn't come into the office last night and instead went to Reid's place? Lenny cared a lot about face time, but damn it, this wasn't fair. I started to feel angry inside. I worked hard on this show — very hard. Was he seriously about to give me a performance lecture?

"The network approached me about doing another show," Lenny told me. "It's a new show that follows people leading double lives. You know, like a guy who has two families that don't know about each other."

"How are you going to get contestants for that?" I asked.

"We're targeting wives and girlfriends that have a suspicion about it. We'll hire private eyes to trail the guys and then we'll nail them. It'll be kind of like an ambush."

"Sounds cool," I told him not sure what this had to do with my performance.

"I want you to be the show runner."

I felt my breath catch. "Are you serious?"

"Listen, I don't like the idea of losing you on this show, but you've pulled in enough blockbuster episodes to keep the show in business for a while. Now I need you to make the next one great."

My face grew hot and I felt like I might cry. All of these years I had felt like I was just hanging on career-wise. My mother was this big celebrity, my father was a hugely successful set designer, and I was just this reject working in the bowels of the business. But somehow on this show I seemed to have found my groove and Lenny was recognizing it. "I don't know what to say."

"You can say yes. We start pre-production in two weeks. Finish out this episode and then take a little time off. Spend some time with that cop boyfriend of yours. Maybe take a vacation. When you get back I need you, all of you, to make this thing great."

*****

Being a show runner was a big deal and it would take a lot of my time. Show runners worked day and night ensuring the show's message was consistent and making sure the episodes matched up. While I wouldn't be out in the field, it would still mean long hours and weekends in the office. It scared me a little, but at the same time I couldn't stop smiling.

I didn't know who to call first – my dad or Reid. I had faced this dilemma before when my car ran out of gas. This time the answer was obvious. I pulled out my phone and sent Reid a text:

Get some wine ready, I have good news. Coming over to celebrate.

I ended the text with a heart emoji in the color red. After all, love was exactly what I was feeling.

ABOUT THE AUTHOR

At the age of 23, after graduating with a Bachelor of Fine Arts degree in film and television from New York University, Jenna Baker picked up from New York and drove west to Los Angeles. It was the same summer that a television series called *Survivor* was premiering. Jenna caught an episode of the show in a hotel room and was instantly hooked. She was so smitten, that she changed her travel itinerary around to ensure she wouldn't miss a single episode.

When she arrived in Los Angeles, Jenna landed an assistant job for a company called Rocket Science Laboratories. They were producing another ground-breaking reality television show called *Temptation Island*. Jenna stayed with Rocket Science for several years moving up from an executive assistant to an associate producer before moving on to other companies to further her career. Jenna worked on numerous reality shows including *Surprise Wedding I & II*, *Married By America*, *Paradise Hotel* and two seasons of *The Swan*.

Working on reality shows was a blast, but it was extremely difficult for Jenna as it meant completely giving up her own life in order to follow someone else's. The hours were brutal and the competition was fierce, but mostly it was the mantra "anything to get the shot" that ultimately forced Jenna to choose a different career path. What she took away from her reality television career was a wealth of hilarious stories about doing anything and everything to make the show work. *Reel Sharpe* was the first book in the "Reel" series followed by *Reel Hollywood* and *Reel Sexy*. The novels allowed Baker the perfect outlet to share her stories and secrets from an insider's perspective while still keeping the content light and entertaining.

Jenna now lives on Long Island with her husband Brandon and children, Austin and Avery.

www.ingramcontent.com/pod-product-compliance
Lightning Source LLC
Chambersburg PA
CBHW051415170626
46809CB00006B/2170